DEPARTURE 37

ALSO BY SCOTT CARSON

The Chill

Where They Wait

Lost Man's Lane

DEPARTURE 37

A NOVEL

SCOTT CARSON

EMILY BESTLER BOOKS

———

ATRIA

New York Amsterdam/Antwerp London
Toronto Sydney/Melbourne New Delhi

EMILY
BESTLER
BOOKS

ATRIA

An Imprint of Simon & Schuster, LLC
1230 Avenue of the Americas
New York, NY 10020

First Emily Bestler Books/Atria Books hardcover edition August 2025

EMILY BESTLER BOOKS/ATRIA BOOKS and colophon are trademarks of Simon & Schuster, LLC

Interior design by Kyoko Watanabe

Manufactured in the United States of America

1 3 5 7 9 10 8 6 4 2

Library of Congress Cataloging-in-Publication Data

ISBN 978-1-9821-9148-1
ISBN 978-1-9821-9150-4 (ebook)

Thinking of Dean Koontz, Richard Matheson,
and Rod Serling.

"Everything is unprecedented if you don't study history."
JAMES RODGER FLEMING

———

"CLICK. BANG. FREEDOM."
T-SHIRT SLOGAN, NAVAL SURFACE WARFARE CENTER,
CRANE DIVISION

OCTOBER 25, 2025

Brian Grayson knew someone was dead almost as soon as the phone rang.

Midnight in Minneapolis. A Marriott by the airport. Brian woke in the dark with a groan of protest—he had three hours more to sleep before rolling out for a 6 a.m. haul to Los Angeles, three blissful hours, damn it.

But the iPhone on the nightstand didn't care, the shuddering of its vibration against the wood more aggravating than the ringtone itself, which was set to the old Oasis song "A Bell Will Ring." No bells should ring at midnight, literally or figuratively. He'd set the phone on Do Not Disturb but there were exceptions for that list: Delta Air Lines and family. The former called more often than the latter, and that was good. Work would need him in the middle of the night. If all was well, his family shouldn't. The ringtone was individual to his seventy-eight-year-old mother—or someone using her phone. She'd heard the Oasis song in Brian's car once and announced that she liked it, and that struck the family as amusing, because the song had been new then and she'd seemed old to all of them.

1

That new song was now twenty years old.

Nobody left in the mix could laugh at aging.

He fumbled out of the tangled sheets and swept the phone off the nightstand. The display confirmed what the song promised: Mom was calling.

Midnight Central time was 1 a.m. on Nantucket, and Melinda Grayson wasn't calling anyone at one in the morning unless someone had died. Brian was so sure of this that he let the phone ring, wondering whose tragedy he should brace for. His father was already three years in the grave, and his mother wouldn't have heard news about Brian's ex-wife before he did, which meant it was either his sister, her husband, or—please, no—their son, Brian's nephew.

Answer it.

But he couldn't. He was thinking about the text message his nephew had sent him not even two months earlier, a photo of his first driver's license paired with an Indy 500 gif. Funny kid, Matt, he was a damn funny—

The phone went dark and still. Son of a bitch. He'd missed it. She needed him, and he'd sat there afraid in the dark and let her call go to voicemail.

It rang again, the screen illuminating and Liam Gallagher's voice crooning, "*A little space, a little time, see what it can do . . .* " over his brother Noel's wicked guitar.

Brian accepted the call and put the phone to his ear.

"Mom?" His voice was hoarse with unshaken sleep.

"Brian." The relief in his mother's voice was nothing but further confirmation of his fears. "Where are you?"

"Minneapolis. What's wrong?" He sat up, swinging his feet to the floor, the sheet dropping from his bare chest. "What happened?"

"Where are you flying tomorrow?"

"What?"

"Where are you—"

"Los Angeles. Why do you— Mom, do you have any idea what time it is?"

"Late. Not *too* late, though."

He checked the glowing red numerals on the alarm clock: 12:07.

"It's past midnight *here*, I think it's plenty late there! What's going on?"

"You can't get on that plane," his mother said.

"Excuse me?"

"Do not fly, Brian. Do not even get on board. Not that plane." She sounded utterly confident and her voice held a grace note of relief, as if she'd caught him just in time. "Promise me."

"I . . . What . . . Mom, what's wrong with you?"

"Nothing's wrong with me. It's the plane. *Your* plane."

Brian opened his mouth and closed it again. Ran his free hand over his face and shook his head. What in the hell was going on? Melinda Grayson was in competition for the world's least superstitious person. The idea that she believed she'd had some sort of premonition felt implausible.

"Did you have a nightmare?" he asked, voice gentle. She'd been alone in that rambling old Victorian since his father died. Too much house, she'd say from time to time, and maybe he should have taken the hint more seriously, should have helped her get out of the old house with all its old memories and into someplace newer and safer and more emotionally sterile. She was seventy-eight years old, living in the house in which she'd been born and in which she'd later raised two kids of her own and lost a husband, and that was a lot for an aging mind to take. There were long shadows and old echoes in that home, and just because the family loved it didn't mean it was the right place for her to be.

"No nightmare," she said crisply, almost curtly, a voice he remembered so well, a tone she deployed the way a herding dog dispensed nipping bites, telling you to move along. "Now promise me, Brian."

"Promise you *what*?"

"That you will not fly. Not to Los Angeles—although I don't think that matters?" A hint of a question to this last bit, the first wave in her surreal confidence. Then she pressed on. "No, it doesn't matter. You stay right there. Understand?"

Understand? He almost laughed.

"Calm down," he said. "Calm down and—"

"I'm perfectly calm. I'm also quite serious. Are you listening to me?"

"Mom, I've got to fly. It's my job. Tell me what happened to make you—"

"You need to listen to me," she snapped.

"I'm listening. But you're not making sense, Mom. I don't know what's made you nervous. Can you tell me?"

"I am not nervous," she said almost indignantly. "I am certain."

"Certain of what?"

"You will die."

The hotel room was too dark and too cold and too quiet. He wanted the sound of humanity, a television on the other side of the wall, a drunk's laugh in the hall, anything.

"Mom."

"You will die," Melinda Grayson repeated, and her voice was so steady that Brian's skin prickled with gooseflesh. She should be hysterical or confused or both, should be anything but calm and assured.

For a long moment neither of them spoke. He was trying to picture her in the house facing the Atlantic, that view from the veranda that had kept them from selling the place so many times, the view that was the singular reason it was a fourth-generation home. Was she in her bedroom or downstairs on the sofa in the book-lined den she loved so much? All those science-based books, no spooky stories for his mother, not much fiction at all beyond Elin Hilderbrand and Elizabeth Strout. His mother was the most practical person he'd ever known.

You will die, she'd just told her son.

Was *he* having the nightmare? He rubbed the knuckle of his thumb between his eyebrows, absorbed the pressure like a reassurance. Awake and aware: good.

"Brian," his mother said, "are you listening to me?"

"I'm *hearing* you. I think that's about all. Because it sure sounds like you're telling me that you had some kind of . . . premonition or something. And that's not like you."

"Indeed, it is not. I think that's important to remember, don't you?"

He didn't respond. What the hell did you say to that?

"I want to ask you a question," she said. "Will you take me seriously enough to answer it?"

Dementia arrived fast with some people, Brian knew that, but there would be indicators, wouldn't there? Things you'd think back on and nod your head at, realizing the overlooked clues. He'd call his sister as soon as this was done; there was no doubt about that.

"I'm taking you seriously, Mom. It's just that what you're saying is crazy."

"Could you give me the answer without the commentary, please?"

He let out a long breath, lowered his hand from his face, and nodded as if she could see him.

"How many times have I asked you to avoid a flight?" she asked.

"Never."

"Correct. How many hours have you spent in a cockpit?"

"About fifteen thousand." The FAA capped you at 1,000 per year, and he had fourteen years with Delta, and flight school behind that.

"Then don't you think, if I were given to *My son is a pilot* paranoia, I would have experienced it by now?"

"I'm not saying you're paranoid; I'm saying—"

"It doesn't make sense: yes, I heard you. You need to hear *me*. You are going to die. Do you have any idea what it feels like to say those words, a mother to her son? Can you possibly imagine?"

Behind him, the air-conditioning kicked on, adding a chilled gust to the already-too-cold room.

"We're wheels up six hours from now," he said. "This late, on that leg, they won't be able to replace me. That's grounding 220 passengers and diverting crew. It creates a ripple effect of—"

"Saved lives. That's the ripple effect."

How on earth could she be so lucid about something so mad? Brian rose and crossed the room and pulled the heavy drapes back, revealing the red-and-white lights of the airport beyond. He could hear the signature hum of a descending 727. The best thing about Delta's Minneapolis hotels was their proximity to the airport. He never tired of watching the planes, and wasn't that strange? Maybe not. If you were lucky, you found what you loved. Brian Grayson loved to fly.

"Mom, you need to explain what happened."

"I am certain, and that is all that matters. If you fly, you die."

Brian watched the 727 glide in, wheels kissing tarmac, slick and smooth and safely on the ground in Minnesota.

"It is one flight," his mother in Massachusetts said. "One day, one flight. If I'm right, you'll have many, many more ahead of you. Or just one. It is that simple. The choice is yours, but—"

"Mom . . ."

"—the responsibility is for all those passengers. Not just you. Imagine that I'm right, Brian. Imagine how you will feel when it happens."

"When *what* happens? What in the hell do you think is going to happen? A crash, a hijacking—*what*?"

It was so silent that he thought he should be able to hear her breathing on the other end of the line but couldn't. He was about to speak again when she cut in.

"I don't know exactly how it will go. I just know that you'll be dead when it's done. You will all be dead."

He couldn't find his voice.

"More than two hundred people," his mother said. "Some whole families, all traveling together, mothers and fathers and children, flying and dying together."

"Stop saying that."

"They will die on *your* plane, which is *your* responsibility."

"Stop!" he shouted, caught by the cocktail of fear and anger.

She fell silent. The clock on the nightstand said 12:10. She'd needed only three minutes to undo a lifetime of trust.

But was that fair? She was the one asking for trust; he was withholding it. Withholding it because to extend it was to believe in something . . . very strange.

Very frightening.

"How are you so sure?" he whispered.

"I don't know," she said. "But I am. Will you trust me?"

He looked from the dark hotel room back out to the blinking lights of the airport.

"Okay," he said. "I'll call out."

"That can't be appeasement, Brian. It *has* to be the truth. Otherwise, I'll have to . . . well, there are other steps I could take, I suppose." She said this as if there were superior plans suddenly taking shape in her mind, and he had an awful vision of explaining himself in a courtroom. *Did my mother call in a bomb threat? Well . . .*

"I promise," he said.

A Hilton in Arlington, Virginia, 3 a.m., when the call came.

Layla Chen, still awake, turned on one shoulder, the over-starched bedsheet dropping to her waist, and looked at the phone on the nightstand. The display was illuminated with a photograph of a smiling woman sitting at a picnic table in the Rocky Mountains, a steaming cup of coffee before her, a buffalo behind her. Cooke City, Montana. Her mother had been oblivious to the buffalo's presence, and the picture always made Layla smile, which was one of the reasons she'd set it as the contact photo. A good picture of a good memory that made her smile.

It wasn't making her smile this morning.

Her mother was calling, and her mother had been dead for sixteen years.

She dismissed the call. The screen went black as the lump in Layla's throat thickened.

I wonder how long they wait to give away a dead woman's phone number? she wondered. She should have already researched this question; couldn't believe that she hadn't. There would be a protocol. What was the waiting time and who regulated it? Was each phone company different? Maybe the phone numbers of the dead were hoovered up by those bullshit robocalling services, the kind that spammed people for credit card or Social Security numbers. She should know.

The screen illuminated again.

Mom is calling.

Somewhere across America, more than five hundred phones were ringing. The rest of them belonged to commercial pilots. The one on Layla's nightstand belonged to the chief archivist of the Defense Advanced Research Projects Agency, better known as DARPA. Layla had insisted on being called at the same time as the pilots. She wanted to know how it felt in real time.

Now she hit the accept button. The phone ticked off the seconds of the sustained call. No hanging up from the other side. No voice, either. Just that promise from her iPhone assuring her that the call was connected. For an awful second, she thought it wasn't working—that the whole system was a failure. Then she remembered she had to speak to activate the response.

"Hello," Layla said.

"Hello, Layla, baby."

The familiarity of that voice was so overwhelming that Layla could not draw a breath.

"Layla?" the voice said. "You don't have to talk. You only have to listen."

It had been sixteen years since Layla had heard her mother's voice, but more than that since she'd heard this version of it, so strong and clear, unencumbered by pain—or pain pills.

"It is a very important night, ahead of a more important day. You need to know that, baby. Everything changes today."

Remember that she is not real, she's just a voice—not even that, she's an imitation of a voice. No soul. So test the system. React as any of the pilots might.

"Stop this," Layla whispered. It was so hard to speak. She stood up, the oversize T-shirt she'd worn to bed rising up her thighs, skin prickling, stomach knotting.

"Listen," her mother's voice said, "if you ever loved me, you will do that much. Just listen."

If you ever loved me ... How often had that been the first line ahead of some random request or mundane instruction? Circumstances didn't matter to Sara Chen when she issued that weighty preamble.

If you ever loved me, you'll empty the dishwasher.

If you ever loved me, you will not get that tattoo.

If you ever loved me, you'll clean the cat's box.

If you ever loved me, you'll take a week of vacation so we can see Yellowstone together before my treatment starts.

Alone in the night, Layla Chen sank to her knees beside the hotel bed.

Her dead mother's voice said, "Under no circumstances, Layla Leigh, can you fly today," and Layla's breath was snatched away by shock. Leigh was not her middle name; Leigh was a joke from the summer she'd started to listen to country music because her best friend Melissa loved it and pleasing Melissa was everything that year. Her mother had teased her, telling her she wasn't sure that Layla Chen was going to go over well in Nashville, so maybe she'd need a stage name.

"*Layla Leigh*," she would drawl in a remarkably proficient Southern accent, "can play not only the gee-tar, the banjo, and the fiddle, ladies and gents, she can positively *wail* on the har-mon-i-ca."

Layla had known the system was good, but this was *too* good. Less imposter than ghost.

In Virginia, 2025, Layla pressed her forehead against the nightstand. In impossibility, time unknown, her mother said: "Today is either the beginning or the end. I'm not sure. But you must not fly. Promise me you won't. Promise me now."

Layla grasped the bedsheet with her free hand, knotted it in her fist. Did not speak.

"*Layla.*" Sharper now, chiding, a voice that had snapped Layla's eyes up from the phone or computer so many times—one that guaranteed her mother's patience was thinning.

"I need that promise," Sara Chen said, and Layla could feel the undeniable reality of her mother's presence, as real as the racing heartbeat beneath her breast.

"I promise," Layla whispered.

"Thank you, *Měinů*," the voice of the dead said, and it was that Mandarin closer, meaning *beautiful girl*, that made Layla slap the phone down on the nightstand. It was too good, damn it. The AI system imitating her mother was so good that, even if you knew what it was, it cut you to the core.

The phone went dark.

Layla gathered it in trembling hands and punched at the display. The phone was alive but the call was ended. Her mother was gone.

No, no, no. She was not your mother. You know this. You . . . know . . . this!

She pulled up recent calls, tapped the number, and put the phone back to her ear.

"Your call cannot be completed as dialed."

Good.

Very good.

Layla lowered the phone, chest rising and falling with deep, edge-of-panic breaths, and forced a brittle laugh.

"It worked," she whispered. "Holy hell, did it work."

They had come up with plenty of spooky shit over the years at Sector Six at DARPA, which was an intersecting point of elite engineers and deeply paranoid thinkers, but still, she hadn't been ready for that.

She drank a tiny bottle of vodka from the minibar, which seemed like the least she could do to celebrate after saving the world, then picked up a second phone, this one company-issued, and called a phone number in Langley, Virginia. Her breathing was steady and her voice was clear when she delivered a short, crisp message.

"Seeker Script is operational."

ASH POINT, MAINE
OCTOBER 25, 2025

"People like to talk about UFOs when they talk about Ash Point," the sunburned man with the wild white hair said, facing the camera squarely but keeping his eyes downcast. "That's nonsense. But the danger isn't."

His eyes came up, found the camera, and held it.

"Instead of looking for trouble from another world," Abe Zimmer said, "folks would be well advised to look closer to home."

"Love it," Charlie Goodwin said from behind the camera. "Perfect, Abe. That's gold."

The old man's stern face fractured into a smile that made his previous intensity seem imagined.

"You sure? I never like seeing myself on camera."

"That's why you have me," Charlie said, and she paused the video and stepped away from the tripod on which her iPhone rested, facing the old pilot and the rusty, eight-foot-high chain-link fence behind him, which was adorned with weather-beaten signs warning away trespassers, promising criminal charges, and asserting the authority of the federal government. Beyond the fence was a long ribbon of runway, the only part of the facility that looked fresh, with unmarred asphalt, repaved every two years on the taxpayer's dime. The handful of low-slung concrete buildings that flanked the runway were abandoned, their steel doors draped with chains and padlocks, the windows boarded up.

Welcome to Ash Point, Maine, property of the Office of Naval Research.

Charlie Goodwin, seventeen-year-old cinematographer in the making, hated everything about the place except for the stories. Well, the stories and the view. If she turned away from the runway and the rusted fence, she'd be facing the breathtaking vista of the North Atlantic, waves breaking on granite ledges beneath a cobalt sky. Abe Zimmer's tall tales were better than the view, though, and filming them helped keep Charlie, a Brooklyn kid from birth who'd been forced to move to rural Maine by her father less than six months ago, from losing her mind and hitchhiking home. She'd picked up 10,000 followers since posting her first conspiracy video. The public loved a paranoid old man, and Abe Zimmer looked straight out of central casting.

"Ignore the camera," she instructed him. "Be natural: Let your eyes go where they want."

It was more effective when Abe didn't look into the camera. He had the keen squint of the former pilot he'd once been. Watching that gaze flash around the desolate old base was by turns compelling and hilarious, as was the way he'd lower his voice to a dramatic whisper before asking a rhetorical question.

"Should I start with the construction of the base?" he asked.

"No, I want the story of the wreck. The anniversary is coming up. That's when we'll have the most views."

Abe scowled. "You told me you were going to do a real documentary, like Ken Burns, not that TikTok shit that the communists want our eyes on."

Damn it, why wasn't she recording? That was a perfect line: she could see viewers jamming index fingers as they hit "Subscribe."

"The social channels are samples for crowdfunding, Abe. You know this."

He grunted, spat into the weeds. He was dressed in faded jeans and an olive T-shirt that said *BUFF Brewing* and had the silhouette of a B-52 soaring over a pint glass. Between the shirt and the windblown white hair, he couldn't have been styled better, and she hadn't even had to ask. Natural content—that was Abe Zimmer.

"Yeah, yeah, funding," he said. "Okay, so I just talk you through the wreck like you've never friggin' heard about it?"

"Exactly like that."

He sighed, and she thought she was about to lose him, so she pressed: "We'll finish in the taproom. Dad told me there's fresh Tail Gunner on tap."

"Well, let's quit bullshitting and get on with it, then," Abe said.

Tail Gunner IPA was what held Charlie captive to this place, although nobody had paid a dime for one yet. Her parents had been determined to turn their love of craft beer into a career. There were a few hitches to the plan. Foremost: Charlie's mother was the brewer, and she was dead. Her dad grasped the chemistry and had the formulas that her mother had left behind from years of study, but there was a difference between having your grandmother's recipe card and her pie, or between holding blueprints and drawing them. Talent was not a chain-of-title possession.

How did you explain this to your own grieving father?

Not that Charlie hadn't tried. Oh, how Charlie had tried.

The whole idea was madness. No matter how wonderful the beer was—Charlie's limited sampling suggested it was adequate but not exceptional, and her palate was already more refined than her dad would dare to consider—his chosen location was a clinical example of stupidity. Even in peak summer season, Ash Point was remote for tourist travel, more than an hour north of Bar Harbor and Acadia, a desolate peninsula in what was known as "Downeast" Maine, a reference that had something to do with the way wind currents carried sailors downwind and to the east even as they traveled north, into colder and emptier waters.

It was there, on tall cliffs above those cold, empty waters, that BUFF Brewing was to be born. Its success formula: cold beer and old planes. The "BUFF" in question was the B-52 Stratofortress, and Charlie Goodwin had been young when she learned that the nickname "BUFF" did not, in fact, stand for "Big Ugly Fat *Fellow*" but "Big Ugly Fat Fucker." Her mother taught her this. Dana Goodwin, maiden name Hightower, had been a military brat, growing up on Air Force bases, and her grandfather had achieved a moment's notoriety for the inauspicious achievement of flying a B-52 right into the side of a Maine mountain.

Oops!

That had been the title of the first of Charlie's TikTok and YouTube videos featuring the wreck site.

The story of the B-52 had faded from the public consciousness in a blink, but it lingered in Hightower family lore. This generations-old tragedy was what led Charlie's father, fresh off his own tragedy, to pack up his daughter and move to Maine. He was addicted to grief, not alcohol. The potential brewery had been his wife's dream, and why should a little thing like her death get in the way of that? Then kismet happened: Greg Goodwin encountered Abe Zimmer. In the type of plan that could only be formed while consuming alcohol, Greg and Abe agreed to a brewery and museum hybrid. The people would come for the beer, but they would learn of the forgotten heroes.

It would have remained talk, as the geographic cure usually should, until Dana died and Greg began to blame the city itself for her death.

He and Charlie left Brooklyn in June, arriving in Maine to impossibly cold weather for the first month of summer, and although Charlie was outraged, she strived for patience. She knew the move was born of heartbreak. She had tried to go along. She really had. The videos were a lifeline, and her father didn't appreciate them, because he thought they were making light of sacred history. But good news today: Greg was gone. Her dad was off for a brewing festival in Wisconsin, and that meant Charlie had the whole weekend to shoot.

She wasn't about to waste it.

"Roll on three," she told Abe, counted three beats, then gave him a closed fist to indicate she was filming. None of this technique was real, but it *sounded* real, and that was all she needed to sell Abe on her legitimacy.

He began to stroll beside the rusty fence and the freshly paved runway, moving quickly, his wiry frame seeming built for speed. He was shorter than Charlie, but he always swelled up and announced that he was perfect pilot height.

Those poor tall bastards can't handle the g-forces like me, he would say. He was infinitely proud of his posture, and the ramrod bearing made him seem almost as tall as Charlie, who was five nine.

"Date was October 28, 1962," he said. "Everyone was worrying about the shit going down in Cuba, but locals who were paying attention were also keeping an eye on Ash Point. Because, for a supposedly closed facility, it was awfully friggin' busy. They'd added an electrified fence. You can still see the conductors."

He pointed, and Charlie pivoted to capture the end of the lane that led off down the peninsula, the blues and grays of the coast tapering to dark layers of pines pressing close to the road.

"Now you tell me, why does the Navy add an electric fence and guard tower to a closed facility?" Abe asked. "Doesn't take a detective to answer that question. During the Cuban missile crisis, this airfield was as busy as a New Orleans whorehouse on Mardi Gras."

Thank you, internet gods, Charlie thought. *You have smiled upon me. I can already see the merch.*

"Now, it had been Indian summer, about like you see today," Abe continued, striding ahead. "Clear blue skies, warm temperatures, the whole bit. Then came the twenty-eighth, and the clouds started to come in. After the clouds?"

He sneaked a glance at the camera, unable to help himself.

"After the clouds came the plane," he said, voice dropping. "Tail number was 60-3730, but the name was the *Loring Loonatic,* spelled like the bird. They had the paint job on the cockpit, you know, to personalize the plane. The bomber was based at Loring Air Force Base in Aroostook County, near Limestone, up in border country, nothing around but hundreds of miles of forest, some owned by the timber companies, some owned by the government, and maybe— *probably*—some owned by both."

Yes, yes, yes! Charlie wanted to shout. She had to bite her lip to keep from smiling. Abe needed the audience to take him seriously or he'd grow petulant. You couldn't laugh during one of his tall tales. He demanded credulity.

Abe reached out to trace the old fence with his fingertips as if summoning memories.

"When Ash Point was built, they said it was a radar station. Well, you tell me: Why does a radar station need a runway like *that*?"

He paused and gestured at the expanse of tarmac.

"We knew they were up to something, likely had to do with Loring and the North River Depot and nuclear weapons. There were a hundred different spook projects going on in the woods up here in Maine, what with us being so far away from watching eyes, and the locals being known as a discreet type."

Charlie fought the smile back again. Abe Zimmer loved to describe Mainers as the original mind-your-own-business breed—even while gossiping about everything he'd ever heard, new or old.

"The storm that blew in that October was like nothing I'd seen before and nothing I've seen since. We're used to rough weather. A nor'easter is no more exciting than a cloudburst to us. But what they had that day was the type of storm modern folks would call a 'bomb cyclone.' One of those hundred-year storms that seem to happen every other damn day, but now people can't seem to remember last week, let alone last year."

Charlie made a beckoning gesture, trying to keep him on track. Once Abe got going about the way society had changed, he was liable to run her out of battery before he got back to the plane wreck.

"Ayuh, so Indian summer turned to a black sky and fifteen-foot swells," Abe said. "The wind was *howling*, and first there was sleet, and then there was snow, and then . . . then came the B-52."

He turned and eyed the hillside as if he were watching the plane descend all over again.

"She came in roaring and never slowed." He made a steep sweeping motion with his hand. "You could hear the impact for miles, and if you lived close enough, like I did, you could feel it in your bones, right in your gut. My father and an old boy named Norbert Cyr jumped into a Jeep and drove for the wreck site. I went with 'em."

This time the pause didn't seem intended for drama. It felt reflective. Charlie was about to nudge Abe when he spoke again.

"We found the only survivor," he said. "He'd ejected, but his chute didn't deploy. His ejection seat landed in a thicket of pines that all collapsed inward . . . "

He made a gesture with both hands, bending his fingers toward one another.

"And he stuck right up at the top. We fished him out. Hadn't so much as had a chance to begin looking for the others when the boys from the base showed up. DARPA, although it was called ARPA back then. Now listen: the man we found was *alive*. Looked right at me with the brightest blue eyes I've ever seen, before or since. Then the military claimed him and next thing you know, there were no survivors at all. They said everyone had ejected and been lost at sea. But I know what I saw! And it's past time that someone admitted why Ash Point still exists at all, inactive but under military control. Take a look at that runway."

Charlie panned over the clean tarmac as the easterly breeze scoured dust across its surface.

"The Navy repaved that last year," Abe said. "Same as they have every two years for the past six decades. Now you tell me: Why would they do that?"

"Cut," Charlie said. "Perfect, Abe. Perfect."

They crossed the cracked asphalt and entered the BUFF Brewing taproom, which had once been a service station built by an enterprising local on the one road that led to the airfield at the end of the remote peninsula. Once the military moved out, the service station and the saltbox-style house behind it were left behind like battlefield casualties. When the property came up for sale, it stayed up for sale. Time went by, the property price plummeted, and Greg Goodwin's therapy sessions did little for his grief or his growing paranoia about the city. No crime rate data could deter him from an overwhelming fear—not after his wife picked the wrong store on the wrong day. Coincidental tragedy wasn't something he could wrap his head around; Dana's death had to *mean* something, and he decided it meant the city was rotten and his duty as a protector was to remove his daughter from the threat.

Where to go?

Off to chase a dead woman's dreams.

They'd moved in three years after Dana Goodwin's death, and the meager solace that time had provided to Charlie evaporated with the transition to the strange place. Now she lived in an apartment above a brewery that wasn't even open, adjacent to an airfield that hadn't functioned in decades. Everything about Ash Point revolved around an absence. She needed only to endure two semesters and escape to college. Survive and advance, she told her friends back home. It was like a tournament—or a prison sentence.

When she followed Abe Zimmer into the taproom, she saw Lawrence Zimmer waiting on a barstool and had to hide a grimace.

Lawrence was Abe's grandson, Charlie's classmate at beautiful Cold Harbor High, a school whose mascot was—you couldn't make this shit up—the Crustacean Sensation. Lawrence would regularly wear his letter jacket with the cartoon logo of a muscular lobster across the back, and he didn't even wear it ironically. He was one of those *Go, team! Hoo-rah!* guys who seemed like he was auditioning for a reboot of *Happy Days* or some shit. Potsie Weber with a fishing boat. He wasn't unattractive—actually, he'd probably be cute if he didn't have a buzz cut that suggested he was in ROTC, tall and broad shouldered, built like a basketball player. He had strong features, a nice smile, and observant eyes that were a lovely shade of blue—downright pretty, in fact. The only problem with Lawrence was just . . . *him.* His door-opening, *Pardon me, miss* behavior, his thoughtful silence in the classroom paired with enthusiastic clapping at the pep rallies, made him feel like as much of a caricature as the lobster mascot on his jacket. The most infuriating thing about him, Charlie thought, was the way he always watched the new girl as if he were rooting for her, as if she were a cause that needed a champion.

Gross.

"Where have you been?" Lawrence asked his grandfather. He acted like a chaperone to Abe. His father had joined the merchant marine and stayed gone, and his mother, Abe's daughter, taught first grade. Charlie had never seen the father, but Lawrence surely had inherited his height from that side of the family, because he towered over his grandfather and seemed to feel that the extra inches granted him superiority. He was always checking on how many beers Abe had enjoyed and giving little sighs of disapproval.

"Been telling stories you should know by heart, if you bothered to pay attention," Abe said breezily.

"Is she letting you review them before she posts them?" Lawrence asked. He had notebooks spread out on the bar in front of him, an iPad propped above those, immersed in homework. If he wasn't practicing for one of the three sports he participated in, he was studying, like a bot designed to replace a normal teen.

"What's that supposed to mean?" Charlie said.

"If it's his story, seems like he should get a say in how it's shared."

"He's the one telling it!"

"But you're editing it."

"And to think," Charlie said, "most people would say your grandpa is the conspiracy theorist of the family."

"It's not a theory. The editor is more important than the—"

"Oh, hush," Abe said. "It's all to the good of the cause. TikTok will win the day for the communists if we let them, sure, but before that happens, I might as well raise some money for the museum."

"Right," Lawrence said. "The museum."

He and Charlie both glanced at the vaunted museum space. It consisted of a roped-off area featuring a dozen framed black-and-white photographs, two rusty props from an unknown plane, and the signature piece: a B-52 ejection seat. A hulking piece of olive-colored metal with a red headrest, drab harness belts, yellow levers, and footrests that looked like something from a wheelchair designed by Satan, the ejection seat was Abe Zimmer's prize. He was convinced that it would bring paying tourists and hadn't taken kindly to Charlie's suggestion that they charge five bucks to tip people backward in the seat and pour tequila shots down their throats to turn the old wreck into a moneymaker.

"I saw that done with an old dentist's chair once," she'd said, a regrettable confession that led to a conversation with her father about where, exactly, she had encountered a dentist's chair and a tequila bottle. Charlie maintained her standard excuse: TikTok. Everything was on TikTok! Gosh, Dad!

"We're gonna demo the ejection sequence here shortly, but first I need to wet my whistle," Abe said, heading around the bar.

"It's not even nine in the morning," Lawrence said.

"He's a grown-up," Charlie said. She couldn't stand Lawrence's holier-than-thou attitude. He was so *earnest* all the time. Not good video content. "Dad just put fresh Tail Gunner on tap, Abe. He wanted your opinion."

"See! Drinking's not a problem if it's a profession," Abe said, grabbing a mug and heading for the tap handles.

"Is your dad off for his brewing festival?" Lawrence asked, regarding Charlie through solemn blue eyes that always held the expression of a judge on the verge of issuing a bench decree.

"It's a business conference," Charlie said. "They determine the proper pricing of different hops and malts and discuss commodities."

"Is he flying or driving to the business conference?"

"Are you auditing his expenses?"

"No. But if he's flying today, he'll be delayed."

Charlie blinked. "What?"

"There's been a big ground stop. Nationwide. It was on TV all morning."

"Huh?"

"A ground stop is when the FAA—"

"I know what it is!"

"Well, there's one today. A software glitch or systems trouble or something. Full national stop."

"Your dad will be just fine." Abe waved a hand impatiently at his grandson as if he didn't want Lawrence agitating Charlie. The idea that she might be considered emotionally tender was annoying.

"I'm not saying he won't be fine," Lawrence said. "It's just that—"

"I'm not worried; I just want to know what's going on," Charlie snapped. The truth of it was that she was worried—a little.

Lawrence shrugged. "I didn't read all of it."

"I thought you said you saw it on TV?"

"Yep."

"Do you *read* the TV?"

"I do when it's muted and the captioning is on," he said evenly.

Abe tipped his mug at the 45-degree angle that he claimed allowed for the perfect pour, pulled the tap handle forward, and began to fill the mug with beer.

"Probably was TikTok that caused the problem," he said. "Infected the systems. Chinese aggression. You can't say I didn't call it."

Charlie picked up the remote control and turned on the TV that was mounted in the corner of the room.

"What's CNN out here?" She didn't watch much TV, just used her phone and iPad.

"Oh, put on the real news, not that godless BS!" Abe barked, and Charlie heard Lawrence sigh softly.

"It's 232," he said.

Charlie punched in the channel and dropped the remote back onto the bar, prepared to have to wait for the FAA story to cycle back up in the breaking news, if they hadn't already moved on for good.

There was no wait.

"What is the price of one sick pilot?" a blond female anchor asked the camera. "Not much. But what is the price of five hundred sick pilots? According to the Nasdaq, S&P 500, and Dow Jones Industrial, billions of dollars and counting. Trading indexes are plummeting this morning as news of the callout effort by pilots for all major American carriers began. The Air Line Pilots Association has adamantly denied that this is a coordinated labor effort, but no one is saying what else it might be. All we understand is that the impact will be felt by a lot of Americans today, as the FAA has now implemented a full ground stop while officials assess this situation. All departures have ceased nationwide."

That explains the clear sky, Charlie thought, remembering how empty and blue it had been outside: no contrails from jets out of Logan or Bangor or Halifax.

"The White House and Pentagon have not responded to requests for comment, although we are being promised a briefing is forthcoming. Every major American carrier is affected. It's too early to say what is happening right now, but it is not too early to say travelers are dealing with a major headache."

The camera cut away from the news desk to show the Minneapolis airport, and then Phoenix, and then Houston. The terminals were packed with frustrated people, almost everyone looking at a phone or talking into one, some people sitting on the floor.

"That's enough of that," Abe announced, and muted the TV. "We don't need to worry the girl, Lawrence."

"*The girl* is not worried," Charlie said. "Just curious."

She had to stop herself from taking out her phone to text her dad, though. In the weeks after her mother's murder, she'd texted him constantly when he was away from home, and now she blamed that in part for her existence in Ash Point. If she'd been braver at the start, maybe he wouldn't have overreacted to the city's dangers.

"For the record," Abe said, "fear is a wonderful thing. American

25

resilience is rooted in our capacity for alarm. It's one of the great strengths of our national character. Why, think of Paul Revere."

"Paul Revere had real news to deliver," Lawrence observed. "He wasn't alarmed; he was reporting facts."

"You're missing the point, grandson. Negative thinking encourages preparation."

"Quick," Charlie said, "let's start digging a bunker."

"You laugh now, but someday you won't. Your generation has immediate knowledge but no wisdom."

"But the problem with *your* generation—" Charlie began, and Lawrence cut her off.

"Please, please, don't feed the beast," he moaned.

Charlie ignored him. "The problem with *your* generation is that you're alarmed by the wrong things. Your capacity for alarm has exceeded the demand."

"Give me one example."

"Pronouns," Charlie said, and then fluttered her hands overhead like a ghost from *Scooby-Doo*: *Wooo-oooo-ooo!*

"Pfft." Abe waved her off. "I leave that bullshit for unsophisticated thinkers. What I'm trying to tell you people, Generation Snore or whatever you call yourselves, is that you can't sleepwalk through a nightmare."

Charlie and Lawrence exchanged a puzzled glance.

"I think you can," Charlie said. "If you're sleepwalking, there's an inherent chance that your dream is a nightmare."

"Horseshit! Dreams come during REM sleep, when the body is paralyzed."

"I don't even know what we're talking about anymore," Lawrence said.

"The great gift of fear," Abe said, pulling the tap handle again, topping his mug of morning beer. "If you maintain a proper skepticism of all things—the Big G not excepted—then you're prepared for trouble. You kids aren't ready for trouble because you've never seen it. Hell, you were born after 9/11. You have no memory of vulnerability. That's a dangerous way to live."

"Wait—are we supposed to be afraid *for* the government or afraid *of* it?" Charlie asked.

"Both," Abe replied without hesitation.

"That's just paranoia."

"Nah," Abe said. "If you're alarmed about enough things, one of them is bound to be right eventually."

Charlie couldn't help but laugh. "There's a T-shirt slogan."

Lawrence didn't seem to share her amusement.

"You came in here to film, didn't you?" he said.

"Roger that," Abe said, setting down his mug, beer foam flecking his mustache. He went to stand beside the ejection seat while Charlie adjusted her tripod.

"Okay, Abe," she said, "tell us a little bit about the rumors surrounding Ash Point."

"Hell, there were all kinds of rumors. You know how it goes in a small town. Or I suppose you don't, since you get all your news from videos. But there was a time when people had to gossip face-to-face. Dark days, I know." He belched, then wiped his mouth. "We can talk rumors later; let's get to the ejection sequence. We need some action. Lawrence, man your post."

When Lawrence stood up from the bar and walked to the ejection seat, Charlie saw he was wearing his letter jacket, the big, muscular cartoon lobster grinning at the world from his back. She snickered. The Crustacean Sensation. Her followers would love that.

As Lawrence fastened the harness belts that secured him to the ejection seat and then placed his feet into the ankle collars that restrained his legs, looking like Hannibal Lecter being denied a snack,

Charlie was immersed in the task of filming, oblivious to the muted TV behind her. She had fans to worry about. Content didn't generate itself. They'd reboot the FAA system and get the planes in the air, her dad would head home, and all would be well.

Later, she would remember that feeling as if it had belonged to another girl in another life.

CRANE, INDIANA
SEPTEMBER 1961

The future of warfare—if not humanity—changed on a hot August day on the grounds of a naval base more than 1,000 miles from the nearest ocean. The discovery involved a single scientist and a model airplane.

The Crane Naval Surface Warfare Center had been created in World War II and now covered more than ninety-seven square miles. During the war they'd made rockets, missiles, bombs, flares, fuses, and detonators. By 1943, chemical weapons had been added, beginning with mustard gas, and a decontamination station was added. What was once temporary became permanent. The Second World War ended, but then conflict began in Korea, and Pentagon planners eyed the threat of the Soviets, weighed the risks in Vietnam and an ascendant China, and poured more money into the facility at Crane. Newer weapons came and went. Some of these were disclosed publicly; others were not.

The least interesting building on the sprawling base was, no doubt, Microfilm Storage Building #45, a bland concrete structure that was, on the surface, exactly what it claimed to be: an archive filled with thousands of canisters of film stacked on long metal shelves. Beneath the surface, in a cavernous warehouse of nearly 25,000 square feet, was a massive laboratory referred to by those select few in the know as "Hazelton's barracks."

Dr. Martin Hazelton was a tall, trim man with salt-and-pepper hair and a sharp, angular chin. He would've been handsome enough for the passing resemblance to Cary Grant to be noticeable were it not for his perpetually harried quality. During the war he had been a physicist in Oak Ridge, Tennessee, and Los Alamos, New Mexico, among the many whose calculations served in development of the atomic bomb. His expertise was the impact of electromagnetic energy on electronics.

Once, this had been a question of atmospheric research. The electromagnetic threat came when pilots flew into storms.

That changed with Oppenheimer.

Now there were vital questions surrounding nuclear war, and Marty Hazelton was tasked with just one: If an atomic bomb was detonated over the continental United States, how might planes in the air be shielded? What he did in Microfilm Storage Building #45 looked much like what American boys did on rainy Saturday afternoons. He built and painted model planes.

What happened then was a little different: he flew his radio-controlled models into a cloud of high-voltage current.

The paints and epoxies he used were reflective blends designed to shield electrical components. Ordinarily, he worked with models of the B-52. Sentimental, perhaps, as it was his little brother's plane—Hank Hazelton was an Air Force pilot—but the B-52 was also the nation's apex predator, its most capable nuclear bomber.

On the other side of the world, the Russians put nuclear warheads on rockets and dug silos deep into the earth, while Marty Hazelton flew toy planes into homemade clouds to watch their electric brains fry. Sizzle and crash, sizzle and crash.

He did not feel foolish.

The problem delighted him because he was sure it could be solved. One of the great unspoken truths of World War II was how *exciting* it had been. The nation had been united in a way it might never have been before and likely never would be again, and much of the world had joined America in both sentiment and strategy, and what emerged from that moment, well . . .

"'Now I am become Death, the destroyer of worlds,'" Oppenheimer had said after the Trinity test.

How unseemly, against that backdrop, to speak of excitement. And yet any scientist knew that it was true. Certainly, they knew it at General Electric and Westinghouse and RCA, at Boeing and Grumman and NASA. Everything was a race. "Show your work" became "Let's give it a shot."

This approach wasn't necessarily foolish. Many of the greatest breakthroughs in the history of science had been made quite accidentally. Mold spores appeared in a petri dish and then penicillin was discovered and health care would never be the same. A chocolate bar melted in a chemist's pocket and microwave technology clarified. Film was forgotten in a drawer and radiation scientists were handed Nobel Prizes.

This was how it happened: hard work and deep thought met happy accidents. "Holy curiosity," Einstein had said. Einstein, the German. What might the world look like had he stayed in his home country? What great American skylines might've turned to ash? One could never know. You could only seize the opportunity with the right attitude, and the right attitude was always—*always*—curiosity.

Marty Hazelton's holy curiosity hadn't waned, but he had to admit it had been a very unproductive stretch of results. The trouble was shielding an object in motion. You could harden a building with properly reinforced concrete, and you could armor land-based components with a Faraday cage that dispersed the electricity, but for a plane, neither was practical. Marty was sure there was a simpler approach in a reflective shield.

Am making good progress, he lied cheerfully in a telegram to the Pentagon, the office of Admiral Ralph H. Cutting, his ultimate superior at the Office of Naval Research.

On September 25, President Kennedy addressed the United Nations, saying: "Today, every inhabitant of this planet must contemplate the day when this planet may no longer be inhabitable. Every man, woman, and child lives under a nuclear sword of Damocles, hanging by the slenderest of threads, capable of being cut at any moment by accident or miscalculation or by madness. The weapons of war must be abolished before they abolish us."

Marty listened as he sat at one of his long modeling tables, scraping at the freshly sharpened tip of his #2 Ticonderoga pencil with his thumbnail while waiting on yet another experimental epoxy to dry. The latest included silver nitrate. You added and subtracted and tested and observed; this was all that could be done.

Add, subtract, test, observe.

Move forward.

The life of a scientist. Of anyone, really. But there came a time when the subtractions outnumbered the additions. Aging meant that the brain became less and the body matched it or one outpaced the other—but subtraction was the only promise. Had his problem-solving mind peaked? Most great mathematicians had their significant breakthroughs in their twenties. Violin prodigies excelled in their teens. Those years were far, far in the rearview mirror.

When he finally came back into the moment, he glanced at his thumbnail and saw there was a fine gray dusting of pencil lead across it.

Graphite, really. What was called "pencil lead" didn't involve any actual lead. It was a mixture of clay and graphite.

He leaned close to the messy graphite dust pile he'd made, drew in a breath to blow the dust out of sight and out of mind, then stopped. Hovered with his pursed lips close to the dust, like a man on the verge of a kiss.

Graphite was an underrated substance. It was a good conductor of electricity and heat. Put to proper pressure, it could be converted into a diamond; put to proper heat, a diamond could be turned to graphite. Electricity applied parallel to the basal planes of graphite was conducted well, but electricity applied perpendicularly made the substance a thousand times *less* conductive. Likewise, it conducted heat well in the parallel and *insulated* it in the perpendicular.

Remarkable.

The problem with graphite was producing it in a stable material. Say, a pliable sheet, something that could be molded and shaped. This was why the bulk of such a fascinating substance went into nothing more exciting than pencil lead. Then again, it had been with a pencil that Einstein wrote $E = mc^2$, so you couldn't say the substance had been a complete waste of potential.

Marty leaned back, studied the dust, and then looked at the Scotch tape resting on his desk.

He tore off a small strip, lowered it carefully to the dust pile with nimble modeler's fingers, and lifted the pencil-lead dust clean from the table. Held the graphite-smudged transparent tape up to the light. One of the fascinating things about graphite was its ability to absorb light from all visible spectrums.

He turned to his model B-52 and placed the graphite-coated tape on the wing.

Foolish.

And yet . . .

An insulator and a conductor, and one with fascinating implications.

That afternoon, Dr. Martin Hazelton requested a sample of high-quality graphite from his procurement clerk at the Office of Naval Research, then spent days laboriously flaking enough of it off to coat every square inch of his model B-52 with copper tape and graphite. He had no real theory about what it would do: this was the fun of it.

Research science was a marvelous job.

The electric arc field Marty had constructed at the far end of the warehouse was really nothing more than an oversize Jacob's ladder, a school science fair experiment on steroids. Massive transformers powered twelve-foot-high rods that looked like the uprights of goalposts on a football field. Between the goalposts sparked enough voltage to kill a man on contact.

He'd incinerated a lot of taxpayer dollars between those goalposts.

As he launched his radio-controlled plane and flew it across the expanse of MSB #45, he had the passing feeling of sorrow that he always felt just before they fried. He sometimes had to suppress a wince when he heard the sizzle of their electronic brains.

When this model plane hit the high-voltage cloud, there was a distinct crackling sound, sharper than any he'd heard before, one that seemed to come almost from inside his own skull, and then a remarkable thing happened.

For an instant, brief but undeniable, he could see the wiring within the plane *glow*, a bright, iridescent web of blue lines, like an X-ray image of the plane's insides. The blue was the color of St. Elmo's fire, offering a perfect schematic of the plane's wiring. Around the web of bright blue wires, the rest of the plane turned to a cloud of gray dust, one that reminded him of a mayfly hatch on a Maine pond, forming a collective shape in the outline of the plane, but full of undeniably distinct, individual parts.

Buzzzzz.

The little motor hummed; the plane passed through the electric current and then seemed to pop back into its previous form with an audible *snap*: no smoke, no glow, no trace of damage. A toy once more.

Marty was so astonished that he almost flew the plane into the concrete wall. He adjusted the controller at the last moment, brought the plane around in a tight turn, leveled it out, and landed it.

He cut the electricity and went to inspect the plane. While he couldn't swear to it, he thought there had been a rearrangement of the pattern in the graphite dust beneath the tape, almost like seeing different fingerprints on a card—close matches but not exact. He turned the battery off, turned the battery on. Started the motor. Stopped it. Started it again.

The plane was utterly unscathed.

That day, he ordered more graphite.

Have holy curiosity.

ASH POINT, MAINE
OCTOBER 25, 2025

The trouble came, as it historically had come at Ash Point, out of the sky.

Charlie was lazing in an Adirondack chair outside the taproom, scrolling through TikTok and waiting for the day to warm up—although days didn't seem to truly warm much in Maine in October—when something glimmered in her peripheral vision and made her look up from the screen.

The sky was a high bright blue, so vivid it almost hurt, one of those days when a photo would look color-doctored, it was so perfect. Charlie had to shield her eyes as she sought the glitter that had drawn her attention. Once her vision was shaded, she spotted it again: a sparkling silver dome drifting right to left, spat out of the cloudless sky.

It was a balloon.

A big balloon. Even up high, some hundred feet or more off the ground, its unusual size was clear. It was a perfect circle, white disrupted by silver seams, like the black lines on a basketball. As it drifted, it spun, and the silver seams threw sparklers of reflected sunlight. It was still inflated—didn't seem to be losing any air at all, in fact—and yet it was descending rapidly.

Holding its shape perfectly but nevertheless dropping as if it had been pierced, the balloon crossed over the roof of Charlie's house and carried on toward Spruce Hill. It seemed to be accelerating and descending at the same time, like a remote-controlled plane with an operator.

She turned and looked at the water. The bay was empty. There were buoys marking lobster traps in all directions but no boats at work. The tide was out, and the rocky beach smelled of wet sand and seaweed and decaying fish—that uniquely low-tide odor—but the rocks were as empty as the water. If someone was operating the balloon, they were a long way off. Was it a drone, maybe?

A drone was intended to return to its pilot. The balloon sure didn't seem to be; it looked like it was going to crash right up on the hill. Well, not crash, exactly—just . . . land.

Another five seconds, maybe ten, and then it was out of sight, down somewhere behind the signature spruce trees that guarded the high ridge. The sunlight that had illuminated those odd silver seams lost contact with them in the trees, the balloon's glow extinguishing like a lightbulb at the flick of a switch.

"What the hell?" Charlie muttered, and then, too late, looked at her phone. Damn it, she'd been so distracted, she'd missed taking a video. That would've been a fun one: *UFO over Ash Point!*

Where had it come from? Impossible to determine. But she knew where it had gone down: right by the wreckage of the old B-52.

She looked back at the plate glass windows of the taproom, saw only her own reflection, and hesitated. Abe and Lawrence were in there. Ordinarily, Charlie would never consider asking Lawrence Zimmer to join her on a trip up Spruce Hill. Today, though, she felt a strange sense of unease at the idea of pursuing the balloon by herself.

But asking for company was ridiculous. She went up Spruce Hill all the time—it was her daily hike when the weather was nice—so why on earth did she want companionship now, just because a balloon had drifted in?

It didn't drift in. It landed. There's a difference.

"Oh, sack up, Goodwin," Charlie muttered to herself, using Abe Zimmer's phrase for all moments of required courage, and then she walked to the Kawasaki ATV her dad used for running back and forth from the house to the brewery. Charlie mocked the Kawasaki relentlessly on her social channels, but in truth she loved riding it, wind in her face, hair fanned back. It made her look ridiculous, she knew, like someone who owned a meat smoker and knew the whole cast of *Yellowstone*, but it was fun, a secret guilty pleasure in her forced rural existence.

Another thing she privately appreciated about Ash Point was the wreck site itself.

Up there, she had memories of her mother. Each winter since the crash, a group of locals made the frigid trip up the mountain on snowmobiles for a Christmas vigil at the wreck site. That tradition began with the Zimmer family and others who'd helped with the rescue effort. Most of those locals were dead now, but the ceremony continued, and Charlie found that touching. There was something beautiful about remembering dead strangers, especially when you were generations removed from their suffering.

Mostly, though, what had been beautiful was her mother.

They made the trip up from Brooklyn every year for the ceremony, and back then Charlie had found Ash Point intriguing, the way you could feel about an awful place when you were only visiting—like, say, Alcatraz. Perspective changed a great deal when it became your home. While she'd certainly never cared about Ash Point the way her mother did, Charlie's throat would still tighten when the group lit their candles and stood together beneath the forty-foot-tall piece of the massive plane's tail that had caused all the trouble. It was called a vertical stabilizer. It didn't stabilize so well in all conditions. A blizzard was one of them. The anniversary ceremony was held in the winter because the Zimmers wanted to honor the dead in the snow, the way it had been on the day of that freak October storm.

The plane had come from Loring Air Force Base in northern Maine, flying low over the wilderness to simulate the tactics needed to evade Russian radar systems, and it turned out that flying low created turbulence that stressed the stabilizer. Stressed it so much, in fact, that it was sheared right off the plane.

Flying without a tail meant looking for a place to land in a hurry, and Ash Point's airfield represented the crew's last best hope. They'd missed it by a quarter mile. That sounded like a lot until you looked at that vertical stabilizer, which was almost as tall as the five-story brownstone Charlie had lived in, and imagined piloting a plane without it, flying over an ocean and through a blizzard. Charlie's great-grandfather had performed an almost epic act of heroism.

For one man, if Abe Zimmer was to be believed, he'd even delivered. Abe's version of the survivor strapped into the ejection seat, regarding his rescuers with ethereally bright blue eyes, was one of the most popular elements of Charlie's videos, but of course it was bullshit. When or why he'd started to tell the tale, she couldn't say. Maybe it was the booze. He was always pouring another beer. Once, Charlie had asked her father if Abe met the definition of an alcoholic. It had taken Greg Goodwin a long time to answer.

"I think he's still holding the bottle instead of the other way around, Charlie," he'd said at last. "But it's definitely closer than you'd ever want to get."

Charlie didn't care about that, though. What she cared about was Abe's storytelling. He was the perfect messenger for the hilariously bizarre legends of Ash Point. He had been a pilot in the Navy and later for a small commuter airline that took summer people out to the islands from Portland or Bangor. His family had been lobster fishermen, but he always said he'd never cared for the water when the sky was right there above it.

On a day like this, it was easy to understand him. The sky was sapphire, and the few leaves that still clung to the trees were bright red with defiance, the neighbor's fields showing orange splashes from remaining pumpkins. Charlie loved fall. It was the most beautiful season and the saddest: a vibrant, heroic, and futile fight ahead of an inevitable onslaught called winter. The defeat was coming, but you wouldn't know it today, when the sky was high and blue and the leaves flared and the breeze had a tang of decaying apples and cool water.

On up Spruce Hill she drove, chasing the strange balloon, the Kawasaki thrumming against her thighs, the ocean breeze sharp on her face. It was exhilarating. She wished she had someone to share it with, but there was no way to explain the feeling to her friends back home. It looked laughably lame until you did it yourself.

Up over a steep lip of rocky earth and then down the other side, just enough of a drop to put a roller-coaster thrill in her stomach, and then she was facing the first ribbons of ripped metal from the plane, and the balloon that rested in a tree overhead. She parked and killed the ATV's motor, and the silence of the spot cloaked her. The place where the plane had broken apart seemed like an acoustic void, a hollow in the earth where birdsong and breezes didn't reach. It was unfailingly cool here, and the sunlight filtered through trees, creating a shifting, dancing quilt of light and shadow. The place felt, Charlie thought, the way an empty church did.

She wasn't sure why her deepest connection to the purpose of a church came when it was empty. She knew only that it was true.

The plane had leveled a stand of pines and punched a pocket

into the side of the ridge. Bits of debris littered more than an acre. It had been a very large plane, traveling very fast when it hit. While the wreckage alone was impressive—daunting, even: a set of landing gear and wheels dwarfed the ATV—it still didn't do justice to the original plane's size. The Stratofortress was 154 feet long when intact, with a 189-foot wingspan. Charlie had never seen one in person, but she'd read a lot about them to inform the menacing voice-over narration for her videos. It helped to have granular detail, as any quality ghost-hunting show demonstrated. The audience must grasp the most salient detail about the B-52 Stratofortress: they were freaking *huge*.

They were also still in use—not just the design, but the actual planes, which blew Charlie's mind. How could you feel good about using a plane built in 1959 to defend a country in 2025? But the U.S. Air Force kept rehabbing them and flying them. They'd been built as long-range, nuclear-capable bombers in the Cold War, but they'd been used for about every purpose imaginable for a big plane, from bombing in Vietnam, Iraq, and Afghanistan to open-water rescue operations.

Apparently, most of them worked pretty well. Just not this one.

Today, though, Charlie's interest wasn't in the wreck; it was in the balloon. The balloon had landed in a tree, still perfectly inflated, round and fat, like a ripe cherry tomato. The breeze was blowing off the water, but the balloon barely moved, just rocked slightly, almost as if it were happy to be up there. The tree was a slender birch without lower limbs, meaning climbing it was impossible, and the branches that had caught the balloon were at least twenty feet off the ground. She wouldn't be able to reach it with a stick. She didn't understand how on earth it was caught so securely when it looked so light and flimsy.

"Just pop already," she told it.

The balloon shook slightly, from side to side, like a fat cartoon bear. A fat *laughing* cartoon bear, mocking. Charlie turned away. The wind off the North Atlantic would take care of it soon enough, and she'd be happy when it did. There was something about its inexplicable appearance that made her anxious, and she hated that. She had never been a nervous kid, and she was determined not to become one now, not even alone in Maine, her father halfway across the country, not even after what had happened to her mother.

She would honor her mom by sitting for a while at the wreck site, where they'd spent many quiet hours together. The hollow where the balloon had come down was, eerily enough, the closest spot to the cockpit. Charlie didn't like the cockpit—it felt too close to the terror, to the tragedy—and so she was sitting with her back to it, looking out at the sea, when the radio crackled.

For a moment, she thought she'd imagined it. The *rasp, rasp, rasp* of static that should then be punctured by a voice.

No voice came, just the crackling white noise.

She turned in the direction of the sound and fixed on the shattered remnants of the big plane's cockpit.

Crackle, crackle, crackle.

No.

No fucking way.

Crackle, voice, crackle.

Yes way.

Charlie walked toward the sound as if unable to resist its pull, and on her way across the shallow blast crater that was now filled with fallen leaves, she felt no fear—felt nothing at all, really—just that physical pull, incontestable, moving her like iron filings in the presence of a magnet.

She knelt beside the shell where once a pilot had sat. The shattered remains of the old radio were in there somewhere, along with a single, rotting spiral of cord, likely a microphone cable. She leaned

43

closer, trying to track it through the shadowed interior. The crackling static cleared, silence returning for a long moment as if to set the stage.

Then came a human voice, well defined, strong, and feminine.

"Charlie, this is your mother. You must not fly today."

It had been a long time since Charlie had screamed, truly *screamed*, and she wanted to now, but she was too terrified to make a sound.

Instead, she turned and ran.

RAVEN ROCK MOUNTAIN COMPLEX, PENNSYLVANIA
OCTOBER 25, 2025

The United States director of national intelligence, a bald man with gray-blue eyes and a chest adorned by countless ribbons, was not happy with Layla Chen.

They were connected on a secure video call, him in the Pentagon, Layla at Site R, otherwise known as the Raven Rock Mountain Complex, a bunker complex in the Blue Ridge Mountains that existed to provide continuity of government in the event of a nuclear or biological attack. The president was not yet present, but Layla Chen was, because Raven Rock's communications system, maintained by the 114th Signal Battalion, was among the most secure in the world, and her current conversation with the DNI was among the most classified conversations in American history.

"Unprecedented," the DNI, whose last name was Hanover, was saying, fine beads of sweat shining on his bald head. "Utterly unprecedented."

That was redundant, Layla thought, but she chose not to point it out. She was doing her best to be patient, which wasn't easy, because

Layla needed to get the hell off this call and get some answers. Hanover was a smart man but also a bureaucrat, and he'd have to deal with the in-person meetings today, starting at the Oval Office. Layla didn't envy him that.

"I cannot fathom," Hanover continued, "that DARPA took such steps without consultation of the Joint Chiefs."

"The consultation was conducted years ago," Layla pointed out. "The system is designed to react as needed."

The system in question was Seeker Script, which was one of Layla's favorite DARPA classified toys. Conventional thinkers would call it artificial intelligence or perhaps a deepfake. Within DARPA, it was known as a "character composite creation," a polite way for saying the same idea that the term "deepfake" conveyed. There were thousands of domestic airline pilots. All of them had mothers. Many of those mothers had been gracious enough to provide social media with samples of their voices, uploading videos to Facebook, Instagram, YouTube, TikTok, and other platforms. Sometimes this was done through their accounts. More often it was done through the accounts of children, grandchildren, friends, neighbors. The data could be scraped, archived, and repurposed. With fairly simple software—at least by DARPA standards—those voices could be prepped with a script and a purpose and then the AI system could handle the dialogue. It was no different than the technology currently being used by chatbots to provide everything from tutoring assistance to mental health counseling to digital romantic partners. Yes, those existed. Layla Chen still thought the latter was a more disturbing idea than anything DARPA had conceived of doing with AI—and she'd been in some wild meetings.

Seeker Script relied on predictive language models to engage the pilots and deliver a clear message: Do not fly.

"The President must approve something of this magnitude," Hanover said.

"Seeker Script was approved by a prior administration. The system is entirely dependent on automated deployment. It was activated by satellite signals indicating the in-flight presence of a lost nuclear weapon."

Hanover started to speak, stopped, then took a breath before he asked the obvious question: "What lost nuclear weapon?"

"The signal corresponds to a B-52 used in Project Kingsolver in 1962," Layla said, doing her damnedest to maintain eye contact.

"What happened to the plane?"

"It disappeared, sir."

"What does that mean? Crashed, fell into the sea, what?"

"We have no idea, sir. Kingsolver was conducted as an effort at invisibility."

There was a long beat, the kind that would ordinarily prompt her to check the connection, but she knew connectivity was not the problem here. Shock was.

"You people can't be serious," Hanover muttered. Hanover, though, knew that DARPA Sector Six was a group of very serious people. Seeker Script had been designed for only the most perilous moments, those in which domestic air traffic needed to be halted without a presidential proclamation—or, more accurately, explanation. Seeker Script was a smoke screen, and one that Layla Chen was enormously proud of, considering it could be achieved with minimal human actors and maximum impact, all while affording elected officials an opportunity to point fingers in any direction they wanted. Deployed effectively, Seeker Script was controlled chaos. It appeared to have been deployed to perfection.

"*Měinǚ*" . . .

Yes. Perfection.

There were other, easier options for clearing the skies. A simple "software glitch" could handle most of it—and had in the past. Seeker

Script was an elevated measure, one that allowed the government to blame an enemy actor. This was reserved for the possibility that combat tactics might be required, at which point the American public would need to know more than that their flights to Orlando had been delayed. If, say, a bomb went off following the grounding of domestic flights, it was crucial to be able to say those actions were not mutually exclusive; rather, they were the clear and coordinated efforts of . . . someone else.

Anyone else.

Domestic tranquility relied on a little bit of paternal secrecy, time to time.

"Tell me that this may be an equipment malfunction," Hanover said, a desperate, imploring tone creeping into his voice.

"We don't believe it's a malfunction. That was the initial hope. The satellite appears to be in good operating condition, however, and reading a consistent signal."

"Then where is the fucking plane?" Hanover said.

A fine question. Layla could feel a pulse behind her eyebrows, tendrils of pain in her temples, like the warning shots of a migraine. Not today. She could not afford to have a headache today. None of the most important people in the world could, and while most of them were known to the public, many were not. Take for example, NASA's planetary defense officer—a real job with a sexy title. Layla Chen's job title was less sexy—officially, she was DARPA's chief archivist—but the reality was something closer to Czar of Old Mistakes. Her role was risk mitigation for decommissioned projects. When DARPA ended a project, it didn't mean the project simply went away. Satellites stayed in orbit, lasers reflected, that kind of thing. The technology traveled. You did what you could to monitor your mistakes, just in case one of them reared its head and unintended consequences demanded swift attention. Project Kingsolver, circa 1962, was a particularly interesting little mistake, as it involved the loss of a nuclear bomber.

Not so shocking, really—the United States had publicly admitted to losing seven nuclear weapons over the years—but Kingsolver was more delicate. That plane had been vanished intentionally. Had the mission gone as planned, it would have returned and landed.

Sometimes, missions did not go as planned. Now a satellite was announcing that maybe Kingsolver had done so after all. Just slower than anticipated.

Layla sipped water, then said, "We are working to ascertain that, sir."

"If there is no plane, then the alarm is false." Hanover's voice sought authority but was unable to overwhelm the fear.

"There could be a gap," Layla said.

"A gap. Between the signal from a plane and its existence?"

"Correct. This one came from Admiral Cutting's team with the Office of Naval Research, working with a physicist named Hazelton. Have you been briefed on that background?"

"I have. I don't believe any of it, but I have."

Layla was inured to incredulity after years of reading about the various moon shots DARPA had taken with everything from bombs to lasers to robot dog warriors. "Then you understand as much as I do at this moment. I have a team diving into Dr. Hazelton's archives with the hopes of learning something new, and I assure you we are working as fast as is humanly possible."

"Fast is not good enough," Hanover snapped. "Do you understand what is happening with the markets?"

"I'm sure it is not ideal for Wall Street." Layla tapped a pencil off the desk, trying to tamp down her impatience. She did not have time for this conversation. None of them did.

"How long are we supposed to keep airspace clear for a ghost plane, Dr. Chen?"

"I'm not sure, sir. If that signal is registering, the plane should appear."

"Appear from *where*?"

"Again, sir, excellent question, and I dearly wish it was one I could answer. The results of Project Kingsolver are problematic, however. We understand only that the plane came off the board. We do not know where it went. Attempts to replicate or reengineer the effort were consistent failures."

Those eyes bored into her, so intensely that he seemed to be in the room, but she was very alone. Outside, three sentries with assault rifles paced on the other side of a steel door.

"What is DARPA's recommendation to the Joint Chiefs?" Hanover asked at last.

"Maintain the ground stop indefinitely." She saw him wince. "And take measures to shut down all communications from Naval Air Station Ash Point."

Hanover blinked, cocked his head, as if he'd misheard.

"NAS Ash Point."

"Yes, sir."

"That base has been closed for years."

"Yes, sir. We would still recommend deploying electronic measures to jam any and all radio or cellular communications from the area."

"Fine. And we should physically secure the space."

"We recommend against that, sir."

"Why?"

"Because if that plane lands, its crew is likely to be . . . quite confused. But not incapacitated."

"Say it in English, Dr. Chen."

"We have to consider that they'll have the ability to launch."

"That's impossible."

"It requires consideration, sir."

Hanover put a hand to his eyes, then lowered it quickly. That ribbon-adorned chest rose and fell. He did not want to believe her, and she knew that, but they'd met many times, and he knew better than to call her a fool or a fraud. Certainly, he knew better than to accuse Sector Six of sowing trouble. They existed to suppress old sins, nothing more. Sector Six was there to make sure that America never paid for a mistake made in the name of research.

They'd been successful for a very long time.

"NAS Ash Point remains under the Navy's control?" Hanover asked.

"Correct. It is unoccupied, but the runway is accessible. That's a good thing."

Hanover rubbed his right temple.

"You don't want planes or helicopters in the mix?"

"We would recommend against it. Heightened caution, yes, but . . . "

She didn't need to finish. He was already nodding.

"How many civilians in the area?"

"Minimal. The base is closed, and the site is extremely remote, at the far end of a peninsula accessible by a single road. The only private property on that road is an old service station and farmhouse recently purchased by a Greg Goodwin of New York. The FBI has wonderful news on that front."

"What's that?"

"Goodwin checked into a hotel in Wisconsin last night. Reservation was for two; we believe his daughter is traveling with him. The property is empty."

"All right. Ash Point will go dark immediately. By the time I'm back on this line, I expect much better clarity about Project Kingsolver."

"Yes, sir," Layla Chen said, leaving the obvious unspoken: if there were clarity about Project Kingsolver, they wouldn't be here today.

BLOOMINGTON, INDIANA
DECEMBER 1, 1961

Marty Hazelton's undoing, although of course he didn't know it at the time, as few men ever realize when they've made their last wrong turn, was born out of nostalgia.

Nostalgia brought him to a tidy town square beneath incandescent Christmas lights. The town was Bloomington, Indiana, and although it was only forty minutes from Crane, he rarely visited. He rarely left the base, period, obsessed with the potential of his graphite-shielded plane.

The problem was the substance. The graphite needed to be laboriously applied, it was expensive and challenging to source, and Marty had yet to determine a successful method of applying it that didn't involve copper tape. The Pentagon was hardly impressed with the notion of taping pencil dust to a fleet of bombers with 189-foot wingspans.

"Must bring this concept to scale swiftly," Admiral Ralph H. Cutting telegrammed tersely on September 6, 1961, the same day the Soviets broke their nuclear-testing moratorium and detonated a weapon twenty-six miles above the earth. It was the most aggressive step yet in the menacing showdown between the United States and the U.S.S.R., nuclear saber-rattling taken to outer space, and no one was excited about model planes. They wanted actionable aircraft that could carry real bombs, and they wanted them *now*.

For the life of him, Marty couldn't think of a way to do it.

He tried mixing the graphite dust with paints and epoxies and polymers. They sizzled and burned. He tried the copper tape on its own, curious if he'd overestimated the importance of the graphite. Sizzle and burn. He tried to mold plastic with graphite. Sizzle and burn.

Marty spent almost all his waking hours in Microfilm Storage Building #45, and his mind remained there even when he slept, dreams in which he'd solved it, only to wake with the haunting realization that he was no closer. Then, on December 1, the day the Department of Defense began distributing black-and-yellow fallout shelter signs to the buildings that were to be used in the event of a nuclear attack, a light snow fell, Bing Crosby's "White Christmas" played on the radio, and the truck driver who delivered graphite mentioned the Christmas lights in Bloomington to Marty.

"It's pretty. Whole canopy of them covering the town square. You should go."

Idle conversation, but the image he'd conjured passed its spark off to that damnable thing called memory, and suddenly Marty was recalling the day he'd taken his brother to see the Christmas lights in Nashua, New Hampshire, in the winter when they stayed with their grandparents because their father was dying in a Boston hospital.

Marty was seven years older than Hank, and because of that there were few childhood experiences that had been truly shared. Marty was a scientist by trade and spirit, and Hank was everything opposite: an athlete, a fighter, a raconteur. And a believer. He believed in the righteousness of battle, in the ultimate exceptionalism of America, in faith and family. When a president spoke, Hank Hazelton applauded. The very idea of a president struck Marty as patently absurd after Oppenheimer's work. In the end, humans were all atoms, and science cared not a whit for one collection of atoms over another. To live a life dedicated to some human leader, human cause, or human passion . . . well, how could you look at that and view it as anything *but* absurd?

There were memories, though. Memories were vexing winds. They were nothing but neurons and synapses and electricity, of course, but still they *felt* like something more. The way a smell or a song or a sunset could transport you back in time to a place in which you'd been guided more by the heart than the head.

This was what sent him driving through the Indiana fields in search of a good whiskey and a Christmas memory.

It was all farmland until he reached Bloomington, a quaint college town that was, of late, becoming a manufacturing hub. RCA had a facility where the first mass-produced color televisions were built for an enthralled nation—as well as components for equally enthused military consumers. Westinghouse had a plant for electrical capacitors. The proximity of these factories to the Crane naval base delighted most locals. The intersection of Crane, RCA, Westinghouse, and a major research university meant progress.

All different kinds of progress. The color television was one flavor. The atomic bomb was another.

Bloomington was a charming town, centered around a lovely limestone courthouse with a domed roof. A weather vane shaped like a fish topped the dome. So far from the sea, and yet they'd gone with a fish. Of course, there was also a naval base just down the road. That made Marty smile wryly. Maybe the fish made more sense than people thought.

The Christmas lights reminded him of that night in Nashua with his brother. It was a night he'd prefer not to remember: the last one of his father's life. On a typical Christmas, they'd have been home in Boston, or maybe ice-skating by the tiny cottage on the Maine pond called Rosewater where they spent summers and occasional winter holidays. Instead, they'd been with their grandparents in New Hampshire because their father didn't want his sons to watch him die, and they'd gone to Nashua because their grandparents didn't want them in the house to hear talk of death. There were funeral arrangements to plan, and estate matters.

"Go to town and see the lights," their grandfather had instructed. "Howard's drivin' in. You boys can ride with him. Have some fun."

Howard was a neighbor, and he didn't seem fond of children, accepting Marty and Hank into his ancient, wheezing truck without a word. The truck had homemade bed rails and a heavy smell of leaking oil or maybe gasoline. Their grandfather tried to hide the dollar he passed off, as if it might be more special to the boys if they didn't know their chauffeur was on the clock.

It was a quiet ride, light snow falling, Howard smoking his pipe so furiously it seemed as if he thought it fueled the truck's fragrant engine.

"Be back in an hour," Howard growled after parking beside a snowdrift nearly as tall as the truck's bed. "I got no tolerance for waiting."

He hadn't yet cut the engine, seeming determined to soak up every bit of heat before stepping into the cold dark. Maybe he wouldn't get out at all, just sit there behind the wheel and smoke until his dollar had been earned.

Marty assured him they'd be back on time, then guided Hank off the bench seat and down onto the ice-covered street before turning back to thank the neighbor. Howard never looked up. He had his matchbook in his gloved hands as he spoke three last words around the stem of his pipe: "Don't get lost."

Marty nodded, clanged the door shut, and then stood looking at Hank, uncertain of what to do, the way he so often was when left in charge of the child brother with such unbridled energy. Hank packed a snowball and pegged it off the brick wall of the mill building beside them, howling an enthusiastic "*Strrrriiiiike!*"

"Let's not do that," Marty said, because the grumpy neighbor was still glowering at them through the windshield as he struggled to relight his pipe, the old truck still chugging away. Marty took his brother's hand and tugged him down the street, toward the towering white pine that had been erected in a small park below the mill and along the river, adorned with lights that were still dark.

They made it half a block before the truck blew up.

It went up as the Christmas lights went on, a synchronicity so astonishingly perfect that it would forever trouble Martin Hazelton's refined scientific mind. Many in the town thought there had been some connection: a thrown spark, an ignition. But the incandescent bulbs used on the Christmas tree along the river were more than two hundred feet from the truck—Marty knew because he later went back to measure—and there were no overhead lines where the neighbor named Howard had parked his truck that smelled vaguely of gasoline. There'd been his own match, of course; that likely had done the trick. Or perhaps the spark had come from within the electrical system of the truck? Not impossible. At any rate, it certainly had not come from above. The winter sky was blameless.

But it had *seemed* to be a shared burst of light; it had *felt* simultaneous. The intellectual understanding hadn't paired with the emotional experience. The Christmas tree lights were plugged in; the Christmas tree burst to radiant life; the neighbor named Howard's truck exploded. Not separate events but joined.

Amazing, how you could feel so certain about fiction.

What Marty remembered best was standing flat-footed in the snow while his brother—his nine-year-old baby brother—ran without hesitation for the burning truck. The crowd gathered by the riverbank and the Christmas tree screamed and hollered but even grown men were not yet reacting, and there was young Hank Hazelton racing across the icy street and into the fire. The flames were already over the cab, foul smoke billowing above, crackling menace below, fire feasting on the wooden bed rails, all the glass blown out and glistening against the snow, and yet Hank rushed right for the driver's door, tugged on its searing metal handle.

Later, they would run cool water over burns that made a perfect outline of the door handle on his palms.

On the other side of the door, the corpse sat upright and smoking. From where Marty stood, motionless as the crowd surged around him, he could see the flesh melting from the man's open mouth in blackened ribbons. That night, while Marty held his brother and tried to soothe him to sleep, Hank would whisper, "His teeth were still white," and Marty would wonder if that could be true.

It turned out it could be.

Strangers had pulled his brother away. Only after they had acted did Marty finally move, a delay so long that to recall it even forty years later made him wince. How fearless Hank had been. How frozen Marty had been.

Neither of them knew yet that their own father was dead. They would find out the next morning, and Hank pestered their mother about the timing.

"He went right around six, dear," she'd said, clueless to the meaning of it.

There *was* no meaning to it. Marty knew that. The problem was that Hank did not. Hank, somehow, was convinced it was all of a piece. The Christmas tree lights came on, the truck exploded, and more than a hundred miles away their father's heart offered its last blood to a lost cause.

Or had it gone in reverse order? That was Hank's question for Marty.

"Do you think that when Daddy closed his eyes the truck blew up?"

Marty had told him sternly that such talk was both foolish and morally wrong, although his sense of a moral world was already wobbling by then.

"I tried to save him," Hank had said, speaking of the neighbor, Howard, and Marty assured him he knew that—that everyone knew that; there was no question that Hank had been very brave.

Neither of them spoke of what Marty had been, standing flat-footed behind the crowd, watching the corpse burn.

They never did speak of it. Not then, not later. There was no point.

And yet, decades later, Marty had to suppress an urge to call Hank, who was stationed on an air base in Hawaii, and ask him what he had thought that night. When he'd reached for the scalding metal handle, had he gotten a glimpse of Marty in the side-view mirror, standing there impotently?

Was I a coward? Am I a coward?

He would not call Hank to ask a fool's question, but some sentimental part of him that he loathed wanted a fresh set of lights to blink on and transport him.

Take me back.

Back to the way it was. Back to the land of unmade choices.

Wasn't that Christmas, in a way? Longing for the past? Sure it was.

He stepped out of the car into the Indiana night, cinched his trench coat tight against the chill, and looked up and down the street as his breath fogged the air. He spotted a cocktail room called the Dandale near the corner of Walnut and Kirkwood, right on the square.

Perfect. He was nearly there when a blond woman jostled past him, head down, hustling against the cold, and then turned to him with an apologetic smile.

"Sorry! I'm just—"

"Cold," he said, and then smiled as she laughed and nodded. A stray snowflake frosted her hair. She was young and pretty and they reached for the door handle of the Dandale at the same time, shared another awkward laugh, the laugh of strangers, and Marty held the door for her.

The cocktail room was small and cramped and perfect. There was a long mahogany bar and a few small tables and booths, with a piano wedged into the corner of the room. There were only three open seats at the bar, two together and one separate, and Marty hesitated, waiting to see which one the blond woman would take. If she picked the stool that was by itself, it would be a clear sign that she didn't wish for him to sit beside her.

She took one of the open pair instead, then gave him a half glance that said the choice was his. He took the stool beside her and moved the menu aside as she set a handbag and a paperback book on the bar. Marty stared at the book.

The Sirens of Titan by Kurt Vonnegut.

"Have you heard of him?" the blonde asked.

"No," Marty said. "But I know a Bernard Vonnegut."

"That's his brother. They're from here. Well, not Bloomington, but Indiana. Indianapolis." She removed her gloves and rubbed her hands theatrically. "I need a warmer. What are you having?"

"Scotch."

"That's a little strong for me. I'm Marilyn, by the way. Marilyn Metzger." She offered her hand.

"Marty Hazelton." He accepted her slim, cool palm.

"Marilyn and Marty. Names close enough that we ought to be able to remember them."

She ordered a vodka soda and Marty ordered a scotch and waited to see if she would pick up her book and divert her attention. When she didn't, he sought for small talk, which was never his strong suit.

"So, Marilyn, what brings you to Bloomington?"

"What makes you think I'm not *from* Bloomington?"

A fine question, and yet he'd found himself certain she wasn't.

"I meant downtown," he lied. "To . . . to this place."

"To talk with strange men in a cocktail room? What type of lady must I be?"

"No, no, I—excuse me. I apologize."

She laughed, delighted at his embarrassment, teasing.

"I'm *not* from Bloomington. With this suntan, in November, you think I live in Indiana? Some detective you'd make."

And with that, she forced him to consider her skin, to take a good look. Yes, she had a deep, sun-kissed glow.

"California," he said, trying to recover his footing and flirt as easily as she was doing. He'd never been natural at it. "You're a starlet masquerading among the Midwestern rubes. If I had an ounce of popular knowledge, I'd have recognized you immediately."

She gave a little snort and lifted her drink. "You've got it. Now name the movie."

"The one with Bogart."

"They were all with Bogart. Warner Bros. worked the poor man to death."

"The one where he's a gangster on the run."

"Again, I'm afraid you'll need to be more specific."

"*High Sierra*—that's it."

She put a hand to her breast in mock shock. "Ida Lupino? You do know how to make a girl swoon."

Marty knew damn well he'd never made a girl swoon. Not because of his looks—he was a handsome man, and knew it—but because he'd never had any aptitude for the required easy charm of courtship.

"Not California," Marilyn said. "Florida. And I'm a journalist."

"Oh? What's the story?"

"The house of magic!" she said jubilantly. Then, voice lowered, conspiratorial, "That's branding for General Electric, you know. They're expanding their Bloomington factory. I don't think it's such a magical place."

"Oh, you're wrong," Marty said. "I spent some time in Schenectady, where the headquarters are. There was magic up there. Some of it was courtesy of Vonnegut. Not Kurt—Bernie. Do you know him?"

"Only of him. Kurt works in public relations for the company. I've met him a few times. Tell me, what *magic* did you get up to with his brother?"

Marty smiled and said, "We built a blizzard."

It was fun to watch her gape.

"You're lying."

"I'm not. But he deserves most of the credit. Well, he and Vincent Schaefer and Irving Langmuir. You've heard those names?"

"You made it snow," she said, ignoring the question. "You're serious?"

"I'm serious. It wasn't all that exciting." Although in truth it had been. Such heady times, there in the GE headquarters in Schenectady after the war, where anything was viewed as possible and where some of the greatest minds in the world had been assembled.

"You're either a liar or no fun at all," Marilyn told him.

"We did help a snowstorm along," Marty acknowledged. "I wouldn't say we *caused* it. A rainmaker cloud can be seeded to produce more rain—or snow, as it were. But first you require the cloud."

"And how do you—what was your term—'seed' it?"

"Well, you can use ground-based generators set on mountaintops at high altitude. But in the earliest days, we were simply dumping dry ice into the clouds by hand from the back of a plane." He laughed at the memory. "Schaefer was the one who hit on the generator design. They worked together with a wonderful, scatterbrained, brilliant man named Irving Langmuir. Irving was the biggest dreamer of the group. I remember he once said that changing the weather had greater potential than the atomic bomb."

He wished he hadn't brought up the bomb.

But she didn't seem nonplussed, saying quickly, "And you're convinced it works? Seeding the clouds?"

"Absolutely. There are some people downstream of the Catskills who are further convinced, but General Electric would rather not talk about that."

"What do you mean?"

"Cloud seeding caused a hell of a flood downstream," he said, and then smiled only because she did first. There was something feline in her smile, a glimmer both beautiful and dangerous. "The reservoirs in the Catskills feed New York City, so that was the big idea: make it rain more over the Catskills, eliminate the drought in the city. And it worked. The problem was the flooding along the way."

"Was the company sued?"

"Oh, yes. I think it was settled out of court."

"And now you—" she began, and he interrupted her only because he did not want any questions about what he did *now* because he couldn't answer them. He could say plenty about the old days of making rain, but nothing of the new days of destroying planes.

"I'll have to read the book," he said, tapping the cover of the paperback. "I really did enjoy Bernie Vonnegut. A funny fellow, quick with a joke, but also a genuinely brilliant man. The notion he had to seed clouds with silver iodide, for example, accelerated things so quickly. That was the—"

He stopped talking abruptly, suddenly almost unaware of the beautiful woman's presence. He was remembering the generator design that Vonnegut and Schaefer had come up with. It was an ingenious and simple device that fed a long cotton cord through a propane-fueled flame after the cord had been saturated in silver iodide and sodium iodide. The cord remained impregnated with the solution even when dry and could be fed through the flame using a battery-operated motor, at which point the solution was vaporized, turned to smoke that seeded the clouds.

"That was *what*?" Marilyn prompted.

"A hell of a design," Marty muttered, and then he took the cocktail napkin, withdrew a pencil from his shirt pocket, and set about sketching the generator, ostensibly to explain it to her, but more as an excuse to let his mind run.

He had failed to find an efficient way to make the graphite dust adhere to the planes. What if he was going about it all the wrong way? Forget the plane entirely.

What if you could shield a cloud and fly a plane into it?

He ordered another whiskey and sketched the way things had looked over the Berkshire Mountains when he and Bernie Vonnegut had built the blizzard in 1947, and if the blonde named Marilyn thought he'd gone a little too breathless and was talking a little too fast, well, that was fine.

Nostalgia for Nashua, New Hampshire, and a trip to see the Christmas lights in Bloomington, Indiana, might've been just what he needed.

No—what the *world* needed.

———

Marty didn't leave the base again in December.

On Christmas Eve, he completed construction of a silver iodide generator at the far end of the warehouse. It was essentially the same design he'd first encountered in the labs of General Electric. That was when the operation known as Project Cirrus had really begun to take off, and the early results were impressive—and controversial. A few farms downstream flooded and the rainmakers fell out of favor fast. But they'd hardly gone away. Project Cirrus had moved from GE to the Naval Weapons Center in China Lake, California, and while the rainmakers were still hard at work, their efforts were a good deal more classified now.

The generator's smoke formed a fine cloud of silver iodide crystals. This met a basic fog machine operated from scaffolding above the generator, turning the far end of his warehouse into a small, supercooled cloud, which he electrified.

Into this cloud he fired graphite dust.

He could have constructed it all within a week if he'd had the lab team he'd once enjoyed at Los Alamos, but those days were in the past, and he was fine with that. He enjoyed working in solitude. The holidays helped. Most of his research colleagues left Crane for visits to scattered families. Even Wyatt Dixon, his right-hand man in the graphite research, took Christmas week off.

"Don't work through the holiday, boss," Dixon said. "Surely you've got family to see."

"Just my brother, and he's in Hawaii," Marty said, and it was only then that it occurred to him that he'd forgotten to send his brother a Christmas gift. He felt terrible about that, but he also didn't know Hank well enough these days to guess at what the man wanted. Nothing, probably, other than to be remembered, which was precisely what Marty had failed to do.

Well, there was one thing. Maybe the only thing.

The watch on Marty's wrist. Their father's old watch, the one he'd been wearing when he took his last breath. The watch was a Webb

C. Ball, the company born of tragedy. Webb Ball set off to develop a reliable system of timekeeping after two trains collided outside of Cleveland, Ohio, because one engineer's watch had stopped for four minutes. Eleven men had been killed in that wreck.

Timing, as they said, was everything.

The watches that came out of Webb C. Ball's response to the tragedy were beautiful, with Swiss movements and leather bands. Once a tool, they were now striving for upmarket luxury status. Marty Hazelton doubted that many modern buyers even knew the story of the train wreck. His little brother had loved the watch, but their father wanted Marty, the eldest son, to have it. The undertaker had removed it from Robert Hazelton's wrist following the open-casket viewing, and there had been something—how awful was this for a scientist to admit?—unsettling to Marty about clasping on the very timepiece that had been on his father's when the last heartbeat pulsed.

It would mean something to Hank to have it, and since Hank was the only one of them with children, there was a chance of extending the legacy.

So he sat down at his desk, pushed the modeling supplies out of the way, and jotted a quick note, explaining that he'd been thinking often of Hank and his family—the whitest of lies, that—and then adding his hope that the watch would be passed down, one generation to the next. He wished his brother safe flying, as he always did, knowing full well that even a peacetime flight in a B-52 could turn deadly, with accidents always possible. It was this last bit that gave him pause, and he looked at his modeling table and smiled.

I've added a little something special, he wrote, *the latest and greatest in super-duper nano technology, guaranteed to protect its wearer against all ills! I called it Rosewater.*

Hank loved Rosewater Pond and thus he would love the name,

and Marty certainly didn't wish to confess the first name for the substance that had risen to his mind unbidden: Nashua Nightshade. There would be nothing funny about that to Hank, who still bore the scarred palms from that awful night.

He unclasped his father's watch, rubbed it down lovingly with a silk cloth, and wound it one last time. It would wind down before it reached his brother, but it was the ceremonial aspect that mattered, not the practical. He thought of his father, kissed the watch face once—glad to be alone in the big empty warehouse, with no one to observe his lapse into the sentimental—and then set about shaving graphite dust and applying it to the ancient, cracked leather band and the back of the watch casing with tiny, meticulous squares of tape. Then he wrapped the watch, boxed it, and mailed it off to Hawaii, where it would arrive some two weeks later.

He himself had received only two Christmas cards: one from his brother—on time, of course—and one from Marilyn Metzger. It had been a postcard showing a winter blizzard in the New England mountains.

Was this one your fault? she'd written. *Wonderful meeting you, and Merry Christmas! I'll be back in Bloomington for more interviews at G.E. early next year. Perhaps we can meet again? Marilyn.*

The note thrilled him—and scared him a little, frankly. He wanted nothing more than to spend time with a beautiful, bright, wickedly clever woman. Yet he was unlikely to be able to make the time. Project Kingsolver was all-consuming. His one escape to the Dandale had been the last of its kind, he thought.

Then again, it had been helpful.

On Christmas Day, he fired the generators. Fog met silver iodide met electricity. A storm cloud was born. He added graphite dust.

Into this, he flew his plane.

When the model hit the cloud, he saw the blue spiderweb of wires

67

and heard the distinct crackling sound that seemed to come almost from within his own skull.

Then there was nothing.

Not the sizzle of a wreck, not the buzzing motor of success. Silence.

He'd lost sight of the plane completely. He set the controller down, killed the electric current, then the generator. Gradually, the room cleared, the smoke dissipating until he could see the concrete wall on the opposite end of the basement again.

The floor between him and the wall was bare and empty. He walked to the wall and looked for an impact mark. Nothing. Turned around and stared at the floor again, sure that he'd overlooked the wreckage somehow.

Nothing.

No plane.

Not even a trace of ash.

He had, somehow, simply *incinerated* the thing by adding graphite dust to the electrically active cloud.

This was not, militarily speaking, helpful. No one in the Pentagon was awaiting a telegram from Crane announcing the great news that Marty Hazelton, their resident EMP genius, had managed to come up with a way to destroy his own aircraft both faster and more thoroughly than ever.

Good news, fellas! Now watch while I burn money. Who's got a key to Fort Knox?

That was one response, sure. The budget mattered, and he knew it, but . . . he could make a plane vanish.

That was no small thing.

Charlie's terror at the sound of her dead mother's voice carried her down the mountain and halfway to the taproom before sanity swooped in, took the terror out at the knees, and told her what she should have known from the beginning: it was a prank.

And a pretty damned good one, she had to admit. The location was both her sacred spot and a spooky one. The use of her name, the instruction not to fly a wrecked plane? Magnificent.

The reference to her mother, though?

Not clever. Not cool.

Just fucking cruel. She hoped whoever had done it didn't know about her mother, had somehow missed the whispered news that the new girl's mom had been murdered in the city.

Charlie, this is your mother.

No, it was not her mother. And yet . . .

There had been a trace of something familiar about it. If she'd spent more time up there, rather than panicking like the frightened

69

girl they wanted her to be, she might've determined who the speaker was. Instead, she'd fled.

Had the voice come from the balloon? No. It had come from something in the cockpit. The balloon was simply the thing that had been used to draw her up there, and she'd fallen for it. From the balloon to the radio to the voice, it was all a very good prank. Except for that last, cruel touch.

She tried to tell herself this, but the voice that knew better was stirring despite her best efforts to tamp it down. The balloon was awfully elaborate for any of the kids from school. Maybe the balloon hadn't been part of it? Just coincidence. The voice could've been planted in the plane, she went up there enough, sure, that was it.

That balloon is not a coincidence, she thought.

But what in the hell else could it be?

She rode the ATV into the taproom parking lot, then idled it, stood, and rotated so she was looking back at the mountain. The balloon sat in the tree with its odd, placid motionlessness, as if the wind couldn't touch it anymore. Nothing moved. No one laughed.

Yet.

It's all on camera, she thought. *That's the point. Not only can they enjoy it; they can share it. Watch Charlie scream! Hilarious!*

She lifted both hands and shot a double bird at the mountain.

"Post that one too!" she screamed.

As if on cue, there was a crunch behind her, and she turned to see Abe and Lawrence stepping out of the taproom, staring at her.

Perfect.

She groaned and flopped back down onto the ATV seat, then wiped her eyes, realizing suddenly that they were hot and damp. Had she *cried*? Really? *Oh, please, don't let that be on video.*

"Charlie?" Abe called.

"Yeah, what's up?" She tried to sound casual. She didn't look at

Lawrence, because he was the type of guy who would want to help, like the captain of the congeniality squad, and Charlie needed no help. A reputation for toughness could be rapidly undone, and she couldn't allow that.

"You okay?" Abe asked.

"What?" She gave him confusion.

"Look a little upset."

"Upset? No, no. I'm fine. Just fine."

Abe and Lawrence exchanged a glance.

"Showing Spruce Hill your middle fingers just because you're feeling fine?" Abe said.

Crap. They'd seen that.

"It's a dance move," Charlie said. "I can show you the TikTok videos."

"I'll pass," Abe said dryly, the breeze fanning his wild white hair back from his face. "I was gonna take Lawrence to town, get a hanging kit for those pictures I found of the base back in '59, add them to the museum's collection. You want to come along?"

"No, thanks."

"I'll let you drive the truck," Abe offered. "You ought to experience a classic once in your lifetime."

His truck was ancient, a 1971 Ford Sport Custom pickup truck he called "Blue" because of its signature blue-and-white paint job.

"I don't want that pressure," Charlie said. "Go on, do your thing."

It would be great if they left. Then she'd be alone with the balloon.

Wait . . . maybe not so great.

"Have you heard from your dad today?" Lawrence asked, and Charlie cringed, knowing that he'd read her uneasiness. She did not need the Crustacean Sensation's steadying claw around her shoulder.

"I don't need to check in with my dad every ten minutes," she said distractedly, looking down at the throttle of the ATV and her hand, literally white-knuckled around the grip. Her heart was still hammering from the voice in the plane. One great prank, sure. One fantastic fucking—

"I know that. It's just good if he's not flying today," Lawrence said.

"Huh?" She refocused on him.

"The ground stop is still going on. Sounds pretty serious. If he was supposed to fly today, it might not happen."

The ground stop. Right. She'd forgotten about that.

"I guess I should text him," Charlie said, swinging off the ATV.

"We can stay a few minutes," Abe said.

"You don't have to."

But she didn't mind when they followed her inside. The TV was still playing, muted. Charlie sat at the bar, pulled out her phone, and sent her dad a text—or tried. The message—RU going to be able to fly home?—stuck, unable to get a signal. That wasn't abnormal at Ash Point, or anywhere in Maine, but in the taproom she should be on Wi-Fi. She checked the settings, confirmed she was connected to the router, and tried again.

Nothing.

"Damn it," she muttered. "No signal. Lawrence, do you have it?"

He checked. "No bars."

"Were you on Wi-Fi earlier?"

"Yeah." He picked up his iPad, tapped, frowned. "It's out."

"How's the TV still on? That uses Wi-Fi."

"I paused it. Maybe it's not live anymore."

He picked up the remote and pressed Play. The broadcast resumed, and he went to fast-forward to see if he could catch up to the live broadcast, but Charlie stopped him.

"Hang on, I want to see this."

CNN had cut away from the airport views to a split screen with the blond anchor on the right and a lean man in a pilot's uniform on the left.

"We're joined now by Captain Brian Grayson of Delta Air Lines," the anchor said. "Captain Grayson, you were supposed to be in the air right now, correct?"

"That's correct."

"Can tell you our viewers why you're not?"

The pilot shifted uneasily, wet his lips, and let out a strained chuckle.

"I, um, I need to say first of all that I'm simply able to relay my own experience, okay? But it is my understanding that my experience is not unique today. I know this from several discussions with colleagues. We all experienced the same thing."

"And what was that, sir?"

Grayson looked like he wasn't sure he wanted to answer.

"We took our sick days after we got calls in the middle of the night from our mothers," he said, and Charlie felt a knot in her gut.

"Pardon me?" The blonde went wide-eyed, even though she'd clearly been prepared for the answer.

"Well, my mother called my cell phone last night, just after midnight, and told me not to fly my plane today. It was a strange call: she was upset, and I . . . I don't know how to say this, but I was kind of *compelled* by her. By the force of her concern, you might say. But the big problem is, she says she didn't make the call. She has no memory of it at all. I've got the call time on my phone, I can see that it happened, and yet she insists that it did not. And this is—as impossible as it sounds—the exact same scenario that many of my colleagues experienced."

"Identical calls?"

"In the big picture, yes. The call and the nature of the conversation."

"What, exactly, did your mother say?"

"Um, well, she denies saying anything, as I've explained. But my mother's *voice* said, 'Brian, do not fly today.'"

There was one thing the toughest new girl at Cold Harbor High could not afford to do: faint in front of an audience. There was only one way to make such an event worse: faint into the waiting arms of Lawrence Zimmer, the Crustacean Sensation himself.

But that's what Charlie Goodwin did.

ARLINGTON, VIRGINIA
OCTOBER 25, 2025

Layla Chen left Raven Rock via helicopter, flew to a secure complex in Arlington, and was escorted into a bland building that held the archived documents of the nation's most classified operation. There, in a windowless room three floors belowground, a team of four—two men and two women with suitably high security clearances—were busy trying to explain the steady radio pulse from a plane that did not exist.

"Any ideas?" Layla asked Betsy Kreuzer, who'd started her career as a CIA analyst before migrating to Sector Six. "I mean, *any*?"

"There is only one way to trigger that alarm," Betsy said. "It was designed by one of our team, a woman named Iris Stoka, and it was built as a fail-safe, requiring a human hand to flick a manual switch. We've never had a failure from the Stoka system. The satellite believes the plane is inbound. We have no reason to disbelieve the satellite."

"Want to guess what Hanover had to say about it?"

"That we'd better be wrong?"

"In so many words, yes. Could we be?"

"Sure. But if we're not?"

Layla nodded, watching the others in the room click away on their computers, scouring old files that had been digitally uploaded, while an open laptop on a metal utility table showed a satellite readout with a red dot indicating the steady, pulsing ping of Flight 3730, last seen in October 1962.

"Let me see the Hazelton file," Layla said. She'd read it before, but that had been years ago, and at the time the only thing that stood out in the file was the seemingly insane notion that Dr. Martin Hazelton had been given an opportunity to test at all. That he'd also been given an atomic bomb for the occasion wasn't really his fault—or even his decision. Events had conspired against Hazelton's preferred timeline, as Layla recalled.

Cuba, 1962. That kind of event. The type that turned tests into actionable missions and rolled atomic bombs onto experimental planes.

"We've got all the digital scans pulled up," Betsy said. "Physical documents are being retrieved."

In the far corner of the room, a metal gate separating the archives slid open, a mechanical *beep, beep, beep* sounded, and then a small forklift pulled into view, two wooden pallets balanced on its extended front arms, carrying it like an offering. Paperwork and manila folders were packed tightly between the wooden frames of the pallets. The forklift pulled up to within a few feet of the women, then the operator lowered the pallets. When they contacted the cold concrete floor, dust billowed up. Layla blinked and turned her head, let the dust clear, then knelt beside the pallets, daunted by the sheer quantity of documents. If there were answers in here, they should have already been found. What could she possibly unearth in an hour, a day, even a week?

The collection didn't comprise the notebooks, blueprints, and binders she typically saw in the archives but standard mailing envelopes. Hundreds of them. Thousands.

"What the hell are these?"

"Letters," Betsy Kreuzer said. "From Hazelton to his brother."

"*All* of them?"

"Every single one."

"Holy shit," Layla whispered, withdrawing one yellowed envelope, which was postmarked from Crane, Indiana, and addressed to an air base in Honolulu. The date on the postmark was December 1961.

"We can give you the haystack," Betsy said. "But I can't promise you the needle."

Layla sat back on her heels and gazed up at the pallets, her dry mouth now having nothing to do with the dust.

"How big was the bomb on that plane?"

"A 3.8-megaton Mark 39."

"Quantify that."

"Approximately three hundred times greater yield than the one we dropped on Hiroshima."

Layla pivoted to face Betsy, but the other woman would not meet her eyes.

"We publicly admitted to losing four of those bombs over the years," Betsy said. "This was number five. *Is* number five."

That correction to the present tense was terrifying.

"You've read the Hazelton file more times than anyone alive," Layla said.

"Probably. Yes."

"Is that plane coming back?"

Betsy hesitated, then said, "He was a brilliant man," and left it at that.

CRANE, INDIANA
SUMMER 1962

The year 1962 passed in a blur that Marty Hazelton scarcely registered. Other than the occasional letter to his brother, he had almost no contact with the outside world, while at Crane his work moved from the basement of Microfilm Storage Building #45 to a hastily cleared five-acre test site down a long jeep road, hidden from view of everyone on the property. Sentries guarded his test site and his building, and the procurement clerk at the Office of Naval Research was no longer prone to hesitation when Marty's requests came in, no matter how expensive.

In the first five months of the year, he built and vanished a hundred model B-52s in his electrified clouds. By then he'd stopped using the word "destroyed" in his private notes and replaced it with "vanished." "Destroyed" didn't suffice. Destruction left evidence of what had been.

His models grew larger. His storm clouds grew larger. By March, he was flying a model with an eight-foot wingspan into a cloud at the end of a football field–size test site.

It vanished without a trace.

Admiral Ralph H. Cutting came in person to watch that one. There was a smile on his face that reminded Marty of Lewis Strauss—which was unfortunate, because Strauss always seemed too hungry for the bomb and too skeptical of those who thought philosophically or morally about the consequences of it.

"Imagine," Ralph Cutting said to Marty, "a squad of MiG fighters going out like that. Flying into a cloud, and that's the end of them."

Less than twenty-four hours after Cutting returned to Washington, Marty was notified that his lab budgets would be "met without question. Proceed with haste."

In April, the first underground nuclear missile base in the world became operational in Colorado when nine Titan I missiles—some of their crucial components had been manufactured on the grounds at Crane—were delivered to Lowry Air Force Base. That same week, Bob Dylan performed his song "Blowin' in the Wind" for the first time, and though Marty loved the song, he had trouble disconnecting it from his memories of the fallout maps they'd studied after Operation Teapot in 1955, in Doom Town, where mannequins representing American families filled quaint suburban-style houses. *The answer, my friend, is blowin' in the wind*—indeed. And these days, most of the answers seemed to be radioactive.

On April 25, 1962, the United States ended its moratorium on nuclear testing at the cheerfully named Christmas Island in the remote reaches of the South Pacific. Operation Dominic commenced with hydrogen bombs dropped from B-52s out of Naval Air Station Barbers Point in Hawaii. Hank Hazelton dropped some of the bombs.

Marty learned this in June, when his brother sent him a letter and a gift. In the letter, Hank reported the spectacle of the bombs as *almost beyond words—ethereal, that's the best I can do. Picture the most vivid* display of the Northern Lights we saw as boys in Maine, only warmer, red and orange, dancing and alive.

Marty didn't need the description. He had been in the air on November 1, 1952, when the first thermonuclear weapon, Ivy Mike, was detonated at an island called Elugelab in the Pacific. By the time the skies cleared from a flash of light so brilliant that the memory still made Marty close his eyes and turn his face, as if its power could be averted all these years later, the island was gone as if it had never existed, and the mushroom cloud rose, and rose, and rose, spreading into the stratosphere.

No, he didn't need Hank's words for the visual. He shook off the memory, one that always threatened to unmoor him, and returned to the letter.

The plane didn't miss a hitch, Hank wrote.

She flew steady and the instruments didn't stutter. But there was the damnedest thing. The hands of Father's watch spun. I can't say when it started, exactly, because I was plenty distracted by the incredible display of light. But at some point, I looked at my wrist and saw the hands were spinning, hour and minute, slow and steady, as if I were manually adjusting the time. Rolling it forward. This went on for maybe three or four minutes, according to the onboard clock, which never changed. Then it simply stopped, and the thing started ticking away, reliable as ever. When we were on the ground again and I had the chance to look it over, I couldn't find a problem. The mechanism is sound, and it ticks away just as it always did. I reset the time without trouble. But I don't mind telling you, brother, that the damn thing rattled me. I can hear your voice now, saying "superstition is the enemy of science" and telling me to "ask the right question" and then coaching me to an explanation. I wouldn't mind hearing one! But you know me, the kid who was always scared of the campfire stories, so you won't be surprised to know that I've not felt right about the watch ever since. I certainly don't wish to fly with it again. That feels risky, somehow. (Are your eyes rolling so fast they're whirling like props by now?)

Laugh as much as you like, and I'll look forward to laughing with you sometime soon, hopefully with a beer or two to aid us along. Until then, though, I'd like you to have the watch. Don't worry, I'm not afraid of it—there's superstitious and there's loony, and I'm only one so far—but it meant so much to Father that I feel guilty leaving it in the drawer. I'd rather you wear it. And I'd much rather you explain to me what in the hell happened with it, because this dumbbell brother of yours hasn't the faintest idea!

In the package was the watch Marty had sent him at Christmas.

Hank hadn't bothered to remove the graphite-and-tape shielding. Maybe Hank had appreciated his brother's gesture as something deeper than a joke. Maybe he simply hadn't taken the time to remove the tape. Either was possible. He could be both lazy and sentimental.

Marty wound the watch.

Tick, tick, tick. No problem.

He pulled out the crown. There was no second hand on the old model, so there was no immediate way to tell whether it had stopped. He put it to his ear, heard no ticking. Pushed the crown back in. *Tick, tick, tick.* His brother had claimed it kept perfect time, but Hank wasn't the most diligent of observers. He ran too emotionally hot; distraction bubbled in his blood. Not so with Marty. He decided to time the watch against his own Elgin. They were showing the same time now; perhaps a day or a week would change that. One crucial thing about setting a watch was that you always wanted to roll the hands forward, never backward. Springs, like time, wanted to press on whether you did or not. It was easier on the mechanical components to work with their design and not against it.

Marty could easily imagine Hank becoming distracted enough to move the hands backward. Hank was impatient. Why make twenty turns forward when ten backward would do? Yes, Marty could almost picture it. Blame not the tool but the operator. Perhaps if he mimicked the distraction, he could produce the same result.

He unscrewed the crown again, slid it out, and—although it pained him to ignore the watchmaker's wishes—turned the hands backward ten minutes, then screwed the crown snug again.

Tick, tick, tick.

It was one of the few tests he could perform. One thing he was not about to replicate in his warehouse in Indiana, even with the resources of the Navy at hand, was the sky above Christmas Island on the day of the nuclear tests.

He put the watch back in its box, thinking he'd check it against his Elgin the next day, then closed the box in the desk drawer and read his brother's letter again, trying not to visualize that aurora Hank had seen through the cockpit glass when the nuclear warhead detonated.

Almost beyond words—ethereal, that's the best I can do.

It was, Marty thought, the most Hank-esque response to such an awesome sight. He'd given the image both supernatural quality and, perhaps, imbued it with hope, writing of its beauty.

A bit different than Kenneth Bainbridge's remarks after the Trinity test, the ones Marty recalled so often: "No one who saw it could forget it, a foul and awesome display" and "Now we are all sons of bitches."

Trinity was not so long ago, and yet it was an epoch when it came to weaponry. The world was moving fast, and Marty Hazelton was supposed to be doing the same, because someone needed to protect the people. Including his own little brother.

Time to get back to work.

He put the letter in his desk drawer and then carried on with the serious business at hand: his model airplane, paid for by the United States Navy.

He fired his generators, turned on the electric current, stood on his insulated mat, and turned on the battery-operated plane. Painted on the wing was the model's number, which represented the total number of tests Marty had conducted with the graphite-seeded clouds: 418. He flew it across the room with steady, practiced hands, and watched it sizzle and disappear.

Poof.

One more plane, vanished. Different voltages, different graphite volumes. This was all that Marty knew to do: keep playing with the conditions until some clarity emerged. He logged the details and then he left Microfilm Storage Building #45 to get some lunch.

The plane was on his desk when he returned from lunch.

He mistook it at first for a fresh model, one awaiting testing. Then he crossed the room and saw the serial number painted on the wing: #418.

Have holy curiosity.

ASH POINT, MAINE
OCTOBER 25, 2025

Charlie had fainted only once before, and it was, of all places, in an aquarium. She was with her mother and her grandparents, all three dead now, and on a trip to Chicago they visited an aquarium and stopped in front of an exhibit of South American fish that were extraordinarily vibrant, tinted with seemingly every hue on the color spectrum. The day had been long and the crowd was dense and Charlie began to feel lightheaded, a strange, sudden sensation. She shifted closer to the glass, thinking it might help if she put her palm on the coolness of it, even though she'd heard the instruction not to touch anything. She was reaching for the glass when she saw the dying fish, the one she would never have noticed if she hadn't physically reached for it. The fish, which was on its side, suspended above the rocks that lined the bottom of the display, gave a lurching roll and twitch of a single fin, and its dying eye met hers.

Down she went.

Later, her mother and grandmother assured her that it had been the heat and the crowd. What heat, Charlie wasn't sure, because the aquarium was a cool place, and the crowd had been no more intense than any subway car, but even at nine years old she didn't want to tell them that she'd fainted because she'd locked eyes—an eye, anyhow—with a dying fish.

That she'd been convinced, in that last half second of consciousness, that she was sharing a final moment with another living thing, that it had *looked* at her, and found her, known her.

She didn't tell them about the fish at all.

And she vowed, silently, that she would never faint again, because waking had been such an awful sensation. All those faces swimming back into clarity, all those concerned eyes, and then she realized that she was down on the floor and everyone else was standing—everyone except her mother, who was kneeling beside her, calling her name, saying—

"Charlie! Charlie!"

It was the same sensation all over, only the voice wasn't her mother's; it was Abe Zimmer's, the old pilot crouched beside her on the fake wooden floorboards of a brewery, no tropical fish in sight. Nothing in sight except for—*Oh, no*—Lawrence Zimmer.

Charlie sat up fast—too fast—and for an instant her stomach lurched and she thought she might worsen this disaster by tossing her breakfast right onto Lawrence's varsity jacket. Based on the way his brow furrowed and he leaned back, he must've had the same instinct, but then she got her palms on the floor and the world steadied around her again.

"I'm fine!" she barked, as if it were somehow their fault that she'd fainted.

"Easy. Just stay down and breathe, okay?" Abe said. "Good news is you didn't hit your head; Lawrence caught you."

Lawrence caught her? Great.

It was all mortifying, and even though she felt dizzy and sick and wanted nothing more than to stay down, she grasped the leg of a barstool and pulled herself upright.

"Thatta girl," Abe said. "Not the first time I've seen a good lady haul herself off the floor using a barstool."

"Awesome," Charlie said, and then she sagged onto the stool and sucked in a few deep breaths, trying to process both the humiliation of the moment and the reason for it. The TV was dark, but the news came back to her.

The pilots.

The ground stop.

The mother calls.

Only they hadn't been from the mother. The pilot, Grayson, knew that because he'd talked to his mother. Charlie knew that because her mother was dead.

"Your dad's okay," Abe said. "Remember, kiddo, he's on the ground, safe and sound."

That made her wince, because it was awful to have them think she was such a shrinking violet that the mention of trouble with her dad's travel plans would prompt her to swoon.

"It had nothing to do with that."

"Well, you sure did drop when—"

"It wasn't the damn TV!" she snapped. "It was . . . "

They were both watching her, waiting, Abe with his perpetual pilot-eyed squint, and Lawrence with his perpetual pep rally face. She had to give them something.

"It was the balloon," she said, and until the words were out of her mouth, she'd almost forgotten about the balloon entirely.

"Say again?" Abe said.

Charlie waved an exhausted hand at the windows.

"Someone flew a dumb balloon into the trees above the wreck. I drove the ATV up there to look at it, and then some asshole had planted a speaker in the wreck, and they . . . " The explanation was merging with the memory now, and it sparked a rage that felt good, the anger pushing the humiliation back. "They pulled a really dumb fucking prank, okay? They pretended to be my mom."

Abe's concern shifted from bewildered to incensed, his eyes narrowing.

"What's this?"

"Some idiot thought it would be funny to scare me by talking like it was my mom's voice coming from inside the plane wreck, because that's real funny, right? Mocking a murdered woman—that's a great joke!"

There was a long beat of silence, and then Abe spoke again, his voice low.

"This happened this morning? Right before you came tear-assing down on the ATV?"

She nodded.

"What's the balloon got to do with it?" Lawrence asked. He'd gone to the window and was peering up at Spruce Hill.

"I don't know. Maybe it was to draw me up there? Maybe it made the voice. I have no clue. Probably it was a drone. Something they could use to take video of me. But I'm going to find out who it was, I promise you that."

She looked at the TV, which was still dark, and picked up the remote.

"We're all caught up," Lawrence said. "Live broadcast is gone. Went out with the Wi-Fi, I guess."

"Shit!" Charlie dropped the remote and checked her phone. No bars of cell signal, and while the router was still connected, the internet was out. Just perfect.

"Mind your language," Abe said, but his voice was detached and his eyes were dark, mouth set in a grim line. "I'd like to know who'd imitate your mother's voice. I would like to find the son of a bitch and kick his ass up over his shoulders."

"Mind your language," Charlie said, and Abe grinned.

"Let's go up there," Lawrence said. "I'll get the balloon down. We shouldn't just let it blow away and get lost. If the wind shifts, it could end up in the water."

"You good to move?" Abe asked Charlie. "Or maybe Lawrence and I can head up there and you can lie down and—"

"I'm fine!" Charlie snapped.

But when she stood up from the stool, she did feel dizzy, and she thought of the aquarium, the way that fish had rolled over and fixed its last stare on her, and she wanted to sit back down—would have if not for Abe and Lawrence Zimmer staring at her as if she were fragile. Feeling the weight of their anxious eyes on her and needing an excuse for the way she'd leaned on the bar for support, she stretched out, grabbed the mug that Abe had been drinking from, and pulled it toward her. There was maybe a quarter of the beer left, and she downed it all, managing not to wince against the bitter IPA taste, then lowered the glass and turned back to them, daring Abe to criticize her.

Instead, he nodded with somber approval.

"One for the shooting hand," he said. "I get it."

"Meet you at the balloon," Charlie said, and then she walked out of the taproom without waiting for them. She felt better as soon as she was outside. It was cooler now than it had been earlier, the bracing wind welcome after her experience in the taproom.

They followed her out and faced Spruce Hill. It took Abe all of two seconds to spot the balloon, even at this distance. Whatever age had taken from him, his eyes were still remarkable.

"That's a big one."

"Yeah. They flew it up there and got it stuck."

"What do you mean, 'flew it'?" Lawrence asked.

"It didn't drift the way a balloon would. It came down over the water and then kept getting faster, like it was, you know, descending. But it's still inflated."

Abe frowned while he pulled a cigar from his pocket and lit it.

"Strange."

"You'll see what I mean when we're up there." Charlie walked toward her ATV. "Follow me as far as you can."

She liked leading the way. It restored the sense of control and courage that the day seemed determine to sap from her. As soon as the Kawasaki's engine turned over, she felt stronger. Abe's old pickup could make it about halfway up Spruce Hill before the rutted lane became too steep and rough, but Charlie would be able to ride all the way to the top. That was good, because it would give her some privacy, a moment alone to process a day that was becoming very strange very fast. She accelerated, blond hair fanned out behind her.

When the motor quit, it went without so much as a sputter. One second, she was twisting the throttle to a responsive, throaty growl; the next, all was silent, and the power steering was gone, leaving her to wrestle suddenly heavy handlebars as the four-wheeler rolled to a stop.

"Are you fucking kidding me," she said under her breath as Abe clattered up behind her in the ancient Ford.

"What's the matter?" he called.

"Nothing. I mean, I don't know." She shifted into neutral, then turned the key, just as she had thousands of times before. There was always a half-second pause, then the blink of the instrument display illuminating between the handlebars, and then the shudder of the engine starting: turn, click, roar.

Now it was turn, click, nada.

"Was it gassed up?" Abe asked.

"Of course. And it's not just the engine: the accessories won't even come on." She flicked the headlight switch on and off to make her point. There wasn't so much as a glow.

"Battery shouldn't cut out on you in the middle of things like that," Lawrence said, climbing down from the truck to help, which was precisely what Charlie did not want.

"I know it shouldn't."

He leaned over her to inspect the Kawasaki's blank display. "Could be you rattled a wire loose somewhere."

"It was running fine!"

"We'll get it figured out," Abe called from the truck. "Lawrence, roll it on over by the shed for her."

Charlie looked up to where the silver balloon rested in the birch.

"It can wait. I want to get that down."

Abe Zimmer grinned. "That thing sure vexes you, doesn't it?"

Vexes. That was one word for it.

"I'd like to get it down," she said. "That's all."

"Well, climb in Blue, then. Good thing we got a vehicle we can rely on."

Charlie started to climb in the bed, not wanting to squeeze onto the single bench seat with Abe and Lawrence, but the pilot wasn't going to have that.

"Get in the damn cab!"

Charlie sighed and climbed in. Lawrence held the door for her, the perfect cringeworthy gentleman, which meant she had to get in the middle, pinned between them. The truck was fragrant with the smell of cigar smoke.

"Funny thing 'bout your four-wheeler," Abe said. "It conked out same as you did, not a word of warning!"

He chuckled, and Charlie swallowed her ire as he dropped the gearshift into drive. A hard wind gusted, blowing bits of fine dust over the asphalt and peppering them off Charlie's abandoned ATV. Up on the hill and high in the tree, the balloon seemed impervious to the breeze.

Abe blasted the old truck up the rutted hill. Sitting in the middle with nothing to grab hold of, Charlie couldn't keep from bouncing airborne and landing nearly on Lawrence's lap. She wriggled away fast, then bumped into Abe, knocking his cigar ash to the floorboards.

"Careful!" he snapped, as if it were her fault that he was smoking in the truck.

They parked on a steep incline about thirty yards from the top and walked the rest of the way. The balloon was still stuck in the same limb, fat as an overripe blueberry, sitting indifferently against the stiffening coastal breeze.

Abe put his hands on his hips and gazed upward, peering through a cloud of his own cigar smoke.

"It's a weather balloon."

"How do you know?" Lawrence asked.

"Because I've seen 'em, grandson; how in the hell do you think I know? Eyes and ears, boy, eyes and ears. Use them and you'll find it's quite a world. Don't even need to look at your phone, hard as that must be for you to believe."

Lawrence ignored this, and he and Charlie stood and watched while Abe paced beneath the balloon.

"Look there," Abe said, "it's even got a radiosonde."

"A *what*?" Charlie said.

"See that little box in the branch down below?"

Abe pointed. Charlie followed his extended finger and spotted a small, white box resting against the tree, tethered to the balloon by a thin line. How had she missed that while taking pictures, and how had Abe spotted it so quickly?

"That's a radiosonde," Abe said. "It takes the atmospheric measurements: temperature, humidity, that kind of thing."

"You're sure?" Lawrence said, and his grandfather shot him a pitying look.

"One of the fun things about flying a plane for the United States Navy was that they taught you a little bit before they allowed you to take off in their equipment."

"Uh-huh." Lawrence's tone suggested the infinite patience of a listener who had endured this tale many times before.

"We launch nearly a hundred thousand of them each year just in this country," Abe continued. "It's called a 'sounding,' technically, but the point is you put the thing in the air. The U.S. and Europe put 'em into the sky twice daily."

"If there are that many going up," Lawrence said, "how come we aren't finding them all over the place? I've never seen one before. Or even heard of them, for that matter."

"Hard to believe there's still something new in this world for you, I know," Abe said. "Stay tuned, there might be something new tomorrow too."

Lawrence ignored him and returned to his unanswered question. "How come we don't see them all the time?"

"Well, the globe's bigger than you might expect. Lots of landing zones, and most of them in the ocean. But the devices are cheap, and they're one of the best methods of measuring the upper atmosphere that exists. I know you two think Elon Musk invented the sky, but I swear it's been there longer."

"The wind's up," Lawrence murmured. "Why doesn't it just float out of there?"

"Exactly!" Charlie said.

"Likely snagged a limb," Abe said around his cigar. "We'll pop her loose. You got a fishing rod?"

"Dad does."

"With one of my patented surf casts, we'll have that sucker hooked, guarantee you. Take Lawrence down and fetch me a fine rod with good action. I don't intend to waste that old Zimmer magic on a Zebco."

He mimed a dramatic casting motion, and Lawrence walked for the truck, leaving Charlie with little choice but to follow, since the Crustacean Sensation had no idea where her father's fishing equipment was stored.

"Grab me a pint while you're down there!" Abe hollered after them. "I get parched in the sun."

Charlie gave Abe a thumbs-up. She was hurrying downhill because Lawrence had started for the passenger side, meaning he intended to open her door again, which was the last thing in the world she wanted or needed. She hustled past him, sliding into the passenger seat and banging the door shut.

"Damn it, that's a vintage truck door, not a submarine hatch!" Abe shouted. "Stop flexing your muscles!"

Charlie held up her hands in a gesture of apology while Lawrence got behind the wheel and started the engine. At least this time Charlie got the passenger seat to herself, safe from any inadvertent bounce into his lap.

Lawrence looked grim. He must take after his father's side of the family, because—say what you wanted about his grandfather's drinking—at least Abe had a sense of humor. Lawrence, with his thoughtful silence in the classroom paired with enthusiastic clapping at the pep rallies, felt like as much of a caricature as the lobster mascot on his jacket. He wasn't a real person. Or whatever was real about him he hid down deep. Perhaps he came alive out on the water, Charlie thought. He was going to follow his father into the merchant marine— already had a scholarship to the Maine Maritime Academy—which seemed like a waste of a valedictorian to Charlie, but maybe it was the dream at Cold Harbor High.

As they drove down the hill, Lawrence said, "Are you feeling better?"

"I'm fine. That was a weird thing. Sorry. It was dumb. Won't happen again."

"It's not like you had a choice," he consoled her, unaware that he was highlighting the most frustrating aspect. Charlie wanted control, and control was about having choices. Lawrence wasn't wrong: when you fainted, it wasn't a matter of choice. That was why it was so upsetting.

She told him to park in front of the equipment shed, which was filled with unopened boxes from the Goodwins' Brooklyn apartment. They hadn't gotten much out after arriving. Greg had been too distracted with the grand plans for his brewery, and Charlie didn't see the point of unpacking reminders of home. She had no desire to settle in. She knew where the fishing equipment was because that had been one of her father's futile attempts to engage her in the glories of the Maine coast. She'd tried to humor him, heaving a sparkling silver hook tipped with a clam strip into the water as the tide came in—and she had to admit it was a little exciting when a fish actually took it—but once she'd landed it, she had to take the hook out, and the sight of the fish on its side in the sand reminded her of the dying one she'd seen at the aquarium.

After that, she'd let her dad do the fishing while she shot video with her phone.

"I don't know which one he wants," Charlie said, pointing at the cluster of rods leaning against a set of steel shelving. "This one's pretty long."

"That's a fly rod. Grandpa will waste the whole day trying to hit something with that, and he won't hand it over to me until we're both exhausted." Lawrence selected a stiffer rod and then picked up the tackle box. "That balloon is really weird."

"Right? Maybe it's a Chinese spy balloon."

"Don't tell that to him; he'll believe you. Next thing you know, the Coast Guard will be out here, listening to him talk politics."

Charlie laughed. Okay, Lawrence had *some* sense of humor.

"If the balloon is weird," he continued, "the voice from the cockpit is even stranger. That's a mean joke. Really mean. Because of . . . " He frowned, trying to find a way to put her mother's murder into words, which was *not* something Charlie could endure.

"It was just stupid," she said, turning away. "No big deal."

She went to the truck and got in the passenger seat while he put the fishing rod and tackle box in the bed. Her dead ATV sat like a taunt. She checked her phone: still no signal. Lawrence got back behind the wheel and started the old truck's engine.

"We're supposed to grab Abe a beer," Charlie reminded him.

Lawrence put the truck in drive. "He doesn't need it."

"Who's the grandpa in this relationship?"

"It's not even noon," Lawrence said, a sharpness to his tone that told Charlie she was on family business and should tread lightly. The problem was, Charlie had never been one to tread lightly.

"Let me guess," she said, "you're not a partyer."

"Are you?"

"When I want to be," she said, although in truth she wasn't. She'd done some drinking, tried a few edibles and once a vape pen, but she never liked the feeling of being buzzed or high, because with it came a lack of control. "There's no place *to* party out here that's not a keg by a gravel pit or bonfire on the beach or whatever."

She'd heard kids at Cold Harbor speak of both, but she hadn't been invited to join them—which was just fine, because of course she wouldn't have.

"You went to a lot of clubs in New York, I guess," Lawrence said, and when she shot him a look to see if he was mocking her, his face was impossible to read.

"When I wanted to," she lied.

He gave that considerate nod of his, one that didn't betray his real thoughts. She didn't speak to him the rest of the way up the hill.

Abe was waiting beneath the weather balloon, and the first thing he noticed was the lack of beer.

"Did I not request a pint?"

"I forgot," Lawrence said. "Sorry."

"'Forgot' and 'sorry'—two words that are real popular in the Navy, let me assure you. Captains love those two."

Lawrence shrugged, and Abe sighed and took the fishing rod from him.

"Get a nice heavy jig out of that tackle box and watch the magic happen."

Lawrence selected one of the chrome-colored, weighted hooks from the box and tied it on to the end of the line while Abe eyed the balloon.

"Secret is all about touch. Finesse. You've gotta feather it in there, like this."

With that, he whipped the rod backward and then stepped forward and extended his casting hand—but the rod remained behind him, the tip bending toward the earth, the hook snagged on a hunk of the old fuselage.

"I told you not to leave that much slack!" Abe barked at Lawrence, although he'd said no such thing. Charlie was tempted to record this—the Zimmer family balloon-fishing expedition would be a viral hit—but she managed not to reach for her phone. Lawrence freed the hook, Abe grunted and reeled the jig up a little higher, then tried again.

This time the jig whipped through the bare branches overhead, struck the balloon, and caught.

"Boo-yah!" Abe shouted. "There was a reason they called me Old One-Shot when I took gunnery practice."

"But it took you two casts," Charlie said.

"And what kind of gun on a plane only fires one bullet?" Lawrence asked.

"Mortars, wiseass," Abe said.

"It would seem pretty easy to hit something with a mortar."

"Well, let's see you do it, then! You kids like to outsource criticism more than sweat. We went from the Greatest Generation to the Grate*less*, I tell you."

"Ungrateful?" Lawrence said, earning a withering look from Abe.

"I was making a point."

"Oh. Sorry. I missed that." Lawrence smiled in Charlie's direction, and she caught herself smiling back, then looked away.

"It isn't as easy to hit a target with a mortar as you might think, and besides, I was a pilot—only took a little gunnery practice to show those boys a thing or two," Abe said, reeling the line taut and testing his hold on the balloon. "And if you've been paying attention, you'll have observed that we have yet another Abe Zimmer Mission Accomplished right here, and you kids were lucky enough to see it in person. Count your blessings, not my casts."

He heaved the rod up over his head and walked backward. The monofilament line tightened, and for a moment Charlie was certain the balloon wouldn't budge, that it would refuse Abe's line as easily as it had ignored the wind.

Then it popped free.

Immediately, the balloon started to drift upward again—the way it always should have, staying high and avoiding the trees—and suddenly Charlie was afraid that they'd made a terrible mistake, setting it loose. Abe began reeling furiously, as if he were Quint aboard the *Orca* in *Jaws*, only his nemesis was hooked in the air, not the water. The balloon seemed to fight back; by the time Abe had it down low enough for Lawrence to grab, there was a fine sheen of sweat on the old pilot's face.

"That's a whole lot of work," he said between wheezing breaths, "to prove what I've already observed. It's a weather balloon with a radiosonde."

The device that Abe called the radiosonde was nothing but an old cardboard box with metal staples used to attach the threads that bound it to the balloon. The box was white and there were serial numbers and a block of text in blue ink printed on the side.

Charlie lifted it and heard something shift with a metallic rattle.

"The sensors are inside," Abe said.

"What does it say?" Lawrence asked.

"'Radiosonde, Navy stock number R217-3730-712,'" Charlie read. "'This instrument was released by a weather station and carried aloft by means of a sounding balloon. When the balloon burst, the instrument descended slowly to the ground on the parachute.'"

She glanced at Abe, who held his palms out, indicating he couldn't explain the reason the balloon hadn't burst. She read on.

"'While aloft, the instrument transmitted radio signals which indicated the temperature, humidity, and pressure of the atmosphere through which it passed. The finder of this instrument may salvage it for parts or dispose of it in any convenient manner. Bendix Friez Instrument Division.'"

She turned the box over and her eyes drifted to the numbers stamped on the upper left-hand corner of the box: *12-11-1962*.

"That can't be a date," she said, and Abe and Lawrence leaned closer.

"It sure looks like a manufacturing date," Lawrence said. "And everything about the box is old-fashioned."

He was right. Even the texture of the cardboard felt different—thicker and smoother than the cheap packaging she was used to—and the fasteners used to hold the threads to the box were flat, round brads, made with metal. It didn't resemble modern packaging.

"Well, it sure hasn't been up there for sixty years," Abe said dryly. "They can float a long time, but I think a half century is pushing it. Could be someone put up an old unit."

"Why?" Charlie said.

"Hell, I don't know."

"And why did the balloon come down?"

As if in answer, the breeze gusted and Lawrence had to tighten his grip and battle the balloon back down. He'd just wrestled it into control when a high, harsh sound pierced the air. The wail of a siren.

It came from behind them and below. From the brewery.

From her home.

"What the hell is that?" Charlie asked.

"That's the scramble horn," Abe said.

"The what?"

"The Klaxon." Abe's voice was soft with wonder, and while he spoke with his standard self-assurance, this time the knowledge seemed to unsettle him.

"What's the Klaxon?"

"The siren for battle stations."

The three of them stood together, listening.

"Well, I'll be f-bombed," Abe said. "How did that old thing activate?"

The only answer was that wail from the ancient air horn, one that called to mind old movies of pilots racing to planes—and raised the fine hairs on Charlie's arms and neck.

"Okay," Abe said. "Let's go down and figure out how to shut that thing off."

"Take the balloon," she said.

Abe looked surprised, but Lawrence nodded. There was a reassurance to his expression, a hint that he shared her unvoiced concerns. There was something very wrong here.

"I've got it," he said, and for the first time she was glad he was there.

The three of them walked downhill as if heeding the siren's call.

Battle stations, she thought, and suddenly she wished very badly that her father were home.

Or her mother.

ARLINGTON, VIRGINIA
OCTOBER 25, 2025

Layla Chen was immersed in the Project Kingsolver files with Betsy Kreuzer when a sentry interrupted with a call from the director of national intelligence.

Hanover had left the Situation Room, and he was unhappy.

"To say the President and the secretary of defense are skeptical would be an understatement," he said. "They're aware of the reputation of Sector Six, but what you're asking for is—"

"Unprecedented," Layla finished for him.

"Unreasonable," he countered, though she thought he'd adjusted on the fly. "I'm trying to keep agencies foreign *and* domestic happy and blissfully ignorant. Everyone has questions, Dr. Chen. Seeker Script was perhaps too effective. It's being viewed as adversarial."

"That's the point," Layla said, watching as Betsy Kreuzer pulled up a digital scan of a classified file from 1952, an operation known as Ivy Mike, in which the world got its first taste of a thermonuclear weapon. Detonated over remote islands in the South Pacific, Ivy Mike was hardly a secret—it was filmed by a professional studio, with a voice-over provided by western actor Reed Hadley—but many of the resulting discoveries had been secret. Into the mushroom cloud flew three F-84 Thunderjets, a mission dubbed Red Flight, outfitted with filters to collect debris from the cloud for sampling. They encountered severe turbulence and lost their instruments due to the electromagnetic intensity. The first pilot returned safely and delivered his samples. The second pilot, flying blind, all navigation tools rendered useless, was unable to locate the tanker plane needed for refueling, at which point he attempted and succeeded in a treacherous dead-stick landing. The third plane crashed into the Pacific, the pilot's body never recovered.

While the Department of Defense and the White House scrambled to handle the public relations crisis, the samples collected by Red Flight were whisked away to Los Alamos for study. For three years the results were kept secret. In 1955 the United States announced the discovery of two new elements, einsteinium and fermium. Other substances remained classified, as did the presence of a civilian on board Red Flight, one Dr. Martin Hazelton, who was then five years away from heading a mission code-named Project Kingsolver.

The average American in 1952 knew the name Ivy Mike. The average American in 2025 did not. And no civilian had ever known the name Project Kingsolver. It was Layla Chen's job to keep it that way.

"You do understand the gravity of my mission," she told Hanover, unsurprised but still disappointed that the director of national intelligence dared to question Seeker Script. The results were on the ground of every airport in the country. *You try doing that without declaring a national emergency,* she thought. *You guys wouldn't have had a chance.*

"I don't need to be reminded of the gravity," Hanover said. "What I need is a way to reassure all concerned parties that Seeker Script was not an act of war, some foreign party hacking our domestic airlines. We've got the good folks of Google telling us they've spotted 'unusual activity' in Iran and the Microsoft security team agrees with the CIA that it was undoubtedly Russia. Meanwhile, the President understands it was our action but has to explain the situation—and when it ends. Not just to the Joint Chiefs or the airlines, Dr. Chen, but to the American people. To the world."

Maybe we should've explained before we launched Project Kingsolver in 1962, she thought, but she said nothing. Security and secrecy were bedfellows. Times changed; human nature did not.

"I don't know what I am supposed to offer here," she said. "My role was making sure Seeker Script existed—and worked. It clearly did. Brilliantly."

"A bit too brilliantly. You must give me a plausible excuse for the scenario that doesn't escalate tension with Iran and Russia."

"No pressure."

"Full pressure. I need *something*, Layla."

He never used her first name. They'd known each other for many years, and he was always formal. She liked Hanover. He was a serious man in a business—politics—that was becoming dangerously unserious.

"Move 37," she said. "Blame the system, not its creators."

"Clarify."

"The most famous moment in the history of artificial intelligence came when the AlphaGo system competed against a human grandmaster in a logic game that is considerably harder than chess. The human grandmaster was shocked when his AI opponent broke with all conventional logic and made a choice that is now known as Move 37. The choice was not a mistake. It was merely a departure from the known chain of logic."

"This is supposed to help me."

"Yes. Suggest that we're still in the process of identifying the creator but have credible intelligence that the action was not hostile—merely a mistake of the machine. The CIA and the FBI have been studying defenses against deepfake calls for years. Perhaps one of those systems went awry and tested itself."

"That's taking ownership for a disaster," Hanover said.

"The alternative is making an accusation we know is false. Blaming Russia or Iran is not without risk."

"No one will like this."

Layla was silent.

"That's the best you have?" He sounded weary, defeated.

"It's an option that could be explained. The PR side of the matter is not my expertise, sir."

"I know it. Meanwhile, where is the plane, Dr. Chen?" Formal again. "Where is this invisible B-52 you seem so sure will reappear?"

"I don't know, but I'm working to understand how it got here. This call, important though it may be, is not maximizing my time or talents, sir. You know this."

He knew it. Sounding disgusted and exhausted, he ended the call. Layla sat back and closed her eyes, feeling Hanover's fatigue as if it had been a virus. How was she supposed to fix a problem that had been created long before she was born?

Layla Chen had not intended to be with DARPA. The private sector was the plan, the military as implausible as the notion that she might actually become a country music star.

A DARPA recruiter had found her smoking a cigarette outside of a loading dock during a college job fair in Chapel Hill. The recruiter didn't have a lighter. Layla did. Cue the forced small talk. The whole conversation took maybe ten minutes, and Layla was left with a brochure and a vague notion that this woman really believed cancer would be eradicated by artificial intelligence and that the military would lead the way, just as it had with the internet. Everyone used the internet on a daily basis; few remembered that its first name had been ARPANET, born with a million dollars reallocated from missile research. Other early hits from ARPA included the AR-15 rifle and a defoliation spray called Agent Orange, but ARPANET had the greatest global impact. Layla suspected the best decision—and the most symbolic—that DARPA ever made was to fade quietly away from the reputation of inventing the internet. Let the wunderkinds of Silicon Valley and Seattle occupy the minds of the American public when it came to tech; let the pundits focus on social media and online shopping rather than the origin story of the ultimate distraction machine in human history. It was better for everyone.

When Layla made her way to Sector Six and became the unofficial Czar of Old Mistakes, tasked with inventorying and tracking the failed efforts of the agency, she decided less was more where publicity of DARPA's role in shaping America was concerned—and make no mistake, she was a fan of DARPA. If human societies could outlast human nature, which was very much an open question, it would require help from the agency.

She would never have been there if not for the forced small talk over that cigarette, the recruiter dutifully asking Layla what she'd studied—applied physical sciences major, aerospace studies minor—and then asking her how someone so smart could still choose to smoke cigarettes.

Layla, who was never more cynical and world-weary than when she was twenty-two, a tendency of many a college senior facing final exams, had waxed eloquent: "We live in a society that feeds us mental junk food all day long and calls it media, feeds us real junk food and calls it nutrition, and I'm supposed to worry about a cigarette?"

Her senioritis might have been obvious. Her bullshit certainly was. But the recruiter's eyes brightened.

"You should join us," she had said, handing the brochure over. "In fifty years, it won't matter whether you smoked your whole life and never went to the gym. We'll fix your immune system, rearrange your genes, replace whatever needs replacing."

She'd been smiling, joking . . . and yet not completely unserious. The recruiter believed in the power of technological innovation to address damn near anything. She focused on cancer only because they were both smoking cigarettes when they should have known better. There are few better excuses for human error than faith that someone else is developing a fix for your bad decisions.

The conversation with the recruiter wouldn't have lingered had it not been paired with another conversation the next day. This one, a call from home. The first of Layla's mother's many trips to the oncologist had occurred.

Layla had pulled the DARPA brochure out of the garbage within minutes of hanging up.

Now, years later, in a fortified archive in Virginia, returning to the file of Dr. Martin Hazelton, she couldn't help but wonder what might have happened to Hazelton if his own father had lived. If he hadn't been in Nashua, New Hampshire, during his junior year of prep school, in a nation on the verge of war, with all the redirected research dollars that lay ahead, what would have become of a mind like Hazelton's?

Impossible to know.

"We didn't treat him well," she said to Betsy Kreuzer as she read of Hazelton's final years.

"His story is not a recruiting tool, no," Betsy said, and though it was meant as agreement, it hit Layla hard. Betsy had no idea what Layla had been thinking of, and yet there it was: recruitment, the loading dock and the cigarette lighter and the woman who thought computers would cure cancer.

"What?" Betsy said, sensing Layla's discomfort, but before Layla could explain, they were interrupted by the opening of a steel door that led to an exterior air lock, changing the pressure of the room and ruffling the ancient letters of Dr. Martin Hazelton as if the old envelopes were coming to life. Two sentries entered, both in full tactical gear, rifles slung over their shoulders.

Two minutes later, Layla was on a helicopter again, flying back to Raven Rock, told only that the Air Force had a confirmed visual of a B-52 over the North Atlantic, a plane that had no known departure base and ignored radio contact.

She never did get to explain to Betsy Kreuzer how she'd come to work for the Department of Defense because of a cigarette break.

INDIANA
SUMMER 1962

Marty had not left Crane for more than a month when a postcard came from Marilyn Metzger.

Do you remember me? she wrote. *I'll be back in town the first week of August. It would be lovely to see you again. Shall we say the Dandale at 5 on August 3? I'll be there—only mildly heartbroken if you stand me up.*

Not only did he not wish to stand her up; he couldn't get away from Crane fast enough.

By then he knew that his vanished planes would return for his dead father's radioactive watch—and only the watch.

He had vanished 159 models, and he'd succeeded in bringing 33 back. They reappeared—unharmed—at precisely the minute the watch caught up to real time. Set the watch back fifteen minutes, the vanished plane would arrive in fifteen minutes. Set it for ten hours, sleep through the night, and you could meet the returning aircraft over your morning coffee.

He was leery of studying the watch in the way it demanded to be studied—disassembled and analyzed and rebuilt. The process felt—

for reasons he couldn't articulate because they were too ridiculous for a scientist to consider—almost certain to diminish the watch's power. Its magic.

There was no such thing as magic, of course, so he *should* disassemble the thing . . . but he couldn't.

The closest he came to tampering with it was to cautiously apply the red and black leads of his voltage multimeter to the face. Two things happened simultaneously: the meter offered its highest possible reading, 50,000 ohms, and the watch's hands twitched. Next, he applied the leads from a dry cell battery to the watch face. There was a brief spark-and-glow response, like a failed match strike, and then the hands began to spin swiftly—and backward.

He pulled the leads away, and the watch stabilized, ticked forward.

Fascinating.

And . . . frightening? He wasn't sure why he felt that way, but he did.

On the first Friday in August, he sat alone at the bar at the Dandale, wondering if Marilyn Metzger would indeed show up. He had a scotch and checked the door each time it opened, gusts of humid summer air colliding with the overmatched air conditioner. The patrons of the Dandale seemed to be the courthouse crowd. Lawyers and clerks, prosecutors and judges, chatter about this docket or that. He ordered a shrimp cocktail and a cup of French onion soup to make himself look more purposeful and less lonely, glanced yet again at the watch on his left wrist. There were two W. C. Ball 1924 vintages in his possession now. He'd purchased a perfect twin of his father's watch the week after the plane reappeared, along with a half dozen other makes and models.

It had not taken long to eliminate possibilities. You could keep your Rolexes, Bulovas, Heuers, and even the rest of your W. C. Ball vintage 1924 models. They were timepieces, nothing more. The watch that would change the world had belonged to Robert Hazelton before it left his dead wrist and moved onto that of his youngest son, who'd flown it in nuclear skies.

Ethereal, Hank Hazelton had called the light. One day, Marty thought, he'd be able to tell his brother what an ethereal sight truly was: the return of a vanished airplane. He wasn't ready to tell anyone that just yet. The Navy knew he could vanish a plane, but they had no clue that he could summon one back using an old wristwatch that had been exposed to radioactive skies.

Why was he still holding off on sharing such revolutionary intelligence?

Maybe because the word "holy" came before "curiosity," the way Einstein had said it. If you lost that adjective—or traded it for another—it became a different game. The great man didn't say, "Have ruthless curiosity," and, more and more, the race for superior weaponry felt that way.

He was so lost in his own thoughts that he didn't notice Marilyn Metzger when she finally arrived. He'd stopped turning to look at the door with each opening and closing, was aware only of the gust of summer heat, and then she sat down beside him. She wore a simple navy dress, a sterling silver chain tracing down her neck to her collarbone, bright against that sun-kissed skin. She was carrying the Vonnegut book again.

"Don't worry," she said, "I'm not that slow of a reader. I brought it for you."

"That's very kind."

The bartender appeared. "Cocktail, ma'am?"

"Vodka soda, please."

The bartender mixed and poured. The piano player played "You'll Never Walk Alone."

"How goes the writing?" Marty asked.

"Splendid! I've been to seven factories, three research labs, and even to Washington. There's excitement about all things GE, let me assure you."

He couldn't tell if she was mocking the company.

"They achieve great things," he said, trying to allow the same ambiguity into his tone and failing. If anything, it sounded like a repudiation.

"Oh, I know it. The House of Magic. A lovely term, bravo to the marketing team, but there's nothing *magical*. It's merely a matter of speed of technology and controlled messaging. What we—the consumers, the civilians—understand about the technology is back here . . . "

She extended her slender hand and placed her left index finger on the polished wooden bar top. There was still no ring on her left hand. Marty was almost embarrassed by how quickly he checked.

"And the scientists, they're out here." She moved her right hand down the bar, farther from the left, and closer to Marty. She smiled, her eyes alight with humor and charm, and slid her right hand rapidly down the bar top, like a piano player finishing off a song with a flourish, which brought her body down close to his.

"Speed," she said. "Speed and controlled messaging make it seem like magic."

He looked down into her face, the mischievous curl of her mouth, which was close enough to be kissable.

"Then," she said, not retreating, and lowering her voice to a playful whisper, "we add the computers. Talk about speed. And what happens then?"

She stretched far enough to her right that the neckline of her modest dress fell away from her chest, and then she crawled her piano player's fingers teasingly over Marty's arm and on across the bar, stopping when her hand was perfectly aligned with the spot where his belt buckle rested beneath the bar.

"Checkmate," she said, and tugged twice on his tie before pulling back, retreating to her proper, perfect posture on the stool, and laughing with what seemed genuine delight. "Start with a lead, add computers for speed, report your inventions when the time is right, consumers and shareholders remain in awed delight. That is the secret of the House of Magic!"

"You're probably right about that," Marty allowed. "The controlled messaging, anyhow. Quarterly reports, you know."

"Ah, yes, the market. What do you think they haven't disclosed?"

"This quarter? I've no idea."

"I mean, what have they never disclosed, because they never can? The Big Secrets! Capital *B* and capital *S*, you know." She laughed at her own joke, and he smiled again, but he was feeling suddenly uncertain. There was an edge to her that he didn't remember from their Christmas meeting.

"Again, I've no idea," he said. "You're the reporter. What do you think?"

She used her drink as an excuse to turn from him. Took a long swallow, swirled the ice once before setting it down, and then straightened the coaster, her eyes on the bar when she said, "Have you heard of Flight 19?"

He was glad she was looking away.

"No," he said. "What does this Flight 19 operation do?"

She turned back. "They're not an operation. They were a squadron. Five torpedo bombers, Grumman Avengers, that flew out of Fort Lauderdale on a clear, bright day for a simple training exercise . . . and disappeared. The largest search in history didn't turn up so much as an oil slick. One of the first planes in the air to search for them disappeared, too, with nine men aboard, but it's commonly believed that one exploded. An unfortunate but entirely natural coincidence."

"I recall the story," he said, hoping to put an end to it.

She gazed at him with cool, steady eyes. Drummed her fingernails on the Vonnegut book, the pages softening the sound to something like a gentle rain.

"No trace was left of those five planes. They just . . . vanished. No wreckage, no fuel streaks, not a single life jacket."

Marty knew he should leave, but he sat rooted to his stool, unable to fathom how fast it had all turned.

"Here's an interesting thing about the planes," Marilyn continued. "They were all missing clocks. Don't you find that strange?"

"I suppose. Most pilots do wear watches, though."

He suppressed a wild desire to cover his left wrist with his right hand, hiding the W. C. Ball from her view.

"Well, I find it strange. Their final radio transmissions were even stranger. They couldn't seem to orient themselves over the water. They debated which way was west, yet the afternoon sun was shining, and any child knows how to find west in America when the sun is up. They complained that their instruments weren't working. At one point, someone says, 'Nothing looks right.' Then, at the very end, another man says, 'We are entering white water.'"

The bartender stepped up, one eyebrow cocked in question, and pointed at Marty's glass. Marty nodded. Marilyn matched him. Neither of them spoke while the bartender fixed the drinks. When he was gone and they were alone again, the piano player in the corner started in on a Hoagy Carmichael number, and Marty turned back to Marilyn.

"So what's your angle on it? The connection to General Electric. The House of Magic."

Trying for charm, the ease with which he'd spoken to her back in December, when she was smiling. She wasn't smiling anymore.

"Don't you think that we'd both benefit from a little honesty at this point, Dr. Hazelton?"

Cocooned in the cheerful chaos of the piano and the bar chatter and the sound of cocktail shakers, Marty Hazelton and Marilyn Metzger might as well have been alone.

"Who sent you on this goose chase?" he asked softly.

"My fiancé. His name was Robert Riley. He was a radioman on one of the bombers in Flight 19. Don't you remember the manifest?"

Marty remembered the name Robert Riley. It was awful that he'd ever forgotten it.

"I think you understand that I'm going to have to end this conversation," he said. "I don't know what led you to me, but it was a regrettable mistake."

"If you think you're going to run back to that base at Crane and hide behind its gates, you're in for a surprise."

"I'm not hiding. But I am leaving." He signaled for the bartender. "I'm sorry to hear about your loss. I truly am. But—"

"Why were you there?" she asked, leaning so close that her blond hair swung forward and grazed his shoulder. Her lips were set in a hard red line, her eyes feral.

"I'm sure you're a fine reporter," he said. "I have no doubt of that. And I understand that Flight 19 was both tragic and, to some people, mysterious. But it was a regrettable accident. Your fiancé's commander made a mistake. The only mystery of Flight 19 is one of human behavior: Why did the others follow him so long when they knew he was wrong?"

"Bullshit," Marilyn said, not softly.

Marty stood, dropped cash on the bar top, and stepped away.

"I'm sorry for your loss." He put on his hat and pulled open the door of the Dandale, leaving the cool of the cocktail room for the furnace of Indiana August.

She followed him. He wasn't surprised, but he was agitated. He felt badly for her, but he couldn't handle any more questions, wanted her to simply go home and grieve. Flight 19 had vanished seventeen years earlier, though. She'd been grieving for a long time. He wondered, as he walked to the car, pretending to be unaware of the clap of her heels on the sidewalk, just how young she must have been when her beloved took off from the Naval Air Station Fort Lauderdale. Robert Riley, radioman, had been very young. Nineteen, if Marty's recollection was correct, little more than a boy.

A tragedy.

But not a conspiracy.

He pushed his way through a group of kids carrying ice cream, stepped down from the curb, and was reaching for the car door when Marilyn caught up to him and snatched the keys from his hand.

"Are you out of your mind?" He whirled back. The children with the ice cream were watching them curiously. Marty grabbed the door handle and the metal, baked in the sun, seared his palm. He had a flash memory of Nashua, the truck exploding, his little brother racing for it.

His teeth were still white, Hank had said of the corpse.

Marty turned on his heel and walked away, crossed the square while a car screeched brakes and a driver honked.

"Talk to me!" Marilyn shouted after him.

He kept walking, his brow damp with sweat. She could have his keys; she could have the damn car. Dr. Martin Hazelton would have no trouble finding transportation back to his naval base. But, once there, he would have to do some explaining. He'd done nothing wrong, but any pause for explaining this sad woman was also a disruption in the work, and the work could not be disrupted, not with the world on the brink, atomic tests rattling the skies and obliterating islands.

Behind him, he heard her heels rise to a clatter on the concrete as she broke into a run.

"Oh, for the love of God," Marty snapped, turning back. She hadn't been prepared for him to stop, so she barreled into him, hit him hard enough that he took a stumbling step and then they were falling together. He got his left hand out and caught a light pole in time to arrest their motion. Her momentum drove them backward while the light pole kept them upright, and they spun like dancers. By the time they were stable her face was close to his and it would have looked to all the world as if he were holding her tight in a lover's embrace.

All the world, of course, could not see her furious, huntress's eyes. Those were for him alone.

"*All right*," he whispered harshly. "Walk and talk. Ask your questions. They're a fool's errand, but I've got two options here, and one is to have you arrested, do you understand?"

"Arrested! Why, I'd love nothing more than a day with you in a courtroom, with the public on hand to watch and listen!"

"It won't require a courtroom," Marty said evenly, "and there will be no one on hand. I promise you that."

She stared up at him, and for the first time she seemed the slightest bit unsure of herself. He gazed back, steady, the promise in his eyes. She pushed away, straightened her dress.

"It's a fine threat, but I'm well acquainted with due process."

"You won't get it. There will be a room prepared for you in a state hospital if I'm required to make a single phone call."

Her eyes darkened, fresh interest—or fear?—in them. Marty turned from her again. This time he walked slower. She matched his stride. They'd gone a block before she spoke again.

"If it is as you say, that Lieutenant Taylor made a mistake and four other pilots followed, chasing him right up to their deaths, then why were you there at all?" she said. "Because I know what you do."

"You know nothing of what I do."

"You make the weather. You've admitted that to me—bragged of it!"

"I bragged of nothing. And I never made the weather; I merely played a small role in . . . in altering it. That's no secret."

"The project might not have been, but your role was! Why no media for you? Why does everyone know Langmuir but no one knows Hazelton?"

"I let General Electric have the newsprint. The shareholders love it."

She grasped his arm, and he kept going, stride steady, almost dragging her along. He headed north on a side street called Lockridge Lane, walking toward a tall limestone house that loomed in the shadows. It looked refreshing and cool on a day that had grown impossibly hot.

"They flew out into a bright, clear day," she said. "Hours later, a massive burst of turbulence swept over the sea. The airport weather station in Miami recorded hurricane-force winds at eight thousand feet. And there you were!"

Marty sighed. "They did not fly out into a bright, clear day. There were billowing clouds and a strong southwestern trade wind. Already you're proving yourself a better fiction writer than journalist."

"Clouds be damned, there should have been no hurricane-force winds that day, and you *know it*, because you fucking *caused it!*"

This time she jerked his arm with such force that he spun back to her. They were standing in front of the tall, Gothic-looking limestone house. The yard was flanked by massive elms, and he was grateful for their shadows. He removed his handkerchief, mopped sweat. Looked up the street, saw no one. Closed his eyes, took a breath.

She is grieving. She is grieving and she knows nothing of reality. If she did, she'd be asking much better questions. So be patient.

"I have caused storms," he said, opening his eyes again.

"I know it."

"I did not cause that storm. No one did."

120

"Bull—"

"Shit, I know, everything I say is apparently a lie. Yet you're here accosting me in pursuit of the truth, you say? Is that not what you want? Or is everything about *you* a lie, including your relationship with Robert Riley?"

"How dare—"

"If it is not, then you want the *truth*, correct?"

She glared at him, said nothing.

"The truth is that an accident happened and a squadron leader made a poor choice. Was I there? Yes. Can I ensure that we were *not* responsible for the weather? Yes. Flight 19 flew into weather that had no help from man or chemistry. I'm sorry."

"I don't believe it." Her jaw was set, but he saw a hint of a tremble there.

"It is the truth."

She looked at him for a long time before she said, "It is hot and I want an ice cream."

Like a child.

"Then you should have it," he said. "May I have my keys?"

"When you've paid for my ice cream."

"I'm trying to show charity. I would hate to see—"

"He was nineteen years old," she said, and her voice nearly broke.

Marty Hazelton gritted his teeth and looked up at the limestone house, where windows reflected the descending sun and gave the place the look of some gray creature watching him with golden eyes.

"I met him on the first day of school when I was five years old," Marilyn Metzger said. "We grew up together. I don't remember a time before him. Only the time after."

"You're not going to find him," he said. "You don't get him back."

"I know that. I'm not a fool. I want to understand how he died, and *why*."

He looked into her haunted eyes.

"I will buy you an ice cream," he said.

———

Long after her fiancé vanished, Marilyn Metzger took a job at a newspaper in Savannah and was assigned to write an anniversary piece about a hurricane that had battered the city in 1947.

That was the first she'd ever heard of Project Cirrus.

Savannah had sued both the U.S. government and General Electric, convinced that the 1947 hurricane had been redirected into the Georgia coastline after the storm was seeded with dry ice deployed by a B-17. The hurricane's path had swung by 90 degrees, turning the storm into a battering ram for their town. While GE and the Navy claimed innocence, one Miami meteorologist declared the storm's sudden shift "a low Yankee trick."

As Marilyn Metzger researched the debate, she came across the presence of Dr. Martin Hazelton, a Project Cirrus scientist. Of all the people involved, he struck her as having the most interesting path, from Los Alamos to Oak Ridge to Doom Town and then Crane, a naval base in *Indiana*, of all places, and the public was told only that it was a handy place to store ammunition, nothing to see here, move along. She visited Crane and convinced a sentry to call her if Dr. Hazelton ever left the base.

"I told him I was an old friend of your brother's, and it had to be a surprise," she said as they sat at a diner called Ladyman's on Kirkwood Avenue, eating ice cream sundaes as if they were teens on a date. "You made the mistake of telling him you were off to Bloomington to see the Christmas lights."

If that reflected the security at Crane, Marty thought, the Navy should be delighted that he didn't leave the base more often.

"We did not cause the trouble for Flight 19," Marty told her while the sun cast pale pink light on the sidewalk. "Project Cirrus was a failure. A fascinating experiment, but a failure. We did not redirect a hurricane into Savannah."

"There are plenty of people in Georgia who think you did."

"There are plenty of people in Georgia who think the Confederate cause was righteous and a football game between college boys is sacred. I'm content to disagree with Georgia."

She shifted, smoothing her dress, flustered. She'd been on her quest for so long that to hear it was for naught must be devastating. She pushed the ice cream away, a tacky pool of melted sugary stickiness.

"When you threatened me tonight—" she began.

"I did not mean to—"

"When you threatened me tonight, you weren't bluffing. You'd have followed through if I'd asked the right questions. Tell me, what's the name of *that* little endeavor? Not Project Cirrus or Project Skyfire. But there is one. And if I'd simply said it, we wouldn't be sitting here, would we? Not both of us, anyhow. Not me."

The phrase "Project Kingsolver" floated through his mind, and when she nodded with grim satisfaction, he had the disturbing sensation that she'd *heard* it somehow—had read his mind.

"I'll say the right name soon, and maybe you'll be more forthcoming when I do. I'll give you a week to think about that." She rose. "See you next Friday, Dr. Hazelton. Five o'clock at the Dandale? It feels like our spot now, doesn't it?"

All this so breezily.

"You're out of your mind, Miss Metzger," he said without rising.

"Oh, no, my dear." Her smile seemed to pin him in place. "I'm on a mission. It's quite different. Ask any American. There's no such thing as madness if one is on a mission."

"Go back to Florida," Marty said, and he meant it, but she simply smiled and put her hand on top of his and gave it a little squeeze that lit nerves his body had forgotten.

She withdrew a small silver cigarette case from her handbag, snapped it open, and shook out a cigarette.

"If I were you, I wouldn't show up without a little . . . incentive."

She pursed her lips to accept the unlit cigarette.

"Here's your incentive," she said. "A monkey will be arriving Monday."

He blinked, utterly bewildered.

"When the monkey arrives," she continued, "he'll have come from Cleveland, and while his identification will be serial number 5709, to the folks back there, he was called Jimmy. They tell me he's quite smart. Why, he might even respond to his name."

She lit the cigarette. Smiled as the tip glowed red. Said, "That's pretty good intel, don't you think?"

Then she pushed through the door, the bell above it tinkling, and Marty sat above his dish of melting ice cream and watched her walk, swaying her hips, and vanish into the night.

The Klaxon siren went off as abruptly as it had come on.

They were down from the mountain, Lawrence clutching the balloon in the bed of the truck, and the tires had just touched pavement when the air horn stopped. The silence it returned to them felt deeper, stranger.

"Guess they called off the attack," Abe joked, but Charlie couldn't force a smile.

"How would that thing come on? I've never heard it. Why now?"

"I'm not quite sure," Abe admitted, pulling into a parking spot in front of the taproom. "Maybe there was a short or a loose wire."

"That's what you said about my ATV."

They both looked over at the Kawasaki. Then there was a thump and a rustle from the bed of the truck, and Charlie glanced in the side-view mirror and saw that Lawrence had hopped out and was wrestling the tangled lines of the radiosonde free. The balloon drifted above him. Charlie popped the door and stepped out into the stiffening breeze.

"What do you want to do with this thing?" Lawrence asked. "Should I just pop it?"

"No!" Her answer came out too fast and firm, and he snapped his eyes over.

"Why not?"

She wasn't sure. She didn't particularly like the balloon—in fact, she wasn't sure that she didn't *dislike* it—and yet harming it seemed like the wrong decision. Almost dangerous.

"I want to get some videos of it. My friends are going to love that thing."

"Great. I hauled it down so you can make TikToks."

"What's your problem? You held on to a string and rode in a truck. I would've done that if I'd known it was such a big deal."

"Whatever. Just tell me where to put it."

Charlie hesitated. "Tie it to the truck?"

"Like hell!" Abe barked. "Blue is a fine-tuned piece of machinery, not a damned anchor."

Charlie sighed. "Use my ATV. It's no better than an anchor today anyhow." She checked her phone. No hint of signal. Cell service was bad at Ash Point, but never *this* bad. "I want to see if the Wi-Fi is back up."

She already knew it wouldn't be, though. Knew it in her bones, a guarantee. On the morning she was murdered, Dana Goodwin had proclaimed her daughter to be a "very perceptive girl." She'd then cautioned that this perceptiveness would be a problem for Charlie, not a solution.

They'd been talking about algebra homework. Or, rather, they *should* have been talking about algebra homework, but Charlie digressed into an elaborate theory that the assignments were becoming longer and the grading more severe because her teacher, Mr. Wentz, was getting divorced. He was all smiles at the front of the room, where they could face him directly, but the workload and grading conducted in private hours felt almost punitive.

She was venting about this while her mother gathered canvas shopping totes for a quick run to the bodega down the block, a fifteen-minute stop.

"You're a very perceptive girl," Dana Goodwin said, her back to Charlie. "But that doesn't always help you. Let's say you're right—and, by the way, I suspect that you are. Does it change anything? Knowing why he's grading more harshly doesn't change the requirement to do the work, does it?"

Charlie grumbled that it *should* change it; after all, it wasn't Charlie who'd had an affair with the basketball coach.

"We do *not* know if that is true, and we will not repeat the rumor," her mother said. "Now, answer the question."

So Charlie had grudgingly acknowledged that, no, the psychological motivations did not alter the assignment. With that, her mother leaned down and kissed the top of Charlie's head, a distracted, glancing touch to which Charlie didn't bother to respond, not even with so much as a look up from her notebook. Her mother promised they'd have spicy Thai lemongrass soup for dinner, a Charlie favorite, and then Dana Goodwin walked down the stairs, up the sidewalk, into the bodega, and took a misfired 9-millimeter bullet to the abdomen.

By the time Charlie heard the sirens—which she ignored because it was Brooklyn and sirens were white noise—her mother was already dead on the floor, her femoral artery blown apart, her blood slickening the dirty tile, two lemongrass stalks resting beside her hand.

Among the many things that Charlie couldn't stop wondering about in the aftermath was how perceptive she really was if she hadn't felt the need to look her mother in the eyes as she left. Shouldn't she have offered a *Be careful* or *I love you* as Dana departed? How perceptive could she be if she'd ignored the sirens, even when it was clear they were right down the street? How had she never once thought, *I hope Mom is okay.*

The conversation lingered as only last words ever can, so on this October day, standing in the empty bar of an isolated brewery, refreshing a phone that could no longer communicate, Charlie Goodwin couldn't help feel that lack of perception stinging her again. She'd said the most casual farewells to her father before his trip, largely because she hadn't wanted him to freak out at the idea of leaving, determined to project a calm that he could absorb. Now she wished she'd said more, even if it had made her seem younger, weaker, whatever. Was there anything weak about being afraid for those you loved? Of course not.

And still she'd sent him on his way with a shrug and an eye roll as he implored her to lock the doors and windows, check the batteries in the smoke detectors, and respond to his texts promptly.

"I hate this place," Charlie whispered now, as she unplugged the router for the third time, desperate for a connection that would allow her to reach her father.

No luck.

"What happened to the radiosonde thing?" she asked. Lawrence and Abe were standing by the circuit breaker, Abe searching in vain for a reason that the Klaxon had gone off.

"It's still there," Lawrence said. "Tied to the balloon."

"Let's bring it in. I want to open it up."

Lawrence looked at Abe, who shrugged.

"Anybody have a knife?" Charlie asked.

Lawrence slid his backpack off the bar, unzipped it, and rooted around, then came up with a pocketknife. Charlie took it and left the taproom, cut the radiosonde free, and returned carrying the box. She set it on the bar.

"Doesn't weigh much."

"Shouldn't," Abe said. "Just some simple instruments."

Charlie folded the knife and handed it back to Lawrence, then hooked her thumbnail under the metal brads that held the box shut, pried them up one by one, unwound the thread beneath them, and lifted the cardboard lid.

The box held a watch, nestled in a folded piece of notebook paper.

"What in the hell?" Charlie said.

She reached in and pulled the watch free. The vintage face had simple hands that were blued like a gun barrel and a single word— BALL in all caps—etched across it. The band was worn, filthy leather that appeared to have been taped back together. No, Charlie realized as she held it closer, it had simply been wrapped with tape, dozens of meticulous tiny squares of it, and beneath the tape was strange black dust. She picked at the edge of a square of tape with her fingernail and her fingernail came away sooty, as if she'd reached inside a cold woodstove.

"What is that?" Lawrence asked.

"No clue."

"Lemme see," Abe said, and Charlie was happy to hand the watch over. She wiped her fingers, but the dust only smeared from one to the other, trapped in the whirls and whorls of her skin.

"Look at that," Abe said, checking the device against his own wristwatch. "It's right on time."

"That's creepy," Lawrence announced, and Charlie glanced at him with surprise. He was the resident skeptic of Ash Point, always giving one of his patented sighs when she and Abe got going on the Skunk Works legends, Grumman and the RAND Corporation and ARPA. Hearing Lawrence proclaim the watch creepy seemed to deepen its menace.

"This has to be seventy years old if it's a day," Abe said, studying the watch, lifting it close to his eyes, then lowering it. "Maybe older.

But what in the hell they did to the band, I can't figure. It's all taped up. Back of the casing is too. Only the tape is filthy."

Charlie rubbed her thumb and index finger together again, feeling the strange, dusty film.

"Hold it up again," she said.

"What?"

"When you lifted it into the sunlight a second ago, it didn't look right."

"Didn't look right?"

"Just do it!"

Abe lifted the watch to eye level again, bringing it into the shaft of bright sun angling through the plate glass, and this time Lawrence sucked his breath in. He saw it too. The watch glowed. It didn't reflect the light, but seemed to *inhale* it, a brief but undeniable glimmer.

"I'll be damned," Abe said, and then he passed the watch back and forth through the shaft of light again. Each time, the sunlight seemed to contract, like something dark taking a bite out of the sunlight.

"Stop doing it," Charlie said as Abe readied for yet another pass.

"Why?"

"I don't know. But stop it."

Abe and Lawrence exchanged a look, and then Abe lowered the watch to the bar top.

"Rest of the box is empty?" he asked.

Charlie and Lawrence peered inside. The notebook paper was about the size of a dollar bill. Lawrence plucked the paper out and unfolded it. There was writing scrawled on it, the letters meticulous for the most part but every now and then jagged, as if the writer had been jostled:

Survival = Find storm cloud, fire nightshade, set watch backward and add voltage. You will catch up.

"Fire nightshade," Charlie read, feeling a prickle. "What is that?"

"I think 'fire' is a verb here," Lawrence said.

That wasn't any more reassuring, but she thought he was right. Find a storm cloud, fire the nightshade, verb form, as in ignition. Yes, Lawrence had a writer's eye. Fire nightshade . . . to survive.

Charlie slipped her phone out of her pocket and checked for texts, any update from her dad. Nothing. No signal. She tried to send him another message: You okay? Things are weird here. Maybe you should come home?

But the message froze, trapped in the strange digital amber that was now Ash Point.

RAVEN ROCK MOUNTAIN COMPLEX, PENNSYLVANIA
OCTOBER 25, 2025

The B-52 that had departed Loring Air Force Base on October 28, 1962, reappeared just before noon on October 25, 2025.

It came back into the sky a hundred miles off the coast of Maine, flying north by northeast.

The vanishing of the B-52 conceived of by ARPA and the Office of Naval Research had been intended as a show of force the Soviets would have to recognize as the ultimate in warfare supremacy, a game changer of the highest order. You couldn't fight an opponent that wasn't there. The problem was that the United States still couldn't explain what had happened to it, and the intended six-minute test flight had gone on for sixty-three years.

Now it was back.

The plane was identical to the photographs and grainy video of the missing aircraft, right down to the custom logo, a loon with a single red eye staring from beneath the cockpit. The eight huge Pratt & Whitney jet engines thrummed, propelling the plane at 280 knots across the North Atlantic.

Layla Chen, watching through a satellite video feed, had to remind herself to breathe.

The others with her seemed less awed than afraid.

The secretary of defense wanted badly to shoot the plane down over open water. The director of national intelligence warned against that. The Air Force and Navy representatives waited on orders. The CIA provided intelligence. The president of the United States simply wanted to know what in the hell was happening and how it could be stopped without impeachment.

They turned to DARPA Sector Six for input, and Layla Chen begged them not to intercept the aircraft.

"If it worked," she said, "then the crew on that plane will want to land. We have preserved an airstrip for this purpose for nearly three-quarters of a century. Let it play out as intended."

"What are the odds the bomb is still functional?" the president asked.

"I'd say they improved dramatically, considering the plane is functional."

No one could dispute that.

Behind, above, and below the bomber, F-16 fighters trailed at a safe distance. Each was armed with missiles that could destroy the B-52 at the press of a button. One version of events. Another, if the Mark 39 thermonuclear warhead was intact, was that the F-16s were armed with matches for the fuse that would create the worst nuclear disaster since Chernobyl.

That was one risk. The other, perhaps greater risk—at least in Layla Chen's mind—was losing the opportunity to study the plane. The bomber buzzing over the cold open ocean was the single greatest achievement in military science. Maybe science, period. It certainly was the greatest weapon ever devised.

Imagine, she thought, watching its black shadow over the green-blue sea, *if Cuba had turned hot in '62, or a shooting war had broken out over Berlin in the eighties, or North Korea launched last year, the way we thought they might. This plane would still have appeared. We would have had the last shot, no matter what. And if the enemy knew that . . .*

"It is banking south by southwest," an Air Force colonel named Collins said via video feed from his post in Colorado. "Returning toward the American coast."

"Do you understand what this means, Dr. Chen?" the defense secretary asked.

"Yes," Layla said. "It's doing what it was supposed to do."

"Which is what?" Hanover asked.

"Return to Ash Point. We just need it to fare better than its decoy flight."

"Come again, Dr. Chen?" This from the president.

"We crashed one," she said, hardly aware of the president, able to ignore the leader of the free world because she was so fascinated by the sight of the B-52. "We had to do that to explain the one that went missing. We can't afford to let this one come down the same way."

Silence as everyone considered the implications of that.

"How many vessels are within the current fallout zone?" the defense secretary asked.

A pause, then someone from naval intelligence answered: "We're seeing fifteen. All civilian. Fishing boats and freighters. We have one sub in the area; the Russians have two. All three are nuclear capable."

"We have to let it land," Hanover said.

Layla, barely listening, watched the plane making its lumbering arc over the North Atlantic and back toward the Maine coast. Incredible. Absolutely incredible. Martin Hazelton had done what he had promised, and what he had promised had been madness, less a science experiment than a *Twilight Zone* episode.

"I think it is crucial to realize that Captain Hightower is maintaining his flight plan," she said. "If he's rattled, he's not showing it."

Captain Hightower had been born in 1934. There was no way he could possibly be commanding this bomber, and yet . . . someone was.

"How many were on the airplane?" Hanover asked.

"Only three. It was a skeleton crew, due to the risk."

"We need to assume that we're being conned," the defense secretary said. "That's something I'd like to get a fucking assessment on. Who is tricking us here?"

No one responded.

"He intends to land at NAS Ash Point?" the president asked.

"Correct," Layla said.

"What is he expecting the situation on the ground to be?"

"A good deal different from what it will be, considering he's more than sixty years off target."

"I do not understand why this plane was launched without even the possibility of radio contact. That's insane!"

"It was the decision of Admiral Ralph Cutting," Layla said. "He died in 1970, so we can't take it up with him."

She understood Cutting's logic, or at least what she'd read of it. A mission so classified that it was almost a guaranteed disaster was better conducted in silence. No one needed radio transcripts from a panicked pilot who was attempting to vanish in midair—not the Soviets, not the Americans.

"What's the Sector Six recommendation?" Hanover asked.

"Let it land," she said, and immediately there were murmurs of discontent. "If it doesn't land, you can use . . . whatever the limited roster of options will be at that point. But if it lands? If it lands, you've got the keys to the next century of global security sitting on an abandoned runway in Maine."

Everyone looked vaguely ill, seasick passengers on choppy water.

"We need to secure that airstrip," the president said. "It should have already been done."

"It can be secured within minutes when they touch down," the defense secretary answered. "Delta Force is on the peninsula. We are following the Sector Six recommendations in keeping the airfield empty for the purposes of reassuring Captain . . . reassuring the pilot. He was promised an empty runway."

He couldn't bring himself to say Hightower's name.

"What is the civilian presence in the area?" the president asked.

The defense secretary fielded this one.

"Minimal. Ash Point is located at the end of the peninsula, one road in, one out. Incredibly isolated country. There are lobster boats offshore and some sailboats. Airspace is clear. Delta Force has procured county public works vehicles and closed the road using a guise of emergency sewer line repairs. There are, however, possibly civilians already beyond that checkpoint. One truck is parked on private property near the airfield. That is registered to an Abraham Zimmer, a local resident, and there is a Subaru registered to a Greg Goodwin, also local, although we can confirm that Goodwin is off the property. We've already severed comms from the peninsula and Goodwin's vehicle was successfully disabled with a targeted EMP weapon. Zimmer's truck is a problem, as it is apparently too old for the EMP approach to work."

"If the plane lands," the president asked, "how long will Delta need to secure it?"

"Ten minutes. This is if we adhere to Sector Six's recommendation not to utilize any aircraft, including helicopters."

The defense secretary was clearly not a fan of that recommendation.

"That plane is armed with a live nuclear warhead, and the crew was prepared to use it when they launched in '62," Layla said. "I stand by the recommendation not to disrupt Captain Hightower's crew with aircraft. Let them land, and give them a moment to breathe. Otherwise, if rattled, they're on to Cuba."

"Cuba?"

"To drop the bomb," Layla said. "We must control that aircraft or reassure the crew swiftly. The alternative is . . . suboptimal."

"Suboptimal," Hanover echoed. "One way of putting it."

No one asked Layla Chen's opinion for the remainder of the call. That was fine. She wasn't sure she could have answered if they had asked. She could simply not take her eyes off the plane.

How? she wondered, a single-word question on loop, one that had haunted DARPA for decades. Project Kingsolver had worked, but . . .

How?

INDIANA
SUMMER 1962

The monkey was delivered to Microfilm Storage Building #45 at a quarter past eight on Monday morning, August 6. Wyatt Dixon brought him to Marty. Dixon, who was a middling scientist with a morbid sense of humor, wheeled the monkey's cage in and said, "Welcome to Crane, Laika."

Laika had been the name of the dog the Soviets put on Sputnik 2, the first living creature to orbit the earth. A mongrel from Moscow, her survival in the alleys and on the harsh, frigid streets suggested a toughness that would serve her well—but certainly not bring her home. Her death on Sputnik 2 had been accepted as inevitable, a necessary sorrow.

She was a sacrifice.

"C'mon, Martin, lighten up," Wyatt said, seeing the revulsion in Marty's face.

"We don't want to borrow Soviet work," Marty said, trying to downplay his reaction. "We lead the way, Dr. Dixon; we follow no one."

"Certainly not. What's your suggestion, then?"

"I don't think we need to trouble ourselves with a name."

Marty squatted in front of the monkey's cage, and the creature immediately moved toward him. A thin paper bracelet was wrapped around his left wrist. A serial number was stamped on it: 5709.

Marty's throat felt dry.

"A name worked for Able," Wyatt commented, lighting a cigarette. "Out and back."

Able had been the first primate to travel into space and return safely, just three years earlier. His predecessors had not been so lucky; a rhesus macaque named Albert II had died on impact when a parachute failed to deploy.

"Maybe we stick with the Able theme," Wyatt said. "Call him Possibility. Better yet, call him Certainty. After seeing those mice, I'm betting the house on him. Where the hell he goes, I can't tell you, but I'm sure he's coming back."

Marty had vanished six mice in his models so far. He'd almost hoped they would return as nothing but bones and charred fur. Not because he wanted to see any creature die—he was a scientist, not a sociopath—but because he was also no fool. There were progressions. In science, you often started with mice, but you rarely ended with them.

They didn't come back charred, however. Didn't come back with so much as a trace of variance. Every measurement, from size to heart rate, remained stable. The mice were all in his building at Crane now, kept in six separate cages, and each day he inspected them one at a time, hoping to see . . . something.

Some change. Any change.

Because change would slow things down.

"We'll call him Jimmy," Marty said, and at that, the monkey threw his head back and clapped his tiny hands.

Wyatt laughed. "Guess you picked a winner, boss. I'll be damned. He likes the sound of that, don't you, Jimmy?"

The monkey clapped again, made a delighted, shrill chirping sound, then dropped to all fours and regarded Marty with his head inclined forward and slightly sideways, as if he were studying a problem. His mahogany eyes gleamed under the fluorescent lights.

"Is the plane ready?" Marty asked.

"Sitting on the runway as we speak."

The runway was a strip of packed earth in a five-acre field surrounded by tall oaks. It was a twenty-minute jeep ride over rough terrain simply to reach it, as far from prying eyes as Marty could go.

"What voltage are you going to put him through?" Wyatt asked.

"Should be 175,000."

Wyatt Dixon whistled. "Brace yourself, Jimmy."

The monkey gave a dismissive wave with his furry left hand, a *Fuck off* gesture if ever there were one, and Wyatt burst into laughter.

"He's a card."

"What's the wingspan on the plane?" Marty asked.

"We're all the way up to twelve feet now, holding the proper angles and proportions."

"Good."

"They sent a video camera," Wyatt said. It came out of his mouth like a casual aside, and when Marty looked at him, Wyatt was busying himself with a cigarette, his eyes down.

"Who did?"

"Admiral Cutting's office."

"I'm supposed to record this one?" He wasn't surprised. He had resisted the demands for weeks, making impassioned speeches about the security risks of transporting film that could fall into the wrong hands.

"Actually . . . I am," Wyatt said, eyes still on his cigarette.

"Excuse me?"

"They'd like us both to watch this one. You run the show, of course, and all I do is run the camera." He forced a laugh. "The monkey might be better with the camera. Maybe I should go on the plane."

"No," Marty said.

"I'm kidding."

"No," Marty repeated, and this time his voice rang in the big building. "We will not film a damn thing."

Wyatt Dixon finally faced him. "Marty . . . they told me to. Ordered me to."

"My process has been approved by—"

"*Ordered*," Wyatt repeated. "You know, the kind of thing that, if refused, has consequences up to and including court-martial?"

"I outrank you, and it's my lab and my project," Marty said. "So what you will do is report my insubordination to Admiral Cutting's office. Then you will let me deal with the fallout."

An unfortunate word, in these times of mushroom-cloud math.

It was silent for a moment. Even the monkey had gone still. Smoke rose and dissipated in the high-ceilinged room.

"The fallout might be bad," Wyatt said, and there was a note of genuine concern in his voice that Marty hadn't anticipated. It touched him. He'd refused to grant this man any status as a true colleague, and yet Wyatt seemed worried for him. "I'm afraid it might be *very* bad, Marty. They seem to think you're"—he hesitated—"losing control of the operation."

"It's my operation. I fly the planes and I record the data and share it. How on earth could anyone think I'm losing control of it?"

"Because the data you *do* share is awfully damn impressive."

Unspoken in his emphasis on "do" came the question: What wasn't being shared?

Marty looked at Wyatt for a long time, then loosened his tie and said, "I know it. That's why I need one more run. Because they're coming. You know this as well as I do. They'll come to see me prove my work, and if it doesn't go off as promised"—he waved his hand around the lab—"I'll get shut down. If it does go off as promised, they'll take over. They know as much as me. The graphite coating, the voltages, the results."

This was true enough—omitting only the watch.

"I know that it works but I don't know *how*, I can't explain enough yet, and they'll come in and take command. I want to understand as much as I can before that happens. You get that, don't you?"

Wyatt's shoulders sagged.

"Take the video at least, Marty. I'll give you space. One more time, even though I don't like it. But you've got to take the video and pretend I did my job."

Marty nodded. "All right. And thank you. I just want . . . a little more time, that's all. It's not a trust issue; you know that."

"Sure," Wyatt said.

Marty turned back to the cage. On the other side of the bars, Jimmy, #5709, of Cleveland, regarded Marty solemnly, as if they were partners in an endeavor of great importance.

Maybe, Marty thought, he was as smart a monkey as advertised.

———

The launch site was on hastily cleared acreage that had once been a homestead. Before the military claimed the land during World War II, Crane had been a tiny farming village. The remnants of an old cabin remained, along with the weathered boards of what might have been a corncrib, or perhaps a woodshed? Hell, Marty didn't know. He'd have passed the place without a thought on another day. Lately, though, he found himself wondering about the past more frequently, felt its breath on his neck.

He set up the camera and looked back at the dusty jeep where Jimmy the monkey waited in his cage. The monkey was holding on to the bars of the cage with his hands, eyes fixed not on Marty or the camera or the remains of the cabin but on the plane, as if he understood that was why he was there.

It was a brutally warm day, several weeks without rain, and dust shimmered beneath a sun that sat high and bright in a cloudless sky, the rough earth dry and cracked underfoot.

I should make some rain, Marty thought idly. *Do some good for the farmers around here.*

The waiting plane was the largest replica yet. The battery packs that would power the plane skyward were tucked beneath the wings, making the scaled-down jet engines seem as if they were truly important. Marty imagined his brother's response to seeing a plane with both replica jet engines *and* an oversize prop on the nose and could almost hear Hank laughing.

Then he looked down at the watch on his wrist and thought that, no, Hank probably wouldn't do much laughing today.

Hank didn't know about any of the testing at Crane. More than once, Marty had begun composing a letter in his mind, but he'd never set pen to paper, even back in the days when he might've been able to get a letter off the base without it being read by someone else. How to begin? *Dearest Brother, thank you for the watch. You may be interested to know that it can salvage a destroyed plane, reassemble it, and return it in denial of all rules of physics, chemistry, and biology, a complete refutation of science as we know it. Good trick, right? Anyhow, what's new with you?*

No, he wasn't ready to send a letter. He'd written plenty, though.

The monkey let out a sudden, shrill squawk, jolting Marty's attention back to the present.

"Ready to get on with it, Jimmy?"

The monkey clapped his hands . . . but he seemed less enthused than he had in the warehouse, and his eyes never left the plane.

Marty checked the focus to ensure that he had a wide-enough angle to capture both the departure and the return flights—already he was sure it would return—and then walked in front of the camera.

"This is Dr. Martin Hazelton, and it is August 6, 1962, at . . . " He checked the time, then regretted it, because he did not want to draw any attention to the watch. " . . . uh, 13:07 here. The air temperature is 93 degrees Fahrenheit, and the winds are westerly, five to ten miles per hour. I will be attempting the first flight of Project Kingsolver with a primate on board. Dr. Dixon and his team have assembled the model. This plane, like the others, is equipped with a radio transponder that will be activated once the plane is out of the visible range."

"Out of the visible range" was the phrase he'd coined for "vanished." It sounded much more scientifically satisfying, he thought—or at least less terrifying.

The radio transponder held no significance at all. It was Marty's shell game, a way to hide the secret of the watch while he worked frantically to understand it. He needed some explanation for his ability to summon the aircraft back from the beyond. He'd picked radio signals because he knew the Navy was fascinated with them already, and labs at Crane were developing missile guidance technology. It was important, Marty thought, that the scenario passed the sniff test. He was like a hypnotist working in reverse order. *Do not look at the watch. Anything but the watch.*

"All right," he said, squinting at the camera as a breeze cut over the field and lifted pollen and dust. "Bear with me here while I ready for launch."

He wished, belatedly, that he'd thought to get the monkey in the plane before the camera was rolling. Doing everything alone, as Marty insisted upon, meant some things could slip your mind, and one of those things was the walk with the monkey. What if Jimmy fought him, bit him, escaped into the woods? All of that on film. What a treat.

The monkey didn't fight, though. He sat back calmly on his haunches while Marty got the cage out of the jeep and onto the ground. When he unlatched the door, he positioned himself squarely in front of it, braced for an attempt at escape, but Jimmy merely extended his hand, reaching for him.

Startled, Marty accepted Jimmy's hand and the monkey stepped out of the cage but didn't let go, matching Marty's stride and reaching high enough to keep his furry, warm little fingers clutched around Marty's.

Somehow, this was worse than if the damn thing *had* bitten him. As Marty walked the monkey across the field and in front of the camera, he had a sudden, acute memory of Hank when he was so young that he'd been instructed to hold Marty's hand when they crossed the street. The monkey clung to him, every bit as trusting, as they walked to the plane.

Inside the mocked-up plane was a single small seat. A harness would bind the monkey backward, securing him in place for whatever came next.

"Okay, Jimmy," Marty said, and, too late, realized he'd uttered the name for the camera—and anyone who watched the film. He thought about making up some explanation, but he'd never been a natural liar, so he didn't say anything more as the monkey clambered aboard and into the seat as if he understood precisely what was desired.

They say he's very smart, Marilyn Metzger had said.

The monkey was still holding on tightly to Marty's index finger. His tiny fingers were smooth, the backs of his paws lined with coarse hair that felt like the bristle brush Marty used to shine his shoes. Looking down at the monkey meant looking down at the W. C. Ball watch on his wrist, which gleamed in the sun, and for a moment he felt inexplicably dizzy.

Then he gently pried the monkey's fingers away from his own and cinched the harness tight. When the canvas belts snugged, the monkey made a soft wheezing sound.

"All set," Marty whispered, and his voice was hoarse.

The monkey looked into his eyes, patient and trusting. Marty rose swiftly, his knees popping, and turned away from the plane. The camera on the tripod faced him down with the unblinking attention of the monkey below and the high sun above.

"Let's get on with it," Marty said to no one, and his voice cracked. He cleared his throat, smoothed his tie against his chest. "Good luck, number 5709."

He thought he managed a smile for the camera, but he wasn't sure.

His base station was a folding plywood tray table with a radio controller, binoculars, clipboard, and pen. He picked up the radio controller and pressed the button that made the big propeller whirl. When the prop spun, Jimmy let out a soft whine. Marty kept his eyes down when he turned up the throttle dial, and then the prop was louder, and the monkey's sounds couldn't be heard anymore.

Down the field, two aluminum antennas waited. Between them, 175,000 volts sparked and danced. Beneath them, the generators hummed, pumping silver iodide crystals and graphite into the air, an old-school, World War II–era smoke generator, an M-1 design just like the one Vince Schaefer had demonstrated in the Catskills. It stood six feet high and weighed more than two tons when loaded. The smoke cloud from the generator would expand a mile in this wind, coating the valley. Employees on the base knew to explain Marty's clouds as the result of "ordnance disposal," a ruse that worked fine in a place where people detonated old bombs on a regular basis.

Marty started the plane. The big model rolled forward, its tires wobbling over the uneven earth, caught a gust as it crested a slight hill, and went airborne, tilting side to side, then smoothing out quickly. If the monkey reacted to takeoff, Marty couldn't hear it over the clatter of the generator.

Onward and upward the plane flew. Fifty yards, sixty, seventy, eighty—and then into the electrified field. St. Elmo's fire, electric blue lines, a web of wires.

The monkey screamed.

It was a piercing sound—brief but shrill, even across the distance and above the rattling smoke generator—and Marty jerked. The controller fell from his hands, clipping the side of the folding table and thunking into the dust below.

The plane vanished. The monkey's scream went with it.

Marty, aware that he was on camera, knew that his response had seemed anything but calm and collected. Then again, he hadn't observed anything quite like this. The model planes sizzled but they never screamed. The mice hadn't made any sound at all.

Or at least none that he could hear.

The scream had surprised him. He wondered why. What did he *think* it felt like, flying into a force field of electrical current?

He walked back to the camera, taking care to look unbothered, though he wasn't sure how convincing it was. His heart was too fast, his breath too short. Maybe they wouldn't be able to tell that from the film.

"Project Kingsolver Test 217, with primate 5709, is underway at"—he looked at his watch—"uh, 13:21. Field conditions remain consistent. Both plane and primate are, as you've seen, no longer within the visible range. Voltage encounter was 75,000. I will wait five minutes, leaving the camera untouched, and then I will activate the radio transmitter to summon the aircraft's return."

He hadn't considered how much time to elapse on this test, but five minutes felt right, and he needed the excuse to walk behind the camera so no one would see him adjust his watch.

If he didn't adjust the watch, Jimmy was staying . . . out there.

Out where? What is it like? How does it feel?

The questions were enormous. The answers would be fascinating. Maybe awful?

He took a moment to light a cigarette and smoke it, staying in front of the camera, keeping his eyes downfield, squinting into the summer sun, and then he wandered off, hoping that he seemed distracted, the classic absent-minded scientist. He circled around the camera, unclasped his father's watch, and checked the time. It was right on schedule, never missing a tick, the way it had always run.

Except, of course, for the day above Christmas Island and Johnston Atoll. Marty hated to think of his brother in those skies. He himself had been aboard one of the three planes that had flown into the mushroom cloud to gather samples from the debris from Ivy Mike, and at that point in his life he'd resigned himself to the necessary pursuit of nuclear research. It was a race, and peace required power.

That was what he'd thought until he saw the instantaneous vanishing of an island where life had flourished. So much history, so much mystery, so much beauty—all gone in a flash.

He'd had a tough day after that flight, and not simply because the flight itself was terrifying and one of the three planes had crashed, the pilot killed, his body never found. Sadly, that wasn't the terror that lingered in Marty Hazelton's mind. What he remembered was the light, and the mushroom cloud, and the sense of things that could not be undone. What he remembered was how the island had gone missing.

He'd been unable to shake that while he sat on the plane, awaiting decontamination, and wondering what substances had been collected from the cloud. He thought a lot about Einstein during that wait, and about the arrangement of "holy" before "curiosity." For the first time, he'd doubted the atomic endeavor. Late to that party, of course—Oppenheimer was already out of favor for his reluctance to pursue thermonuclear weapons—but Marty loved science.

Once there had been an island called Elugelab. Then along came science. The island was gone now, forever gone, and science had left a radioactive cloud in its place.

How far was too far?

The answer wasn't his to give. It wasn't even America's to give. That was the problem. The arms "race" implied an end, a winner. Nobody could win this one. They could only extend it. If they finished it, everyone lost.

Once there was an island . . .

Eleven years after Elugelab had been vaporized, Marty Hazelton unscrewed the crown of his dead father's watch, rolled the hands backward, and then restarted the watch.

Tick, tick, tick.

He'd killed three minutes in front of the camera, so he set the time back only two minutes. Then he walked to his folding table and scooped the radio controller off the ground. Set it on the table, glanced at the watch, making every effort to look casual. One minute to go.

Tick, tick, tick.

He could feel his heart hammering just beneath his tie, which had blown across his shirt, the wind so warm that it chapped his lips. He smoothed the tangled tie, then moved to the small radio transmitter. It was a stainless steel cube with a single button and a red light. The frequency was already set. The boys at the Pentagon were extremely interested in the frequency. Marty expected they were testing any number of different frequency ranges on different planes in different locations, only to be enormously frustrated by the failure to replicate his results at Crane. The thought almost made him grin.

You can play with the frequencies, fellas, and you can use the graphite shielding, but you can't account for the third leg of the stool because you don't know about it. My little secret.

For now.

When the minute hand clicked forward, he tapped the transmitter's button. The red light came on. He realized he was holding his breath. The transmitter didn't matter, but by pretending it did, the ritual became real. Down the field, there was a single pop, sharp as a bottle rocket, and the plane burst back into view.

This time, the monkey did not scream.

Dead, Marty thought. *He is dead, I pushed this madness too far, and this is good, very good, because I'll have time to get my hands around it now.*

But then the plane was down, its wheels bouncing over the hillocks of seared grass before it came to a stop directly at Marty's feet. The monkey, Jimmy, #5709 of Cleveland, Ohio, looked first to his left, then to his right, then fixed his gaze on Marty and let out a soft, shivering sigh.

What have you seen? Marty wondered with awe. *What have you felt?*

The monkey, of course, would have no answers. That was the problem. The Navy would want someone who could speak—and soon.

"Well, Jimmy . . . how was it?" Marty asked, trying to keep his voice light.

The monkey made no sound. It was also the first time he declined to clap at his own nickname. A nickname that Marty had just screwed up and used on camera for the second time. No matter. He could come up with a story to explain it away if anyone asked.

The monkey appeared unharmed. He would undergo a battery of tests now, extensive blood workups and physiological study, and perhaps they would find a change that had not occurred in the mice, but a visual examination indicated no changes. His range of motion was full and fluid, his fur uncharred, his eyes clear and bright.

Too bright.

Was that an illusion? Something Marty had projected onto the animal because he felt the animal must show *some* indicator of the remarkable journey he'd just taken? Maybe.

But he couldn't help the prickle that crawled across the base of his skull when the monkey focused on him, his brown eyes seeming more vivid.

Marty turned back to the video camera on the tripod, tried to smile, and said, "Number 5709 is back with us, safe and sound. So is his aircraft."

He walked to the camera, shut it off, and then returned to the plane. He loosened the straps of the canvas harness. The little creature remained cooperative, demonstrating no panic or trauma, acting like the same intelligent, curious beast he'd been before the launch. The only change was the most minor behavioral shift: when the monkey climbed out of the plane, he refused to take Marty's offered hand as he had on the walk from the jeep to the plane.

For some reason, late that night, sleepless, Marty would remember that, and it would trouble him.

ASH POINT, MAINE
OCTOBER 25, 2025

I took Charlie longer than it should have to realize that Abe and Lawrence were scared.

After everyone had handled the watch and read that creepy note—*Survival=Find storm cloud, fire nightshade, set watch backward and add voltage. You will catch up*—the room had gone silent. Abe sat and drank, staring at the watch, while his grandson busied himself with futile efforts at rebooting the router. Charlie checked her phone, turning it off and back on, an equally pointless endeavor. She gave up and put the phone away.

"Abe."

"Hey, kiddo." He spoke to her as if in greeting, as if she'd just arrived.

"This is all really fucked-up."

"That's a big ten-four, Jolly Rancher."

"What does that mean?"

"It means I agree." He focused on Charlie with fresh clarity. "Much as it pains me to admit it, your little iPhone would be awfully handy right now."

"It won't work," Charlie said.

"I've tried rebooting," Lawrence added. "Everything is out."

"I see that. Usually, it would make me laugh, watching you two act like the sky is falling just because your videos aren't loading. Today . . . well, I'd like to know what's going on in the rest of the world. Maybe we should go into town. What do you think?"

It was a long drive down a lonely road off the peninsula to Cold Harbor, a cluster of little shingle-sided buildings near the water, weathered gray from winter winds. A market, a gas station, a post office, a wharf. The kind of place that made for great postcard and calendar photos but didn't offer much. Would it be better there than here? Maybe, if only because they wouldn't be all alone. And yet she didn't love the idea of leaving.

"I guess," she said. "I don't know."

Watching her, Lawrence said, "You think something is wrong. Like, really wrong."

"Do you not?" she shot back. "First the FAA thing, all those weird calls to the pilots, then our phones go dead, and the internet does, too, and on top of it all we get a balloon with an old watch and a note about survival! Yes, I think something is really wrong."

She looked at the black screen of the TV, desperate for it to turn back on. She wanted to watch a press conference or a presidential address, see someone in control.

"Let's put on the radio in the Subaru," she said. "It's got XM; we'll be able to pull in whatever satellite signals we want, no Wi-Fi or cell signal required."

"Good idea," Lawrence said.

She grabbed the keys from the hook by the door and Lawrence followed her out. Abe stayed behind, beer mug in hand, his eyes back on that old watch.

Charlie and Lawrence crossed the parking lot and went up the driveway that led between the old service station and the decrepit saltbox house that was supposed to be Charlie's next home if her father ever finished remodeling the bar, which seemed unlikely at his current pace. The apartment above the taproom was fine by her, because she had no intention of remaining in Maine long enough to move anywhere else. She'd applied to Chapman, and that meant Southern California was calling, a whole new life waiting next fall, college classrooms and film screenings and southern sunshine; she'd be *gone*.

She had believed that until today. Now, for a reason she couldn't articulate but that seemed to compress her lungs, she wasn't so sure. For a place of blue sky and soft sea sounds, Ash Point felt draped with dread, and there was something about the spot that felt eternal to her now, a trap that hadn't yet been sprung but would be soon.

Or maybe it already had been. Maybe she was as lost to the world as the world was to her, and that was why she knew better than to encourage Abe to take them into town. Ash Point wouldn't release them. They'd never make it off this peninsula.

"You okay?" Lawrence asked. His deep-blue eyes were fixed on her in that penetrating way she ordinarily hated. Right now she didn't mind it so much. It was certainly better than being alone.

"Worried about my dad. That's all."

"I understand that. I can't get a text out to my mom, and she's not even ten miles away. With your dad being all the way in Wisconsin . . . anyhow, I understand."

She realized that he had no idea where his own father was at this moment. Somewhere across the endless ocean. The odd maturity of Lawrence Zimmer, the quality that made him seem lame most of the time, probably had a lot to do with growing up feeling like the man of the house, with his dad out to sea on a cargo freighter or oil tanker for months at a time. Abe was around, sure, but Abe was not the most reassuring presence, even when sober.

"Maybe they've got the planes back in the air by now," she said, and they both looked at the sky, a reflex. It was empty.

Eerily empty.

She lifted the key fob for the Subaru and clicked the unlock button absently, distracted by the unbroken sky. Only when she tried to open the driver's door and found it locked did she realize the fob hadn't worked. She punched the unlock button again. Nothing.

"What the hell?"

"Use the key," Lawrence said.

Charlie stared at the fob, a flush creeping over her cheeks. This *was* the key. You unlocked the doors with the remote and then the car sensed the fob's presence and allowed the push-button starter to fire the engine.

"Here," Lawrence said, and took the fob gently from her, then pressed down on the back of the plastic case, which released the top half, like a space shuttle separating from its rockets. He withdrew the silver key from within and grinned.

"You know how it works from here?"

"Very funny," she said, and took the key from him and opened the door, grateful that she managed to stick it in the lock on the first try. She'd never had to use a physical key on the car, and she had a bad feeling about what that meant.

She slipped into the driver's seat, put her foot on the brake pedal, and pressed the starter button.

Nothing.

Not a chime, not a beep, not a light. Not even so much as the dashboard alert that no key fob was detected.

"It's dead," she said, her voice dull and distant. "Just like the ATV."

Lawrence leaned in, brushing against her as he searched for the hood release, then popped it. He walked to the front of the car, lifted the hood, and stared inside.

"Battery's connected. Nothing's burned up. Try again. There should be something, at least a click or a warning light."

She tried again.

"Nothing."

He slammed the hood, and when she saw him through the windshield, his face was stricken.

"This is fucked, Charlie," he said, and the fear that had been scampering back and forth through her body like a trapped mouse picked up pace.

"What do you think is happening today?"

Before Lawrence could respond, Abe bellowed at them from the taproom door.

"Is it dead?"

"Yeah," Lawrence called back, and then he started for the taproom, and Charlie followed, carrying the useless car key. When they passed her ATV, she refused to look up at the balloon, and the chill she felt when she walked beneath its shadow came from deep within her.

"It won't even turn on the accessory mode, let alone crank the motor," Lawrence told Abe. "Just like her ATV."

They went back in the taproom, and nobody said anything when Charlie locked the door behind them.

Please let me be paranoid, she thought. *Please let me be having some kind of mental breakdown.*

Wouldn't that be nice? She was owed a breakdown, damn it! She was a seventeen-year-old girl—a seventeen-year-old girl with TikTok, that brain-rotting app; it was inevitable that she was psychologically damaged beyond repair from her mere existence as a teen female with social media, based on the pundits. Throw in the murdered mother and the move to Maine, the new school and new friends (no friends?) and her father's distraction. Sure, she was having a breakdown! It was hard to imagine anything else.

But the old man and the young man watching her were experiencing the same reality, and they were also afraid.

"Let's assess the scenario," Abe said. "Abnormal, sure, but—"

"No phones, no internet, dead vehicles, and that weird-ass balloon? I don't think 'abnormal' covers it!" Lawrence's voice sounded the way Charlie's chest felt: high and tight.

Abe turned his pilot's gaze to his grandson, and Charlie thought she saw Lawrence take some small measure of relief in the sharp glance. He, too, wanted an authority figure.

"We can explain some of it if we stay coolheaded," Abe said.

"It's the balloon," Charlie said. "It's a spy balloon, like the Chinese one over the Rockies that freaked everyone out a few years ago. Remember that?"

Abe sucked in on his lower lip and pinched it between his teeth, brooding.

"Don't think it's a spy balloon."

"Are you kidding me! It's not a coincidence! First there's the balloon, then the electronics go out, and then—"

Abe lifted a hand. "You're out of sequence. First there were the phone calls to the pilots. The fakes ones. Those happened overnight, before the balloon showed up."

"Right, I know that," Charlie said, although in fact she had forgotten.

"Also, spy balloons are much bigger. This situation with our electronics feels more like the result of an EMP. Electromagnetic pulse. A nuke detonated up in the atmosphere can take the grid down in a blink. Those can also be natural, a simple coronal flare—a sunspot, basically."

"It wouldn't account for the calls, though," Lawrence said.

"No," Abe said unhappily. "It wouldn't."

Charlie tucked her hair behind her ear and insisted, "The problem is the balloon."

"I don't know about that," Abe said.

"Well, there is *something* wrong with it! That creepy note and watch? And the radiosonde thing has a serial number from the fucking sixties and—"

"Hey."

"Oh, are you kidding me? We're gonna worry about my language while the world is ending?"

"The world isn't ending."

"It sure feels like it!" Charlie shouted.

That brought them all to a stop. For a moment they stared at one another in silence. Then Abe said, "Let's make sure gravity still works."

"What are you talking about?"

"The beer lines." He walked behind the bar.

Lawrence lifted his hands, exasperated, and Charlie shook her head. She turned to the front windows, looked out to the water and clear sky, all that bright blue, and found herself wishing for thunder and lightning, an eclipse, a meteor, any form of natural explanation for the day. Instead, the bucolic scene offered its postcard-perfect view as if in mockery. Down in Brooklyn, her friends would be posting responses to her videos about the evils of Ash Point. Even if she could see them, she wouldn't be able to muster any snark about the place. There was nothing funny about Ash Point today. The new things were dying and the old things were rising.

"Beer lines still work!" Abe announced with such gusto, you'd have thought he'd solved the whole dilemma.

"Terrific, Abe. That's just terrific."

Lawrence, ignoring them both, walked to the light switch and flicked it up. The room flooded with light.

"How does *that* make sense?" he asked. "Everything is out but the lights?"

Abe said, "Microchips."

Lawrence turned to him, thoughtful, and nodded.

"You're right. The lights here are old. They need electricity, but not microchips."

Abe pointed out the window. "Exactly like my truck. Blue still runs because she was built in 1971. Electricity, yes; microchips, no. That's the difference."

"What would cause everything with a chip to fail?" Charlie asked.

"An EMP. Or maybe spyware."

"Or some kind of AI weapon," Lawrence said. "Like whatever caused those calls."

"Wait," Charlie said. "Doesn't your truck have a radio we can use, then?"

Abe gave her a rare hangdog look. "I took it out with the eight-track player. Kept meaning to put a new head unit in it, one with Bluetooth and such, but . . . well, I've got so many projects."

He promptly finished his beer and reached for the tap handle again.

"Don't get drunk," Charlie said. "Not now, Abe, please."

Abe looked up, his eyes patient and paternal.

"I just want a cold pint before I drive Blue up the road to see what the situation is. When I find out the rest of the world isn't missing a beat, and it's only the three of us fools who think there's trouble, it'll be nice to blame the booze! Then I can say I'm not crazy; I'm just drunk."

Charlie couldn't return his smile. Whatever waited up the road was going to be bad. She was sure of this. She was a very perceptive girl. Ask her mother. Oh, wait. There would be none of that.

Charlie, you must not fly . . .

"Abe . . . are your stories about the plane crash really true?" she asked. "I mean, I know you enjoy telling them, but did you *seriously* see a survivor in that ejection seat?"

The humor drained from his face.

"I did. They pulled him out of the tree and got him in a gurney and put a sheet over him, but I got a clear look, and I know he was alive. I'll never forget it. His eyes were blue and bright. *So* bright. A bad kind of bright."

"Why would they have lied about it?" Charlie asked. These were questions she'd put to him many times before, but back then her focus had been on funny social media content. The answers didn't seem funny now.

"I've been trying to answer that question for more than a half century," Abe said. "I have not the faintest idea why they lied. I just know that they did."

He put the beer down, hitched up his jeans, and walked to the window.

"We've got an operational decision to make, and I've never been a fan of autocracy, so I'll open this up to votes: Do we all go, or do I go alone?"

Charlie looked at Lawrence. Neither of them spoke. What was better: the safety of the taproom or the possibility of help down the road? What waited in Cold Harbor? Was the quaint little town still the same place, or were things worse there? If people were freaking out, the isolation of Ash Point might not be so bad.

"If the situation out there is good," Abe said, "then I won't have trouble coming back here to share the pleasant news. If it's bad?" He paused. "If it's bad, we're all going to have a tough time, and I don't want to die feeling foolish about giving up a safe, secluded place and putting two kids into the unknown."

"Hey, hey," Lawrence said. "Who said anything about dying?"

"Power of negative thinking, grandson. Prepare for the worst and hope for the best."

"We should stick together," Charlie said, but it was too late now:

they hadn't voted when Abe gave them the chance, and he had filled the silence with an executive decision.

"If there's trouble out there, we'll be driving right into the teeth of it," Abe said. "The only thing I like less than an island from a tactical perspective is a peninsula. But that's what we've got."

He unlocked the front door and stepped outside.

"Wait!" Charlie yelled, but he lifted a calming hand to indicate he wasn't leaving yet. He walked to his truck, opened the passenger's door, and then rooted around in the glovebox. When he stepped back, there was a gun in his hand.

Charlie's heart began to thunder.

Abe returned to the taproom, opened the cylinder of the revolver, and turned it to face them, showing the five bright brass backings of the cartridges inside.

"If you need them," he said, looking Lawrence dead in the eyes, "use them. And don't waste them."

"Abe . . . ," Charlie started, but she couldn't finish the thought. His expression was firm, his mind made up. He snapped the cylinder closed and passed the gun to Lawrence before turning to her.

"You were right, kiddo: I *am* afraid. If all the trouble was out here, I'd say we pile into the truck and ride out together. But it isn't. The airport shutdowns were nationwide, and we don't know what's happened out in the world since then. I don't like that. So I'm afraid to stay and I'm afraid to go, but I can't do both, can I? Best part about having a team? Options. We'll divide and conquer."

He reached out and squeezed her arm.

"I'm a paranoid old man," he said. "We both know it. So let me play my role, okay? I'll go into town and tell the crazy stories about the balloon and the watch and get laughed at. Once I know it's safe and that the joke is on me, I'll come back. Hell, I'll bring pizza. We'll have a party and make a video for your friggin' TikTok fans."

He gave her a crooked smile that couldn't hide his fear. She felt as if she might cry if she tried to speak, so she didn't say a word.

"I'll be back in a half hour if all goes well," he said. "An hour, tops. If it gets any longer than that, then there's been real trouble. At that point . . . "

Silence. He didn't have any idea what to recommend.

"At that point," he continued at last, "I'd remind you that there are bomb shelters underneath the buildings on that old airfield. They're not pretty places, but they serve their purposes."

Lawrence hadn't said anything. He gripped the revolver tightly.

"Lock the door behind me," Abe told him, "and give me an hour before you make your next choice. You're a smart kid. You'll make the right one."

Lawrence nodded. His jaw trembled.

"Just think what a fine story I'll have when this is done," Abe said, forcing a grin. "I'll drink on this one for years to come. A lot of people have given up on my old material, you know." He winked at Charlie. "I need fresh content, right?"

"Be careful, Abe," she whispered. "Please."

"Never tell a pilot to be careful."

He squeezed her arm once more, gripped his grandson by the shoulder and looked at him for a long, tender moment, then stepped out into the sunlit day.

Lawrence reached past Charlie and locked the door.

On the other side of the glass, Abe pulled his cigar from his pocket, relit it, and then dragged on it until he had a good smoke going. He studied the sky all the while. His gaze lingered on the balloon.

At last, he went to the truck, climbed inside, and started the engine. He lifted his hand in a salute, but he didn't look back at them before he pulled out of the parking lot and drove off alone down the long, dusty road that led away from Ash Point.

INDIANA
SUMMER 1962

Before ringing Marilyn Metzger's room, the hotel clerk wanted to know Marty's name.

"Tell her it's Jimmy from Cleveland."

"Yes, sir."

When the clerk repeated this on the line, Marilyn's lilting laugh was loud enough that Marty could hear it. She was a puzzle. Convinced that she was dealing with the gravest of issues, and yet she laughed often and easily. How?

"Go on up, sir. Elevators are on the left. Third floor, room 33."

The door was open when he arrived, and Marilyn Metzger, dressed in a pale blue dress, stood with her back to it, pouring scotch into a tumbler glass.

"Forgive the presumption," she said without bothering to turn, "but I assume that after the day you've had, you might be ready for a tipple."

"You don't know anything about the day I've had," Marty said, stepping into the room and closing the door. "I haven't made a report to Cutting yet, so unless he has a surveillance team on me, you know nothing. Or maybe you sneaked out to Crane yourself, climbed a tree?"

"I loved climbing trees," she said with a nostalgic sigh. "Broke my ankle falling out of one when I was nine. You know what I did then?"

"Stopped climbing trees."

She turned to him, smiling. "Learned how to climb with a cast on my foot."

She leaned against the high windowsill, her back to the city. The curtains were open, and the windows looked out across the tree-lined streets that bordered the campus.

"Your drink?" She lifted it but held it close, making him come to her. He could smell her perfume, something floral and perfectly faint, the kind of teasing *Is it even there?* scent that made you want to lean in.

"Jimmy from Cleveland," she said. "I liked that one. You come across as a humorless man at first, but that's not the truth."

Marty said, "Who do you work for?"

"The United States, same as you. You should ask what I want. That's the question that matters."

"Okay. What do you want?"

"To know how it's done, for starters."

"How *what* is done?"

"How you make airplanes disappear."

Her voice was so loud that he cringed. She looked from side to side, faux surreptitious, then stage-whispered, *"How you make air-planes disappear."*

"We're about to begin repeating ourselves," he said. "And I won't—"

"No we're not. We're moving right along." She sipped her drink. "The Telstar 1 satellite is down. It will be announced soon, but nobody will say the truth: our own atomic tests in the Pacific fried it."

"You're some newspaper reporter," Marty said wryly.

"Oh, relax. That wasn't all a lie. I have written a few articles. They were specials for the *Oak Ridger.*"

Oak Ridge. Of course.

She sat down on the small settee by the window and patted the cushion beside her.

"Let me tell you my real story. Then you can decide whether you want to run away or have me arrested—or both."

He meant to say no. He really did.

But he sat down beside her.

What Marilyn Metzger had wanted, always, was access to secrets.

"It turned out to be fortunate," she told Marty, "that Robert and I hadn't gotten married yet. I think, with his name, I never would have been granted my first job in the Department of Defense. But, lucky for us, all he'd left me with was a kiss and a promise. Not even a ring."

When she arrived in Washington, D.C., she had $32 in a checking account and a list of jobs that she believed would require security clearance.

"Typist or secretary positions," she said. "Except for the janitor spots. I applied for three of those. I really liked the idea of having keys."

The janitorial work had been given to men, and Marilyn Metzger, who disclosed nothing of her missing fiancé in the interviews, was hired as a phone operator for the Navy's procurement division. She did good work. Two years later she won a job at the Pentagon, the massive five-sided military administration building on which construction had begun on September 11, 1941. By the time Marilyn entered the building, it was home to the Department of Defense, a brand-new organizational merger of the Army, Navy, and Air Force. She intended to stay there for as long as it took.

"As long as what took?" Marty asked when she told him that.

"To learn the truth of Flight 19."

A car passed on the street, and she took the opportunity to look away from him, gazing out the window behind her. She was sitting on a blush-colored settee with her legs crossed.

"Now I am the personal secretary of a United States admiral," she said. "Do you want to guess which one?"

He strived to look indifferent.

"Admiral Ralph H. Cutting," she said.

Marty nodded, then finished his scotch. *Run*, his brain told him, but he didn't move.

"There's more in the bottle," Marilyn Metzger said, watching him.

"It can stay there."

"You sure? You look a little peaked."

"I'm sure."

"Are my bona fides convincing enough for you?" she asked. "Or do you need more? Jimmy should've spoken for me, no?"

For some reason, her teasing tone incensed him.

"There wasn't much to giggle about, watching Jimmy today," he snapped.

"He didn't make it?" She seemed shocked, and Marty felt a ridiculous burst of pride, a sense of *She trusts my work* even though he didn't understand his current work any better than he understood this woman.

"He made it."

He hadn't wanted the whiskey but found himself pouring a stiff belt of it anyhow, thinking of the way the monkey had refused to accept his hand after the plane returned. Such a silly thing, and yet it lingered.

"Congratulations," Marilyn said. "You're changing the world."

"I don't know about that."

"Come on, Dr. Hazelton. Nothing will ever be the same. That must mean something to you, even though we're just arrogant stardust."

Marty lowered his glass. Frowned. That phrase . . . it was something he'd often thought but never said, or at least never said aloud, except for maybe one time—one time that taught him better.

Then he got it. With the memory came a better understanding of her.

"You read Cutting's notes from Offutt," he said.

Offutt Air Force Base was in Nebraska, headquarters of the Strategic Air Command, the nerve center of the American nuclear triad, and in December of 1960 Marty had been one of a few dozen people who'd been convened in a bunker complex there to listen while the nation's highest-ranking military leaders walked through the likely results of a nuclear exchange with the Soviets. They'd sat on wooden folding chairs in front of a cement wall, several stories high, and watched as giant maps were unfurled with solemn ceremony, and then one speaker after another climbed the scaffolding to point out various targets and explain the death tolls associated with each one. It was a singularly grim day, one that made Pearl Harbor feel like the Fourth of July. The topic was nothing less than the end of civilization.

A plan for it.

Marty had not been asked to speak. Later, after the formal sessions concluded, he met with a smaller group and answered a few questions about the winds, then was asked if he agreed with the casualty assessments and if he saw any room to mitigate the impact in, say, China, if a target in Russia were struck. Marty's response was that he could quibble with some of the calculations but didn't see the point.

Cutting pressed him on that, saying that, with the death toll in a nation that wasn't even the direct target, the calculations damn well mattered. Marty's response was clipped and measured.

"It would have mattered in 1951, Admiral."

In 1951, they'd been armed "only" with atomic bombs—not thermonuclear bombs. For all the horrors of Hiroshima and Nagasaki, those weapons were muskets compared to what had followed. The bombs that had killed tens of thousands had been replaced by bombs that would kill millions in a blink-fast, broiling flash. The United States now had more than 20,000 in a still-expanding arsenal, and a single one dropped on Moscow would leave 10 million dead. The Soviets could respond in kind. The Rubicon had been crossed.

We're all a collection of the same thing that will destroy us, sir. Atoms. That's human life, plant life, and it's also the bomb. Nothing but stardust. We just happen to be the most arrogant stardust.

Marilyn Metzger seemed grimly pleased that he remembered.

"I didn't just read the notes," she said. "I was there. One of five women in the whole place. World ending is a man's game. But Cutting wanted me there."

"Why?"

"Because my memory is better than his, and he knew that no one was allowed to keep transcripts of what was shared in that bunker."

True enough.

"That phrase: 'arrogant stardust.' It stuck with me. Because it was so . . . defeated."

"It was hard to sit in that place and not feel some futility," he said.

"I was there and I wanted to fight!"

"Fight for what? It won't be victory. Deterrence demands the counter launch. Equal opportunity extermination."

"Exactly," she said. "The victory is in avoiding that. Imagine vanishing a plane and promising—*really promising*—that you could bring it back. Not next week, not next year, but a hundred years from now. What's the limit, do you think? How far can you go?"

He wasn't sure. He'd wondered about this a great deal.

"I can't vanish a plane," he said.

"Martin." Chiding, the disappointed-teacher voice. "Imagine if America could say to the Soviets, 'Go on, launch your missiles, but our leaders, the men you hate so much, won't be here. They'll have *vanished*, truly vanished, off to return at a time of their choosing.' What do the Soviets do then?"

"Say, 'Nice try,' and issue their launch codes. Because you're pre-supposing a personal goal, leader versus leader, assassination rather than annihilation. The nuclear game is beyond that."

"You're wrong. Mad kings with rivals? There's nothing more personal. Each country has plans for leadership, some fractional percentage of the population who survive and rebuild."

"And that's a laugh," Marty said. "It'll take a thousand years for the soil and water to purge our poison when an all-out nuclear war is done, and whatever society emerges won't remember what ours looked like. Or care."

"Why don't *you* care, damn it! *Care* before that happens!"

He was surprised by the sudden venom in her voice. Her body had gone rigid, the muscles in her neck taut, her up-thrust chin trembling ever so faintly with righteous rage.

"I care," Marty said. "But I don't make the rules."

She burst off the settee and paced the hotel room, bristling with anger.

"I'm so sick of academic discussion around the end of the world! Planes disappear, cities are flattened, nations build bunkers, and you little men in your little laboratories lift your hands and say, 'It wasn't me.' Don't any of you *feel* anything?"

He didn't answer. What was the point?

For a long moment there was silence while she stood there glaring at him and he sat, waiting her out. When she suddenly crossed the room in three swift strides, he was utterly unprepared, and when she slapped him across the face, he never so much as lifted a hand in defense. The blow rocked him good, stunned him.

"Did you feel that?" she hissed.

"Yes," he said. "Thank you, I did."

When she reached for him again, he tensed, expecting another blow. Instead, she gripped the back of his head and pulled his face to hers and kissed him, her lips soft and warm, a flick of her tongue gliding between his own lips, quick as a snakebite. Then she shoved him away and stepped back.

"What about that?"

He stared at her, speechless, the sting of her slap on his cheek obliterated by the touch of her mouth on his, that grazing tip of her tongue.

"Arrogant stardust," she said. "That's all the human race is to you. Yet we fight and we fuck."

He winced a little at the ugly word, and she seemed pleased by his reaction.

"Explain it to me," she said. "How all animals behave that way; we just evolved a little faster. No magic to it, just math."

Marty reached up and rubbed his cheek. The slap would leave a bruise. He hadn't intended to touch his cheek, though; he'd wanted to touch his lips.

"Have you ever been in love?" Marilyn asked.

He hesitated, then shook his head. "No. Not truly."

"I was afraid of that. I don't think a man who has never been in love can save the world. Ever wanted a child?"

"No."

"Why not?"

"Because I think we're rushing toward the bottom of the funnel, and what would be the point in bringing a child into the world at that moment?"

He was braced for her next onslaught, be it physical or verbal, but she softened and, he thought, maybe even nodded.

"You've found something *sacred*; don't you understand that?" she said, voice scarcely above a whisper. "I don't need you to admit it, but

I've seen the files. What you can do with those planes—it's supernatural, almost, a phenomenon that can't be explained—"

"I'll explain it," he said despite himself.

"Why do you need to?"

He blinked, bewildered. "Because I don't understand it yet."

She laughed a cold laugh again. "Why do you think we're here?"

"Who? The two of us?"

"All of us! Do you really see no higher?"

"You're talking about God?" he asked, uncertain, and she put her face into her hands, exasperated. He stared at her and thought of the monkey refusing to touch his hand. She whirled from him, stalked across the room to the bed, and plucked a paperback book from the nightstand. Vonnegut again.

"If you need to explain something so badly," she said, pulling a picture free from the pages, "then explain *this*!"

It was a black-and-white photograph of a Japanese child—boy or girl was impossible to tell because so little was left of their hair or flesh—reaching out from beneath a pile of stone rubble. Hiroshima, after the first bomb fell, or maybe Nagasaki, after the second.

"This," Marilyn Metzger said, "is what happens when we solve for X. How much more powerful is the hydrogen bomb than what we used here?"

"Roughly a thousand times," Marty managed, his throat dry. "The bomb we dropped on Hiroshima was a stick of dynamite compared to what we have now."

She returned the photograph to the pages of the Vonnegut paperback with the gentlest of touches, like someone handling an ancient treasure map.

"We flattened two cities, ended a war, and imperiled the world. And now we *race* the Soviets for superiority. I love that word. The space *race*, the arms *race*, everything a contest, which implies what?"

173

"Someone wins."

"No," she said. "It just implies that it has an end."

She was standing close to him now and the light was low and he wasn't sure if there were tears in her eyes or if that was merely the dark, dancing reflected light. He couldn't bring himself to leave the room. He could be court-martialed for this conversation, and still . . . he wanted to be with her. It had been so long since he'd had someone to talk with—really talk.

"What do you want?" he asked.

"To go on the plane. When you test it."

He said nothing.

"The human test is coming," she said. "And I will be there. When the time comes, make the argument for using me, all right? That's all I ask."

Again he offered no response. They faced each other, standing beside her bed in the dim light.

"I'm sorry I hit you," she said.

"It's fine."

"I'm not as sorry I kissed you."

His throat made an audible click when he swallowed.

"I wanted to see you feel something," she said. "I still do."

He wanted to reach for her. He wanted to run from her. Which to do?

In the end, he didn't make the decision. She came to him, and when she kissed him the second time, her tongue parted his lips fully, and the taste of her was no longer a trace but full and glorious. They kissed, swaying beside the bed, lips together but bodies still inches apart, and he couldn't bear that any longer, so he slipped his hand in her hair and cupped the back of her head and pulled her to him, chest to chest, feeling the heat of her all along him like a current.

When she reached behind her, he thought she meant to remove

his hand, so he released her and stepped back, flustered. She hadn't been swatting his hand away, though. She'd been reaching for the zipper of her dress. When she slipped out of it and stood before him, wearing only the bra and panties, he felt a shiver that seemed to come from within him, and she saw it, smiled, and took his hand.

"Feel something," she whispered as she pulled him down onto the bed.

And he would. Of course he would. But every time he'd been with a woman, even while in the throes of the physical pleasure, he simply couldn't seem to get all the way out of his own head. It was one of the things he hated about himself, and as he lowered his mouth to her breast and slid her underwear down her thighs, aching with lust, he was afraid it would be the same with her: that the missing fraction of him that always hovered above, an observer, distanced and alone, would remain. Even when he climaxed, he would think of choices and risks or, worse, of dying stars and pointless days, that funnel of despair.

Instead, his mind emptied as he slipped within her. He felt only her warmth, and it washed the world away, and a greater gift he'd never known.

ASH POINT, MAINE
OCTOBER 25, 2025

Time seemed to slow once Abe was gone and Charlie and Lawrence were alone.

She sat at the bar, mindlessly checking her phone, unable to keep from trying. Lawrence paced the front windows, his grandfather's gun in hand.

"This is driving me crazy," Charlie said.

"It's only been twenty minutes."

"It feels like forever!"

He didn't argue.

She opened her texts, saw the undelivered I love you messages waiting for her father. Would they ever go through? He didn't need to read them to know that she loved him. He knew. Right?

She closed the message app and opened the camera. Everything worked except for communication—or escape from Ash Point. It was as if someone had targeted those precise functions and removed them. Disable the car, the ATV, the internet, and the cell signal. Why? And how?

"The camera works," she said aloud, just to say something, because Lawrence's silent pacing was stressing her out.

"Terrific," he said. "When my grandpa comes back, keep him out of your damn videos, all right?"

The contempt in his voice startled her.

"What's up your ass?"

"Nothing."

"Uh, that wasn't nothing, dude."

He turned to her, his jaw working as he gritted his teeth and seemed to ponder whether to speak. Charlie beckoned him, a *Hit me* gesture.

"Do you not think anyone here sees your videos?" Lawrence asked.

"Why do I care if they do? I make them for my friends back home, but I don't care if—"

"Oh, we get it," he said hotly. "It's pretty clear who the videos are for and who they're making fun of."

Charlie rocked her head back. "What are you talking about? I don't make fun of anyone. I'm talking about Ash Point! Like, my own property! The place where I live!"

"We *are* the place where you live!"

She gaped at him, stunned that he wasn't getting it.

"I'm talking about the plane crash and the airfield. Evidently you're so self-absorbed that you somehow think it's about you, but—"

"Meanwhile," Lawrence cut in, his voice an obvious attempt to imitate her narration from the TikTok videos, "the locals carry on, oblivious to the evils of Ash Point. While the terror falls from the sky, their eyes are on the sea, clueless to the world around them, mindlessly hauling lobster traps. Rare is the one who bothers to look up, let alone ask the right questions. Let's bring in savvy sky watcher Abe Zimmer—if we can get him to lower his beer mug—because he is the one who counted the corpses on that fateful day."

Holy shit, he'd memorized it. And hearing it come out of his mouth, even though he was mimicking her, was profoundly unsettling. Because . . .

Because she heard it now.

She sounded awful. Not to people back home, they'd all laugh, but to people here? To Lawrence?

"It's a joke," she said. "That's all."

He was nodding with a grim smile, and she heard her own words again, and, yes, he was right, damn it. It *was* personal. She'd meant it to be funny, but a solid test for whether something was witty or mean was if you needed to cherry-pick the audience.

"Meanwhile," Lawrence said, "my grandpa friggin' loves you. I get to hear how damn great you are, how you listen to his stories, ask him questions, and I've never once told him that you're only asking them so you can humiliate him."

"That's not true!" Charlie cried, and she meant it, because Abe had been nothing but kind to her.

"If we can get him to put down the beer," Lawrence began again, and she lifted both hands to silence him.

"Okay, okay, I'll cut that. I promise. If we ever get a signal again, I'll delete the old ones. And if . . . look, the next time I interview him, I'll do it differently."

Lawrence looked away, the anger gone from his eyes.

"You were about to say *if* you get to interview him again," he said softly.

"No."

But she had been, and they both knew it. She wasn't sure she'd see Abe again. It was crazy to feel that way, and yet she did.

Lawrence cast a troubled gaze at the empty road down which Abe's old truck had vanished.

"I should've gone with him. It wasn't right, sending him out alone."

"I know," Charlie said, and her agreement seemed to surprise Lawrence. He sighed, then crossed the room to the little museum area that excited Abe so much. There was an old pair of binoculars on a shelf there, a relic of the Korean War, one of Abe's surplus store finds, and Lawrence picked them up.

"What are you doing?" Charlie asked.

"I want to get a look at the end of the road," he said. "Maybe we can see . . . something."

He was getting stir-crazy waiting, and although Charlie thought about reminding him that Abe had told them to keep the door locked for the first hour, she didn't.

"Okay," she said, and then she slid off the barstool. Lawrence was at the door, gun in one hand and binoculars in the other, when she stopped him.

"Hang on. I don't want to leave this behind." She gestured at the radiosonde with the old watch and strange note.

"Use my backpack," he said.

Charlie unzipped it and loaded the radiosonde carefully inside, then put the backpack on her shoulders. Lawrence rolled the dead bolt back, pushed the door open, and then walked out of the taproom and into the empty parking lot, blinking against the bright sunlight, gun in hand.

The old service station that would someday be BUFF Brewing faced the airfield across the road, which was to the east. Abe had driven out and turned right, heading south. At the end of the parking lot, he'd made another right, onto the only road that existed for the next three miles, a stretch of asphalt that led from the end of the Ash Point peninsula back to the mainland, where a Y-shaped intersection offered routes north and south. There he would have headed south, toward Cold Harbor. North led to Lubec and the Canadian border crossing.

It was a lonely place.

A strong sea breeze undercut the sun's efforts and carried a chill through the deceptively bright day. Charlie shivered, and Lawrence saw it.

"You want my jacket?"

"No, I'm good. Do you have to hold that gun? It's freaking me out."

Lawrence put the revolver in the pocket of his Cold Harbor High varsity jacket.

They stared up the road in the direction Abe had gone. It was empty, steep embankments falling off on either side, weeds weaving in the wind. There was never any traffic down to Ash Point, but the road had never seemed more isolated, like the end of the earth. The pavement seemed white in the sunlight, and Charlie thought suddenly of Abe's description of the sole survivor he'd found in the snow all those years earlier.

The wrong kind of bright.

She shivered again, and this time it had nothing to do with the wind.

Lawrence lifted the binoculars to his eyes. Adjusted them. Frowned.

"Do you see anything?" she asked.

"No. Well . . . this is weird."

"What?"

"It looks like there's a ROAD CLOSED sign down there. You know, like a construction zone? There's definitely an orange sign and some cones." He stepped farther down the road. "I think there might be a dump truck or something down there too? It's hard to tell."

He lowered the binoculars and scanned the surrounding area, then nodded at the top of the embankment across the road, where the fence protecting the runway stood with all its rusty warning signs.

"Let's climb up there and get a better look."

Charlie hesitated. The hill wasn't far away, but it was also out in the open, exposed, and she suddenly missed the dim taproom with its solid walls and locked door. Lawrence was walking across the road toward the airfield, though, and Charlie trailed him, not wanting to be left alone. He was already on the other side of the fence—not a difficult task, considering how many gaping holes the decades had opened in it—and striding onto the tarmac. Ahead were the concrete block buildings that had once housed the radar stations, barracks, and armories of Ash Point. One stainless steel structure had switchback stairs like a fire tower, and at the top was an oscillating red antenna, a giant dish. Transmitting or receiving? She had no idea. Abe Zimmer was obsessed with that antenna, endlessly pontificating about its potential classified purposes. The thing creeped Charlie out on a good day—and this wasn't a good day.

Overhead, the blue sky was darkening in the west, with plump white clouds that bore gray underbellies, and the wind was picking up off the water. When Charlie looked longingly back at the taproom, the weather balloon weaved as if with excitement, tugging impatiently at the cords that bound it.

Let me go, it seemed to say. *The fun has just begun!*

Lawrence was standing on the runway, binoculars back to his eyes.

"Can you see it better?" Charlie called.

"A little. These old binoculars suck, but . . . Charlie, it looks like the road is closed. There are work trucks down there but nobody's working."

"Weird. It's a Saturday, and the pavement down there is fine."

For a moment Lawrence didn't answer. Then he said, "I can see Grandpa's truck."

"*What?*"

"His truck is right on the other side! It's just behind the utility truck, sitting there, empty!"

He lowered the binoculars and turned back to her, ashen.

"He never would've left his truck, Charlie."

No, he wouldn't have.

"Maybe it died, like my ATV?" she ventured, but that didn't make sense, because Blue had been running fine.

"If it died, he'd be walking back to us," Lawrence said.

They stared at each other, unspoken questions and deep fears hanging in the air, and Charlie was just about to say that they needed to go back to the taproom when a low moan came from the sky. She looked up, saw nothing but those white clouds with the gray bellies, mismatched, as if they carried a storm below and a peaceful day above. The sound deepened, moan to roar.

"Look!" Lawrence cried, pointing northeast, over the water. Charlie followed his extended arm and then she saw the plane, a wicked-looking black silhouette with long, swept-back wings. It was a big plane. Very big. It was also descending and banking southeast, putting it in line with the airstrip.

"Lawrence . . . is it going to land?"

"No," Lawrence said, but he sounded unconvinced, and he should have, because seconds after he issued the denial, the plane's landing gear opened.

"Holy shit," Charlie said. "It's a B-52."

That was the only type of plane she possibly could have identified. She'd looked at enough photos of them over the years, and since her move to Maine she'd made nearly daily trips up Spruce Hill to see the wreckage. The B-52 wasn't something you could confuse with any other.

The inbound plane descended steeply, targeting the long runway. Coming right at them.

It wouldn't matter whether the pilot saw them or not—he could hardly swerve a plane to miss them.

"Run!" Lawrence shouted.

Charlie ran. The roar of the jet engines came on, tornadic. She made it off the tarmac and went stumbling into the weeds, tripped, and fell, skidding through the sandy soil on her elbows. Lawrence helped her up and they stood together, backed up against the fence, while the plane touched down.

The enormous landing gear kissed the pavement and suddenly the plane was barreling right past them. A bright yellow parachute unfurled behind it, ballooned full, and acted as a drag to help slow the bomber. The jet engines, four on each side, shuddered, as if disappointed to be landbound once again, and then fell silent.

Naval Air Station Ash Point was back in business.

INDIANA
SUMMER 1962

The morning after he left Marilyn Metzger's hotel room, Marty was summoned from Microfilm Storage Building #45 to meet with Captain Dwight Fremont. Fremont ran the base's security operations.

"What's it about?" Marty asked the sentry who brought him the news.

"No idea, sir."

Marty left his lab, walked through the heat to the security building, went up the limestone steps, and entered. Captain Fremont was standing in front of a window in the hall. When Marty opened the door and a shaft of light fell over the dark walnut floors, Fremont turned his broad, linebacker's shoulders and gave a grunt that Marty couldn't read as a greeting or a repudiation.

"Dr. Hazelton."

"Good morning, Dwight," Marty said, and then wondered why he had insisted on poking the bear, because Fremont, a faithful servant of protocol, liked his rank mentioned.

"Come inside," Fremont said, and they entered his office, a small room with a desk, two chairs, a bookcase, and a single window flanked by a globe and an American flag. On top of the bookcase was a model of a frigate, one of the sailing vessels that had been the country's first navy ships. The desk was bare except for the telephone and a thick manila envelope. Marty sat facing the desk, and Fremont took his time settling in behind it, folded his hands atop the manila envelope, and regarded Marty with a sorrowful gaze.

"I hate to disturb your work. I understand it is of the highest importance."

There was more than a hint of skepticism to the statement.

"I appreciate that," Marty said mildly.

"Yes, sir. Very important. Maybe more important than I'd realized."

Marty crossed his legs and straightened his suit jacket.

"Oh?"

"I just finished a meeting with our friends at the FBI," Fremont said, seeming to enjoy the taste of that sentence.

Marty waited. Fremont seemed disappointed that no question came, and he had to press on alone.

"They have been surveilling a Soviet spy," he said. Waited a beat, got nothing, and then added, "A woman."

Marty, who had never bothered to so much as verify that Marilyn Metzger was a real name, was somehow immediately unconvinced.

Of course they will blame her, he thought instead, defensive. Was he that easily undone by simple sex?

It had hardly been simple. He could see her again in the darkness, moving beneath him, then above him, then beneath again; could remember the way her back had arched and her hair had fallen across her own lips as they parted when she leaned her head back in what had seemed to be genuine throes.

A spy. Of course. What he should have known from the first, clumsy attempt with the book by Bernie Vonnegut's brother. Flight 19 and Nashua and the secret meeting beneath the Nebraska fields—all the right pawns to prompt a reaction from him. But he'd given her nothing. Hadn't even admitted that he could vanish a plane. If her access to Cutting's office was as high as Jimmy the monkey suggested, she knew the goals of Project Kingsolver, but Marty hadn't shared them.

"Do you have a picture?" he asked.

Fremont gave that grunt again. "Right to it, eh?"

"Not meaning to rush you. It's just that I've met only one woman in Bloomington recently. If it's not her, my lab awaits. A lot of work to be done."

Fremont unwound the thread that held the envelope's closure shut and shook the contents loose, a file cluttered with so many red CLASSIFIED stamps that it would be difficult to read the typing beneath.

"Here she is," Fremont said, and slipped out a black-and-white eight-by-ten photo.

It was Marilyn, standing at a crosswalk on a street in downtown Bloomington, towering elms and an elegant limestone house behind her. She seemed to be looking directly into the camera, although her chin was tilted slightly up and to the right, not so different from the way it had been when she climaxed.

Or pretended to climax. Was a spy's orgasm fake by definition? There was a puzzle. Schrödinger's cat had nothing on that.

"You've met her," Fremont said, unable to conceal the pleasure in his voice.

"I have. She was at the cocktail lounge in Bloomington near the square. The Danforth."

"Dandale."

"That's the one. She's a Soviet?"

"She's believed to be compromised, yes. What did—"

"How long have they been following her?" Marty asked.

Fremont stopped, flustered by being asked for answers when he wanted to offer only questions.

"It's been a long-term operation. She identifies herself as close to high command. We think that's a tactic that would comfort smart men who wouldn't speak to her otherwise."

"Identifies as close to high command, or *is* close to high command?"

Dwight Fremont smiled grimly and tapped one of the bright red CLASSIFIED stamps.

"Sure," Marty said. "But if I see her again, I'll need to be prepared."

Fremont's fat chin nearly quivered with shock.

"See her again? Sir, you're being notified of this situation—this *highly sensitive and classified* situation—in the interest of security. You certainly should not see her again!"

"Did they arrest her?" Marty asked, and Fremont looked exasperated.

"It is an ongoing surveillance detail that may yield a . . . a treasure trove!" he exploded, as if the notion of Marilyn Metzger's arrest was the most absurd idea he'd ever heard. Watching him, Marty was suddenly and utterly convinced that Fremont was not lying but, rather, had been lied to.

He was the right guy to take the bait. The FBI visiting, sharing a report with more angry stamps than a bad child's report card, speaking of spies sipping vodka sodas on the Bloomington square? Yes, Dwight Fremont was just the man. He hungered for real secrets. For a greater role than tending the gates.

"If she hasn't been arrested," Marty said, "that means she may find me again, correct? I'm trying to be properly prepared."

"I would urge you to avoid all contact," Fremont said, and Marty sighed.

"Of course. But if she's a good spy—and it seems she is, based on the size of that report—then she'll initiate contact again, won't she?"

Fremont rubbed his jowls. "The concern expressed to me this morning was that she's had any contact with you already. We need to limit the damage."

"Why didn't the FBI talk to me?"

"Chain of command in an intelligence matter."

"Seems like adding a middleman," Marty said, and Fremont flushed.

"There's no middleman, only protocol. What did she ask you about?"

"Vonnegut," Marty said.

"Who?" Fremont opened his desk drawer, found a pen and pad, and Marty realized he thought he'd been given some serious intel, a spy's name. Vonnegut . . . why, it even had the nefarious ring of a foreigner, nothing like Fremont, a surname that had helped conquer the American frontier.

"Kurt Vonnegut. He writes books. His brother makes rain."

Fremont blinked. "Excuse me?"

"Just what I said. Bernard Vonnegut makes rain. Kurt writes books. They're from Indiana, just like you. The good guys."

Fremont grunted, wrote notes. "What about Crane? Did she ask you anything about the base, your work, our security protocols?"

"No," Marty said. "I would've reported anyone who did that."

"She just wanted to talk about books?"

"And movies. She likes Humphrey Bogart."

"That's all? No conversation about your work?"

"None." It was as if his reflexes now belonged to some other man. A liar—a fool—and possibly a traitor.

Fremont seemed both surprised and disappointed. No doubt he'd been promised more. Marty considered asking him whether the FBI agents had said anything about Admiral Cutting and then decided against it.

"How many times did you see her?" Fremont asked.

189

"Twice. Both times at the bar. Chitchat, nothing more."

If they had proof of something, let it be known.

Fremont wore the look of grim surprise that indicated Marty's answers didn't jibe with what Fremont been told by the FBI, and it was clear that the captain did not have the faintest idea what to do about the disconnect.

"I was asked to make it clear to you that she's considered a true risk," he said.

"Understood."

Fremont braced his meaty forearms on the desk. "The federal hope is that you'll avoid another encounter at all costs."

The federal hope. A propaganda film title just waiting to be used.

"Understood," Marty repeated, and then, just to be done with it, added, "I'm grateful. A bit shocked, of course, but . . . it's a tense world, isn't it?"

"Indeed," Fremont said. "To be clear, though, the request is that you avoid potential encounters for the foreseeable future."

Marty raised his eyebrows. "I'm to stay on the base?"

"That's the request, sir. Until the intelligence operation has concluded."

There it was. The federal hope was that Hazelton would stay home and finish the work. Solve for X. Then hand it over.

Marty sat and watched bruise-colored clouds shift outside the window behind Fremont's desk, and he wondered where they'd come from, and if they were natural. Probably. Then again, just because Langmuir was dead didn't mean his work was. You didn't get to take your work off the board simply by dying. That was why it was crucial to do good work.

He remembered the picture of Hiroshima in Marilyn Metzger's trembling hand.

"Well, Dr. Hazelton, I appreciate your cooperation," Fremont said at length, made uneasy by the silence, the way men who weren't capable of deep thought so often were.

Marty smiled. "I'm afraid there won't be cooperation."

Fremont's bushy eyebrows lurched. "Excuse me?"

"I won't stay on the base unless I feel like it. That's all."

"This is an active intelligence operation! We're talking about matters of national—"

"*I'm* working on matters of national security," Marty snapped, jabbing his index finger off his chest. "Real ones, the kind that turn bone to ash. Detectives chase clues, I do math, and we'll all damned well be best served if that's how it continues! The FBI can learn its fucking role; I already know mine!"

Fremont was so shocked at the outburst it took him a moment to respond.

"I am aware of the importance of your work," he began, slowly and genuinely, as if a reminder to himself that Marty Hazelton was special and must be treated as such. When a man from Los Alamos or Oak Ridge shouted, you'd best keep your cool. *Ka-boom!*

Marty wanted to laugh, had to suppress a smile, which told him just how angry he truly was. He was never funnier than when he was angry, and never angrier than when he was afraid.

"I know you are," Marty said. "And I am aware of the importance of *your* work, and of *theirs*, and so it is with all due respect that I tell you I solved the most important equation of my career on the back of a cocktail napkin at the Dandale, and if that's where I do my best thinking, then *that's* where the Navy wants me to be."

He took a breath, smoothed his jacket, and then added, "Besides, I like their cocktails."

Five minutes later he was walking alone back to his building, and Captain Fremont was on the phone with Washington.

Nobody stopped Marty at the gate when he left for Bloomington.

ASH POINT, MAINE
OCTOBER 25, 2025

Charlie and Lawrence stood against the fence and stared at the B-52, and neither of them spoke. The plane was awesome in the strictest sense of the word. Charlie couldn't imagine what it must feel like to have one visit your town when it meant business, guns firing, bombs falling. Even in stillness, the aircraft projected menace.

"We need to get out of here," she said, but Lawrence didn't answer, and didn't move.

"Lawrence . . . " She tugged on his jacket sleeve. "Come on. We need to go!"

"People are getting out," he said.

Stairs had opened in the belly of the plane, and a single man emerged, seeming miniature against the towering aircraft. Then there was another, and maybe a third and fourth, it was hard to tell, their shapes hidden by shadows beneath the plane.

"Maybe this is good," Lawrence said.

Charlie wasn't sure. The plane was official, and a little reassuring with those U.S. Air Force markings, like a promise of order restored. Still, she hesitated.

"They're going to know what's happening, at least," Lawrence said.

"They shouldn't have landed here."

"Remember that show about the planes that were diverted to Halifax after 9/11?" Lawrence said. "*Come from Away*. That worked out."

"Are you seriously referencing a musical right now?"

"It was based on a true story!"

"Well, let's not sing to these guys right away, okay? Save that for the second act."

"Very funny."

"Just let me ask the questions." Charlie went up the hill and onto the tarmac, with Lawrence trailing. The crew from the plane was still clustered beneath its belly, in the shadows, as if afraid to step out into the sunlight. Even the Air Force seemed confused today. She wondered if they'd been ordered to put down at Ash Point or if they'd been running out of fuel and taken an emergency option. Was the point of resurfacing the runway every few years to keep an active escape route on the Eastern Seaboard? It made as much sense as anything.

"Hello!" Charlie shouted, her voice higher than she'd intended. "Hey! Do you guys know what is happening?"

One of the airmen spun toward her. She kept walking, almost at a run, the pace of barely suppressed panic. Her mind was desperately seeking logical explanations for the plane, but her spine seemed to tingle with warnings about it.

"Why did you land here?" she shouted. "Can you tell us what is happening?"

"What's the broad doing?" one of the airmen said, turning back to look at his crewmates.

Charlie stopped walking. Lawrence bumped into her, but she scarcely registered the contact.

"*Broad*"? Who said "broad"? It wasn't just offensive; it was anti-quated.

Her focus had been on the men beneath the plane, but now she looked up at the aircraft itself, and a chill bloomed in her chest.

"Lawrence . . . look at the logo."

"I see it." He was right beside her, yet his voice sound far-off, numb.

The plane was painted with a loon in profile, the exact same paint job as the plane that had crashed here in 1962, the so-called *Loring Loonatic*. The bird's scarlet eye seemed even brighter against the black paint, as if it were floating against an endless night sky.

"Come on up here, kids," a different airman called, and this voice was kinder, more reassuring than the one who'd yelled the question about the broad, but Charlie didn't move and neither did Lawrence. She couldn't stop looking at the loon. This couldn't be the same plane, of course. There was no way; that plane was in pieces up on the hill above the airfield.

"Come here!" the airman yelled again.

Charlie and Lawrence stayed where they were, silent, staring. The plane's parachute fluttered in the wind, a sound like the snap of a sail. The three airmen started toward them, and Lawrence reached into his pocket, where he'd put Abe's gun.

"Don't," Charlie said.

"Well, what are we supposed to do?" he asked wildly. "Something is really wrong. They shouldn't be here, and what happened to my grandpa?"

The taproom was far behind them, a long run, and even if they made it, locking the door wasn't going to do much good. The front of the building was glass; anyone who wanted to break in would do it.

There are bunkers, Abe had told them, but the bunkers were on the other side of the airfield, behind the plane and the advancing air-men. They were all dressed in olive flight suits, and two of them had

195

sidearms. White men, average height, one stockier than the others, one unnaturally pale, his blond crew cut only slightly darker than his pallid skin. He had blue eyes, very bright.

The wrong kind of bright.

Too late, Charlie thought that maybe they should have run after all, at least tried. Now there was nothing to do but wait—or tell Lawrence to draw the gun.

They waited. The airmen approached warily.

"Who's in charge?" said the point man, who had dark hair cut short like the others, his face lean, his eyes shielded by aviator sunglasses.

The stocky man with the gun in his hand looked at Charlie and Lawrence and said, "Captain, what the fuck is happening here?"

"Ease off on the language," the one in the aviators said.

"The language!" The stocky man barked a laugh, looking around with a wild expression. "You not seeing this place? Where did you put us down?"

"Ash Point," Charlie said. "Do you know what's happening today?"

She suspected they didn't. Dana Goodwin's perceptive girl was beginning to believe what the spine had already told her and the mind had refused: there was something very wrong with that plane, and she understood more about the world than the men who'd just disembarked from it.

The pale one with the close-cropped buzzed hair gave a high keening sound that seemed torn between a whistle and a sob.

"Kid, I've been to Ash Point! This ain't it." But as he peered around, his eyes narrowed and he looked a little nauseated.

The captain was staring at Charlie. She wanted him to take off the aviator glasses. She saw twin reflections of her own terror in his eyes, and that was almost more disturbing than the pale man's bright blue eyes and the stocky man's bright green eyes.

"This is Naval Air Station Ash Point?" the captain asked.

"It was."

"What do you mean, 'was'?" the stocky one snapped, and then the pale one shrilled, "This is all so fucked!" and the captain lifted a hand to silence them. He was focused on Charlie.

"Clarify for me, please," he said.

Clarify for *him*? They'd landed a fucking B-52 at a closed airfield and *Charlie* was supposed to explain?

Lawrence, easing his hand into his jacket pocket, said, "Where do you think you are?"

"I put down at Naval Air Station Ash Point," the captain said slowly. "But it doesn't . . . " He paused, glanced at the empty buildings, eyes roving over the boarded-up windows and that oscillating radar antenna. "It doesn't look right."

"That's a fuckin' understatement!" the pale one yelped.

"They said psych ops," the stocky man said thoughtfully. "That was the word at Loring all week. All the stuff about the cloud was bullshit."

"This is one mother of a psych op!" the pale man said. "This place is closed. Use your eyes! Better yet, listen!"

They all listened. Ash Point, a lonely place on its best day, felt like a ghost town right now, the wind moaning and the distant breakers more menacing than charming, thumping into the rocks as if hungry for them, then whisking back like retracting claws.

Lawrence looked at Charlie. She tried to beg him with her eyes not to draw the gun. He was scared, and there was nothing more dangerous than a scared man with a gun.

"Psych ops bullshit," the stocky man said. "What'd they tell us about the cloud? 'Expect the unexpected.' Okay, this is the game."

The pale man muttered, "I didn't like that friggin' cloud, I don't like this place, and I don't like these kids."

What was the cloud? The day was growing more overcast, but by and large the sky was blue. Not as clear as it had been when the balloon appeared, but . . .

"Charlie," Lawrence whispered, "look at his name tag."

"Huh?"

"Look!" Lawrence pointed at the captain.

The name stitched onto his flight suit said HIGHTOWER.

"No," Charlie said, voice calm, and then shook her head, as if the situation were trivial, unworthy of her time. "This is not . . . no."

The captain stared from Lawrence back to Charlie.

"What's wrong with you two?"

Neither of them spoke.

"Say it!" the captain barked, and his voice was so commanding that Charlie found herself saying it.

"You have the same name as a man who crashed a plane here in 1962."

Silence.

"I haven't crashed a plane anywhere," the captain said at last, "but why did you tell me the year?"

"Because it is October 25, 2025, and something is really, *really* fucked-up today."

The silence thickened like fog. Finally, the stocky man broke it with a wild laugh.

"You gotta give these CIA boys credit!" he shouted. "When they come up with a game, it's good! Close up the airfield, board the windows, and send out a kid to tell you that you're starring in a Rod Serling show!"

"Bellamy," Lawrence said suddenly. That brought them all up short.

"What's that?" the captain asked.

"He's Bellamy. And you . . . " Lawrence pivoted to the pale man. "You're Granville."

Granville said, "I don't get the point of the game."

Charlie shook her head. "It's not a game. You're supposed to be dead. All of you. You took off from Loring—"

"I'm not listening to this," the pale man, Granville, said, turning from Charlie and walking back toward the plane.

"Stop moving, Granville," the captain said. He was doing his best to hide his fear. "Go on, kid. We left Loring and what?"

"And you crashed," Charlie said. "It was a freak storm: snow in October. All of you died."

"Shut her up!" Granville screamed, whirling and rushing toward Charlie. The one named Bellamy caught Granville just before he reached her.

"Damn it, show some composure!" the captain, Hightower, shouted.

But Granville wasn't listening. He was raving.

"Then this little bitch tells me I'm dead and it's 2025! They're playing games and *I'm not doing it*! I'm out!"

The moment imploded when Lawrence Zimmer said: "Soldiers are coming."

Granville and Bellamy ceased their grappling immediately. They all looked at Lawrence, saw him pointing at the far western end of the airfield, and turned in unison.

A group of men in camouflage raced between the long-closed buildings. They carried rifles. They ran low and they ran fast.

There was a pause, one that couldn't have been more than three seconds but felt eternal, and then the captain said, "Grab the kids and get back on the plane, *now*!"

At that, Bellamy's hands found Charlie's arms, and even while she tried to resist him, she was focused on Lawrence, because she knew he would draw Abe's gun and knew it would go badly.

He did draw it, but it was too little, too late, as they say. He never had a chance. The barrel got caught in his jacket pocket, the man named Granville saw the gun, his arm flashed down in a smooth, savage chop, and then Abe's revolver was on the tarmac and Lawrence's gun hand was wrenched between his shoulder blades. Bellamy had Charlie's arms pinned, lifted her feet right off the ground, shoving her forward. She would have fallen if not for his painful grip, and in the effort to keep her footing she found herself stumbling ahead, right toward the plane.

The soldiers pulled up once they realized their targets were in motion. Two dropped into sniper position on the ground, others spread out, but they all stopped their advance. Someone shouted into a bullhorn, the sound clear.

"Captain Hightower, we are friendly! United States Army here, sir. We are friendly!"

Everyone stopped. Charlie almost fell to the tarmac, but Bellamy caught her and held her. They were only a few paces from the steps that led up into the belly of the plane, at least a hundred yards from the soldiers.

"What the hell do we do, Captain?" Bellamy asked.

Hightower didn't answer. He was staring out at the soldiers, who had him in their rifle scopes.

"I don't like this place," Granville whispered. "I don't like it and I don't trust 'em, no matter who they say they are."

"We are coming your way, sir," the voice from the bullhorn said. "Slowly and peacefully. We are United States Army, Captain Hightower. Please relax your men!"

Hightower stayed silent. Charlie was sure he didn't trust Ash Point any more than Granville did, but she thought he'd at least hear the Army out.

That hope was vanquished by the sudden, high whine of a jet engine. All motion on the ground ceased, and all eyes went skyward.

The jet came in fast—breathtakingly fast, a speed that made the B-52's approach seem downright placid—and so low that Charlie could see the individual missiles mounted on the wings. The plane banked and blasted by and then there was nothing left but the echo.

"What was that?" Bellamy shouted. "Tell me what in the fuck kind of plane that was?"

"I don't know!" Hightower yelled. Then, softer, wonderingly, he added, "That's not one of ours, and it's no MiG. So what *was* it?"

Lawrence Zimmer said, "Maybe a Tomcat?"

"What?" Hightower looked down at him.

"Or an F-16? A fighter plane. You know, *Top Gun*, Maverick. Tom Cruise."

Hightower, Bellamy, and Granville all exchanged a look. They had no clue what a Tomcat was, and they definitely hadn't heard of Tom Cruise.

"They're ghosts," Charlie whispered. "Lawrence, they're ghosts."

Lawrence met Charlie's eyes and she saw that he was still hoping for a solution, a way in which the world could make sense again. The ghosts of the three airmen from the crashed flight had no such illusions.

"We're going airborne," Captain Hightower announced. "I don't know what happened in that cloud, but I've got a nuclear bomb under my command, I've got combatants on the ground and unknown aircraft in the sky, and I want my plane in the air."

The next thing Charlie knew, she was being hauled up the steps and into the B-52, dragged aboard the plane by three men who'd died in it six decades earlier.

RAVEN ROCK MOUNTAIN COMPLEX, PENNSYLVANIA
OCTOBER 25, 2025

"You were told!" Director of National Intelligence Hanover bellowed, veins bulging in his temples, tendons taut in his neck. "You were fucking told, repeatedly, no aircraft! Damn you!"

"We wanted a presence," the defense secretary said. "A show of force to keep them from boarding that plane again."

"And how'd that work out?" Hanover raged.

Layla Chen heard them but didn't respond, staring numbly at the screen that showed the Ash Point airfield from a camera worn on the helmet of a special ops soldier. The Loring crew was back in the B-52 and the jet's engines were thrumming to life. On the operator's radio, a commander was shouting at the Delta Force team to hold their fire and hold their position, do not engage, do not engage!

So close, Layla thought. *So fucking close, and we bungled it.*

The impossible plane had been safely on the ground and empty. The Delta Force team had been on the airfield and within a hundred yards. Then came the F-16 flyover, from a plane that the crew of the *Loring Loonatic* could not possibly have trusted, because they'd never seen anything like it, and now the madness was just beginning.

Good luck talking them back out of the aircraft, she thought, and then the big plane began to move and she felt sick.

A show of force, the defense secretary had said. Brilliant. Now the *Loring Loonatic* was about to go airborne again—along with its Mark 39 thermonuclear warhead—likely headed for Cuba.

The kids were a problem. Delta would've taken the plane easily if the kids hadn't appeared. That changed the calculus. The old man in the truck, Abraham Zimmer, had claimed to be the only person on Ash Point, which Layla supposed was a noble lie, considering he'd been grabbed by Special Forces posing as county highway crew. Cool under pressure, he'd unwittingly exacerbated the problem. Had Delta been able to take the taproom and secure the kids before the plane came down . . .

Could've, would've, should've.

"We cannot let it take off," the defense secretary said, and then the president, who'd been shocked and silent while they watched the events unfold, finally spoke up to say that was not an option. Prudent, considering any attempt to stop the plane might end with a nuclear blast that would kill thousands of civilians instantly and, with the prevailing northeasterly winds carrying the radiation toward urban areas, claim many more in due time.

The plane would be allowed to take off.

Then what?

"Passive pressure," the president suggested, as if Layla had voiced her question aloud. "Keep the F-16s visible and wait for the pilot to figure it out."

"The F-16s just scared the pilot back into the air," Hanover said. "I don't know why we think they'd be reassuring to him now."

"We don't know what the pilot *is*," the defense secretary said. "Stop talking about him like he's a rational actor—or even human. That man took off in 1962. Whatever he is now is not normal. We can't assume rational decision-making."

"Everything he's done so far is rational enough," Hanover said. "He followed his flight plan, he got scared by what he didn't understand, and he returned his aircraft to the air rather than surrender it to unknown forces. That's pretty damn clearheaded, if you ask me."

"You're seriously saying that about some kind of fucking ghost?"

"Maybe I am."

"Dr. Chen?"

It was the president, and it took Layla a moment to respond. It was hard for her to stop watching the B-52, which was airborne again, an utterly remarkable thing, one that no one in the room seemed to properly appreciate for the magic it was. They were too concerned with the threat. If they could just get that thing back on the ground for study . . .

"Dr. Chen?"

"Yes. Sorry."

"What's the Sector Six recommendation?"

Excellent question. And unfair. Sector Six kept track of DARPA's possible disasters, but it didn't promise to solve them. Layla opened her mouth to say as much, then stopped. It was not a day for whining. She wanted out of this room. Wanted a drink. Wanted to close her eyes.

Wanted to see that plane up close too. Yes, she wanted that most of all.

Gone for sixty-three years, then back in a blink, unblemished, the crew moving like time stood still . . .

"I'm not sure we have a recommendation," she said, "considering we missed an opportunity on the ground. But I would agree with Admiral Hanover that the pilot is behaving in a rational manner, however implausible that might seem to all of us."

The defense secretary didn't like hearing this, but so it went. The defense secretary also liked to fix problems with missiles fired by drones. The *Loring Loonatic* was not a problem to be fixed with a missile.

"What does that mean to you, based on your knowledge of Project Kingsolver?" Hanover asked.

What she knew of Project Kingsolver did not anticipate what was happening right now. No one had ever been able to explain what had gone right—or wrong—with the lone test flight of Project Kingsolver. The possible exception was Dr. Martin Hazelton, and he wasn't going to walk into Raven Rock to enlighten the group.

"We could consider countering their technology with our own," she said.

"Explain that."

"We can establish a communication link."

"I thought they had no radio."

"We can address that with a drone. DARPA has funded development of drones for crisis communications with the capability of claiming the microphone on a secondary device, such as a laptop or a phone."

"A secondary device doesn't help us much. The plane is from 1962."

"The kids aren't," Layla said.

A pause. Glimmers of hope, the first she'd seen in any of their eyes since Delta Force failed to claim the plane on the ground.

"We won't even need a drone for that," Hanover said. "Depending on the altitude and location, we can simply activate their devices. Do we have the numbers for these kids? It's Lawrence Zimmer and"—he checked his notes—"Charlie Goodwin."

"We've got their numbers. An active MAC address shows the Zimmer kid also has an iPad in motion."

"Put this in action," the defense secretary said.

"I would give that a few minutes," Layla said. "Let Hightower fly in peace for a little while."

"Why on earth would we delay this?"

"Because the crew is likely to be distressed by the very existence of the phones and iPad," Layla said. "They're flying scared right now, and they may need some time to sort out what must feel like a terrifying situation."

This pause extended while everyone pondered a pilot from 1962 seeing an iPhone for the first time.

"Just get the system ready for use," the president said. "Then I will make a direct appeal to the pilot, an explanation. With direct communication, I can convince him to land for the good of his country."

"You might consider an alternative," Layla said.

"What's that?"

She managed to continue meeting their eyes when she said, "I suspect that Captain Hightower would rather hear from President Kennedy."

Someone laughed. The others made no sound at all.

"DARPA can make that happen?" Hanover asked finally. "Kennedy's voice, in a real-time conversation?"

"Yes."

"In genuinely convincing fashion?"

"We got more than five hundred pilots to call in sick because they believed they'd heard from their mothers," Layla answered. "I think that speaks for our capacity to convince."

They looked at one another. Nobody spoke for a moment. Finally, the president took control.

"If John F. Kennedy can land that plane safely, let him do it."

It was October 25, 2025, and the living were deferring to the dead.

No pressure, Jack, Layla Chen thought. Kennedy had come through in Cuba one perilous October long ago. Who was to say he couldn't do it again?

INDIANA
SUMMER 1962

Marty didn't bother to watch his rearview mirror on the drive into Bloomington. There was no need. They'd have watchers downtown if not behind him, and whether the watchers would be genuine FBI agents was a question, but their presence was not.

An active intelligence operation.

He believed that much from Dwight Fremont. Whose intelligence and with what goals, though? Different questions.

He parked a block east of the square, behind a battered red pickup that made him think of the old farmer's truck in Nashua. He walked directly to the Dandale, ordered a drink, and scanned the bar. Nobody seemed to be watching him. Good watchers never did, though.

"Say, may I borrow your phone?" he asked the bartender.

"There's a pay phone outside."

"It's a hundred degrees in the shade out there. Call will take ten seconds and double your tip."

The bartender looked at him sourly. "Better be true on both counts."

"It will be."

The bartender pushed the phone his way. Marty dialed Marilyn Metzger's hotel and asked for room 33. He wasn't expecting her to answer, but she did.

"Vodka soda waiting for you," he said without identifying himself.

For a moment, there was no sound at all, as if he'd lost the connection.

"Is everything okay?" she asked at last.

"Your ice is melting. I'd hurry." He hung up before she could respond.

It didn't take her ten minutes.

She slid onto the stool beside him, smiled uncertainly, and said, "This is a pleasant surprise."

"I had time to kill. Your boss hasn't sent me a fresh monkey. Also, the FBI visited the base to tell me you're working for the Soviets."

She stared at him. "Is this . . . Are you testing me?"

He shook his head.

"The Soviets," she said, and her laugh was so empty that it chilled him.

"Not so funny. Those are federal charges."

"Sure." She didn't merely look unconcerned; she looked contemptuous. It was both unsettling and reassuring—and all of it was deeply, deeply confusing.

"Who brought this crucial news to you?" she asked.

"The FBI, like I said."

"You saw an agent?"

He was nonplussed by her questions. He'd expected to see her back on her heels, whether the accusations were true or not, but she was controlled.

"Not yet."

"Of course not."

"And what is that supposed to mean?"

"Someone truly told you this?" she asked. "You haven't engineered this story as a personal test of me? It would be fair if you did, of course."

"The head of security at Crane told me this!" he snapped. How on earth was he defending his own integrity to an accused spy? The risk he'd taken coming here was madness, but now he felt untethered from reality, because not only was she unafraid of the accusation, she was angry about it.

"Korman? Or Fremont?"

Both names said so easily, so indifferently.

"Captain Fremont," Marty said, feeling vaguely ridiculous that *now* he'd decided to become formal about it.

"Do you think they sent anyone to him? Or was he lying?"

"They said . . . he said . . . " He stopped, flustered, and sipped some of the scotch, then rubbed his forehead and tried to think. The gleam of the light off his watchband seemed too bright. Why had he come here? Why did he keep talking to her? Saying too much—he was always saying too much when she was around—but there was a reason. A way she looked at him, something she knew that others didn't.

"What?" she nudged. "What did they say, Marty?"

"I saw a file."

"Anything detailed? Or was it just the picture and the accusation?"

"It was plenty thick."

"How much of it did you get to read?"

He thought of all those red stamps—too many. Cluttering the pages. Why would you stamp so much red over the text? Maybe because the words beneath the red warnings didn't matter.

"Why do I believe you," he said. It wasn't really a question, just a statement, but she answered it anyhow.

"Because you have impeccable instinct." She smiled humorlessly. "All the lies they wanted me to tell, and then they turn around and tell one about me. Talk about a thankless game."

"What lies?"

"Would you like to see a *real* intelligence file?" she asked.

He didn't answer. He lifted his glass. It was empty. He set it back down.

"Marty?"

"I don't know," he said, and that was honest. "This has all become very distracting. I should be focused on my work, and now I'm here . . . "

He winced, feeling a headache come on. She watched him with surprising tenderness.

"Did Fremont ask you anything about your brother?" she asked.

Marty turned back to her slowly, feeling as if something deep within him had slipped loose, some crucial gear, the flywheel to an intricate clockwork that once broken might never be put back together.

"What did you say?"

"You heard me," she said, soothing as a mother to a frightened child.

"My brother . . . my brother has nothing to do with this," he said, and suppressed a desire to hide his watch beneath his shirt cuff.

"What is 'this'?"

"My work. You. All of it!" His voice had risen, and a few people looked over.

Marilyn put her hand on his arm, light and comforting. "Let's get out of here."

"They likely bugged your hotel room," he said.

"Well, we gave them an earful, didn't we?" Her smile devastated him. She took her wallet from her handbag and put a five on the bar and stood.

"Why did you ask about my brother?" he said, still seated, looking up at her, unsure of himself. Of everything.

"You can read about that," she said. "And then we can talk. What do you say, Marty?"

He wished he hadn't made the drive to Bloomington. And not just today—all the days before, and particularly last winter, when he'd come for Christmas lights and a memory. When she'd looked at him, and part of him had understood that she knew him in ways others did not. How?

Marilyn slid back onto her stool.

"We don't have to go," she said.

"You're damn right we don't. I'm going to have another drink."

"I don't think you should."

He laughed. "A spy's advice. Worth its weight in gold."

But the spy talk clearly disconcerted him more than her.

"What do you remember," Marilyn Metzger asked, "about Doom Town?"

Doom Town. That absurd village in Nevada, the one where they'd brought him to estimate fallout conditions. Why was she suddenly interested in that?

"It was eerie," he said despite himself. "All those houses, real ones, down to the last detail. Rugs in front of hearths, curtains over the windows, and the mannequins . . . fake families, plastic dogs even. It was a strange damn sight."

He tried to sound casual and knew that he failed.

"Be more specific," she said. "What did you do there?"

"Why in the hell are we talking about Nevada?" he asked, roughening his voice.

Doom Town. There had been nothing left of the place. Later, he'd gotten to see the videos, and in the slowed-down footage you could see the houses implode, sucked in on themselves, gone into an eternal cloud of fire.

"What do you remember," Marilyn said, "about Nashua?"

"Royden Sanders is out there, doing top secret work with missiles. Go buy Roy a scotch and leave me alone. The FBI will arrest you before you make it that far."

She didn't so much as blink.

"Not Royden Sanders," she said. "What do *you* remember about Nashua?"

"Not a damn thing."

She seemed sad. And, for the first time, rattled.

"Okay," she said. "Let's go another way. Tell me about your brother."

"I'll be damned if we're going to talk about my brother."

"Where is he?"

Hank was in Hawaii, or he was dropping test nukes over the South Pacific, incinerating islands, but Marty wasn't about to get into all that. Besides, if she really worked for Cutting—Soviet asset or not—she already knew that.

"If you knew the monkey from Cleveland was named Jimmy, you surely know where to find my brother. Let him fly in peace."

She winced, as if the words had hurt her. That puzzled him. Maybe it was the idea of anyone flying that hurt her. Once, her fiancé had boarded a plane and flown off into a blue sky and never come back. He wished she didn't blame him for it, but he understood it. He was about to say as much when she spoke again.

"You're going to need to fill in some gaps."

He barked out a harsh laugh. "You're not subtle for a spy."

She sighed. "Not for me, Marty. To save yourself, and do the work you want to do, you *must* fill in some gaps."

Save himself? He felt another pulse of a headache, looked for the bartender, but his back was to them. Marilyn's vodka soda was almost untouched. He took it and drank. She watched him.

"When did you start drinking?"

"When you didn't finish it."

"I mean in general. When did you start drinking, Marty?"

"College, then the war. It's part of being a man. Don't try to pretend I've got some kind of alcohol problem. It's a cute trick that won't work."

"Tell me when you had your first drink. Just that much."

"Nobody remembers their first drink."

"Everyone does. I was sixteen and it was strawberry wine and I was scared of it, because my cousin drank so much she got sick."

"Men don't remember."

"Every man remembers his first drink. What was yours?"

"I don't know. Scotch, probably. Why are we talking about this?"

"Where was it?"

"I don't remember!"

"Was it in Los Alamos? Oak Ridge? Nashua?"

Why did she keep mentioning that town?

"Did you drink in Nevada? In Doom Town?"

"We all did. Once you see the bombs go off, Marilyn, you wish for a drink."

She leaned closer, suddenly fascinated, as if he'd opened a door to a cabinet of curiosities. "Why?"

"Because of its power. Because it is an awesome and terrifying sight. Ethereal."

He'd used his brother's word and wished he hadn't. He finished her vodka soda and flagged the bartender down and pointed at both empty glasses. The bartender seemed uncertain until Marilyn nodded. Then he brought them another round.

"Tell me about your lab," Marilyn said, and Marty barked out an astonished laugh.

"You really think I'm going to tell you about my lab?"

But he was telling her almost everything else. Why? What was there in her eyes—in her heart, he wanted to believe—that made him feel the need to talk?

"You don't have to tell me about it," she said. "But I need you to *think* about it, at least. What's wrong with your lab?"

What was wrong with it? Nothing was wrong with it.

"Compare it to Los Alamos and Oak Ridge and China Lake," she said. "For that matter, compare it to Schenectady. What's missing from your lab that you had in those?"

He frowned, downed some whiskey. "Nothing is missing."

Then he thought, *Except for the planes, of course—but don't worry, I can bring those back!* A smug smile crept over his face, but when he glimpsed it in the mirror behind the rows of liquor bottles, he didn't like the way he looked. He steadied himself, got grim again. Grim was good. This was serious business, vanishing planes in a nuclear war, and you couldn't trust anyone who went about it with a smile.

"How many people do you see in your lab, day-to-day?" Marilyn asked.

"Why in the hell would I tell you that? You're a spy!"

A few people sitting farther down the bar looked over in surprise, and Marilyn smiled and patted the air, a dismissive, *Nothing to see here* gesture.

She said, "I don't think you have many colleagues. Isn't that strange, compared to Oak Ridge or Los Alamos?"

"This is different. It's very classified."

"The Manhattan Project wasn't?"

His head pounded and his tongue felt thick and as dry as a snakeskin. He wondered why she'd asked him about his first drink. Wondered why he couldn't remember it. Maybe it had been with his father? No, his father had been a teetotaler, and he'd died long before Marty was old enough to cajole him into lifting so much as a champagne glass for a celebration. College—that had been it; he'd had his first beer in college. But with whom?

"You're given no assets to help with crucial, classified work," Marilyn said. "That's strange, isn't it?"

"I have assets."

"Do you know Dr. Dixon's specialty?"

Another name from a classified operation, offered so casually.

"Applied physics," Marty said.

"You've seen proof of this?"

"You honestly believe you'll convince me that my own right-hand man is compromised? I've seen your file; don't forget that."

Unfazed, she shifted closer.

"Think from Nashua, to Doom Town, to Crane," she said. "Tell me what's missing."

"What's missing? A hell of a lot. I was in plenty of other places, and you know it. Schenectady, for one."

She nodded.

"And Fort Lauderdale, though I wasn't doing what you suspect out there. And Los Alamos and Oak Ridge and China Lake."

"Yes, yes, yes," she said in a rising, enthused whisper that gave him a flash memory of her hotel bed in the darkness.

"You probably know more of my biography than I do at this point."

Again that strange look of sorrow flickered through her eyes, a bittersweet expression that confused him.

"You're right about that. And therein lies the problem you must solve."

He could make a plane vanish and return. *That* was the problem he must solve. There were no others that could occupy space in his brain until that one was done.

"I can't tell you where Robert went," he said. "I'm sorry—I truly am—but I can't. I know you think you can break me, that if you throw enough confusion and booze and maybe even sex into the mix, I'll cough up some story of secret ops in Florida in 1945, but there were none."

She swallowed. Rubbed her fingertips up and down the cocktail glass but didn't lift it, just watched the streaks clear, removing the opacity of the frosted glass until the contents within clarified. When she lifted her chilled fingertips from the glass and touched his arm again, he felt the transferred coolness spread up his arm and raise a tingle on the back of his skull.

"I appreciate that," she said. "You would tell me the truth if you could. I believe you when you say it now. I didn't at first."

"Good. Because it *is* the truth."

"Okay," she said, and turned her face to his. "If you can't tell me where Robert is, that's fine. But where is your brother?"

He stared at her. "What?"

"Where is your brother?"

"I'll ask you not to speak of my family, please. But there's also no secret to his location. You work in Cutting's office, don't you? Or was that a lie?"

"It's not a lie."

"Then you can find out where Hank is. It would take one phone call."

"I want you to tell me."

"Why?"

"Because you owe me one, damn you. You lost my Robert. Tell me where Hank Hazelton is."

"They have nothing to do with one another!"

"Then tell me," she urged, and he had a wild desire to smack her right off that barstool, to see blood on her mouth and on the back of his hand. To *hurt* her, really and truly.

Except that wasn't quite right, and he knew it. He hadn't come here to hurt anyone. He'd come here to *get* hurt, hadn't he?

He drank the scotch down. She never took her eyes off him.

"When was the last time you heard from him?"

"It's been a while. I've been busy. You know that."

"*When?*"

"We write letters."

"Both of you."

"Sure." That was an odd question.

"When was the last time you saw him? That's not classified."

"Well, he deployed to Hawaii in . . . hell, it has to be in your file. You tell me."

"You're quite bad with dates, Dr. Hazelton. Can't remember your first drink or the last time you saw your brother."

"You want to know someone who was bad with dates, you should've met Irving Langmuir. He once walked right into a paint can and then carried on, leaving a footprint of paint behind with each step, oblivious, because his head was up in the clouds. Irving was an absent-minded scientist if ever there were one."

He smiled, feeling better about himself. He wasn't alone. There were men like Irving Langmuir who could scarcely remember to put their pants on before they left the house, and yet they had Nobel Prizes. Who was it that said genius and madness were so close that they danced on the head of a pin? Schrödinger? Schrödinger had been close to mad himself, and yet he probably understood more about—

"Give me your best guess," Marilyn demanded. "When did you see Hank last? Or where? Surely, you remember *where* it was."

"This is silliness."

"Tell me where you saw him."

"It doesn't matter!" he hissed, and then there was a sharp pop as the empty whiskey glass broke in his closed fist and a shard cleaved through his palm with exquisite pain, blood dripping onto the bar top.

Marilyn Metzger didn't so much as glance at his bleeding hand. Instead, she put her arm on the bar to screen the scene from view and leaned very close to him, almost as close as they'd been in her hotel room, when their breaths and bodies had become one.

"You owe me," she whispered. "My fiancé vanished over the Atlantic before we could exchange our vows, and you can't solve that one. This one you can. You owe me, damn it! So say it!"

Her voice was intense, but Marty couldn't focus on her words or on his anger or even his painful, bleeding hand. There was something troubling stirring in his mind, rising like a ruby-red cloud, hot and dangerous.

"Was it in Schenectady or Oak Ridge or Hawaii?" Marilyn whispered. "*Where was it*, Marty? Where did you say goodbye to Hank?"

"Goodbye"—that was a bad word. He'd never said . . .

He looked down at the bar. The bottom third of the glass was intact and it was filling with his blood. He needed to wrap his palm, and fast. Needed to get out of there and away from Marilyn, because he was hurt, his hand was badly hurt, just like . . . just like . . .

"Why did you ask me about Nashua?" he said. The question excited her, brought her eyes alight.

"Tell me what you're thinking," she whispered. "*Please.*"

He didn't want to share. It wasn't a pleasant memory, after all. The old farmer, Howard, the truck exploding, and Hank, young, brave, reckless Hank, racing toward the burning truck while Marty stood flatfooted, a trapped observer, never able to even explain what spark had found what fuel source, a witness without answers, and the worst kind of coward.

"Go on," Marilyn whispered. "Say it, Marty. Say it!"

She was watching him the way a baseball fan watched the last hitter in the bottom of the ninth with two outs and two strikes, desperate for a miracle.

"My brother is a pilot," he told her, but his voice was unsteady, and her hope flickered but didn't fade. It was as if her baseball hero had missed the pitch and she'd almost given up until the ball drifted foul and now the batter could stand in there again.

"My brother is a pilot in the South Pacific, and he has seen the awesome power of atomic war," Marty said. "'Ethereal'—that was his word. That one stood out to me, because . . . "

"Because?"

"Well, because it wasn't one he'd normally use. It didn't sound like Hank."

He reached past her with his bleeding hand and grabbed her vodka soda, the cold glass wonderfully numbing on his wound, a pain that seared his palm the same way Hank's must have seared when he wrapped his hand—his brave, foolish hand—around that metal handle and yanked the truck door open in a futile effort to save a dead man, a man whose lips had already melted off his face, leaving white teeth grinning against blackened flesh.

Marty clutched the cold glass and looked in the mirror behind the bar, saw the reflection of the Bloomington town square outside, the one he'd visited all those months ago to see the Christmas lights. He closed his eyes and the image of the Bloomington square disappeared and Nashua was superimposed on his eyelids as if by a movie projector.

His eyes were still closed when he said, "My little brother died in Nashua when he was nine years old," in a voice that was his own but seemed to come from someplace impossibly far away, out of a tunnel of infinite blackness. Inside the blackness, an engine buzzed, the sound of a small plane, and somewhere beyond that, in deeper darkness, a monkey screamed.

Marty made it out of the bar before he vomited. He fell to his knees on the sidewalk, the sunbaked cement like Nevada sand under his hands. When he sat upright, he left a single, perfect handprint in blood on the concrete. Then Marilyn's palm was on the back of his neck, cool and comforting, and he heard her telling him it was okay, heard onlookers asking if she needed help, heard her dismiss them, heard it all but registered none of it, because the other sounds overwhelmed them: the exploding truck, the monkey's scream, and the relentless buzzing of a thousand small motors.

Marilyn took his face in both of her hands and turned his eyes up to hers.

"Let's get to my room," she said, and he knew better than to follow but he walked with her anyway.

AIRBORNE, EASTERN SEABOARD
OCTOBER 25, 2025

They blindfolded Charlie and Lawrence as soon as they were on the plane.

The B-52 was massive yet had a tight entrance. A hatch in the belly led to another vertical metal ladder, like making the last climb up into a fire tower. Bellamy had been tugging Charlie so roughly that she missed two of the rungs completely, feet flailing. Bellamy grabbed the strap of Lawrence's backpack, which Charlie was still wearing, and used the backpack to haul her up into the plane as if she were cargo. The airmen were barking at one another, debating where to put their hostages, but she didn't understand many of the options. One sounded like "wizo" and another was "the dummy bay" and Captain Hightower shot both of those down, but Charlie didn't hear what he chose instead. Then he was gone from view and Bellamy and Granville were shoving them through a series of ever-tightening corridors into what appeared to be the tail of the plane itself.

It was like being in a steel cavern, everything hard-edged, Charlie's elbows and shins smacking metal. For something that was so large from below, the interior was cramped, tighter than the stairwell of her old Brooklyn apartment. They pushed on so far that she thought they were about to run out of plane, and then Bellamy kicked her legs out from under her, upending her and dropping her to the hard deck.

"Hey!" Lawrence cried, and then he was down beside her, dropped even more unceremoniously. The pale man, Granville, re-appeared with an outstretched rag in his hands. Charlie tried to kick him, missed, and then the rag was around her head and her vision was gone. She had a moment of the strangest relief—she'd expected the rag was coming for her mouth, a gag—before the terror of the blindness set in. She started to scream, then stopped herself, bit down on the tip of her tongue. If she screamed, they *would* gag her.

She willed herself silent, waiting in the blackness.

There was commotion and clanging. Shouts that grew distant. Cold air and colder metal. The smell of old oil, searing her nostrils. Lawrence breathing heavily beside her.

Then thunder. A rolling boom of incredible sound that shook everything around them.

She thought of the jet that had flown by, the Tomcat, and was sure that it had returned—and fired and hit. The sound was that loud, the shuddering around them that violent.

Then she felt the plane moving forward in the blackness and re-alized that the sound was the B-52 itself. They were taxiing. Down a runway that had been closed for decades.

I am going to die, she thought. *Going to fly, going to die. My mother's voice told me not to fly, and now I am going to die, fly and die, fly and die, I am going to fly and—*

When they went airborne, she experienced it in a way she'd never felt on a commercial plane. The process was more abrupt and more vertical. She cried out despite herself, thought she heard an echo, only to realize it was Lawrence, reacting just as she had.

The liftoff was so jarring, she braced for impact, unsure of whether it would come courtesy of a missile fired from the Tomcat fighter plane or Spruce Hill itself, the new plane colliding with the wreckage of the old one, making sense of itself once more.

Nothing happened. And yet *everything* happened. The plane was loud and it was violent, the noise of the craft insistent, a ceaseless series of creaks, pops, and twangs, as if the metal were stretching out the kinks. She imagined pieces of the wings coming loose as the plane roared through the air, a trailing debris cloud, chunks spiraling to the earth. She imagined her body being sucked through the fuselage, falling, blasting a Charlie-shaped hole into someone's roof. She imagined death from the air in more forms than she'd have thought possible—and all of them felt plausible.

"Charlie." It was Lawrence, beside her, somewhere to her left.

"Yes."

"You . . . okay?"

"I think so," she said. "Not so sure."

"You're hurt?"

"No. I mean . . . I'm blindfolded on a fucking airplane that crashed sixty years ago, Lawrence. The situation isn't great is my point."

"Right."

"What are these guys, do you think? Ghosts? They're too real for ghosts. Their hands leave bruises, I can tell you that."

Perhaps most terrifying were their undeniable human forms. She could wrap her head around the idea of a spirit capable of slamming doors or bumping furniture around in an attic, but not of the dead who gripped you with warm hands, breathed stale breath in your face, had hair on their knuckles and stubble on their jaws. They were too real to be ghosts and yet they were too impossible to be human.

"They seem to think they're the crew from the plane wreck," Lawrence said.

"They sure do."

"Maybe Grandpa wasn't wrong. Maybe they really did pull survivors out of that plane. All these years, people thinking he's a crazy drunk, and then they show up . . . "

At the mention of Abe, Lawrence's voice wavered and finally faded out altogether.

"He'll be fine," Charlie said.

"No he won't."

"Yes he will. The Army or whoever that was has got him. They won't hurt him."

"You really think so?"

There was something needy and childlike in his voice. On any other day, Charlie would've teased him for it. Today, bouncing around in the bomb bay of an ancient airplane, she said, "I'm sure of it."

Lawrence didn't answer. She wanted to reach for him in the dark, give him a squeeze, a pat, something, but her hands were tied. She slid to the right, jeans rasping over rough metal, thumped against him, shoulder to shoulder. She didn't mind the contact. Strange how fast things could change. The idea of touching Lawrence Zimmer would've made her cringe just that morning and now she was grateful for it.

"You're not . . . bleeding or anything, are you?" Lawrence asked hesitantly. "That guy knocked you down pretty hard."

"Knocked you down harder. I'm okay. Skinned up, that's all. What about you?"

"My arm's bleeding a little," he said, and then rushed to add, "But not bad."

He seemed to be trying to convince himself. She turned toward him as if to check the wound, her eyelashes scraping the oily rag when she blinked, nothing but blackness returned for her efforts.

"Are you sure?"

"I'm sure. It would've been worse if I hadn't been wearing my jacket."

"That stupid lobster coat," Charlie said. "Of course it helped."

"He's a hard shell," Lawrence said, and the joke took Charlie by such surprise that she laughed despite herself, then he did, too, both of them a little too manic. Still, it felt good.

"Didn't help me with the gun," he said softly. "I had a chance and I screwed it up. Sorry."

"You had a chance to get us killed and you screwed that up," Charlie said. "I wouldn't complain about that."

A pause, then: "They seriously think they flew out, like, hours ago," Lawrence said. "It's all a shock to them, like they went through a time portal or something."

"I know. Did you hear them talking about the cloud?"

"I don't like that guy Granville," Lawrence said. "He seems a little crazy."

"I would, too, landing in another century."

"He's different," Lawrence insisted. "The one who accepted it the best was probably the pilot, Hightower. I mean, he was stunned, yeah, but he was coming around the curve, you know?"

"Yes," she said. Hightower had seemed to be coming around the curve. He asked the best questions and was most thoughtful with his answers, showing none of the hysteria of Bellamy and Granville.

"It felt like the Army was waiting on them," she said. "Like they knew it would be there."

"Maybe Grandpa was right," Lawrence said. "Maybe there is a reason they kept repaving that runway."

Charlie thought of all the videos she'd uploaded from Ash Point, all the jokes she'd made. It had been funny, to pretend to believe.

It was not funny to be on the plane.

BLOOMINGTON, INDIANA
SEPTEMBER 1962

Dr. Martin Hazelton had held it all together until Nevada, according to the file Marilyn Metzger showed him. In 1955 he was considered the foremost atmospheric scientist involved in the atomic program. There was debate over whether he was better suited to the potential of weather alteration, continuing with the team Irving Langmuir and Vincent Schaefer had assembled, or to the study of nuclear weapons.

The atomic side won. Dr. Hazelton was transferred out of China Lake and sent to the Nevada Test Site, including a place nicknamed "Doom Town." Marty remembered it well.

What he did not remember so well—or at all until he read of it—was the three-month hospital stay that had followed. There were doctor's notes, photographs, and transcripts of interviews. He wanted to deny them, to look up at Marilyn and call it all a fraud, but he knew better. In his heart, he had always known. He resolved to put the experience out of his mind, and, once resolute, Marty Hazelton's mind was a formidable force.

Not an impenetrable one, though. There were glimmers and flickers, like a recalled nightmare. He didn't dwell on them as he turned the pages. What he wanted was a diagnosis. What he wanted was the science.

Included in the file was a letter from a Doom Town colleague named Dr. Kristof Golden. In May of 1955 he wrote:

Dr. Hazelton has demonstrated a concerning tendency to speak of his brother. His only brother died as a young child, yet Dr. Hazelton now speaks of Hank frequently and in the present tense. Hank, he says, is an Air Force pilot. He speaks of Hank's impetuousness and courage with equal measures of scorn and envy.

The first reference to Hank came when we toured the replica town site in Yucca Flat on the day the mannequins went in. The town was an intricate, eerily lifelike re-creation, with full-sized homes, vehicles, streets, and traffic lights. Everything about the place was compelling and surreal. I took Dr. Hazelton's silence on our first tour as a simple reflection of this experience. As the tour progressed, however, he came increasingly distanced, refusing to engage. In one of the homes, which housed a family of nine and had been staged to create a classic American-village scenario, there was a mannequin of a boy sitting on a porch swing. He was dressed in trousers and a denim shirt and had a blond crewcut and blue eyes. Dr. Hazelton stared at the mannequin for a long time. At last, he said that the boy had an uncanny similarity to his little brother.

We were on our way out of the village when he told me he'd forgotten a notepad and abruptly walked back down the empty street. I followed just far enough to see that he returned to the mannequin of the boy on the porch swing, knelt beside him, and

*appeared to speak to the dummy. I was unsettled by his behavior,
yet if the mannequin was such a compelling replica of his
deceased brother, one could understand Dr. Hazelton's emotional
response.*

*He seemed well the next day, when we launched a pair of
helium-filled Kytoon balloons to obtain weather data. This
exercise was conducted minutes before the first controlled nuclear
detonation. Dr. Hazelton was focused and in total command. He
correctly anticipated a shift in prevailing winds that others did
not. In his prime, Dr. Hazelton was the finest in his field.*

*Prior to testing, he seemed every bit himself. Following
the detonation, which we observed from a shielded tower at a
safe distance, he was more somber. He quoted Bainbridge and
Oppenheimer's remarks from the Trinity test, but I thought little
of that. He demonstrated genuine awe at the display of light
that came from the test itself. This is not unusual; I would have
less trust in a man who did not display awe in the face of such
power.*

*We all deferred to him, as it was known that he had been
the only civilian scientist aboard the Red Flight squadron that
collected samples from the Ivy Mike detonations, and that Red
Flight experienced tragic losses. Dr. Hazelton's familiarity with
the thermonuclear weapons was more personal than most.*

*We later joined the crews that surveyed the resulting
damage of the detonation, which was a grim affair. Crews were
removing the mannequins as if they were corpses, wrapping
them in blankets and placing them on stretchers. The exercise
was a designed study of disaster response. Dr. Hazelton wished
to return to the house where the mannequin that resembled
his brother had been seated on the porch swing. There was
nothing left of the house itself but rubble. Of the "family" of*

nine, six were deemed dead, with the three in a basement shelter estimated as survivors. Dr. Hazelton was intensely curious about this estimation, inquiring about the radioactive cloud and the permeability of the bunker's materials.

At this point, Dr. Hazelton departed in search of the mannequin from the porch swing. He found the remains of the boy's replica approximately 7,000 feet from the house. Both legs and one arm were missing, and the left side of the face was charred beyond recognition. Dr. Hazelton joined crew members in wrapping the mannequin's remains in a blanket and placing it onto a gurney. I was struck by the tenderness with which he undertook the task. I recall turning away from the scene at one moment because it felt utterly intimate.

As we left the scene, he paused, then announced that he wanted to locate the left arm of the mannequin from the porch swing. This was met with some consternation, and I pulled a few men aside to explain that Dr. Hazelton was struck by the mannequin's resemblance to his own deceased brother. Dr. Hazelton searched the debris field, and when he returned, he smiled as if all were well and suggested we have a drink.

This was noteworthy insofar as I had never seen Dr. Hazelton consume alcohol. I did join him for a drink that afternoon—he had several whiskeys, neat—and while our conversation began on the affairs of the day, he soon pivoted to his brother. I listened with growing concern as he told me about "Hank" and his service in WWII and current deployment in a B-52.

The following morning, I returned to our research facility to discover that Dr. Hazelton had launched five additional Kytoon balloons overnight. These launches were unplanned. When I inquired as to what testing instruments he'd launched, his response was nonchalant.

"Letters to my brother. I think they'll make it through. You don't, do you?"

I admitted that I found it unlikely that any letters attached to the Kytoon balloons would reach his brother in Hawaii, and he smiled as if that answer genuinely pleased him, as if he knew better than me.

At 0900 he came to my office and suggested we go for a drink. When I observed the early time and declined, he laughed and said his brother had warned him about men like me, "stuffed shirts" as he put it, and then left the building. I expressed my concern to Dr. Brian Keene, at which point I confirmed that Dr. Hazelton has no surviving siblings. Dr. Keene urged me to speak to the site commander, which led to this request for the written record.

Marty finished the letter and looked up at Marilyn and neither of them spoke. He thought that he should challenge her. She was a spy. They'd told him so. Why on earth would he believe this file?

Because you remember it, he thought.

Yes. He did. That perfect replica of the perfect American town, quaint, like a full-scale model train set. He remembered the mannequin on the swing. The crew cut and the blue eyes. He'd gotten lost in the precision of the paint, how lifelike it was, and somewhere along the line he'd started to wonder what might've become of his brother in an alternate world, one where they never went to Nashua to see the lights.

He'd have been a hero. No doubt about that. Died a hero as a child, so he'd have been a hero as a man. A pilot, maybe. He loved the clouds.

Out there in the high heat of the Nevada day, picking his way through an imaginary town, Marty's mind had begun to wander and, it seemed, never made it all the way back. He remembered the drinking. He remembered, vaguely, talking of his brother, except he hadn't intended to speak of him in the present tense. It was a hypothetical Hank, that was all. But maybe he didn't clarify that for Kristoff Golden. Marty's hypotheticals always required faith that they might work. He'd never seen the point in testing with the expectation of failure. You needed to *commit*. He was the best at that. Ask anyone who'd ever worked with him.

He'd gone back to the porch to put his father's wristwatch on the mannequin's left wrist. His brother had loved that watch. His brother would have received it if he'd outlived their father, but that hadn't come to pass. They died on the same night, miles apart, one in a Massachusetts hospital, one on a Nashua street. Hank's life ended in childhood: a child who'd raced to help a stranger in a burning truck while his older brother watched it all fearfully from the sidewalk, never able to explain what, exactly, had even happened.

A bang, a flash of light, an eternal loss.

Why?

No answers for that.

For some silly reason, out there in Nevada, Marty had decided to pass the watch along to a dummy. It was a sentimental gesture, the kind he wasn't particularly skilled in making.

Then came the blast.

He remembered that. None who saw it would ever forget it, as Bainbridge had said. Awesome power and ethereal light. A tremor in the soul.

The detonation had blown the dummy more than a mile from the porch, but Marty recovered the missing left arm. And the watch. Unharmed. *How?*

"Are you all right?" Marilyn Metzger asked.

Based on these reports, no, he wanted to retort, but all he said was "I'd like to keep reading."

"Fine."

He read on. He'd been in a psychiatric hospital in California two days after his "break with reality" in Nevada, and he'd remained there for twenty months. He remembered the grounds, the smell of the orange trees, the dusky rose light at sunset. The quiet. A respite from the sun-seared testing grounds of Nevada and their catastrophic sounds. The list of experimental medications they gave him was daunting—beginning but not ending with lithium. The electroshock therapy sessions went on for months.

The patient was agreeable to them, provided he was allowed to wear his wristwatch. There had been some debate over the risks of that—might it sear his skin?—but the leather-banded watch did no harm.

The notes of a psychiatrist named Millar compromised much of the file.

"Dr. Hazelton's delusions about his brother persist, but they do not seem to cloud his understanding of any other facet of reality," Dr. Millar wrote in June of 1956.

He continues to study and work. His problem-solving skills remain exceptional. He reads and retains the daily news. His memory for his own life is keen and accurate, with the notable exceptions of his brother's death and the insistent, unwavering notion of his brother's current life as a B-52 pilot. He will not yield on this, and yet he has not demonstrated the slightest inclination to engage in fiction on other topics. In this regard, he is a remarkable patient, unique in my experience, his delusions confined to a single, elaborate, point of life. His intellectual rigor is steadfast. Unfortunately, he brings the same rigor to the delusion.

Amid the doctor's notes came a curt request from Admiral Ralph H. Cutting suggesting that if Dr. Hazelton *could* work, he *should* work.

The psychiatrist pushed back on this, cautioning that it was far too early to know whether the patient would experience further slips from reality and at what cost.

In 1957, the Soviets conducted sixteen nuclear tests, and it was decided that Dr. Hazelton would return to work in carefully monitored conditions on the grounds of the naval installation at Crane. Admiral Ralph H. Cutting took accountability and assured Dr. Millar that he would maintain close supervision of Hazelton.

"We are engaged in a race for this nation's salvation and survival," the admiral wrote. "Dr. Hazelton has both the capacity and desire to aid his country. All necessary protocols for his health will be observed. His fantastic beliefs about his brother are irrelevant to his capacity for work."

Millar pushed back, requesting an additional six months. He was denied.

"Eccentric behaviors are a hallmark of great mathematicians," Admiral Cutting responded. "Dr. Hazelton's fantasy about his brother harms no one, and it may be indulged in the interest of national security. We cannot waste him."

His case manager was to be a woman Cutting trusted immensely, Marilyn Metzger, and there would be a psychiatrist on-site at Crane, Dr. Wyatt Dixon, to provide personal observation.

In September of 1957, Marty flew to Indiana. There, his life and work habits were the picture of routine. Rigor, to use Millar's term. Wyatt Dixon checked in regularly, masquerading as a colleague who would be present as frequently or infrequently as desired. Marty preferred to work in solitude. He was permitted full access to the daily news and free movement inside and outside of the base—though he rarely left—but he was denied access to classified materials regarding the continued testing of atomic weapons. What he knew of them was what the public knew of them.

Admiral Ralph H. Cutting, Office of Naval Research, and Director of Central Intelligence John McCone both agreed that if anyone might conceive an actionable method for shielding nuclear bombers from an atmospheric atomic blast, it was Dr. Martin Hazelton.

———————

At length, Marty closed the file and placed it on the table beside the chair. For a long moment it was silent.

"I should not be surprised that they lied to you about me," Marilyn said. "But it's infuriating nevertheless. Because *they* are the lie, just like me. The only difference is . . . "

She stopped, inclined her head slightly, and then shook it.

"I suppose there is no difference. I felt more for you than the others did, that's all. But that's a selfish judgment, isn't it? So much bias. Perhaps they're right to warn you away from me."

Marty couldn't look at her when he said, "Is the story about your fiancé true? Was he really on Flight 19?"

"Yes," she said. "Yes, that is true. And that's why . . . " She stopped, smoothed her dress, swallowed. "I knew better than to sit down and speak with you directly, of course. That wasn't my instruction. That is, no doubt, why there's concern about me now. I was merely to oversee and make sure there were no problems. But the more I read about you, the more I wanted to meet you."

"Why?" Still not looking at her.

"Because you wrote letters to the dead and sent them into the sky. Fifteen years ago, on a Florida beach, I did the same silly damn thing, a note tied to a balloon string, and sent to ride the wind, and I wanted so badly to nurse the hope that there was a chance. I wasn't as good at hoping as you were. I wanted your belief in the impossible. Just a taste of it."

He finally looked at her. She was sitting with perfect posture, hands folded in her lap, and her voice was so steady, he was almost surprised to see the tears on her cheeks.

"They're going to make you test Project Kingsolver," she said. "You know that, surely."

"Maybe not. Maybe they'll hand the whole project off to someone else." He reached out and tapped the file. "Because of that." He tapped his head with the same finger. "Because of this."

"It has to be you. Because no one else can explain how it's done."

"Neither can I," he said, and he felt the weight of the watch on his wrist like a shackle. The watch was a delusion, surely. Were the planes too? How much had he invented?

"It works?" he asked her, tentative. "It really works?"

"What does?"

"My model planes. They go out, and they vanish, and they come back? That's not a . . . " He wet his lips, forced a smile, and tapped his head again.

"No," she said. "It's not imagined, Marty. Not a delusion. It's very real."

Silence. He looked at the file.

"Will you be in trouble for this? Fired, court-martialed, worse?"

Her laugh was cold and humorless. "I'll be just fine. Supposing that whoever visited today actually *did* come from Hoover's office and wasn't cooked up entirely by your little security chief at Crane?" She waved a dismissive hand. "Cutting's office has rank. The Bureau might not feel that way, but what the Pentagon wants, the Pentagon will get. And right now? They want that trick with the plane to work."

"No matter what warped mind conceived of it," Marty said, and Marilyn's face turned grim, and she did not answer.

"Why did you push me?" he asked. "The book by Vonnegut's kid brother, the questions about Nashua. You could have just handed me the file."

"No," she said. "That would have been cruel. I thought if you got there alone . . . less cruel, certainly."

"But it wasn't alone. You pushed me along."

"Cloud seeding," she said, and, damn it all, he smiled, because it was the perfect answer.

"Did you think I would remember something about Flight 19?"

She was quiet for a long time before she said, "I had my fantasies. My letters tied to balloons."

He nodded. "I'm sorry."

She nodded too. Said nothing.

After a while he said, "Will they let me see you again, or will they prevent that?"

"Do you *want* to see me again?"

"Yes."

"Why? A liar like me? A fraud like me?"

"Kindred spirits," he said, and maybe she smiled at that. He wasn't sure.

"I can't imagine anybody will stop me from seeing you," she said. "Certainly, it won't be Dwight Fremont. If they know I've spoken to you, fine, I'll defend that. If they know . . . "

Her eyes flicked toward the bed, a fast, guilty glance, and then she said, "They don't know anything else."

He wasn't so sure.

"Ralph is coming to see you himself soon," she said, redirecting.

"Ralph?"

"Admiral Cutting. He'll want to watch you. To see how you hold up. Whether you break."

"And if I don't?"

"Then it's on to Ash Point, Maine. An airfield. Your work will be tested with new scope and scale. They will shield a storm cloud and fly a real plane into it."

"With a real pilot?"

"Yes."

Marty ran a hand over his jaw. His mouth was dry, his throat burning from booze and vomit. He was sober: everything he'd gotten down had come back up in a hurry. Outside, the sun was setting over Bloomington, the town tinted with ruby light.

"Who knows I'm crazy?"

"You're not—"

"Who knows I was institutionalized?"

"Enough people, I suppose. But not many. As your work took on more significance, your personal history was . . . diminished."

He almost laughed. "I can imagine."

His intellectual rigor is steadfast. Unfortunately, he brings the same rigor to the delusion.

"Why did you show me this?" Marty asked, gesturing at the classified file.

"So you can make the right decision. I wouldn't ask you to take it on faith. There's a video reel, too, if you care to watch it. Shock therapy sessions."

He wasn't sure if he wanted to watch that.

"What's the right decision, in your mind?"

"I don't know. But I do know that it isn't right to ask you to proceed still believing your brother is out there in his B-52."

Marty felt as if he had crossed a bridge without intending to, and now the bridge had collapsed behind him and there was no path back, only the one ahead.

"When we were boys," he said, "Hank believed I knew everything. His role was the questioner, and my role . . . my role was to provide answers."

And protection, he thought but did not say.

"He had a million questions, and back then I felt as if I had a million answers. What I didn't know, I could learn. I loved teaching him. Once he was gone, I kept the conversations going in my mind. When I heard a question, it was so easy to hear it in his voice. And then I'd set out to find the answer. For a long time I was clear on the situation."

He thought of Doom Town, the dummies awaiting a flash-fire extinction.

"I was always better with the 'How?' questions than the 'Why?' questions."

He remembered the observation tower shuddering beneath the force of the atomic test in Nevada. Remembered the impossible ball of light that had risen over the Pacific. Yes, it was the "Why?" questions that had stumped him in the end. He closed his eyes but the images didn't cease. He saw his brother reaching for a burning truck. He saw a cloud of smoke and flame. His own feet, motionless on the sidewalk. A plastic arm, charred, with a ticking watch still clasped around it.

We cannot waste him, Cutting had written of Marty Hazelton. Marty wondered what the admiral might've written of Hank.

"I never moved, that night in Nashua. My brother was so young, and foolish, and brave. The truck started to burn, and he went toward it like he'd heard a starter's pistol. Faster than any of the men. Even the ones who did move."

He stood and put on his hat. In the dusk, Marilyn Metzger wiped at her eyes. When he extended his hand and said, "Thank you," it took her a moment to reach back for him, and when their hands met, her fingers were damp with tears.

He walked to the door and left the hotel and went out into the night.

AIRBORNE, EASTERN SEABOARD
OCTOBER 25, 2025

Sitting beside Lawrence Zimmer in the shuddering steel coffin that had once been the pride of America's military, Charlie stared into the blackness of her blindfold and thought about her captors.

"I wonder what their rules are," she said. "Are they ghosts or what? Can they die? The plane is real." She thumped the metal with her heel, a dull echo clanging back at her. "It's pretty shitty, in fact. There's nothing J. J. Abrams about this thing. That may be a problem."

"What do you mean?"

"If the ordinary rules apply, then it will run out of fuel at some point. Right?"

"I don't think it uses fuel," Lawrence said. "It didn't stay in the air sixty-three years on a tank of gas."

"Well, I can smell the fuel. It's real!"

He went quiet again, and she knew he was smelling the oil and jet fuel and wondering if she was right and what that might mean.

"They can stay up a long time," he said.

"Evidently."

"I mean, in the real world. If the rules apply, like you said. They can fly all the way to Russia without refueling."

"That's good news?" She was thinking back on the scene at the Ash Point airstrip, trying to make sense of the chaos. In the moment, it had been all terror and reaction, logic lost to emotions. Now, in the cold dark, she had time to think.

"I wonder why the Air Force didn't use the jet again? If they knew this plane was . . . I don't know, coming back or whatever you want to call it—and clearly they did, because they were waiting for it—then why didn't they keep the fighter plane, or bring helicopters, or the fucking Navy, whatever? If they didn't want it to take off, they could have kept it on the ground."

Lawrence didn't answer.

"They're scared of it," Charlie said softly.

"So am I," Lawrence said.

"Yeah. But maybe it's good news."

"How is that possibly good news?"

"It means they won't shoot us out of the sky."

Silence again.

"So it's up to Hightower, you think? He can do what he wants?"

"I don't know. But it seems like they let him do this much. I mean, they could have blown it up. They could have easily killed all those guys on the runway. They were close enough to shoot, and they didn't."

"Maybe they don't die," Lawrence said. "They sure don't seem to age."

Good point. Charlie remembered the pictures of the crew that Abe had found for his museum. The men looked exactly the same as they had in 1962. Well, except for the eyes. Those too-bright, wrong-kind-of-bright eyes.

"Can you use your hands if we sit back-to-back?" she asked.

"Enough to untie me? I don't think I could do it." She could flex her fingers but, with her wrists crossed and tied, she didn't feel dexterous enough to work a knot.

"I bet I could do the zipper," Lawrence said.

"Pardon?"

"On the backpack! My knife is in there."

"Oh." She realized, for the first time, what else was in there: the strange old watch that seemed to drink in the daylight, and the note with its formula for survival. *Fire nightshade.*

"Think you can do it?" she asked, shifting closer. She felt him stretch, testing.

"I can use my fingers okay. I think I could open the pack, yeah. I don't know about using the knife, though. I'd be afraid to cut you."

"We've got bigger things to worry about than cuts."

The statement was braver than she felt, though. The idea of him sawing away so close to her wrists was frightening. Then again . . . she was blindfolded and riding a ghost plane.

"Okay," Charlie said. "Let's dance. Though you don't look like you'd be much of a dancer."

"I'm not bad."

"I'd like to hear a witness vouch for that, but I'll have to trust you. I'm going to turn toward my left, you turn toward your right, and then just scoot back."

She turned away from him, he from her, and then she braced her heels on the shivering steel floor of the plane and prepared to slide backward. Before she could begin, he slammed into her.

"Ouch!"

"Sorry! I should've said on three."

"I knew you couldn't dance." Charlie rolled her neck, shifted, and leaned forward, clearing space for him to reach for the pack. "Okay, words I never thought I'd say, but see if you can find the zipper."

She heard a rustle as he adjusted behind her, then felt his hands pass by hers. A moment later, his searching fingers pressed hard against her butt.

"A miss low," she said as he jerked his hand back as if he'd touched a live wire.

"Sorry!"

"The pack will be located *above* my ass, Zimmer. That's why it's called a *back*pack. It rests on the back. Now try again, and if you squeeze my boob, that's the *front*, and you've overshot."

He reached again, more tentatively, and his fingers found her arm, then moved up to the pack. She felt the straps tug at her shoulders as he clawed at the bag, searching.

"Got the zipper," he whispered, and Charlie thought that she would never have been able to conceive of a day when this was good news, but here she was.

"Tremendous. Now use it."

She wanted him to find the knife, but she wasn't sure that the watch wasn't more important.

Survival—Find storm cloud, fire nightshade, set watch backward and add voltage. You will catch up.

Who had written it, and what did it mean?

INDIANA AND MAINE
AUTUMN 1962

Back at Crane, there was no more talk of a Soviet spy.

Marty kept to his routine but added a new, private project: deciphering his own mind. He wrote memories in his notebooks, working on recall—and reality.

The memories were spotty. There were long, dark gaps. Lithium and electroshock therapy hadn't brought him back but pushed him further away. His recollection of the hospital in California was as a military base, but there had been no troops. He remembered the orange groves and the solitude and spending an enormous amount of time locked in his room. In his mind, he had always turned the lock.

He thought.

Marilyn had sent him back to Crane with a video reel. He waited three weeks before he watched it, not sure he wanted to see its contents. Then he watched it every night for a week. It was a video of his electroshock therapy sessions. He was both thinner and tanner in those days; they'd let him have plenty of sunlight. He looked good, right up until the electrodes went on his head.

In each session he was formal and cordial. In each session he requested his watch, explaining that it helped to calm him.

They let him have it.

During the treatments, his body went rigid and danced at the edge of convulsion, voltage pounding his brain. He was given up to 420 volts. A brain cell typically operated with less than one half of a volt.

Before and after the treatments, he would look at his watch.

He wondered if his faith in the watch was a delusion, no different than the fantasy of his pilot brother. If the watch had no power, though, then other scientists would have matched him by now. They had his materials—the Nashua Nightshade, that blend of graphite and silver iodide, so carefully calibrated—and if that was all they needed, they'd have caught up to him swiftly. It had taken centuries to discover the atom and then, even with the greatest minds in the world, from Marie Curie to Niels Bohr, it had taken decades to demonstrate nuclear fission, or what civilians called "splitting the atom."

Once that had been done, though? Within weeks of the discovery of fission in Germany, Oppenheimer had published the possibility of the chain reactions that became the atomic bomb. In a mere eight months of work on the Manhattan Project, they'd built the thing. Atomic weapons had moved the way Hemingway had described bankruptcy: slowly, then all at once.

Marty thought other scientists could catch up to him with the vanishing act of the planes, but how useful was that if you couldn't call them back? Vanishing them was simply a cleaner bomb—and a more expensive one, limited in battlefield utility. The return of the planes was altogether different.

Supernatural.

Could he believe such a thing? Well. His capacity for belief seemed to ebb and flow more than he'd ever known. The same man who demanded equations for everything had evidently written messages to the dead and sent them heavenward on balloons.

He had more layers than he knew.

He read through all his old notebooks. In the twenty months after Doom Town, he'd become obsessed with studying inertia, an irony that felt almost too rich to believe. Nashua. His inertia. His baby brother burning. The trip home to his grieving mother. Her husband was dead and here came Martin with the news that her youngest child was too. He remembered her face, the way she'd tried to hide the blame. The way she'd failed. She could barely look at him when she gave him his father's watch.

Back to prep school, then off to college. Libraries and laboratories. Never enough books. Never enough questions, problems, things that could be solved. He lived to solve things. Give him a problem, watch him solve it, give him another, please, God, give him another, because if he went too long in his own head . . .

No, he did not question Marilyn Metzger's file. It was, he could almost hear himself telling young Hank Hazelton, a very natural progression. Hank's voice had been useful, offering the questions, those relentless questions. Hank was the voice inside Marty's head that posited possibilities, that demanded answers.

Add enough external pressure, then watch the resulting implosion.

What he found in his own notebooks included an account of the wristwatch that was eerily similar to the version he'd attributed to his brother. Red Flight over Elugelab, the plane rocked by a sudden wave of intense heat. A tremendous mushroom cloud rose more than 100,000 feet into the air, a power so awful that Marty wished he'd never beheld it, and away went the island, replaced by a mile-wide crater where once thousands of years of life had existed. Fish carcasses floated, their skin burned crisp. Singed birds fell to the sea. The mushroom head of the cloud spread out for nearly a hundred miles.

Into the cloud, Red Flight had flown with filters mounted on the wings, off to sample the excitement of what humanity had wrought on the earth. Two of the three made it back. Marty had been on one.

Later, waiting on the plane to be decontaminated, he wrote in his journal of "an ethereal light, an awesome power, the visual incarnate of an intersecting burden between human knowledge and human nature that is hard to reconcile as anything other than the point of no return."

Then he'd described his watch, the hands whirling like mad, and promised to explore the possible causes.

If he'd ever done so, there was no record of it. Not until he'd emerged from the hospital and been assigned to his isolated lab at Crane had he returned to study the watch—and then he'd credited the idea to his dead brother.

There was one very interesting element of the notebook from the Ivy Mike test, although it wouldn't have stood out to anyone other than Marty. The page he'd filled before takeoff was smeared with thick smudges of black powder, as if someone had rubbed the paper with a piece of charcoal.

He looked at that page and recalled the discovery of Nashua Nightshade here at Crane. The idle, nervous scrape, scrape, scrape at the pencil with his thumbnail. His curiosity over graphite, with its unusual electrical response, capable of conducting the current or insulating against it.

He didn't recall preparing the watch, but he was, like many a scientist, given to absent-minded stretches. He also was prone to remembering his mother's cold caution when she handed him his father's watch after the funeral: "Don't let anything happen to it, Martin."

How many times she'd given him similar instructions about Hank.

Now, he looked at those smudges of charcoal-colored dust in the pages of his Ivy Mike journal, then read and reread his own words:

I can't say when it started, because I was distracted by the incredible display of light. But at some point, I looked at my wrist and saw the hands were spinning, hour and minute, slow and steady, as if I were manually adjusting the time. Rolling it forward. This went on for maybe three or four minutes, according to the onboard clock, which never changed. Then it simply stopped, and the thing started ticking away, reliable as ever. Now we are on the ground again and I have had the chance to look it over. The mechanism is sound. I reset the time without trouble. Nevertheless, the interaction between the device and the atmospheric disruption, one with effects we cannot yet begin to quantify, is worth consideration and further study. I shall turn to it in time.

It had taken him a decade and one mental breakdown, but he had.

The end of summer at Crane passed quickly. Dwight Fremont avoided him as if he'd heard they were testing Marty with new viruses. Marty read the newspaper each morning, rewrote the events at night, then read the paper again, testing his memory.

The Soviets had agreed to provide military assistance to Cuba. The White House was not a fan of that. On September 2, all nonmilitary air travel in the United States and Canada was grounded for five hours for an exercise called Sky Shield III, clearing airspace from the Arctic Circle to Mexico as the Americans tested their defense capacity against incoming bombers. Marty wondered what they were really getting ready for. He had some ideas. Ash Point waited.

Also on September 2, William R. Blair died. Not many people took notice. Blair had launched the first radio-equipped weather balloon before going on to develop a little thing called radar. His name was in the paper one day, gone the next. Time moved on. People changed the world, left it, and were promptly forgotten.

President John F. Kennedy visited Texas, where he promised to put a man on the moon. The Soviets warned the Americans not to attack Cuba. NASA announced it would launch a satellite to test the effects of radiation in space.

He tried to write a letter to his dead brother once more.

Hank—

Imagine that our fictional dialogue was something my mind needed to protect in order to think clearly. Imagine that the story about your experience in the skies above Christmas Island was one that I needed to arrive at a conclusion that otherwise eluded my conscious mind. I was never good with stories. I wanted real things, clear math. I envied Einstein's imagination the most. His math made sense; his questions did not. Perhaps I set out to find a way toward that level of imagination, the necessary appreciation for mystery.

The letter felt stilted, forced, an exercise in introspection. He burned it. Hank was gone from him now—again—and it was dangerous to invite him back in.

One week later, a telegram arrived from Ralph H. Cutting's office, saying that Dr. Martin Hazelton's "presence is requested immediately at Naval Air Station Ash Point for advanced testing of your exciting protocols."

Marilyn was among the team members waiting on Marty. He greeted her warmly, making no pretense of distrust, and watched the others take this in. There were nine men and two women, including Marilyn, on the team—and there were three sentries for each of them, providing a round-the-clock deployment of a dozen active guards who never spoke to the scientists. The other woman was a petite, gray-haired, dark-eyed scientist named Iris Stoka who spoke with a faint Eastern European accent. German, Austrian? Marty remembered Fuchs, the man who'd smuggled the Manhattan Project details to the Soviets with a zealot's conviction that it was the best way to defeat the Nazis. It was unfair to doubt Iris, but this was autumn of 1962, the season of distrust, wariness worn like perfume.

Iris Stoka represented a new Department of Defense outfit called ARPA—the Advanced Research Projects Agency—which had been established four years earlier in response to the Soviet launch of Sputnik 1. Additional team members came from the RAND Corporation and Grumman. This was the highest ranks of the top secret Skunk Works teams, men who knew every secret dream of the United States military, let alone every secret reality. Marty knew they'd likely all been briefed on his background, informed about those lost years in California, about the troubles in Doom Town. Direct eye contact was uncommon, and yet, whenever he looked around, he seemed to catch someone staring.

The base was under the command of Admiral Ralph H. Cutting, Office of Naval Research, a veteran of World War II and Korea. Cutting was around sixty, with the lean build of a man who hadn't missed morning calisthenics in decades and a face so clean-cut, it looked as if he shaved with a straight razor three times daily.

Ash Point in autumn was perfect, the hills lit with fire-colored maples and golden birches, the sea sapphire beyond, and the only interruption of the beauty of the isolated peninsula was 8,000 feet of tarmac and a cluster of buildings. The first Nightshade test there used a sixteen-foot-long Grumman test plane, which, according to Marty's math, was probably the outer limit of what he could vanish in a synthetic cloud. Anything larger would require the assistance of Mother Nature—or an atomic bomb.

The Ball watch ticked along on his wrist while the Grumman was started: no batteries anymore; they were cooking with gas now, the plane loaded with testing instruments. Inside the radar station, operators sent out the radio signals that Marty had assured them would call the plane back when desired. They might as well have been shooting squirt guns into the sky.

The big generators clattered to life and filled the sky with a smoke-colored cloud, resembling a thick fogbank. The electrical charge was added by transformers the size of boxcars, with towering poles and arcing current. It was all terribly expensive.

Marty looked out to the forested hills that were slowly vanishing behind the smoke cloud as the generators roared and the Grumman's prop spun. He remembered again the words of Kenneth Bainbridge after witnessing the Trinity test of the atomic bomb: "No one who saw it could forget it, a foul and awesome display" and "Now we are all sons of bitches."

And, of course, there was Oppenheimer's reaction, his mind called to the old Hindu scripture: "Now I am become Death, the destroyer of worlds."

There had been a moment, however brief, when Marty Hazelton had believed the lasting lessons of the atomic bomb might extend for as long as a century. Not forever—he was too dedicated a student of human history to believe that—but a long time. A generation, anyhow. Maybe two.

And yet here they stood, so eager to test the next deadly toy, one they understood far less than the bomb. It had been a mere seventeen years since Trinity. A blink, a breath.

"Let's get to it," Admiral Cutting said, brushing at his ribbon-adorned chest.

Let's get to it. Those were the words with which they'd proceed to change the world?

"'Have holy curiosity,'" Marty said.

The admiral frowned. "Excuse me?"

"Albert Einstein said that."

"Einstein is dead," Admiral Ralph H. Cutting said.

Maybe that is just the right phrase for the moment, Marty thought. *Cutting came through after all.* "Einstein is dead." *Indeed, he is.*

And perhaps holy curiosity had gone with him.

"Okay, then," Marty said. "Let's get to it."

The plane went up, and it went missing.

Nobody's eyes were on him when he adjusted his watch.

Six minutes later, Marty called for a change in radio frequency from the boys in the radar station. A new signal was beamed out of the concrete bunkers of Ash Point and into the sky. Onlookers watched, their held breaths obvious. Marty, his own breathing steady, counted down the seconds with practiced calm.

The Grumman reappeared with a scream.

Admiral Cutting was a different man after witnessing his first live test. Almost immediately, he asked the team meteorologist about the possibility for the next cloud with lightning, one that could work for a real plane.

"We can do it," he said with unconcealed enthusiasm. "*We can actually do it.*"

Marty heard him say "we" and thought, *You and the French mouse in your pocket. There's no "we" here. I can do it, you son of a bitch, me and only me.*

He said nothing. Looked at the weather forecasts. Clear days ahead. Cutting grumbled that they should've been in Florida, where the storms were reliable. Everyone knew damn well why they weren't, though. Florida was awfully close to Cuba. Also, Ash Point had been chosen for a reason. Loring Air Force Base was not far away, and it was home to nuclear-armed B-52s that could fly all the way to Moscow.

"It has to be perfect," Marty said. "I need lightning, and I need a cold cloud."

Iris, of ARPA, rarely spoke during the group meetings, so Marty was surprised when she said, "He's correct."

She thought she understood the process. Maybe even thought she could replicate it. She'd shown great interest in the radio signals, speaking frequently about Marty's last-minute changes to what he called "the return code"—but the signals were useless.

Weeks passed. The Indian summer days drifted on. In Cuba, tensions rose. With each update, Admiral Cutting seemed to add a layer of knotted muscle to his jaw. He stared at the cobalt sky like a man on a life raft lost at sea, desperate for rain.

Marty and Marilyn spoke casually in front of the group, and not at all outside of it. They shared a cigarette break once, and he touched her hand while providing her the light, but that was their only physical contact. While they smoked, he said, "How am I holding up, Miss Metzger?" staying formal, because he knew there had to be listening devices everywhere at Ash Point.

She took a long moment before answering.

"Your family would be proud," she said. "Written any letters?"

"No," he said, and blew smoke. "There's nobody left to read of my exploits, even if I could get word off this base."

He said it with a smile, but her eyes told him, *Good, good, very good.*

In Cuba, spy planes took pictures of suspected missile sites. In Maine, the Ash Point team built artificial clouds and vanished planes, then brought them back. They shared numbers, photographs, wild ideas, desperate for an explanation. Marty was amused by their theories. He was less amused by how hungry Cutting looked, waiting for the right storm.

He found that hunger troubling. Then again, he found most things troubling these days.

On the first week of October, while U.S. marshals escorted James Meredith into his first class—colonial history—at the University of Mississippi and the U.S. Air Force explained to the public that the nuclear testing above Christmas Island in Operation Dominic had created an artificial radiation belt that threatened the safety of astronauts on the pending Gemini missions, the sky above Ash Point was a relentless, brilliant blue. Down below, the team was dismayed. They wanted a cold black cloud so they could test the limits of what Dr. Hazelton had discovered—and weaponize it.

The meteorologist, Rosson, a man from Georgia who pored over the forecasts by the hour, reported good news: there was a depression off the Carolinas that appeared likely to push northwest, meeting the cold waters of the Gulf of Maine and creating the possibility of violent weather. It was five days away, maybe six.

The pressure system dissipated over Cape Cod, and—short of a single, lead-gray day and a light shower—Ash Point remained bucolic.

They vanished another Grumman test model. Iris Stoka sat at her drafting table, staring at the unexplainable reality before her. One day she called Marty over.

"You will shield the cloud with generators mounted on a plane," she said.

"Yes," Marty said.

"And then fly the next one into the shielded cloud."

"Correct." He wasn't sure where she was going with this, because she understood the process better than anyone.

"How long do you think the power of the shielded cloud lingers?"

"I don't know yet."

She nodded, her eyes distant.

"Imagine," she said, "if the same plane that shielded the cloud could reenter it." She sketched a half oval, indicating the 180-degree change of course she envisioned for the aircraft.

Marty saw the point. "It would be more efficient. Less risk all around; less cost."

"So much more than that!" she said. "It could *leap*. Vanish, return, vanish. If the partner were not required, it could leap through time again and again."

She sketched a line that seemed to hop, hop, hop across the blueprint.

Listening, Ralph Cutting's eyes brightened, and Marty thought of Ivy Mike and the incinerated island of Elugelab.

"Let's shield one cloud," Marty said, "before we get ahead of ourselves."

Iris Stoka was a genius in her own right. The expertise that had brought her to the new agency called ARPA was in computers. One afternoon, over coffee, she walked Marty through her vision for a satellite system that worked in constant ground communication with computers below.

"The human operator will soon be a thing of the past. We will look back and laugh at the idea that we ever had human beings in charge of monitoring radar." She paused, then added, "In charge of much of anything, really."

Iris, working off the myth of his radio signaling as the callback mechanism, developed a brilliant system of targeted frequencies, and Marty felt chills when they vanished a Grumman test plane with one of her devices aboard, only to hear the Klaxon activate just before the plane came back. The plane's carefully tuned transmitter spoke to the Ash Point's receivers, activating the alarm before it even found the sky. Iris Stoka smiled then in the way Marty often did, trying to hide her own pleasure at a success.

He pulled his jacket cuff over the watch, a habit that was turning into a tic.

On October 22, Cutting summoned the Project Kingsolver team

to share that President John F. Kennedy had ordered a naval block-ade of Cuba. "Quarantine," actually; that was the word, because a blockade was an act of war, and an act of war with a thousand nu-clear missiles pointed at your shores and cities was not something to undertake lightly.

All the same, it seemed to be moving that way.

"The President has demanded that the Soviets dismantle all mil-itary bases on the island," Cutting said. "He'll explain it to the nation on television tonight."

The Ash Point team watched the president's address together.

"It shall be the policy of this nation to regard any nuclear missile launched from Cuba against any nation in the Western Hemisphere as an attack by the Soviet Union on the United States, requiring a full retaliatory response upon the Soviet Union," the president said in his Boston-tinged tone. He looked good, tall and young and fit, and he sounded good, full of courage and conviction, and yet there was something different about him.

Fear, Marty thought. There was fear to him.

Cutting turned off the television and asked for another weather report. Rosson said that the best chance for storms was several days out. It was then that Marty cleared his throat and requested leave from the base.

This took them all by surprise. Even Cutting was flustered.

"We can't . . . It's such a classified operation, Doctor. You know that better than anyone."

"Of course. But this isn't good for me. Day after day of waiting." Marty tapped his forehead. "I'll need a clear head."

There were advantages to knowing that people thought you were insane. Leverage.

"I just want to take a drive," Marty explained. He thought that if he made it outside the electrified fences that surrounded Ash Point, he might finally have a real conversation with Marilyn. He could be wrong about that, but as a working hypothesis he liked it fine.

"You want to go for a drive," Admiral Cutting said, as if Marty had suggested wrestling a bear in the nude.

"That's right. Down south, toward Camden."

"What's there?"

"Trees and water."

"We're not hurting for either up here."

Marty smiled. "I used to go there when I was a kid. A family retreat."

The admiral winced at the mention of Marty's family, no doubt bracing for a reference to his brother.

"I'm getting tense in this place," Marty said. "All the waiting, now this news from Cuba. I think it would be good for me to get some time alone. Solitude."

Cutting looked at Marilyn Metzger.

"Seems like a fine idea for all of us to have clear heads come test day," she said breezily, as if she were making conversation rather than granting approval.

Cutting gave Marty one day of leave.

AIRBORNE, EASTERN SEABOARD
OCTOBER 25, 2025

There was a moment, after Lawrence unzipped the backpack and located the knife, when Charlie believed they had a chance. A chance to do what, she still wasn't sure—sneaking out of a plane at 30,000 feet didn't achieve much without a parachute—but being free from the ropes and the blindfold was at least a victory of some kind.

Then the footsteps clanged toward them.

"They're coming," Lawrence said. His fingertips were pressed against the back of Charlie's wrists, and she could feel the textured grip of the pocketknife, though she hadn't yet felt the blade, only heard the snick of it opening, a sound that prickled her flesh, knowing that the blade would soon be near—or in?—her wrists.

"Fuck!" Charlie whispered. "Hide the knife."

"Where?"

"Sit on it."

"On the *knife*?"

"I don't know! Do something, though, or you're going to lose it."

Footsteps and voices in the darkness. A clanging echo, metal on metal. Lawrence shifted, using his hands to prop himself up, then scooted backward and sat on the knife.

"You did close it first, right?" Charlie asked.

"Very funny."

She was joking because she was terrified. Humor had always been her reflex response to fear, hence the videos mocking Ash Point. The move had been frightening for her. Snarky video commentary provided the illusion of courage and control. When you taunted something, you could fool others into thinking you weren't afraid of it. Fool enough people, and maybe someday you'd succeed in fooling yourself.

Now, listening to the dead men clatter through the impossible plane toward her, she understood the fallacy of her approach. It didn't hurt to laugh at your fears, but you needed to be laughing at yourself too. Anything else was simply nursing a lie. Eventually lies caught up, and then someone else enjoyed the last laugh at your expense.

Even the dead. Always the dead. You were going to join them at some point; you knew it and they knew it.

If they're real, she thought as Bellamy and Granville's voices became clearer, their footsteps nearer, *then why couldn't my mother's voice have been real this morning? And does that mean . . .*

No further time for analysis, because the ghosts arrived. Someone knelt beside Charlie.

"Good news," Granville said. "The captain wants to see you. I personally wanted to drop your ass out of the bomb bay, but he's in charge."

"Take our blindfolds off first," Charlie said.

"You don't get to make the rules. And he doesn't want to see both of you. Just you."

"We're staying together."

"No, you're not. Captain said, 'Bring the girl,' and your buddy looks pretty damn comfortable right where he is."

"Fuck that! We're staying together!"

"Think you're in a position to negotiate, you foulmouthed little bitch?"

"Just grab her," Bellamy said, sounding exasperated.

Granville grabbed Charlie and heaved her upright. The backpack sat awkwardly, drooping toward her left shoulder, but nothing fell out.

"Drop the bag," Bellamy said.

"I can't drop it, you dumb asshole, my hands are tied. But take it off, because it's killing my shoulders."

Leave it here, she begged silently. *Leave it all with Lawrence—the radiosonde with the watch and the note. Maybe he can figure something out.*

"Should've checked it for weapons," Granville said immediately.

"Like I had time to worry about that," Bellamy said.

"Check it now," Granville snapped.

Bellamy tore the pack from her shoulders.

"I've got homework in it," Charlie said. "See if you can do it for me? We hear a lot about your generation being smarter than us, but I've got my doubts."

"Shut up! Damn you, *shut the hell up!*" Granville shouted. Any reference to the future was the spark that lit his fury. Considering he was dead in the future, that seemed fair enough. She couldn't imagine being a big fan of his situation if the combat boot were on the other foot.

"Calm down," Bellamy said. "Composure, dammit."

"Kiss my ass, 'Calm down.' This little bitch—"

"The captain wants to see me," Charlie said. "Don't forget your orders."

The blindfold meant she was entirely unprepared for the slap, so what would've been a glancing blow took her by surprise. She cried out and fell against the side of the plane, then tumbled into Lawrence.

"Granville!" Bellamy shouted, and then hands were on her, hauling her up.

"Leave her alone!" Lawrence yelled.

The two dead men rifled through Lawrence's backpack, and then Bellamy said, "What in the hell is this?"

Charlie was certain the wristwatch and note were in his hand. Then he tugged her blindfold off and she saw he was holding Lawrence's iPad, looking at it with wonder—and fear.

"It's homework," she said.

"The hell it is." He turned it over in his hands, running his fingers over the edges, inspecting the camera lens. He hadn't even figured out how to open the magnetic case yet. "Some kind of radio compass."

Radio compass?

We are truly screwed, Charlie thought. In her favorite ghost-hunting shows, the ghosts spent their afterlives floating around among the living, observing until they chose to intrude and scare the shit out of someone. Since they'd always been watching, you never had to update them on current events.

"Explain it," Bellamy demanded, lifting the iPad.

"I'll explain it to the captain," she replied. She preferred Hightower. Maybe it was because he was her dead relative. Blood was thicker than time travel.

"Damn right you will." Bellamy dropped the backpack, clutched the iPad in one hand and Charlie's arm in the other, and yanked her away from Lawrence, Granville trailing, his pale face and cut-to-the-scalp hair gleaming in the dimly lit plane.

Lawrence fell out of sight. He still had the knife. But could he use it on his own wrist bindings? That seemed unlikely.

The plane seemed to go on forever, a network of narrow steel corridors that smelled of fuel and oil and seemed to contain random pockets of cold air. Even with the blindfold off, Charlie couldn't see much, because Bellamy was holding her so close and moving her so fast. They passed a metal ladder leading down, and she remembered that the B-52 had two decks. That had been something Abe waxed on about endlessly when he talked about the ejection sequence. She wondered where Abe was now and who was talking to him. Surely no one had fired shots on the lonely road to Ash Point. But Lawrence had said his truck was empty . . .

"Up and in," Bellamy snapped, shoving her up another narrow ladder and into the cockpit.

The world spread out before her, bright and beautiful. The banks of windows showed blue sky and glistening water and forested islands. The clarity of the scene was reassuring—right up until the ghost pilot turned from the yoke to face her.

"Let's talk," Captain Hightower said.

He nodded at the copilot's seat, and Bellamy shoved her into it, lifting her legs to swing her feet clear of the controls. There were wild arrays of levers, dials, and gauges. Flying the B-52 of the Cold War era had required a lot of concentration, with no computers to help.

"She's carrying electronics," Bellamy said. "Granville, show him."

Granville passed the iPad forward. Hightower took one hand off the yoke and accepted the device.

"What is it?"

"It's a . . . small computer," Charlie said, self-editing for terms they might be able to follow. "It belongs to my friend."

She'd never called Lawrence Zimmer a friend before. It had been a long day. He felt like a deeper friend right now than any she'd ever known back home.

"Where was it made?"

Charlie thought that referencing China might be a mistake, the iPad promptly confused for a communist spy tool or some wild shit. Were iPads even from China? She had no clue. They were ubiquitous, that was all.

"I don't know where, exactly. A company called Apple produces them. They also make phones. I've got a smaller version of that thing in my pocket."

Instantly, she wished she hadn't said it. Granville was grabbing at her, his disgusting, hairy-knuckled hands on her thighs, his sour breath in her face. He was groping at her pocket, trying to pull the phone free, when she bit his arm.

"Damn it!" He reached backward, loading up another slap, but Captain Hightower caught his arm.

"Ease off."

"She *bit* me."

"And I'll do it again if you touch me," Charlie said. The phone was halfway out of her pocket now, the camera lens visible. How much of her life had been experienced through that lens? Now it was looking a ghost in the eye, and there was no audience. What a waste.

"Take the phone out. But don't you dare touch my legs again."

Granville reached out warily, like a man petting a cat that had already clawed him, gripped the phone with his fingertips, and slid it clear. All three men marveled over it, whispering muttered concerns. It would have been hilarious if not for the fact that Charlie was trapped 30,000 feet in the air with them.

"It's a phone and a camera and internet," Charlie said.

Their faces reminded her that the internet meant nothing.

"Tap the screen," she said.

Bellamy tapped it, and the screen filled with a photo of a tiger eating a pumpkin; Charlie loved that photo, which had been taken at some big-cat rescue center in Indiana. The image made all three men literally gasp, and not because of the tiger: they were stunned by the clarity. The Polaroid era hadn't offered anything like that. Had they even made it to the Polaroid?

"This is spooky," Bellamy murmured, and the idea of a ghost

finding a phone spooky made Charlie want to laugh, but their faces silenced her. They were grim men. No, they were *scared* men.

She looked away, out at the clear sky, empty of air traffic. Convenient, how the pilot calls had preceded the B-52's return.

Someone anticipated this, she realized. The military had been waiting at Ash Point, and the skies had been cleared. If they'd known it was coming, though, then where the hell were they?

Layla Chen watched the three men aboard the B-52 pass the Zimmer boy's iPad and Goodwin girl's phone back and forth, the image projected on a high-definition LED screen, courtesy of the hijacked cameras on the devices. The scene was surreal but far from fiction, and that meant she needed to pay attention, because there would be an appropriate moment to announce to the ghost crew that DARPA was watching them.

"We should be talking to them now," the defense secretary said.

The microphones on the devices were also live but the Raven Rock team was muted, everyone waiting for the right time to speak.

"No," Hanover replied. "Dr. Chen is right. We need to let them process the situation. Besides, the girl is holding up all right."

"I'm not worried about the girl; I'm worried about the fucking bomb!" the defense secretary snapped.

The girl *was* holding up all right, Layla thought. Charlie Goodwin was impressive. She was clearly scared but she handled herself well, even with a touch of humor that was astonishing given the circumstances. There had been a moment, when she'd bitten Granville, that nearly precipitated forced contact between Raven Rock and the cockpit, but then things settled down, and Layla and Hanover were able to win the argument that more time was better.

"This is a remarkable opportunity to observe them before we intercede. The more we understand of their mindsets, the better our chances of working with them."

And so, down in Raven Rock, shielded from any potential blast of the Mark 39 warhead, they watched and listened and counted on the girl to ask the right questions. She was only seventeen, originally from Brooklyn, recently relocated to Ash Point. This they knew both from her intelligence file and from the testimony of the agitated—and, it appeared, somewhat inebriated—old man who'd been removed from the pickup truck on the road to the peninsula. Abe Zimmer was with interrogators now and not proving particularly useful, asking more questions than he answered.

The Zimmer boy, Lawrence, was nowhere in sight, although he'd been loaded onto the plane with the Goodwin girl. The plane was charting a course toward Cuba that was deeply concerning to everyone.

"The risk rises exponentially by the mile," the defense secretary said, looking at the satellite map showing the B-52's progress: Portland, Boston, New York ahead.

"The risk is already substantial," Hanover answered. "Dr. Chen, are you ready with . . . with Kennedy?"

How to answer that? She had an open laptop loaded with DARPA's finest voice simulation software in front of her, but was it fair to say she was ready to negotiate nuclear warfare in the voice of John F. Kennedy?

"I can use the system when desired," she said, the best nonanswer she could give.

"How much more time do we give them before we activate that microphone?" the president asked.

No one had a firm answer. Initiating conversation was likely to be a one-shot opportunity. It would go well or it would go very, very badly.

"Let's listen a little longer," Hanover answered. "Let's listen and decide."

On the satellite map, the B-52 floated toward America's eastern population centers.

"How did you get here?" Charlie Goodwin asked, voice muffled but clear enough to understand.

"Excellent question, kid," Hanover muttered, and then the president told everyone to be silent.

If Layla's understanding of Project Kingsolver was accurate, Captain Hightower wouldn't be able to answer much about how he'd come to be flying over America in the year 2025, but she was deeply curious about what he remembered. The truth of Project Kingsolver had never been recorded in the files, because it seemed only one man ever understood it all: Dr. Hazelton.

MAINE
OCTOBER 23, 1962

Before Marty left Ash Point in one of the olive-green jeeps, Admiral Cutting stopped him at the gate.

"I need you to know how crucial this mission is," Cutting said. "This project. Your work."

"I'm aware."

"I don't think so," Cutting said. "Yesterday, while the President was speaking to the country, the Soviets tested a nuclear weapon at an altitude of 180 miles above sea level. Preliminary intelligence suggests the entire point of the exercise was to obtain data about an atmospheric electromagnetic pulse. Our bombers are in the air around the clock, Dr. Hazelton. You know that. If there's a way to ensure their survival, it changes the calculus for Khrushchev. For the world. It may well be the one way out of this mess in Cuba."

Marty wanted to dislike this man, and in many ways he did. But Cutting had not sent missiles to Cuba. He was being asked to respond to provocations and situations beyond his control.

The problem was they all were. Including Kennedy and Khrushchev. They were, Marty thought, all still responding to Oppenheimer after all these years. To the invention of world-ending weaponry.

But that wasn't fair, either. Oppenheimer had been responding to Hitler. It went backward like that, on and on, human evil and technological miracles, deadlier weapons in pursuit of peace, a contradiction that seemed as old as civilization itself—and, maybe, destined to end it.

He shook his head, tried to stay focused. Cutting frowned at him.

"Are you all right, Doctor?"

"Fine. I'll take a drive and clear my head."

"Stay focused on the mission. There's a Nobel Prize ahead of you, Hazelton, but first we need to ensure there's a world for such things. We stand at the brink."

"Science or peace?" Marty asked.

Cutting blinked. "Pardon?"

"The Nobel for physics or peace?"

"I . . . well, I'm not in charge of that."

No, he wasn't. But he'd been thinking of seducing Marty with the physics prize, of course. Marty wondered if the admiral knew that Alfred Nobel had died regretting his own discovery, nitroglycerine, because it had been used for dynamite, a remarkable healing substance turned into battlefield fodder.

"Do you know what dynamite means?" Marty asked, his eyes on the electrified fences between him and the glory of autumn in Maine. "Nobel picked the name because it referred to the Greek word for power. But in his original patent, he called it 'Nobel's Safety Powder.' Phenomenal, don't you think? The duality. Nobel's Safety Powder led to dynamite. Away we went."

Cutting's frown deepened, his chiseled features harshening like a rocky cliff collecting winter ice.

"We'll get the right cloud," Marty told him, "and I will shield it, and I will vanish whatever plane you wish. But today I'm going to sit on a dock in the sun and put my bare feet in a cold pond."

Cutting nodded and stepped away from the jeep. The gates parted, and Marty drove past the electrified fence, down the dusty road, and away from the isolated airfield. There were few curious eyes to watch him pass. Ash Point had been selected for good reason.

He wound his way west, then picked up Route 1 and turned left, southbound on the coastal highway, enjoying the topless jeep, the buffeting breeze off the salty sea. A black Oldsmobile sedan fell in behind him in a little fishing village called Cutler. He drove on, pretending he didn't see the blonde behind the wheel.

On through Searsport and Belfast and into Camden, and there he turned west again, away from the water, toward a high, humped mountain with one flattened side facing the ocean. That was Mount Battie. There was a small turret-style tower made of stone on the top of the mountain. A memorial to the soldiers of the First World War. Up there, Edna St. Vincent Millay had written a lovely poem that Marty had once known by heart but could no longer recite. He remembered the opening of another, though, one she'd written in 1942 after the Nazi slaughter in the Czech village of Lidice.

The whole word holds in its arms today
The murdered village of Lidice,
Like the murdered body of a little child . . .

Reading it, he had thought of Hank. He did again now, let the memory come and did not resist it, let the terrible scene in Nashua wash over him as the heat from the fire had. To this day he was unsure of the ignition source. A spark from the farmer's match, yes, but where had the fuel pooled, and how had the single fleck of fire found it?

You could say that didn't matter, and you would be wrong.

Past Mount Battie rose Mount Megunticook, and in the hills southeast of that lay Rosewater Pond, where Marty had taught Hank to dive. Hank, fast and reckless, was afraid of nothing except for heights. Marty, a skilled diver, had endeavored to obliterate that last fear by putting the boy out over safe, deep water and teaching him the fundamentals.

You like to jump on land. You never stop jumping around the house. It's no different out here. Start with that, then. Just jump. Trust the water. Trust me.

Until dusk, Hank had hurled himself higher and harder into the air, whirling, twisting, occasionally so heedless in his sprinting assaults on the rock that he lost his footing and slipped, laughing as he bounced up, oblivious to his bloody scrapes. Marty was afraid, watching him. He called off the practice, distracting Hank with the pursuit of fireflies.

They'd never had a diving contest again.

Rosewater Pond was empty today, as it typically was after Labor Day, the summer cottages closed, their residents back south in Boston or New York, no doubt listening to the latest from Cuba. Marty drove all the way down to the old family cottage. When he cut the engine, he heard the crunch of tires from the Oldsmobile as Marilyn Metzger pulled in behind him.

Marty got out and walked around the property, inspecting the deteriorating cottage. A local man took most of the rental money in exchange for caretaking, and it seemed he was better at the former task than the latter. When Marty finished his circuit of the camp, Marilyn was sitting on the hood of the Oldsmobile, gazing across the pond and into the bright maples and birches. He sat on the hood beside her.

"It is a lovely place," she said.

"Yes. You don't hear the ocean like at Ash Point, but I'll take the pond."

"Solitude," she said. "Agreed. There are too many listeners at Ash Point."

"I'm trying my best not to say anything to alarm them."

Her eyes inventoried him, kind as they could be while assessing for damage.

"Don't worry," he said. "I know Hank is dead. Haven't forgotten that one yet or managed to talk myself out of it again."

"Do you hate me for telling you?"

"No. I thank you for it. How much trouble did it get you in?"

Her face said what he already knew: she hadn't told anyone.

"Does Cutting know you followed me?" he asked.

"Of course."

"He still trusts you."

"Yes. Because you keep working. That's his only concern."

"Ah."

The breeze blew her hair across her face, and she pushed it back.

"Will you keep working when the real plane arrives?"

He didn't answer. The sun was to the west, across the pond, putting a glint off the face of his father's watch. The wind stirred crimson leaves, scattered a few to the water like flower petals tossed into a bride's wake as she passed, honeymoon-bound.

"Cutting tells me the Soviets tested a high-altitude atomic detonation yesterday," he said.

"That's right. It fused more than six hundred miles of *buried* electrical cables, more than a thousand miles of overhead telephone lines, and quite possibly took down their own space station. Modern life in some villages came to an effective halt."

Marty pictured that in America—the electric grid going down, towns frozen, life slowed—and didn't hate the idea. The problem, of course, was that the idea was fiction. Villages without power meant hospitals without power. You couldn't return to the past no matter how badly you longed for it. Time accelerated, walked, then ran, then flew.

He wondered about the monkey with the bright eyes. Wished it could have spoken to him. What was it like out there beyond the vanishing point? The monkey couldn't say. It would take a human to do that.

"Should we vanish a plane with human beings on board?" he asked.

Marilyn didn't answer.

"Well?"

She sighed. "It's a perilous moment. No denying that. Not even if I want to. And I do want to. But I've seen the classified reports, I know all the armaments, and . . . "

"You think it's worth trying," he said when she trailed off.

Silence.

"You don't have to like it to understand it," Marty said. "If I can vanish one bomber, it will be an awesome show of technological superiority. Maybe one that slows this madness down."

Marilyn gave the slowest, saddest of nods.

"I think Cutting is right," Marty said. "And I hate it. But if they're testing high-atmospheric atomic detonations, in this moment? We're close to the edge. To the end, rather."

"They'll keep testing," Marilyn said. "And by 'they' I mean 'we.' There are more nuclear tests scheduled for the Johnston Atoll site today."

Marty stared at her. The world bristled with unprecedented risk, rival leaders weren't in direct communication, and the United States intended to fire nuclear weapons into that fraught moment?

"Yes," Marilyn said, as if he'd asked the question aloud. "One will be from a Thor missile. The other will be an airdrop from a B-52.

You'll love the code name for that one: Calamity. Perhaps someone involved grasps the irony, but I doubt it."

Neither of them spoke for a while. The breeze was peaceful, the mood fretful, a contrast that seemed to electrify the air. Could he back the Soviets off? Maybe. They couldn't fight what they couldn't see.

Could he back the United States off, though? A different question. Marty was tired of being on the side of science, wanted to align instead with the mystery. With awe. With holy curiosity.

"Where is Iris from?" he asked.

"She's consulted widely. Grumman, Raytheon, the RAND Corporation. She's Czech, but she's been here for decades."

Since the war, in other words.

"You don't trust her," Marilyn said.

"I'm not sure. I certainly have no interest in her passport. I don't think she's one for national concerns—on any side."

"Then what bothers you about her?"

"Her brain," he said simply. "She's brilliant."

"That's a good thing."

"Sometimes. Her systems interests, though . . . she'd rather leave the humans out entirely."

"Unmanned planes carry less risk."

"So does an unmanned planet."

Marilyn was quiet. Then she said, "Is it really the radio signal that calls the plane back?"

Marty suppressed an urge to cover his watch.

"Does Iris think otherwise?"

"She seems skeptical. But she can't determine what else is doing it."

So she'd tested and failed. He was not surprised by this. They would never admit that they were trying to make him expendable, but they surely hungered to remove a man of dubious mental health from the point position.

"Well?" Marilyn said. "Do the radio signals work? Is that really how you summon the planes back when you've vanished them?"

Marty was not a liar by nature—there were the obvious moral reasons, along with the mathematical costs of wasted time and misdirected efforts—but he also carried memories of Christmas Island and Doom Town, mushroom clouds, power unchecked. He often wondered what Oppenheimer might've done if given a second chance. What Einstein and Niels Bohr might've changed if they'd flown with Red Flight over the obliterated island of Elugelab.

"It is the radio signal," he said, "but what matters is the ratio of the Nightshade. Some of that is mere instinct. I haven't nailed down the math yet; I'm reacting to the conditions."

"Maybe it's not instinct. Maybe it's magic. Supernatural power, the Almighty, something bigger than us."

Marty turned to her. "How much leverage do I have with Cutting?"

She frowned. "Leverage to ask for what?"

"To be on the plane that vanishes."

Silence. Wind over the water. Her eyes on his like a bird of prey.

"You want to go on the plane?"

"I have to. I can make plenty of arguments for not letting them test with human subjects at all, but I must concede at least a couple in favor of it. Like saving the world. The human element, though . . . " He put his hand on the hood, felt the sun-cooked metal hot under his palm. "That bothers me. If anyone goes, I should be among them."

"I suppose you have that much leverage. They'll refuse initially. But they did the same to Jimmy Doolittle when he asked to lead the Tokyo raid, and who ended up flying the first plane over Tokyo?"

"Jimmy Doolittle."

"Exactly. Why? Because they wanted to bomb the place that badly. I think they want you to vanish a plane that badly." She paused, then said, "I'm sure of it, actually."

They watched the autumn leaves fall, a sound like no other, so soft, so perfect. So slow. There was nothing more underrated, Marty thought, than time passing slowly.

"It's about the Nightshade ratios," he said. "I change them at the last minute. Cutting has to recognize that logic. Iris certainly will."

"I hate that name. Nashua Nightshade."

"I'm sorry." It meant more than he could express to know that she hated it because she knew what Nashua had meant for Hank. For Marty.

They watched the leaves make their languid descent. It was so peaceful a sight, and yet in the end, the leaves always met the ground, dead, their brief, glorious airborne existence ended. It was beautiful as long as you could ignore that.

"Enough leverage for you," Marilyn said softly, almost as if to herself. "Yes, certainly. But enough for me?"

"You still want to go. That remains your private motivation."

"It does." Her eyes were bright and her smile fierce.

He sighed. "Robert is not up there. Wherever that plane goes when it disappears—and I don't know where it is—you won't find him waiting."

"Maybe not," she said. "But I work for the Office of Naval Research under the command of Admiral Ralph Cutting, and my assignment is the protection of all things under the purview of Project Kingsolver. I'll go on the test flight."

"That's insane."

"Of all the people to direct such an insult."

He laughed despite himself.

He was opening his mouth to tell Marilyn that, while he admired her bravery, he would not support it when she spoke first.

"Have you ever made love in the water?"

He stared at her.

"Well?" she said.

"No."

"Me neither." She slid off the hood of the Oldsmobile in a fluid, graceful motion, used the toes of her right foot to slip off the sandal on her left, then reversed it and walked barefoot down the rock and toward the water. She was wearing a charcoal skirt that fell just below her knees and a sleeveless white blouse. While he watched, she tested the water with one cautious toe, then lifted her skirt and waded in. She stood like that, facing the sun and assessing the temperature. Then she turned to him with a smile.

"Exhilarating," she said. "Just warm enough, just cold enough. Perfect."

He didn't move from the car until she slipped the blouse over her shoulders. Then he went in a hurry, clumsy with his shoes and socks, none of her grace. By the time he was free of them, she was naked and waist-deep in the water, the sun at her back, her breasts the pale shade of secret places.

"Does this go in your report?" he said as he unbuckled his belt.

"Ask me that again and I'll drown you."

He hoped her denial was true but didn't know. Then she found a submerged rock and stood on it, clearing the water almost entirely, and he decided he also damn well didn't care. Whatever she knew about his brand of madness, he understood only this about hers: he needed it.

He waded in. The water welcomed him, and then so did she. Exhilarating, just as she'd promised. Cold and warm. Electric.

Perfection was making love in a pond in Maine on the last warm day of autumn.

Somewhere off the coast of Cuba, warships were moving into place, and the world bristled with missiles, and, for a beautiful breath, none of it mattered.

Later, they lay on the rock, naked in the sun, her leg casually entwined in his, and he thought that he could stay right there forever. The sun went down and the shadows came, though, as they always must.

They dressed in silence beneath the pines, and by the time they walked up to the cars, the wind was rising and cold. She asked him no questions and he made her no promises.

"Come what may," she said by way of farewell, and that was all, and enough.

The road back to Ash Point was long and lonely and dark, but her warmth rode with him. When he reached the airfield gate and the electrified fence, there was a new shadow on the runway, the silhouette of a plane larger than any other.

The B-52 had arrived.

AIRBORNE, EASTERN SEABOARD
OCTOBER 25, 2025

"E xplain this!" Granville snapped, holding the iPhone high.

"I already did," Charlie said. "It's a computer and a phone and they're common in our era."

"I'm so sick of hearing that shit!"

"I'm sick of hearing yours," Hightower said coolly. "Get back to your stations, both of you. Leave that thing with me and let me talk to the girl alone."

He turned and looked at them, and though his eyes were hidden by the sunglasses, his bearing seemed to shift, some stiffening of posture that said, *Chain of command, anyone?*

His voice was lower when he said, "Remember that jet? Let's be ready if it returns. Not packed in here like sardines with nobody on the turret gun."

They left.

Charlie gazed at the empty sky and thought that Hightower had asked a very good question: What had happened to the jet? Why wasn't it trailing them right now, the pilot peering in at their cockpit through his masked face, the way it happened in the movies?

Hightower wasn't wearing a mask, though there was one near him, with a hose running to an oxygen bottle that was mounted on the seat. Beside the bottle and below the dizzying panel of gauges and switches were white-knobbed metal levers that made Charlie think of an old-fashioned typewriter, the hammers that struck the page when you struck a key. Each knob had both a number and a letter stamped on it: 4T, 5T, and so on, up to eight. There were eight engines, so that made sense, but she wasn't sure what the *T* meant. "Throttle"? "Thrust"?

Hightower saw her staring and said, "You've never seen this cockpit before."

"No," she said. "I mean, not a whole one."

She didn't want to clarify that she'd seen pieces of the one he'd died in.

"I don't like that," he said softly, "because I want you to be a spy."

"Me too. Then I'd know what the hell is happening."

Shockingly, he smiled. His concern hadn't ebbed, but he smiled, and in that moment she almost forgot to be afraid of him. Almost.

He adjusted two of the white-knobbed levers, which took more muscle than Charlie would've guessed, the mechanical components seeming to resist effort rather than assist it. The plane roared in response, then slowed a little.

"If you have an explanation for what the hell is going on, I need to hear it now," he said. "Because my orders are clear: I've got the rest of this fuel to burn, no more, and unless I can determine things are safe in America, I need to put the baby down on Cuba."

"'The baby'?"

He turned back to her. "The hydrogen bomb."

Charlie felt her bowels stir and chest tighten.

"Look, guy. Captain, I mean. Captain Hightower, you can't do that. You know something is wrong with your mission."

"Oh, it is definitely FUBAR," he agreed. "But orders are orders. We were briefed on it all before we flew into the cloud, and there was no confusion. If things don't look right on the ground, I'm to understand that . . . " He paused, swallowed, set his jaw. "That things didn't work out in Cuba. And then we hit back. Hard. There won't be anything left of that island, I promise you."

He looked very young and very sad.

"Cuba is fine!" Charlie shouted. "There's no problem down there—not one that has anything to do with us; not anymore."

Hightower looked dubious.

"I'm not up here because things were going well, kid. I've seen photographs of missile silos."

"You have no clue. All due respect, but . . . no clue. It all went fine in Cuba, or close to fine. I don't know much about Cuba; they don't really teach that shit, so it couldn't have been that big of a deal."

"Cuba couldn't have been *that big of a deal*?" Hightower echoed, astonished.

"I mean, we know it was, like, a thing," Charlie said, spreading her hands. "But it obviously worked out. Nobody launched from the Bay of Pigs, right? That was the threat?"

"The Bay of Pigs invasion was '61, before the missile sites went up. That was our idea, anyhow. You don't know what you're talking about."

"Well, take some comfort in that! If it turned into a big problem, I'd know, right? It worked out! The country is good. Better than we realize, maybe? There are problems, sure, and bad shit happens every day, and if you watch enough videos, you become convinced it's only getting worse, but . . . " She felt her eyes filling with tears and was surprised by how profoundly moved she was by the simple idea of *home*, of her country, a place that seemed screwed-up in so many ways that now seemed mostly trivial, and certainly, *certainly*, not worthy of a nuclear bomb, no matter where it was dropped on the planet.

"You have a radio," she said. "Talk to someone with the Air Force if you don't believe me."

"I don't have a radio. No comms. We are flying silent."

"*That* was the plan? A nuke and no radio?"

He looked almost offended. "I just volunteered."

"Well, if you don't mind my saying so, the plan sucks."

He didn't seem inclined to disagree.

"You flew out of one era and into another," Charlie said. "Ask whatever questions you want; I'll prove I'm right. I can get real specific for you, because we're family."

For the first time, she'd astonished him.

"*What?*"

"I'm you're great-granddaughter, dude! You're the only reason I've ever been to Ash Point! Everyone makes a big deal about how you . . . " *Hmm*, she thought, *let's tread lightly here.* "How heroic and tragic you were, and whatnot."

"Tragic," he said.

"As far as we knew," Charlie corrected hastily. "And, to be honest, we evidently didn't know much."

Should she tell him about the balloon and the watch? She wasn't sure. They were her trump cards, and yet Bellamy and Granville had ignored them, all their focus on the iPad. Maybe it was better if Lawrence kept them away from the cockpit. They seemed worth holding out, a final power play if she couldn't simply reason with Hightower. For a dead man, he seemed quite reasonable.

He adjusted the yoke and flew through a low, thin cloud. They were over the water, tracing the coast to the far east. Was it still Maine down there, or Massachusetts? Little fishing villages, crowded harbors, lots of islands, but mostly open ocean.

"I don't buy it," Hightower announced suddenly. "Granville is right. This is a psych test, nothing more. What they want to know is how much stress we can hold up to before we drop the bomb. Hell, it's probably a dummy. I should drop it out of spite."

Now, there was an idea Charlie didn't want to put to the test.

"Imagine that I'm right," she said. "Please. Just *imagine* I'm telling the truth."

"You can't be."

"From my perspective, *you* can't be flying this plane! But you are flying it, and I'm working through that, and you could try to do the same. Look at the technology I showed up with." She jutted her chin at the iPad and phone resting at his side. "You *know* that stuff doesn't fit your narrative."

"There's plenty of classified tech I haven't seen."

He was so rigid, unyielding, so infuriatingly on mission.

"Get over a city and then tell me that I'm crazy. The ocean doesn't prove anything. It's mostly the same as the one you flew over sixty years ago, other than the temperature. It *looks* the same. The cities won't. And once you see them, you'll understand." Then she was struck by a brilliant idea. "Fly to New York! The Twin Towers are gone! That ought to prove it! Just fly by and look."

"What towers?"

She stared at him, stunned, then realized that the Twin Towers of the World Trade Center had gone up after he was dead and had come down before she was born. That seemed impossible. The towers had been iconic landmarks in first good ways and then bad, and they'd *both* missed them?

There was the new one, though: One World Trade Center. Hell, there was the entire skyline, so much of it new in just the last few years, each skyscraper reaching higher than the last. Her city. Home. She could explain it to him.

Assuming that nobody blew them out of the sky simply for entering the airspace. She had to count on the mysterious absence of the fighter jet as a reassurance. The Air Force was watching this plane but keeping their distance, and considering she was sitting on top of a nuke, that was probably a hell of a good idea.

"Just fly by the city," she said. "Stay over the water and fly by and . . . look, that's all. You won't be able to call me a liar then."

They flew on, south, toward Cuba.

Then Hightower nudged the yoke toward her, and the big plane banked west.

RAVEN ROCK MOUNTAIN COMPLEX, PENNSYLVANIA
OCTOBER 25, 2025

The president of the United States said, "Fuck me," calmly and clearly.

"We cannot let this happen," the defense secretary said. "Not New York. No. They cannot enter that airspace."

"They're already in it from a fallout perspective," Hanover said. "Close enough to count if a bomb detonates."

"That girl is more of a threat than Hightower is," the defense secretary said. "Telling him to go toward New York. Holy shit, what's wrong with this kid!"

"It was logical," Layla Chen said. "She's making a compelling case."

Everyone stared at her, their lack of agreement a palpable thing. A shame, Layla thought, because the kid was savvy. The visual of the New York skyline was bound to make an impact on Hightower. The price of that impact, however, was an open question.

"It's unacceptable," the president said.

"Let Hightower hear from Kennedy," the defense secretary said. "Now."

The president hesitated for only a second before nodding. "Yes. We do it now."

Layla Chen took a breath and leaned down to her laptop.

ASH POINT, MAINE
OCTOBER 25, 1962

The United States naval blockade off Cuba made its first stop on a Thursday, when the destroyers USS *Joseph P. Kennedy Jr.* and USS *John R. Pierce* confronted a Lebanese freighter, the *Marucla*, and sailors boarded the ship to search its cargo. Khrushchev announced that the Soviet Union perceived the blockade as an act of war and cautioned President Kennedy that "if you weigh the present situation with a cool head without giving way to passion you will understand that the Soviet Union cannot afford to decline the despotic demands of the USA."

Construction of missile sites in Cuba continued. Robert McNamara, the American defense secretary, warned that Soviet freighters were being trailed by submarines—likely nuclear-capable submarines. The United States moved to DEFCON 2 for the first time in history. Strategic Air Command kept nuclear-armed B-52s in the sky around the clock.

At Ash Point, Maine, the weather forecast had the small team excited. A tropical depression over the Carolinas was spinning a volatile warm-air mass toward the cool waters of the Gulf of Maine just as a separate storm front swept down out of Canada, and the two would collide over Maine on Saturday, like clashing superpowers of the natural order. There would be lightning. More than enough electrical activity for the Nashua Nightshade to work its magic on the proper scale to vanish a B-52.

"It will work," Admiral Cutting told the team in the briefing room.

"Do you have a crew ready?" Marty asked.

"Yes. Volunteers who are well acquainted with the risk."

"I don't think anyone is well acquainted with the risk," Marty said.

In another room, on another day, Cutting would have dressed down anyone who dared to question him, but this was Ash Point in autumn of 1962, there was a naval blockade around Soviet missiles in Cuba, and Marty Hazelton could make a bomber invisible. The admiral was not going to dress him down.

"We will be flying two planes," Cutting said. "The B-52 on our airstrip right now is outfitted with generators for Hazelton's Nightshade."

Marty suppressed a wince. It was *Nashua* Nightshade, not *Hazelton's* Nightshade, and now that he knew Marilyn hated the name, he wished never to hear it again.

"That craft will handle the seeding and shielding of the storm clouds," Cutting continued. "The test craft, also a B-52, will come from Loring."

"Why separate launch sites?" Marty asked.

"Because if anything goes wrong, we're going to need to explain it. Loring is part of routine flight patterns."

They all understood the classified nature of their mission, but no one had yet spoken aloud of the possibility of failure.

"I'll need time to familiarize myself with the generators," Marty said. "The largest plane I've ever seeded a cloud from was a B-29, and that was a long time ago."

Silence built, like a room filling with cigar smoke.

"You won't be airborne, Doctor," Cutting said. "We can't have that. You'll be in a supervising capacity right here, of course. It's your show."

"No." Marty shook his head. "I'm not going to allow this first test to happen unless I'm part of it."

"You'll be part of it. You'll have direct radio communication."

"I need to be on the plane."

"That's not an option."

"Do you remember who led the raid over Tokyo, Admiral?"

Cutting's jaw muscles pulsed, that teeth-grinding tension back. "I haven't forgotten the USS *Hornet*. But you're no Jimmy Doolittle. He was qualified to fly."

"When it comes to shielding that cloud, there's no one alive who's remotely as qualified as me. I have to be prepared to alter the dispersal ratios of the Nightshade at the last minute, the last *second*. The lives of the men on that B-52 from Loring will depend on it."

"Request denied," Cutting said.

Marty placed both palms down on the table and said, "I'm afraid we have no path forward, then."

"You're not in charge!"

Marty smiled, a languid grin, unhurried, like the autumn leaves falling at Rosewater Pond, and then said, "That's the problem, Admiral. I *am* in charge. You do not have anyone who has conducted a successful test without me. Everyone in this room knows it."

He stared directly at Iris Stoka and saw the grim agreement in her eyes.

She believes she's close, but she knows she isn't there yet. Maybe she's vanished a few models. Probably. But she damn sure hasn't brought one back.

"You can figure it out, maybe," he said, speaking primarily to her. "But it will take a while. Weeks, months, years? You're damn sure not going to be ready without me in forty-eight hours, and meanwhile, down in Cuba—"

"Enough!" Cutting roared, and then he cleared the room except for Marty and Marilyn Metzger.

"I could have you prosecuted," Cutting told Marty.

"Or you could back the Soviets down for a decade. Pick an approach."

Cutting glared at him.

"He's not wrong," Marilyn Metzger said. "And I'll go on the plane with him."

When Ralph Cutting looked at her, Marty saw the years of trust that lay between them. No warmth, but plenty of trust. He suspected she'd fed Cutting the right decisions many times before, and, moreover, that when Cutting had ignored her advice, it turned out to be the wrong choice.

"I'll watch over him," Marilyn said.

"Dr. Hazelton, you are dismissed," the admiral said. "I'll speak with Miss Metzger in private, thank you."

It was two hours before Cutting sent for him again and said that Marty and Marilyn Metzger would be on the B-52 that departed from Ash Point.

"I'll grant your request," Cutting said, "but your philosophy is disappointing."

"It's in the best interest of the mission," Marty said, because he thought that was what Cutting would want to hear, results-based talk, hoo-rah!

"Bullshit," Cutting said.

Marty cocked his head. "Why do you think I want to go up there?"

"Guilt and poor decision-making," Cutting said without hesitation. "You have a disappointing moral confusion over the idea of accountability."

Disappointing moral confusion. That was a surprisingly interesting take from Ralph Cutting.

"We're going to change the world," Marty said. "Why wouldn't I want to be up there when it happens? It's my work, after all."

Cutting stared at him, rubbed his jaw, and said, "You're a brave man."

That was when Marty understood that Cutting didn't expect anyone to come back from these flights. He'd seen the models, and he'd reviewed the math, but he didn't believe it would work with a B-52.

That night the breeze blew hard and warm, and the swells ran high and fast. It was October 25, 1962, missile site construction continued in Cuba, Soviet submarines continued on course, more than five hundred American fighter planes were prepared to launch, and Khrushchev and Kennedy still had not spoken directly.

AIRBORNE, NEW YORK CITY
OCTOBER 25, 2025

When Charlie's phone rang, the sound was so unexpected that she and Hightower jumped together.

"What the hell is that?" he yelled.

"My phone. Untie me and I can answer it."

To her astonishment, he did. He was less threatened by her than he was by the phone. She picked it up, turned it over, and saw the screen filled with a familiar face.

It was John F. Kennedy, and he looked grim.

"Let me speak to Hightower," the dead president said in his thick Boston accent. *High-towah.*

Stunned and yet somehow moved by Kennedy's sense of authority, Charlie tilted the phone so Hightower could see the dead president.

"Captain," Kennedy said, "you're probably a little shaken up right now, unless I miss my guess."

Hightower's eyes were rapt.

"I've had better days, sir," he said. "But I'm still airborne."

He believed it was the president, Charlie realized. Was that good or bad? So long as the fake JFK wanted him to land without launching, it was good.

Right?

The dead president smiled wryly, and Charlie was struck by his easy charm. Someone had engineered this perfect imposter. The definitive white lie, one that could do no harm. Or so they thought. There was danger in the approach, though. No matter what the intention was, there was always danger in a lie.

"What you three have done," Kennedy said with austerity, "will forever remain a symbol of American might and ingenuity, a defense of freedom unforgettable to our allies and enemies alike. Now we need you back on the ground."

The words were his, scrambled snippets from some speech or another. It made sense, of course, to let his words speak for him, and yet Charlie was troubled by them. The lying felt unnecessary. Hightower wasn't a threat; he was lost.

"I ask you to return to Ash Point, sir, where you will be welcomed as the heroes you are, and fully debriefed," Kennedy continued. "A ground crew is ready for your arrival. I'm sure you have plenty of questions, and I look forward to meeting you myself. On behalf of a grateful nation, I thank you for your service."

Hightower didn't look flushed with pride, necessarily, but he seemed at least soothed by the sentiment. That bothered Charlie. Kennedy was dead, and the world Hightower knew was long gone. The past was painful, but the past was *real*. Telling someone that he didn't have to reckon with the past wasn't kind; it was cruel.

And dangerous.

Hightower couldn't go back to 1962, and how would he feel when he learned what had really happened to John F. Kennedy?

"What happens when we land?" Charlie asked the dead president.

Kennedy stared fixedly ahead, silent, a lag in the response for the first time.

"We will speak again when your airplane is safely on the earth."

"No! Tell us what really happens!" Charlie shouted at her phone. "He's seen Ash Point with his own eyes and he didn't blow it up. So stop lying and tell him what will happen when he lands!"

She'd anticipated objection from Hightower, but he did not say a word. Instead, he listened with interest.

Again there was a lag, time required for the masterminds of this trick to dictate the words that would come out of the fake Kennedy's mouth. There was something wrong with that whole idea, no matter the stakes. They should show Hightower the real president and let him hear the real truth. Wasn't that what you owed a hero?

"Young lady," the fake Kennedy said, "if you will cede communication to Captain Hightower for the remainder of—"

"Tell him what year it is!" Charlie shouted. "Tell him about Dallas, about Oswald; tell him all that!"

Kennedy said, "Captain Hightower, I now command you to—"

Charlie powered the phone off.

"What the hell did you do?" Hightower yelled. "That was the President!"

"No it wasn't. John F. Kennedy is dead, he has been for almost as long as . . . as *you*!"

Hightower was ashen.

"I'm sorry," Charlie said. "I really am. But they're lying to you with a dead president. They put his videos into a computer and spit out a replica. That's all it is: a replica. The real man is dead."

"It's his voice," Hightower said. "I know that voice. I know that face."

"That's the point! They have all the video and audio to make him say whatever they want, and they're picking a lie!"

Even as she said it, she wondered *why* she was saying it. Maybe whoever was putting the words in the dead man's mouth could land this plane and get Charlie off it. Shouldn't that be what she wanted? The *only* thing?

But she remembered her mother's voice floating out of the cockpit of the wreck, remembered how awful it had been, and she couldn't bring herself to feel badly. Fuck them. She would get Hightower to land the plane, and she wouldn't need to impersonate the dead to do it.

The real John F. Kennedy, she thought, would've understood the moral imperative along with the tactical.

"You need to see New York," she told Hightower. "Then I'll turn the phone back on and we'll wait to see who they have to talk to you next."

RAVEN ROCK MOUNTAIN COMPLEX, PENNSYLVANIA
OCTOBER 25, 2025

"We're going to start a nuclear war because of a seventeen-year-old sadist," the defense secretary said. "What in the hell is that girl doing? Hightower was listening! He was *buying it!*"

No one responded right away. They were all numb, shocked.

"It was a bad idea," Layla Chen said finally. "I had not anticipated the girl would resist if she heard the command to land. It was my bad idea."

No one argued that.

"We can't take a shot now," the president said. The satellite map showing the B-52's course confirmed that taking a shot would be a very poor idea, indeed. Goodbye, Boston.

"We can't just let them carry on!" the defense secretary objected.

"I think we have to," Hanover said.

"Untenable risk."

"We're already past the point of untenable risk," Hanover responded. "It is now in the pilot's control." He paused, then added, "And, apparently, the girl's."

"Fallout from hitting the plane will be minimal compared to letting him drop the bomb."

"Catastrophe is not minimal."

"And yet it is still relative."

Math in the atomic age.

There was a beat, and then Layla Chen spoke.

"We have no indication that pilot wants to drop anything. We aren't even sure if the bomb will work if he does. The only way to guarantee failure is to rush toward it. You do not do that in a nuclear scenario."

"We've seen your last idea in action," the defense secretary said. "The Kennedy bit was a very bad idea."

They all waited on the president.

"If he moves off the water and toward the city," the president said, "we must consider it hostile behavior, an act of aggression."

"And take the shot?" the defense secretary pressed.

"And take the shot."

Nobody spoke after that. They just watched the map. Ash Point, where it had all begun, was a forgotten dot at the top of the screen.

ASH POINT, MAINE
OCTOBER 1962

Marty met his pilot on the day the United States tested a Thor missile with a nuclear warhead off Johnston Atoll with the Cuban crisis worsening by the hour.

Earl Dupree, of Pittsburgh, had more than a thousand hours of flying time in the B-52 and carried himself like a man who would catch a live grenade in the air and replace the pin without breaking a sweat. He chewed Black Jack gum, rarely smiled, never laughed. His eyes were alert but distant, a man accustomed to observing the world from above. His skeleton crew consisted of Doyle Donovan, a slender twenty-three-year-old kid from a town called Tomahawk, Wisconsin, and Lester Ewing, from Albany, New York. The skeleton crew was by design, both because of the highly classified operation and because of fear of failure.

On the upper deck of the plane, behind and above the pilot, where the electronic warfare officer was usually stationed, Marilyn Metzger would be seated in a cramped, gear-filled room without so much as a porthole window view. She could see the radar screens and nothing else, flying both blind and backward. None of the B-52's crew seemed pleased that a woman would be on board. If Marilyn noticed or cared, she betrayed no indication.

Marty would be in the copilot's seat so he could see the clouds. Down a long, narrow catwalk and alone in the back of the plane, Doyle Donovan would sit in the tail gunner's plexiglass bubble, awaiting Marty's instructions. The Vulcan cannons that ordinarily fired 20-millimeter shells at enemy planes had been replaced by the smoke generators, loaded with Nashua Nightshade.

The bomber was intimidating even with its eight engines silent. *Loring Loonatic* was painted in script beneath the silhouette of the bird, its sleek black head outfitted with a red eye that glistened ruby-like. Marty had never cared for the tradition of clever names and silly cartoons adorning weapons of war, but it was common. A morale booster, he'd been told. He wasn't sure that good cheer was the missing ingredient of the atomic-bombing age—sanity seemed more likely—but if ever there was a poor advocate for that case, it was a man who wrote letters to his dead brother.

They spent the entire day drilling on the grounded plane, working through the maneuvers again and again, and while Marty's focus was on the smoke generators, Cutting's crew obsessed over the ejection seat maneuvers.

"Pay attention," Marilyn hissed at him during a break. "We argued our way onto the plane despite everyone's concern, and now you're so distracted that you're making them rethink the risk."

He knew she was right.

Ejecting was an exercise that felt closer to suicide than salvation. To begin the operation, the armrests needed to be lifted, exposing a trigger that, once depressed, initiated a series of fascinating mechanical and chemical reactions, as the seat was literally blown into the sky with an explosive charge. A cartridge detonation launched a catapult system that rolled the seat upward on rails, blasted it out of the plane, deployed a parachute, and then threw the occupant clear of the seat.

Marty was impressed by the engineering, the ejection seat its own marvel in a bewildering aircraft, but he had little interest in the safety lectures. His concern was the generators. He was limited to a headset radio and trust in Donovan to disperse the Nashua Nightshade as instructed.

The B-52 from Ash Point would be the first in the air, piloted by Dupree, who was to fly five hundred feet above the storm cloud, shield it, then ascend steeply and bank north while the bomber from Loring flew behind and beneath them, entering the cloud at 465 miles per hour.

At that point, one of three things would happen:

The plane would encounter lightning within the shielded cloud and vanish for six minutes; it would pass through the cloud without encountering lightning, requiring another test; it would not vanish at all, disproving Marty's math and dismaying the Ash Point crew.

There was, of course, a fourth option, though he didn't like to consider it.

The plane might be gone for good. His greatest fear was of a plane that simply disappeared and did not return.

The plane would then be reported as lost, and a search would commence, but what would they find? Not even an oil slick. It would remind the world of Flight 19—if the world noticed or cared. The good news for Admiral Cutting was that the world's attention was focused south, in Cuba. One downed bomber over the North Atlantic would not be a headline story. Crashes were uncommon but not unprecedented with the B-52. At a single air base in 1956, three of the bombers had crashed in eight months, killing nineteen. They weren't even unique stories in Maine. In 1957 a B-52 returning to Loring broke apart in midair, killing eight of the nine men aboard. In

July of '58, another crashed in a field near Loring, once again claiming eight lives. In the first three months of '61, two B-52s carrying nuclear weapons crashed without the bombs detonating—although in one case that required the accidental disconnection of two wires, the only thing that prevented a nuclear blast in Goldsboro, North Carolina.

All this was to say the press and the public would not overreact to one more missing bomber. Luck, not strategy, was the only thing that had prevented Americans from nuking their own nation on multiple occasions, and still munitions factories churned out bigger bombs with deadlier yields.

Can I stop the whole crazy race if this works? he wondered, sitting in the cockpit, listening to Dupree explain yet again the ejection seat deployment process as if Marty were a child struggling with a simple lesson.

The arms race needed to end.

It was going to, one way or another.

Each new report from Cuba was dire. The latest classified information was that Kennedy believed it would take an invasion to remove the nuclear missiles from Cuba. On the other side, Fidel Castro sent a telegram to Khrushchev requesting a nuclear response if the Americans invaded, saying, "However difficult and horrifying this decision may be, there is, I believe, no other recourse."

The American hope—one that felt more tenuous by the moment—was that proper pressure would intimidate the Soviets into submission.

At Ash Point, Rosson launched weather balloons, and Marty Hazelton cleaned his watch.

The world waited for dawn. Some of the world prayed for it.

It was October 1962, and there were no longer sure things.

On a day that would come to be known as Black Saturday, an American pilot in a Lockheed U-2 spy plane that was nicknamed "Dragon Lady" was shot out of the sky over Cuba while traveling at half the speed of sound. While the remains of Major Rudolf Anderson Jr's body and plane crashed to the Cuban soil, a Soviet submarine in the sweltering tropical waters offshore lost radio contact when its batteries overheated. Located by American naval destroyers, the unidentified sub was subjected to a depth-charge barrage designed to bring it to the surface. Cut off from communication, deprived of oxygen, subjected to temperatures above 110 degrees Fahrenheit, and down to one hour of battery life, the submarine's commander surfaced to find his ship facing a flotilla of American destroyers, blinding searchlights, and low flyovers from planes.

Convinced he'd entered into a war that had already begun, he screamed that he would not disgrace his nation or shame his fleet, then ordered a dive and the launch of a nuclear-tipped torpedo, a strike that would have vaporized the entire American task force in the Sargasso Sea—all while more than 3,000 warheads were pointed at Russia from various places on the globe, on planes and in silos and in submarines. Once those missiles went airborne, the Soviets would have responded, unleashing an earth-scouring exchange.

The order to commence that exchange was given on the Atlantic Ocean on October 27, 1962. It was not heeded.

The brigade chief of staff, Vasili Arkhipov, argued with his captain that if war had already broken out, the Americans would not be wasting such time and resources locating one submarine. The tactics of the American ships did not match the scale of devastation. The sub identified itself and demanded the Americans cease their provocations. They received an apology via radio. Vasili Arkhipov, who may have come closer to single-handedly saving the world than any man in history, departed with his submarine crew.

While the world danced with extinction in Cuba, atomic experts were busy reviewing the results of three nuclear tests conducted that very day. Two of those tests were launched by the United States. Over the remote Johnston Atoll, the Calamity mission had gone off as scheduled, and in Nevada a ground explosion was conducted while thousands of tourists drank atomic-themed cocktails on the Las Vegas Strip.

On the secure line between Ash Point, Maine, and Washington, D.C., news of the U-2 takedown and the submarine encounter was relayed and a terse agreement made: Project Kingsolver was to proceed, with exact launch time to be determined by the weather conditions.

Temperatures rose with the sun, but the breeze carried a blade's edge. The sea was laced with whitecapped, rolling swells that broke hard against the rocks, shook themselves like angry dogs, and charged again. Gulls shrieked and circled beneath clouds the color of gunpowder.

Marty watched the tumultuous sea while the wind lashed his face, making his eyes tear as he gazed at the water and wondered about the monkey from Cleveland, #5709, Jimmy. What had he seen? He'd made it back but was different. There was no denying that.

Those eyes . . .

Overhead, the clouds coiled and shifted. There was thunder, loud enough that it startled him, and then he realized it wasn't thunder at all but the sound of the B-52's engines.

The Klaxon pierced the air.

Battle stations.

He made his feet move, feeling too slow already, unable to run, scarcely able to walk. He was afraid but he was moving. He was doing that much.

I'll have to tell Hank, he thought dimly. *I'll have to write him about this whole crazy scene. No, better yet, I'll call him; it's been so long since I've heard his voice. He may know Captain Dupree, might've flown with Donovan or Ewing, might've . . .*

He stopped walking. Looked up at the clamshell clouds, rippled and dark and gleaming, and back at the plane with the loon painted on its nose.

Hank is dead. Come on, Martin. Now is not the time.

When he moved again, it was at a run, the fastest his fifty-year-old legs could manage. On the tarmac, the sound of the plane was deafening, most communication limited to hand signals. An airman slapped a helmet on Marty and guided him into the belly of the plane.

Once they were inside, Donovan peeled off, snaking down the tight catwalk that carried him to his lonely gunner's post in the tail while the others went forward, toward the cockpit. There, another set of ladders waited, one descending, one ascending. Marilyn would already be aboard, harnessed into her seat on the upper deck of the plane, flying backward and blind, a claustrophobe's nightmare. The navigator, Ewing, climbed below, and Marty clambered into the cockpit behind Dupree. Dupree was already seated, chewing his Black Jack gum, stubble shading his jaw, cool eyes indifferent. He barely glanced at Marty.

"Strap in, Doc," he said.

Marty did. He had flown hundreds of hours in dozens of aircraft and all types of weather, yet still the experience of takeoff in a B-52 took his breath away. The plane's sheer power was something felt in the gut, and the noise was overwhelming, the screaming jet engines putting a vibration through the metal decking and fuselage and miles of wires and cables and thousands of bolts that made the plane sound as if it were coming apart. Liftoff, when it happened, was a stomach-dropping sensation of separation from the earth. Then they rose steeply, Ash Point behind them, black clouds before them.

"Hazelton, you there?" a voice crackled into Marty's ear. It was Donovan, back in the tail gunner's compartment.

"I'm here," Marty said. Speaking relaxed him a little, refocused him on the task at hand. The wind battered the big plane, making Dupree's jaw clench as he wrestled the yoke. For all its sophistication, flying the B-52 required an enormous amount of physical effort.

"Loring has departure," another voice said. This was Ewing, the navigator. "Pick us a winner, Doc, and let's try this spooky shit."

He meant pick a good cloud, and since Ewing couldn't see the sky, he had no idea what they were flying into. Marty sat forward.

The storm front was moving in fast, and lightning strobes lit the lead-colored clouds to the left and right, creating a maze of color and shadow. There was a dip so sudden, it clacked Marty's teeth together, and by the time Dupree steadied them out, Marty could taste blood in his mouth. Any of these clouds would work, he thought. All they had to do was seed this crazy sky.

Marty slipped his watch off his wrist and held it in both hands, ready to advance the dial. Dupree saw him, frowned, but didn't say anything. It was easier to hide the watch on the ground, but up here, jolting and jostling, Marty was afraid that he'd misfire somehow, and he no longer cared so much about his secret as he did its success: there were men with families on that plane, living, breathing humans who were about to enter the unknown.

Thunder and wind. Lightning, again and again, above and below, left and right. Plummet and shudder, teeth-snapping, stomach-tossing lurches that threw Marty against his harness.

"Goodness," Dupree said, and though it was the mildest of words said in the mildest of tones, it was the first reaction he'd shown to anything, which made it distressing. Marty could see the tension in the pilot's shoulders and arms.

The second bomber appeared. At first it was nothing but sound, but when Marty turned to his right, he saw the B-52 from Loring. It was a menacing silhouette, the swept-back wings bristling with eight engines, the towering tail stabilizer, and the odd cannons flanking the tail.

Dupree said, "We ready, Doc?"

Marty stared down at the second plane. He was surprised to see what looked like a duplicate of the signature loon painted beneath the cockpit. He'd thought those little quirks existed precisely to individualize the planes. Perhaps it was a squadron approach? He didn't pretend to know the habits of Air Force men. Still, there was something about the plane that bothered him. It looked too familiar. Why was that? All the time he'd spent studying B-52s in the past year, from models to photographs to diagrams, and still he was perplexed. There was something wrong. Something different.

"Doc?" Dupree said.

Marty leaned closer to the window. The clouds shifted, thickened, then thinned again, and, yes, now he was sure.

"Why does it have smoke generators?" he asked.

No one answered. Not in the cockpit, or on the radio. He turned to Dupree.

"Why does that plane have its own generators?" he repeated.

"Doc, I just fly this one."

The plane Dupree commanded was still shuddering through the storm, but Marty was almost oblivious to the turbulence now. He thought of Iris working away at her drafting table, all those sketches of clouds and ascent angles, and the day she'd asked whether a second plane was needed at all. Marty assured her that it was, but his assurance was vague, to which she said:

It could leap. If the partner were not required, it could leap through time again and again.

"What don't I know?" he said now.

"What you don't know is still more than I *do* know," Dupree said. "Now, Doc, we're supposed to fire those generators at your command. Will you give it?"

"Radio that plane."

"They're flying silent."

"What the hell does that mean?"

"Just what I said. That's their mission. Mine is to fire our generators. I don't know theirs."

"Why do they even have generators?"

"Doc, you're asking for intel I don't have!"

Leap, Iris had said, and Admiral Cutting's eyes had brightened at the possibility, imagining a nuclear bomber that could appear and disappear, again and again, something beyond stealth.

Marty's failure, impossible as it seemed considering the circumstances, had been one of imagination.

He hadn't taken it far enough.

And they hadn't waited on him.

AIRBORNE, EASTERN SEABOARD
OCTOBER 25, 2025

When the New York City skyline came into view, Captain Hightower's eyes went wide and distant.

"That's not New York," he said.

"Yes it is," Charlie said. The familiarity of it felt like a dream to her, so close yet so far away.

They flew on. Closer, lower. Still no fighter jets in the sky. They were the last plane on earth, it seemed. Hightower didn't seem to be even remotely concerned about other planes, though. He was staring at the New York skyline with his mouth hanging slack.

"What in the hell is this place?" It wasn't a real question; the words were for himself—vocalized shock, nothing more.

Charlie stayed silent as the mighty, gleaming spires of glass and steel appeared before them. One World Trade Center, Central Park Tower, Hudson Yards, the slender spire of the Steinway Tower, 432 Park Avenue and its brand-new cousin, 270 Park. She knew them all, loved them all. Her favorite thing about the city was its fearless quest for the sky.

Looking at Hightower, she saw wonder and fear shifting in his eyes like dance partners. But at least there was no argument about how this was some hologram the Soviets had conjured to fool him. He knew what he saw was real.

"The tallest buildings are new to you, aren't they?" she said. "But the Empire State Building is still there. Look." She pointed at the stately old building's spire. "And the Chrysler Building."

The Chrysler Building had been the tallest in the world once, and now it was a subordinate on the city's skyline. She tried to think of other landmarks that would matter to him. He hadn't been born so long ago, really, and yet so much of New York had changed. Ten of the twelve tallest buildings had been built in her lifetime. No wonder it looked like a foreign land to him.

"Captain! Holy shit, Captain, are you seeing this?" Granville's voice, just ahead of a clatter of boots on metal, and then he and Bellamy appeared, crowding into the cockpit, wild-eyed.

"Look at it!" Granville gestured wildly at the city skyline. "What in the fuck is it? Where did you take us? Where did they put us!"

"Back to your stations!" Hightower shouted, but Granville wasn't having it.

"I'll be damned if I will! You need to explain this! What did they tell you that they didn't tell us?"

"I got the same briefings and you know it."

"Bullshit!" Granville's voice was shrill. "How are they doing it? How in the fuck are they doing *that*?"

He punctuated the question by jabbing his finger at the New York skyline.

"We're not helping by losing our cool."

"Losing our cool?" Granville gave a hysteric yelp of a laugh. "Man, you put us into . . . into . . . another fuckin' world, I don't know, and you're gonna sit there and tell me not to lose my cool? Fuck you, Captain, *fuck you!*"

"*Hey!*" Hightower snapped. "Back off and get your head together."

That would not happen, Charlie saw. Granville wasn't backing off, and it was clear that he couldn't get his head together. Not right now; maybe not ever.

"Take us back," Granville said. "Back to Loring. Right now."

"Loring is gone," Charlie said, and they all stared at her. "Closed, I mean. It's not an active base anymore."

Granville slapped her.

It was a backhanded blow that smacked her head off the hard frame of the seat and brought coppery blood to her lips. Hightower shouted, punched at Granville's arm, and bellowed for Bellamy's help.

Bellamy did not move. He was staring, transfixed, at the city.

In the cramped space of the cockpit, Granville loomed behind and between Charlie and Hightower, his eyes flicking over the gauges and controls as if considering his options. Charlie had a sudden fear that he would reach for the thrust levers, kill the engines, and send them spiraling toward the water.

"Captain, I'm telling you, take us back."

"I can't, you insubordinate son of a bitch!"

"Bullshit. You know how to do it."

"I don't! And I'm in command of this plane. Get the hell *back to your station!*"

Granville's mouth was a thin, tight line.

"I'm done with this," he said. "Captain, I'm done."

Bellamy looked from one man to the other and gave a sickly little laugh, as if he'd stacked too many things he couldn't believe on top of one another, and now the stack was tumbling on him, a cascade that couldn't be stopped.

"We've got a bomb to drop," Granville said. "If nothing else, we need to do that much. You take me back or I deliver the baby as ordered. Fuck Cuba, I'll drop it here."

The plane's motion seemed to cease with Charlie's held breath, everything trapped and still and unreal.

"Do not give me orders," Hightower said, but his voice had a waver, the kind that the word "bomb" could put into it.

"They've already been given and you know it. We had a job to do."

"Not to bomb the United States of America!"

"That's not the United States of America!" Granville shrieked, pointing at the cockpit window. "It's not, and I won't listen to anyone who tells me it is! You get me back to Loring or I'm going to do my damned duty, one or the other, end of fuckin' story!"

"Bellamy," Hightower said, low and steady, "take control of your crewmate."

Bellamy blinked, then reached for his pistol, but he was shaking and slow and Granville was faster. He grasped Bellamy's gun by the barrel as it came up, then wrenched it free, Bellamy barely even fighting for it, too shocked for a struggle. Granville spun the gun, rotating it so he had it held by the grip instead of the barrel, the muzzle swinging around as they grappled.

The gun went off.

Charlie's scream was high and wordless and overwhelmed Hightower's desperate, pointless pleas for order. He sounded like a judge in a courtroom gone mad, bringing a gavel to a gunfight.

Bellamy fell back, hands clasped to his belly, eyes wide. Blood spurted through his fingers, painted the steel door with scarlet, and when he dropped, he fell sideways, landing on his left shoulder, one booted foot jutting into the cockpit. There was a high, harsh whistling that Charlie realized was coming from a hole in the fuselage where the bullet had exited Bellamy's body and punctured the steel. Its small round opening cast a single shaft of sunlight down on his body, a beam like the eye of God shining on him as he took his last breaths.

Granville gazed back at him with horror and hubris, the *You made me do it* defiance of an abuser paired with *What have I done?* recognition.

"Relinquish your weapon," Hightower said, and even in her terror Charlie marveled at his steadfast faith in formality, in protocol. It was ridiculous in the face of these circumstances, and yet he would not break. He would give the right orders in the right voice until they were all dead. He was the man you'd want to fly the bomb, no doubt about it, but the problem was that they needed the human soul beneath the soldier, because this situation had gone primal. There were no ranks anymore. There was only the weapon—and the hand that held it.

Granville turned from Bellamy. He looked almost childlike, impossibly young and very afraid.

"What have we all done?" he said.

Charlie thought, You *did it, asshole. There's no "we"; it is only you,* but she couldn't say a word, could only sit there staring at him in terror.

"Relinquish the weapon," Hightower repeated, and Granville gave a laugh that turned into a sob.

"*We* are the weapon, Captain. Don't you see that yet? We signed up to become the fucking weapon, and now we are."

He looked out at the city, then down at Bellamy. The airman was slumped against the wall, his neck bent unnaturally, jaw slack, one limp hand over his belly, blood bright on his drab flight suit.

"I'm sorry, old boy," Granville whispered. "Damn all, I am so sorry."

Then he turned to Charlie and lifted the gun. As the muzzle rose, she was sure that he would shoot, a clear, eerily calm sense that death was here and would not be denied. Maybe it was how her mother had felt in that bodega. The last thing Charlie saw before she ducked was Granville's too-bright blue eyes.

The gunshot wasn't aimed at her but at Hightower. The glass of the cockpit window shattered, spiderwebbing, and she screamed again as cold, fresh air blew through the bullet hole like a blast from a pressure washer.

Crashing, we are crashing now, my already-dead pilot is dead again and we are all going to join him, going down now . . .

But the plane was rising.

She lifted her head and saw Hightower still at the yoke, the cockpit windshield split between them, a bullet hole letting in the whistling wind, blood staining its cracked edges. Whose blood?

She looked to her left and saw Granville.

He had fired the gun into his own mouth.

His body shuddered and what was left of his chin trembled, but it was a synthetic motion, not a human one. He was dead, the rough ride irrelevant to him now. His blood trickled across the corrugated floor and mingled with Bellamy's, extended to him like a handshake, an apology that could never be heard.

Beside Charlie, Hightower fought the yoke, steadying the plane, taking it out, away from the city, over the open water. The air smelled of smoke and blood. The gun lay on the corrugated metal floor, and Charlie thought about reaching for it, but what was the point?

Hightower removed one hand from the yoke and pulled his sunglasses off, then ran the back of his hand over his face, trying to gather himself. He swallowed and looked at Charlie, and she finally saw his piercingly bright eyes. The mark of the time travelers, the wrong kind of bright.

"Are you all right?" he asked.

She nodded. The whistling wind, funneled through that small, fractured hole in the glass, blew her hair in all directions. She pointed at the hole.

"Won't the plane go down now?" she whispered. "The pressure or whatever?"

"It would take a lot of holes larger than that to cost us pressure," Hightower said. "They're built to take gunfire. From the outside."

It was quiet as they both considered that idea: from the outside. She thought of Lawrence, tied up in the bomb bay, and wondered if he'd heard the shooting.

Then, with a deep grief, Hightower said, "It broke him. When we put down at Ash Point, it broke him."

Charlie couldn't think of anything to say.

"He volunteered," Hightower added, speaking more to himself than to her. "Knew the risk and volunteered, like all of us. He was a brave, good man. You probably can't believe that, but it's the truth."

They were now well out over the water, the city skyline fading behind.

"I believe it," Charlie said.

When he looked at her, she saw there were tears in his bright eyes.

"Thank you," he whispered.

RAVEN ROCK MOUNTAIN COMPLEX, PENNSYLVANIA
OCTOBER 25, 2025

In the nation's wartime White House, buried beneath the Blue Ridge Mountains, in the Emergency Conference Room, you could hear the soft sounds of the air filtration systems that were supposed to protect America's leadership from biological weapons. It was that quiet. Everyone seemed afraid to breathe, let alone speak.

They'd been ten seconds from launching a missile at the B-52. Maybe five seconds, if the president had rushed. They all knew they could be watching a radioactive cloud roll toward Manhattan at this moment while emergency sirens blared, broadcast networks blinked to alert screens, and the nation's populace exchanged doubts or panic on social media. The ones lucky enough to still be alive.

Many in Manhattan would already be incinerated.

It had been only a few seconds from that.

Then a man who'd been born one hundred and one years earlier had fired two shots with a handgun, and the B-52 banked east.

They'd heard it but not seen it. The Goodwin girl had powered her phone off after the disastrous attempt to talk Hightower down using the voice of John F. Kennedy, but the tech team at Raven Rock were able to activate Lawrence Zimmer's iPad. Unfortunately, it was jammed beneath a seat, the camera offering no vantage point on the situation. The microphone, however, was clear.

They could have used it to speak to Hightower. The president had wanted to. One last, desperate effort.

Then had come the gunshots, and then the plane turned away from the city, and with each mile of distance it gained, the chance of survival for New York increased.

"Do we engage them now?" the defense secretary said at last, breaking the silence.

"No," Layla Chen said, and she knew she was speaking out of turn here, but she had to. The stakes were too high. "It went badly last time, and they're flying in the right direction now."

Hanover agreed. So did the Air Force general who'd been prepared to issue the final launch command. His usually ruddy face was the color of old snow.

The president listened and said, "I want to see them keep flying east. Away from the city."

"We need some contingency plan," the defense secretary said.

"Patience won't hurt," the president said.

"Listening won't hurt," Layla added.

So they listened while the Air Force put Black Hawk helicopters into the air and the Navy and Coast Guard mobilized ships. The president was returning to the idea of passive pressure. Let Hightower see the military, but from a distance. He may, the president reasoned, find a degree of comfort in it, given time.

In a bunker at Cheyenne Mountain, a drone operator had the B-52 centered in his scope, ready to take it out of the sky at any moment.

Layla had a dim memory of the launch code from Project Kingsolver, the three words that Hightower would utter if he intended to drop his Mark 39 thermonuclear bomb: Crown the king.

She shivered.

Across the globe, intelligence reports were flooding in. The Russians were watching, and the Iranians, and of course the allies: Germany, Great Britain, Japan, Israel; all of them had intensifying questions as to what, exactly, the United States military was up to off its own shores.

If they only knew, Layla thought.

AIRBORNE, ASH POINT, MAINE
OCTOBER 28, 1962

Dupree chewed his gum and wrestled his aircraft through the storm, his determined face lit by relentless lightning, while on the radio Doyle Donovan announced his intention to fire the Nashua Nightshade.

"It's my call!" Marty barked into the headset.

"You can ask the admiral about that in person if we survive this, Hazelton, but it's not your call anymore. You wanted a part in it and they gave you a seat, that's all."

"Captain Dupree," Marty began, but Dupree was already shaking his head.

"We're here to test," he said. "And I hope you paid attention yesterday, or God help you."

Yesterday? Yesterday they'd done nothing except drill endlessly on the ejection process.

And then, sudden and sharp, Marty understood.

He looked down to where the B-52 from Loring rode just off their starboard side, no more than five hundred feet below, a precariously close arrangement for all but the finest pilots, particularly in this weather, and watched as the lightning lit up the black plane and made the red eye of the loon painted beneath its cockpit gleam.

"They never meant to land this plane," he said.

Dupree didn't answer.

Marty got it because he'd already lived it. There had been scientists—including three Nobel laureates—on the Manhattan Project who had advocated for a public demonstration of the bomb *before* its military use. Let Japan see it as those at the Trinity test had seen it, they argued. Let them know what power was held.

They had been overridden. The planners determined the best means of showing the enemy the awesome power was a tactical strike.

The Loring plane wasn't going to be tested and returned to base. It was going to be sent forward—and more than six minutes forward. Iris Stoka believed she could do that. She believed it because Marty's lies had allowed her to. Down below, back at Ash Point, Iris Stoka and the Advanced Research Projects Agency were prepared to utilize a useless radio signal to summon back a vanished plane at the hour of their choosing. And then what? Hit Moscow? Cuba?

"Dupree," Marty said, and his voice was hoarse and hollow, "you've got to make contact with that plane."

"I can't, damn it! Not even if I want to. They're flying silent, and that's the game, Doc. I'm not the one running it!"

"There's got to be a way to signal them! Something!"

Dupree's headshake was firm.

"I'm along for the ride at this point. We all are."

"We'll shield the cloud and then eject," Marty said. "Is that it? One plane vanishes, the other crashes, and then what?"

"I don't know!" Dupree's voice went high and harsh, and for the first time Marty could feel the pilot's fear. "You think they tell us? I'm trying to get people home alive. That's all! That's my mission."

"Contact Ash Point!" Marty said. "They don't know how it works. It can't be summoned by the radio signal; that's a lie—my lie. The truth is that plane can't be called back by anyone but *me*, and if I'm not there, it's *gone*."

Dupree's jaw worked at the gum, his hands flexed on the yoke of the plane, and he said nothing.

"I'm spreading this shit with or without you, Doc," Donovan said from the tail gunner's seat. "Be advised."

"No, damn it!"

Silence but for the crackling static of the radio. Marty remembered the way his test planes had fallen, one after the other, incinerated, until the day he'd used the watch.

"Fifteen seconds," Donovan said.

Marty swore, grabbed his father's watch, and pulled out the crown. Rolled the minute hand backward.

One, two, three, four, five, six.

"Deploying the Nightshade," Donovan said, and a fine gray mist joined the clouds below them.

The Loring bomber flew into it.

The flash of light, when it came, wasn't the brightest Marty had ever seen—that had been on Elugelab—but it was the strangest. A dancing, textured rainbow of silverish blue, an extraordinary shimmer that lit up every wire within the plane, filling the dark cloud with an iridescent web of blue lines. Around the web, the plane shattered into a cloud of charcoal-colored dust like a million electrified mayflies hatching.

Then it was gone.

In the pilot seat, Dupree said, "Goodness."

Donovan's voice, high and filled with fear and wonder, came over the radio.

"Holy shit, holy shit, it's gone! It's just gone! It was there and now it's gone and *did you see that fucking light?* Holy shit, what have we done?"

"Get control of yourself," Dupree said, though his own voice trembled. "We've got six minutes to wait, and if it works, we hit them again and give them six months."

Six months? Marty saw the price of his long lie. They believed the bomber could be summoned back with radio signals, and Marty had allowed them to trust so he could protect his secret. He had been content to control the power with the idea that it might die with him, but not that others might die and leave him behind. That wasn't a sacrifice; it was murder.

They would not listen to him—Dupree belonged to the mission—but they might listen to Marilyn. Cutting would, anyhow.

Marty fumbled for the clasp of his harness, unbuckled it, and threw it back. Dupree spun toward him.

"Sit down! Hazelton, damn it, sit back—"

But Marty was gone. He clambered out of the cockpit, smashing painfully against the steel frame as the plane bucked in the wind, and behind him Dupree shouted into the radio, telling them that Marty was on the move. Hopefully, someone at Ash Point would hear it and care. They were heedless and reckless, though, scared past the point of no return by missiles in Cuba and submarines off the Florida coast. They didn't believe there was time to waste convincing the Soviets of what would seem impossible.

As he banged his way through the plane, bouncing from one side to the other, shins and elbows cracking off metal while the craft rocked and rolled, he saw the argument. What photographs would the Soviets possibly believe? What videos? There were none that would convince the Kremlin. Anticipating the hollowness of the threat, the Pentagon had given up on live testing and moved toward live *action*. It was the bomb all over again, Hiroshima without the debates that had predated that decision. Or perhaps there had been plenty of debates, and Marty Hazelton simply wasn't privy to them. That was more likely.

The plane shook left to right. He fell forward, the side of his head striking the fuselage, a thunderclap of a blow that stunned him. When he pushed himself upright, he was disoriented. The plane seemed a maze of shadowy dead-end corridors. He needed to find the ladder. Marilyn was in the electronic warfare officer's seat, on the upper deck, flying blind and backward.

Suddenly there came a sound from the tail of the plane—a far-off but clearly jubilant shout. Donovan, whooping with wild, astonished delight. Marty didn't need the radio to tell him what had happened. The plane from Loring was back.

It had worked.

Now they would the fire the Nightshade generators once more, vanishing the plane with a goal of six months this time, confident that they could recall the aircraft with a satellite and signal when what they needed was a watch.

He couldn't let them try it. There was too much risk. Six months? He couldn't give them that.

He found the ladder to the upper deck, gripped a rung, and heaved himself up. One step, two, three . . . into the hatch.

"Marilyn!"

But she was not there.

The electronic warfare officer's seat was empty. The person Marty most needed had never been on the plane at all.

Charlie was just about to ask Hightower what his plan was when there came a dull bang from behind the cockpit, then an undeniable sound of motion.

Granville, she thought wildly. *He's not dead, and I should have taken that gun. How was I stupid enough to leave him with the gun?*

Then she turned, saw the bodies of Granville and Bellamy still slumped, facing each other in their cooling blood, and beyond them Lawrence Zimmer. His eyes went wide at the sight of the corpses.

Charlie said, "They got in a fight," as if that clarified anything. Lawrence just stared at her.

"There's a lady on the plane," he said.

Charlie had not the faintest idea what he was talking about. Then Lawrence climbed up and there was a blond woman behind him, her flight suit too large, draped on her, her bright eyes fixed on Charlie.

"Miss Metzger, you were told to stay in the EWO seat," Hightower said.

Charlie looked wide-eyed from one to the other, and then understanding arrived wrapped in a memory.

"You're the broad, not me," she said.

She was remembering the way the crew had all stopped beneath the plane at Ash Point. One of the men—*Bellamy?* she thought—had yelled out, *What's the broad doing?* and Charlie had inferred it to be directed at her. He'd been looking back at the plane, though.

"She found me," Lawrence said. "Then we heard the gunshots."

The blonde didn't say anything. She was staring, horrified, at the bodies of Bellamy and Granville.

"You were supposed to stay seated until we cleared you," Hightower said.

"You seem to have greater concerns, Captain Hightower."

Hightower didn't dispute that.

"You might also have a solution," she said, and finally looked up from the dead men.

Hightower gave a snorting, contemptuous laugh.

"Truly," she said. "The boy has Marty's watch."

"Marty?"

"Dr. Hazelton. The boy has his watch and a note. You need to see this."

Hightower glanced back as Lawrence removed the box from his backpack. The same pilot who'd been unable to conceive of an iPhone needed no time at all to recognize the odd box that had floated down to Ash Point.

"Where'd you get the radiosonde?"

"It was attached to a balloon. There was a watch, and a note."

"They came down just before you," Charlie added.

Lawrence opened the radiosonde and passed it forward. Charlie took it, removed the note, unfolded it.

*Survival = Find storm cloud, fire Nightshade, set watch
backward and add voltage. You will catch up.*

"Does it mean anything to you?" she asked Hightower, and she
could see from his face that it meant plenty but wasn't necessarily
reassuring.

He looked at the woman.

"A watch? You kidding me? A *watch*?"

The blond woman's face was almost rapturous. She gazed beyond
Hightower, through the bullet-pocked glass, out to the clear sky beyond.

"He did it," she said. "We're really . . . we're here."

"We are in 2025, according to them," Hightower said.

It was hard to tell whether that frightened her or delighted her:
those eerie, bright eyes could have conveyed either emotion.

"Let me see the watch," Hightower said, and Charlie handed the
old wristwatch to him. He touched it warily, turning it over in the
same fashion as he'd handled her cell phone, as if it might explode.

"What's the nightshade?" Lawrence asked.

"Spook smoke," Hightower said, as if that were a satisfactory
answer.

"What does that mean?"

"It's how they shielded the cloud," the blonde replied. "Dr. Hazelton invented it. A remarkable achievement."

Her voice was soft, awed.

"Who is Dr. Hazelton?"

Now the bright eyes registered clear disappointment.

"You don't know?"

Charlie shook her head. The blonde looked at Lawrence. He
shook his head. She seemed to sag a little.

"That's a tragedy. I suppose I shouldn't be surprised. Admiral Cutting's team could always keep a secret, but . . . Marty should be known. Even in 2025 he should be famous."

Hightower glanced back at her. "You believe them."

"Of course. It was my project."

"Your project was six months," Hightower said. "We're off by six fucking decades."

It was the first time Charlie had heard him swear. Even in the gunfire, he'd kept his tongue.

"Hiccups on the way to history," the blonde said. She could not stop staring out the cockpit. It was as if she were seeing the sky for the first time.

"Two men are dead," Hightower shot back.

"I see that. I'm very sorry."

"And President Kennedy is dead. The girl told me."

"Why," Lawrence Zimmer moaned, "would you tell him *that*?"

"Because they were lying to him," Charlie said. It seemed hard to defend the choice now that Lawrence was here, but she thought if he'd heard the fake Kennedy, he'd have understood. Then again, there were two dead men at his feet and a bullet hole in the windshield, so it was hard to argue that Charlie had orchestrated a success up here.

"I would think he'd have passed by now," Metzger said. "If it is truly the year 2025."

"She tells me he was assassinated," Hightower said.

Lawrence covered his face with a palm, as if the burden of being associated with Charlie were too much to bear.

"Well, he was!" she said. "One year and one month after you guys took off."

"Is she right?" Hightower asked Lawrence.

"Why do you trust him but not me?" Charlie said, but Hightower ignored her and kept looking at Lawrence.

"Yes," Lawrence said. "She's right. I don't know why she told you, but . . . she's right. He was shot by a man named Lee Harvey Oswald on November 22, 1963. President Kennedy was riding in a convertible in Dallas when it happened. Someone killed his brother five years later."

The blonde gaped. "Bobby is dead?"

Lawrence nodded.

"Who shot them? Soviets?"

"I think . . . I mean, there are lots of weird theories and stuff, but I think it was just random people," Lawrence said. "It wasn't a military thing, just crazy people with guns."

"We see a lot of that now," Charlie added.

Hightower took a deep breath, wiped his mouth with his hand.

They were flying over the forested coast, north by northeast, tracking the Maine shoreline, as if he intended to go back to Ash Point. Maybe, with any luck, he did. A ship had appeared in the water below them, long and white, with orange markings on the side. A Coast Guard cutter. In the distance, Charlie could hear a soft *whump, whump, whump.*

"We got choppers in the air now," Hightower said. "An escort would be my guess. We must scare the living hell out of them."

Charlie twisted and saw black silhouettes behind the plane, three helicopters flying tightly together, making a wicked-looking triangle, but keeping their distance. Hightower watched them, impressed.

"Those are new. The world might've gotten worse, but the helicopters got better."

"You believe it now?" Charlie asked. "That it's 2025?"

"I don't understand what in the hell happened inside of that cloud, but I've still got eyes and brains. I saw Ash Point, and I saw that city—I guess it's still New York—and I see you two, and I know that none of it is from my day." He jabbed a thumb at Lawrence. "Well, he might've passed for a kid I knew in '62."

Lawrence straightened as if he'd just been complimented. Charlie couldn't suppress a braying laugh.

"You're such a dork, even the time travelers accept you as their own, Lawrence."

Hightower added, "But we sure didn't have any girls with mouths like yours."

"Those were the days," Lawrence said, and Charlie shot him the bird.

They flew on in silence, the helicopters trailing.

"There will be a drone operator watching you," Charlie said. "Somewhere on the other side of the country, probably, North Dakota or Colorado or someplace; I don't know. But if they want to shoot you down, they won't have to use the helicopters to do that."

"I don't think they'll want to shoot us down," the woman said. "Not with a bomb on board, for one thing, but more than that . . . they'll want the plane." She paused, gazed around with her shimmering eyes, and added, "And they'll want us, of course. We're much more exciting than the monkeys."

"The monkeys?" Hightower said.

The blonde just smiled. It was an empty, cold smile, and it promised Charlie that this woman, whoever she was, knew a hell of a lot more than Captain Hightower had ever known.

RAVEN ROCK MOUNTAIN COMPLEX, PENNSYLVANIA
OCTOBER 25, 2025

"This would be your girl, Sector Six?" the defense secretary said.

"*Your girl*," Layla thought. What an interesting way to phrase it. As if DARPA had birthed the whole problem. They'd had some help, and Layla was just trying to put the genie back in the bottle.

"That would be Marilyn Metzger, formerly of the Office of Naval Research," she said. "She was an overseer of Project Kingsolver."

"What was she doing on the plane?" the president asked.

"Experiencing it," Layla said, and then lifted her hands, palms out, at their skepticism. "I didn't authorize the decision. I wasn't born yet."

"She sounds levelheaded," Hanover said, a trace of hope there.

"She generally was," Layla said.

"Generally?"

"There are some criticisms in her file about her relationship with Hazelton. She also made some overtures about Flight 19 that caused consternation in the fifties."

"Flight 19?"

"A group of torpedo bombers we lost in 1945, with her fiancé on board. Once she was with the Department of Defense, though, her record was impeccable."

"What do you think she wants to do?" the president asked.

"I have no idea, but her initial read of the situation is a good one. We don't have any desire to shoot the plane down, we do want it back on the ground, and we will be very interested in the survivors."

No one said anything. Layla suspected everyone in the room was imagining what the lab tests might show about the plane and the people inside it. Invisibility. Time travel. Powers long thought beyond the reach of science.

"I almost hope the Chinese are listening to this," the defense secretary said. "Can you imagine what they're thinking?"

"Do not voice that thought again," the president snapped. Then the cockpit voices came back to life in the B-52, and Raven Rock went silent once more, because the group on the *Loring Loonatic* was formulating a plan.

AIRBORNE, EASTERN SEABOARD
OCTOBER 25, 2025

They'd flown in silence for a few minutes before Captain Hightower said, "Okay, Metzger, let's hear a plan."

"Marilyn," the blonde said.

"What in the hell do I do, Marilyn? It being your mission and all."

She was quiet, watching the sky.

"You've got Nightshade generators to fire, don't you?"

"Yeah, I've got them."

"Then we could try to leap. It would take us out of this moment, anyhow. For better or worse. But I think we can only go forward. That was Marty's understanding."

Charlie was silent. The letter in her hand rustled in the whistling wind from the bullet hole in the cockpit glass. Lawrence grasped the doorframe, balancing above the dead men, while Marilyn Metzger stood on the other side, separated by the blood streaks on the floor.

"Let me read the letter again, please," she said.

Charlie passed her the note. The woman read it slowly, thoughtfully, and Charlie found herself enchanted, watching those incandescent eyes. Who *was* she? If Charlie survived—a big question—she would find out. Marilyn Metzger and Martin Hazelton.

There were more boats in view below now, gunmetal gray, their bows cutting frothing white wakes.

"Can you add voltage to the watch, Captain?" Marilyn asked.

"That's the easy part. I can also fire the generators, assuming nobody shoots me out of the sky for trying. But are we supposed to take the kids with us?"

Everyone was silent.

"I suppose we will have to land," Marilyn Metzger said, but it was clear she didn't love the prospect. She also had refused to get out of the plane on the runway at Ash Point, Charlie realized. It was as if she was determined to remain in the sky.

Hightower said, "What do you think happens if we put it down again?"

"Everyone I knew is likely dead by now, of course, but I can offer some guesses. You may not want to hear them."

"Make them anyhow."

"We will disappear. They'll be more interested in the plane than us, but they can't have us out and about, either. Simple risk-and-reward calculus says there's greater benefit to secrecy concerning our return than a public declaration. We'll have to remain a secret unless more has changed about our approach to black ops over the years than I assume."

She looked at Charlie and Lawrence. "Have you ever heard of Project Kingsolver?"

They shook their heads.

Marilyn Metzger's electric eyes looked unsurprised.

"I think that speaks volumes. We were a secret, we've remained a secret, and . . . " She stopped, cocked her head. "Have you heard of *any* time travelers?"

"*The X-Files*," Lawrence said. "A bunch of movies. Stephen King wrote a—"

"She means real ones," Charlie said.

"Correct," Marilyn Metzger said.

"Absolutely not. No one has admitted to trying it in real life."

Marilyn Metzger sighed and nodded. "There you go." She reached forward and touched Hightower's shoulder. "We may be one of a kind. But it's not a kind they can admit to producing."

"Nevertheless, the kids have nothing to do with it," Hightower said. "And the land down there is still the United States. If I have to put this plane somewhere, I'd rather do it there."

"I don't know if that's a good idea," Charlie said.

"*Charlie!*" Lawrence hissed, shooting her a *What are you doing to me?* glare.

"I don't think it'll just be them who disappears," Charlie said. "What she said makes a lot of sense. The country can't just parade them out for a press conference and say, 'Good news, we launched these people back in '62 and we lost them, along with an atomic bomb, but then they came back!' They'll never admit that. And two of the people are dead! That's definitely a bad look. So, do you think they'll let you and me tell the story? No way, dude. Your grandpa was right. Ash Point is a successful secret because people work hard to keep it that way. They're not going to give up just because the plane lands. Those guys on the runway—the soldiers? They didn't look like a welcome-home party."

"This child," the defense secretary said, "is the greatest threat to national security since Benedict Arnold."

But she's not wrong, Layla Chen thought. *She is not wrong.*

"Dr. Chen, do you think it's possible for the aircraft to—what did Metzger say? Leap?" Hanover asked.

"I can't say, sir. But we didn't think it was possible, or at least likely, for them to return at all. Here they are. That tells us they have a chance."

"What is the watch they keep referring to?" Hanover asked.

"I have no idea, sir."

"It can't be a physical watch," the president said. "It's a code word, surely."

"I don't recall that code word from the Kingsolver files."

"We'll find it in there," the defense secretary said. "Because they can't be talking about a fucking wristwatch. Implausible."

They were listening to a conversation between time travelers, and this asshole wanted to say what was plausible? Layla Chen bit her tongue.

The audio feed from the Zimmer boy's iPad came alive again.

"They'll also have to admit that the calls to the pilots this morning were fake," Charlie Goodwin was saying. "That won't be a good look, either."

"This kid . . . ," the defense secretary groaned.

Very smart, Layla Chen thought. *Very, very astute read, Miss Goodwin.*

"What calls?" This voice, softer, was Marilyn Metzger's.

"They made all these fake calls—like the one from the President. Remember, I called it a deepfake?"

Hightower murmured something inaudible.

"Anyhow, they faked these calls to ground domestic planes all over the country this morning," Charlie Goodwin continued. "They were busy blaming that on hackers from Russia or Iran last we saw. I don't know if the story has changed, but I doubt those countries had anything to do with it."

"Is there a way to take just the girl out?" the defense secretary said. "Leave the plane intact but shut her up?"

"Quiet," the president said.

"And then they did the same thing with your plane wreck, or whatever wreck was supposed to be your plane. I don't understand that. But a voice came out of the radio in that wreck, and it was my mother's voice." She paused. "It was good. *Really* good. Way better than the Kennedy fake, honestly, because the tone was right. The voice really seemed to know me."

Layla Chen's neck prickled, the fine hairs rising on her arms.

"What was the goal of that operation at the wreck, Dr. Chen?" Hanover asked.

"There was no operation, sir."

"But she's describing Seeker Script."

"I understand that. Seeker Script was deployed only through cell phones, and only to pilots."

"So now she's lying?" the defense secretary said. "The little shit is actively lying to them to keep them from landing? Unbelievable."

Layla didn't respond. She was thinking of Move 37, the artificial intelligence departure from logic that she'd urged Hanover to use as a cover story that morning. Possible. Except you needed a phone. Didn't you?

"Do we attempt to activate the microphone and engage with Metzger?" the president asked. "She seems the most informed."

"Certainly the calmest," Hanover added.

"Let's give it a minute," Layla said.

"The voice of patience over here is going to get us into real trouble," the defense secretary grumbled.

"Impatience is what put that plane in the air to begin with," Layla said. "I would like to hear more about Metzger's understanding of the project."

"I think they'll land," the president said. "And when they do, we'll need an explanation ready for why this plane was in the air at all. There are countless witnesses and videos showing it off the coast of New York. How do we explain that plane without giving away the whole game?"

They all looked at Layla. She considered, then said, "There's a historic B-52 that tours around to air shows. Probably a few of them."

"We have one at Barksdale now," the Air Force general confirmed.

"Get it in the air," Layla said. "We'll borrow a page from Project Kingsolver, only this time we won't crash the damn plane. That was always stupid, although the idea was to provide some comfort to their families."

"What do you want to do with the Barksdale plane?"

"Use it as a decoy. We'll secure the Loring B-52 for analysis; then we'll land the Barksdale plane at Ash Point and make a public statement in front of it. The story will be that the Barksdale plane lost its radio contact due to age-related equipment malfunctions and caused us some understandable consternation when it remained airborne and silent, so we used military resources to force the landing. We'll have the pilot address the media to explain the situation."

The president nodded. So did the defense secretary.

"Very good, Sector Six," Hanover said with a trace of a smile. "Very, very good."

"Now we just need it on the ground," the president said.

Yes. That one little detail remained.

AIRBORNE, ASH POINT, MAINE
OCTOBER 28, 1962

Marty pulled himself into the EWO seat, the one where Marilyn Metzger was supposed to be, and sat numbly, listening to the faint voices crackling through a headset microphone without reacting to them.

They'd been in it together, he thought.

A lie, a betrayal. A way to make the weapon work. Keep Hazelton happy, keep him going. The mission was everything. She'd told him that herself. Why was he so shocked that she'd never climbed aboard the plane?

Because she came just as far as me to have the chance, he thought, and then he thought that he understood.

She'd boarded a plane. Just not the decoy. She was on the real deal.

Crackle from the microphone. He blinked, picked up the headset, put it on.

" . . . he's gone. Hazelton is gone." Dupree's voice.

"Get him back!" Cutting's voice.

"We've got to eject and we've got to do it soon. I cannot order my men to leave their stations."

Marty listened, detached and distracted, but glad that Cutting was on the line. He would be able to answer the only question that mattered.

He keyed the mike.

"Hazelton here."

A static-heavy pause, then: "Get back to your seat, man! Damn it, we're going to eject!"

That was Dupree.

Marty said, "Admiral Cutting, you there?"

"I'm here. Listen to him, Hazelton."

"No. Too late for that. You need to listen to me. Was the other plane armed? The one we just vanished?"

Static and silence.

"Admiral, I need to know. Because you don't understand it. Nobody does. Not you, not Iris, nobody. If you give me the wrong answer . . . I can't imagine the consequences."

"The plane is armed," Admiral Ralph H. Cutting said. "Not my call, Hazelton. It was not my call, and it may save us from a catastrophe in Cuba. The history books may not account for Ash Point, but the Russians will."

Marty closed his eyes and bowed his head. He was scarcely aware of Cutting demanding that he to return to the cockpit.

They'd armed a plane and sent it to the other side of time. Manhattan Project logic applied to Nashua Nightshade, forced by the Cuban crisis. No time to demonstrate, only time to detonate. World-ending logic, if it went sideways.

He stared at his father's watch, that singular watch that had gone mad in the sky above Elugelab when they dropped the world's first thermonuclear weapon, then survived the blast at Doom Town on a mannequin's wrist. Perhaps it wasn't singular. Perhaps he could create another like it by exposing it to the same conditions. But those conditions were exquisite and precise. Unique. And they created exactly one watch.

The plane creaked and popped, those sounds of living metal.

"Hazelton!" Cutting's voice, harsh on the radio.

"Yes, Admiral. I'm here."

"Where is 'here'?"

"The EWO seat."

"Then strap in and prepare for ejection. Do you understand me?"

"Is Marilyn on the other plane?"

Silence.

"She got something for overseeing Kingsolver," Marty said. "She got a promise, didn't she?"

"You're going to eject on Dupree's command," Cutting said. "That is an order, Hazelton."

A man far below, shouting out orders. It was almost funny.

"Of course, sir," Marty said. He was trying to determine why they were ejecting. It seemed so dangerous, so wasteful. Why was it worth it? And then he saw: one plane goes missing, and it would be explained as the crash of the other. Of course. Because what was the alternative? Telling the truth would cause quite a stir. Telling the truth to the families of the men on the plane? That wouldn't go over well. You'd have questions, interviews. You may well have a Marilyn Metzger among the grieving, and she certainly could cause some trouble.

"They want six months?" he said into the radio. "That's what Iris and her team think they can provide with the radio signals?"

"Hazelton, you need to confirm my order."

"Confirmed. Tell me if it's six months."

"That's classified," Cutting said.

What a perfect fool.

Marty removed his watch. What was the worse choice for Marilyn and the crew of the Loring plane who'd volunteered for this mad mission, to burn up like so many others on doomed test flights or to go on to an unknown future? Depending on how things went in Cuba, they might reappear in a gray sky, the sun clouded by ash, the landscape below a charred tribute to a good world ruined. Or maybe they would land to a cheering crowd. He couldn't say.

But he could give them a chance. Not by hand-winding the watch—there wasn't enough time for that—but he remembered his test back at Crane, the way the hands on the watch had spun backward when he applied a little voltage. It was not difficult to find electrified low-voltage wires in the B-52. There were miles of them. He removed his headset and tore the wires loose from it, then stripped them of the rubber insulation and twisted the frayed copper threads into solid leads.

Then he touched them to the watch face.

Spark and glow, and he swore he heard a hum, and felt a dull tingle deep in his palm, as if the watch were drawing the marrow from the slender bones of his fingers. The watch's hands spun backward instantly—and quickly. He tried to keep count as the hour hand passed the 12 again and again, but it was too fast, a blur.

Even if he could keep track, what was the right time to select?

The Wright brothers' test flight at Kitty Hawk had been in December of 1903, not even sixty years ago, and here he sat in a jet that could cross the Atlantic and drop a nuclear weapon. The unimaginable became the ordinary so swiftly. The new century had dawned without flight and progressed to bombers and rockets and would soon, some believed, lead to the landing of a man on the moon. If the world didn't burn, there would be great things ahead.

Ashes or answers. Humans would solve great mysteries in the

years to come, or they would die trying. Maybe they would die because they solved them.

The hands spun, spun, spun. Minutes and hours merged to make days and weeks. Months became years. He could not imagine what Marilyn and the men from Loring might find upon their return, but they would make it there. Out of his cloud, obeying his watch? Oh, yes, they'd make it. He couldn't say the same for anyone down below, but that, of course, was out of his control.

You were given only so many gifts. It was up to you to handle them with care.

He removed the leads and pushed the crown in.

Tick, tick, tick.

The *Loring Loonatic*, somewhere beyond time, was readying for descent.

He put the watch in his pocket and got to his feet, holding on to the side of the plane for balance. There was one thing left to try, one last act of madness. He didn't believe it would count for much, but he didn't see what it could hurt, either.

AIRBORNE, EASTERN SEABOARD
OCTOBER 25, 2025

"What was it like when you were in the cloud?" Charlie asked.

"Peaceful," Marilyn Metzger said before Hightower had a chance to answer.

"It didn't feel long? It was just . . . ?" Charlie snapped her fingers.

Marilyn shook her head. "Not that fast. It was just the sensation of flying, a lovely sensation, calm and . . . " She stopped talking, looked down at the dead men at her feet, and then seemed to think better of the pleasant description. "Captain Hightower, what was your experience?"

"About the same," he said softly. "I was flying with control, and the sky was calm, and I knew we'd come out on the other side. The kid is asking questions about time, meaning did it feel fast or slow, but that requires *thinking* about it. I don't remember thinking about time. Did you?"

Marilyn Metzger shook her head.

"I was very relaxed. I was very calm. Time was not a problem."

"Agreed," Hightower said. "There were no problems that even entered my mind until we were out of the cloud and I was coming down at Ash Point. I saw the runway and I knew to go toward it. That was all. Instinct. Then the world came back. Not my world, but a world that needed to be dealt with."

They flew on. The coast was growing more familiar by the mile, and eventually Charlie saw the long black ribbon of runway that was Ash Point. Home. The coastal waters swarmed with rescue craft, and black helicopters hovered. Everyone was waiting to see what happened next. Nobody wanted to take the shot at the B-52, and the B-52's pilot didn't want to drop the bomb. Lots of risk, zero trust. It was, Charlie thought, a neat little replica of Cuba in October 1962. What was the expression? History doesn't always repeat itself, but it often rhymes?

Marilyn Metzger was right, Charlie thought. They would all disappear when they landed. The B-52 had real time travelers on board. That was a big secret. If they'd kept it for more than sixty years already, they weren't going to be in a hurry to give it up now. Dana Goodwin's very perceptive girl was alive and well, seeing all the things that waited for Hightower and Metzger on the ground, black sites and silence, certainly no televised address about a hero who'd lifted his hand on the eve of the Cuban missile crisis. There were too many decades of deceit behind them for that.

"There's another way for us to get home," Charlie said. "We can eject."

When they looked at her, she pointed down at the chaos of rescue craft in the waters off Ash Point.

"Think they'll miss us? No chance. And it will be a hell of a lot harder for them to make us disappear if we come out of this plane in front of a bunch of witnesses. You can't fake that. It's too big, like the moon landing."

Marilyn Metzger said, "We landed on the moon?"

"You talk too much, Charlie," Lawrence said. "You really need to learn when to shut up."

"Yes, we landed on the moon," Charlie said, "but that's irrelevant. If we parachute out of this plane, in front of all the people down there, it's going to be impossible for them to just grab us and hide us. It's a different world than the one you left. Everyone and everything has a camera. There will be hundreds of videos of us coming out of the plane."

Hightower shook his head. "Too dangerous. Not many survive an ejection from this plane."

"Survival is evidently in my DNA," Charlie said. "Look at you! Talk about beating the odds."

This time Hightower didn't laugh—or even smile. But he looked thoughtful.

"Besides," Charlie said, pointing at Lawrence, "he's practiced."

Lawrence blanched, but he nodded. "That's true."

Hightower said, "You've *practiced*?"

"I sit in the ejection seat and reenact it. It's supposed to be for your museum."

Hightower blinked. "My museum."

"That's right," Charlie said. "They have an ejection seat that Abe—Lawrence's grandpa—makes this big reenactment out of, every step of the sequence. The only difference is, he never actually moves."

It felt like a profound difference. She could picture Lawrence sitting in that silly chair that no longer felt so silly at all, and suddenly she was very glad she'd taken the video of him, no matter her motives at the time. In a strange way, she felt as if she'd already gone through the process.

"I might not have ejected in that seat, but I've been skydiving more than fifty times," Lawrence said, warming to the argument. "Started with a tandem jump and then went solo. My grandpa insisted on it."

Speaking of the man he'd left on the ground, Lawrence choked up a bit but pressed on. "He wanted me to be a pilot, you know."

A quiet indecision pervaded the cockpit.

"Marilyn?" Hightower said.

"It's your plane," she answered.

"It was your mission."

She shook her head. "I won't . . . I can't make that call."

"All right," Hightower said at length. "This was a volunteer flight, and it still is. I'm not giving any orders. You want out, it's your vote."

Charlie looked at Lawrence. He was so pale, he appeared bloodless, but he nodded.

"Okay," Charlie said, and the act of speaking the single word felt foreign, something she wished she'd practiced. She was already that numb with fear. "We go out, and you two go on."

Marilyn Metzger didn't look sold yet. She scanned the blue sky.

"We don't even have a storm. There's no way it works. You read Marty's letter. We'd need a storm to even try to vanish. Fire those Nightshade generators into a sky without electricity, and you'll waste it."

"I can find a cloud," Hightower said.

Charlie had a sudden, horrible thought.

"What if their strategy changes once you're alone? What if, once we jump out, they shoot you down?"

"They won't," Hightower said calmly and without hesitation.

"How do you know?"

"Because he's got a friggin' nuclear bomb on board," Lawrence said.

"That's one factor," Marilyn Metzger acknowledged. "There's another, though: ARPA will want to see if we can make it on our own. That was the dream of Project Kingsolver."

"You mean DARPA?" Charlie asked, and Marilyn frowned, perplexed by the term.

"Whoever's in charge of secrets," she said. "I'm quite sure some-one still is."

Hightower was smiling faintly—and maybe a little bitterly.

"You agree," Charlie said.

"Yes. Oh, do they want us on the ground? Sure. But if someone out there knows we're supposed to have another choice, then I can guarantee you they're curious to see what happens if we take it."

Charlie was suddenly ashamed that she'd ever believed he'd flown into a mountain. He was far too good a pilot for that, she thought.

"You'll need the watch," Charlie said.

"Yeah," Hightower said. "We will."

Lawrence opened the radiosonde and passed the watch to Charlie. She handled it delicately, studying the way it seemed to inhale the sunlight rather than reflect it. When she rubbed her thumb across the worn metal surface, a thin layer of grime marked the whorls of her skin.

"How do you apply voltage?" Marilyn said. "That's part of it."

"They made that easy when they pulled my radio," he said, and pointed to the gap in the instrument panel where wires with taped ends dangled. "Just undo the tape for me, kid, will you?"

Charlie did it. It took a while, because her hands were shaking.

"That's fine," Hightower said when the wires were bare. "Let them rest like that."

Charlie sat back, and Hightower said abruptly, "We're really family?"

She'd almost forgotten that she'd tried to explain the family tree, then given up when he didn't like being one of the dead limbs up in the overstory.

"Yes. My mom was so proud of you, and I always made fun of that, because all you did was hit a mountain."

Hightower looked sharply at her—and then laughed. It was such a

359

wonderful, rich sound. A man's laugh, deep and a little coarse; a laugh that Charlie's subconscious could have no memory of, and yet somehow it carried her mother within it. DNA was a fascinating thing.

"Did you ever meet Sarah?" Hightower asked.

Charlie started to say *Who?* but caught herself. Sarah was her great-grandmother.

Sarah was his wife.

"No," she said. "But I knew your daughter. I knew Ruth. She was the nicest person I ever met."

His jaw trembled ever so slightly, but he kept his eyes steady on hers.

"Tell me something about her," he said. "Something real."

"She loved Christmas carols," Charlie said. "She loved everything about Christmas, really, especially snow on Christmas Eve; that was her favorite thing in the world, but she liked the music a whole lot. She drove everybody nuts with that. It started on Thanksgiving and she never turned it off until January."

He turned away from her, and his Adam's apple swelled as he swallowed, and then he didn't say anything for a long time.

They flew east, banked, came back west. The water off Ash Point was calm and clear except for the rescue boats, with more seeming to appear by the minute, each with distinct military markings.

"Okay," Hightower said. "The skydiver's in charge now. You're going to have to listen to him. I can't go with you down there."

He turned to Lawrence. "Prove to me you know the ejection sequence."

Lawrence jumped in, chapter and verse. They were going to do this, Charlie realized, looking at the sea below them, which had never seemed so imposing, so powerful. They were really going to do this.

Or die. One or the other.

RAVEN ROCK MOUNTAIN COMPLEX, PENNSYLVANIA
OCTOBER 25, 2025

Raven Rock was in an uproar, everyone talking over one another, responding to the wild card in the deck that was Charlie Goodwin.

It had been, Layla thought, a truly brilliant countermeasure. It would be awfully hard to make the girl and the Zimmer boy disappear once they parachuted out of a B-52 in front of witnesses and live-streaming cameras. There would be too many video sources to shut down. It was a hard scenario to control.

"Dr. Chen, give us an option here," Hanover demanded.

The room went quiet. They waited, everyone's eyes on her.

"There are two," she said.

"Yes?"

"We concede that the girl just won the game, and we shift to a posture of explanation and negotiation. We get in front of the story, claim the kids stowed away on the plane from Barksdale—something along those lines—and then deal with negotiating their silence once we have them secured. That's one option."

"The other?"

Layla met first Hanover's eyes, then the president's.

"They don't have to survive the ejection. It's entirely possible that they won't, regardless. But that could become a guarantee."

The defense secretary liked it. She could see that.

"The girl has pushed us here," he said. "She has made it a zero-sum game."

"I think we had a little to do with that," Hanover said.

"Nevertheless, it's the scenario. And we can't assume that any negotiation for silence will be successful."

"I think it will be," Layla said.

"Why?"

"Because who on earth will believe their true story?"

Silence. The president nodded.

"It's one hell of a risk," the defense secretary said.

"It's also one hell of an opportunity," Layla said. "Imagine what the kids can tell us. The research potential is remarkable. We got to watch Donovan and Dupree for another fifty years after the first Ash Point flight. Tremendously interesting blood labs."

"That's if the kids survive," the president said.

"Yes," Layla agreed. "We had mixed results with the first Ash Point ejections, but that was a different situation. In fact, we still have no idea what transpired on Hazelton's flight. No one ever will. All we know is we had to carry his remains down the mountain in a basket."

No one responded to that.

AIRBORNE, ASH POINT, MAINE
OCTOBER 28, 1962

Among the cloud-testing gear that Cutting's team had not wanted Marty to bring aboard the B-52 was a folded weather balloon and a radiosonde. They were ordinarily launched from the ground, not a plane, and they were never dropped from a B-52; yet they'd allowed him to bring it aboard, which had struck him as a pleasant surprise at the time. Now he understood that they were happy to appease him because they'd had no intention of honoring any of his wishes.

Go ahead and pack your toys, Doc. Whatever you need.

He found the balloon where it had been stowed, opened the radiosonde, and ripped the instruments out, leaving an empty box behind, then withdrew the pocket notebook he'd carried with him for so long. He had no time to write, so he scribbled what bare minimum instructions he could, knowing it would likely mean nothing but wanting to release at least a chance of remedy into the world of pain he'd helped create. He folded the paper, placed it in the radiosonde box, added the watch, then tied the box shut once more.

That was the easy part. The balloon, even uninflated and folded, was a different matter. It was cumbersome in the best of conditions, and the B-52 was no longer experiencing the best of conditions. Each time Marty got his footing, the plane's sudden motion threw him back to the steel floor. He gave up and settled for crawling, dragging the balloon over one shoulder like a camper who'd given up on getting his tent back in its bag and set off for the parking lot with dignity abandoned.

The ladder to the cockpit was, ironically, the easiest part of his journey, the rungs giving him a solid grip. Then he got his head up to the cockpit level and almost blew backward.

The pilot's seat was gone, and wind screamed through the open hatch above the place where Dupree had once sat.

The pilot had ejected. Alarms were blaring and insulation blew about. It was cacophony and chaos and yet it was not bad news: there was a hole in the plane, and that was what Marty needed. All he could do was get the balloon out of the plane and let it take the watch with it.

He thought—a hypothesis, nothing more, but one worthy of testing—that the balloon, left free to drift, a partner to winds, might have a chance at finding the shielded cloud.

Perhaps that would be worth nothing. Then again . . .

Have holy curiosity.

He tumbled from the top rung of the ladder into the narrow bay between the access hatch and the cockpit, entering the wind tunnel. The plane was out of the cloud and descending fast. What of the watch, then? What of that wonderful little mystery? All he knew was that he could not let it return to the clutching hands on the ground. He would give it to the sky, and if the sky wished, the sky could give it to the sea.

Humanity could find its own fucking watch.

But that's not right, he thought as he tugged the weather balloon's silvery folds up the ladder, hand over hand, like a sailor hoisting the mainsail. *They can't all be blamed for the few, and Marilyn and that crew surely can't be. They raised their hands in an hour of need. They deserve the best effort in return.*

He crawled into the cockpit and looked up at the open hatch. The black clouds coiled and twisted like undulating snakes, lit occasionally by forked tongues of lightning. The air was frigid, peppering his upturned face with fine particles of sleet.

Sleet and Nashua Nightshade, maybe?

He pulled the radiosonde up and pinched the box between his feet to secure it. The twine looped between the brass brads held the top shut, the watch and the note inside, and for a moment, looking from the frail box to the furious sky, he was overwhelmed by the certain futility of it all.

Then he remembered Donovan's triumphant whoop when the bomber from Loring had reappeared. He remembered Dupree's soft *"Goodness!"* and the way his jaw hung slack, the omnipresent chewing gum forgotten, and he remembered Cutting's hungry eyes back on the ground at Ash Point when the first Grumman test plane had returned.

Doubters, all of them. Doubters no more.

Marty bunched balloon fabric in his open hands, tucked his palms beneath it, and then pushed it upward, offering it to the open hatch like a supplicant.

The storm snatched it. The thin cords tethering the radiosonde to the balloon whistled through his hands like fishing line screaming off a reel as a shark hit the bait, and he was scarcely aware of his ring finger separating from his left hand, there and then gone, a nub of white bone and bright blood in its place. He parted his hands as the threads scorched open crimson lines on each palm, and then the radiosonde thumped over the floor, clipped him once on the underside of the chin, like a last, lukewarm uppercut from an opponent as the bell sounded, something for you to remember between rounds, and the balloon vanished, taking his father's watch with it.

The last time he saw the balloon, it was filling with air, tugged upward like a parachute, no helium to hold it aloft, only the whims of the wind. Then it was gone from view.

He crawled into the copilot's seat. There was a yoke, and he knew it could be engaged, but he didn't know how and couldn't bring himself to care, because he couldn't land the B-52.

He could eject. That was still possible. He'd been through so many repetitions of it on the tarmac, over and over, while Marilyn hissed at him to pay attention. He thought he remembered the steps.

He wiped a bloodied lip with a bloodied hand and sat back in the seat and closed his eyes. The wind punched hard. The big plane bellied into the gust and then dropped, nose down, then up, slamming left, then right. As the bomber slalomed, Marty slid to the floor, scraping over the jagged remnants of what had once been the pilot's position.

He kept his eyes closed.

He wished, suddenly and almost painfully, that he had met Captain Hightower and the crew from Loring. He wasn't sure what he might've told them—could he have said their sacrifices were worthwhile?—but he would've liked to shake their hands and say thank you. He would have liked them to know that he had done his best, and if all he'd left them was a mystery, well, it wasn't for lack of effort.

Maybe it wasn't all that bad, either. Mystery had its benefits. Mystery and hope were as close as lovers.

He'd have liked to tell Marilyn goodbye. To say that he understood her choices. She wanted to be in the sky—always had—in pursuit of the impossible, which was a beautiful thing. He bowed his head against the storm and wished for the wind to carry her a simple gust of goodwill. It didn't seem like too much to ask.

When he opened his eyes, Hank was laughing at him.

His brother sat behind the yoke, broad-shouldered and lantern-jawed, with that tall, strong build that made strangers scoff whenever Marty insisted that once upon a time his baby brother had been so scrawny, the family had worried he'd forever be a runt.

"Lighten up," Hank said. "Didn't I tell you we were going to be fine?"

Sure he had. Marty didn't remember when, exactly, but the time-line didn't matter, did it? Trust did. Faith. Hank's grin was so con-fident, it rendered his face positively serene, and his grip, when he extended his large, unblemished right hand to Marty's, was strong enough to bend steel.

They shook, and then Hank laughed a wild, exhilarated laugh, like the one he would give when he broke the surface of the pond at Rosewater after a dive so reckless, it stole Marty's breath. He released Marty's hand and re-gripped the plane's yoke and flew on through the darkness, grin never wavering. He was a wonderful pilot, and you could breathe easy when he had control. It was good to be with him again.

There was a single, sharp smack of warm wind, like the one that met you at the screen door on a summer morning, a hint of spruce on the air, and then they flew out of the black cloud, and the sky ahead was blue and clear.

AIRBORNE, ASH POINT, MAINE
OCTOBER 25, 2025

Charlie had never jumped out of a plane before, and while she knew they were not at a particularly high altitude, it still felt impossibly high, beyond any hope of survival, parachute be damned. As Hightower and Lawrence blathered away about timing and hatches and something called an actuator, she heard it all but couldn't focus, couldn't look away from the ominous sea. The waves looked like insignificant ripples from up here, but down there they were big, rolling punishers, the same water that had drowned thousands—millions?—of people across the centuries.

"Hey," Hightower said. "Hey."

Belatedly, Charlie realized he was speaking to her.

"Yes?" she said.

"It's time to go," he said gently. "You've got to follow him."

"Oh. Right." Her heart was hammering, and she was sure that if she stood, she'd faint.

"You'll make it," Hightower said.

"I know."

He assessed her. "I can land. If you're not up to it, I can put her down, and deal with whatever's waiting for me. Hell, it'll be a hero's welcome, I'm sure."

In the movies, Charlie thought. In the movies it would be, yes. Stories cleaned things up. The real world was different. There were bad days and bad people and bad timing. Trips to safe places on your own street that ended with sirens. Nobody was letting the pilot from October of 1962 have his hero's welcome, even if he'd earned that. She was sure of it, and so was he. They came from different worlds, but some things stayed the same. Power was one. Secrecy was another.

She looked at Marilyn Metzger. The woman with the radiant, wrong-kind-of-bright eyes gazed back.

"We can land," Marilyn said.

Charlie shook her head. "We'll be fine." She swallowed, wet her lips, and then forced a smile. "Don't drop that bomb, guys. Nobody has in a long, long time."

"Keep it that way while we're gone," Hightower answered.

"We're trying."

He smiled. "All right, then. When you open my museum, don't let them say I just flew into a mountain, okay? Make it a little more . . . compelling than that."

"Trust me," Charlie said, "that will not be a problem."

Hightower shook Lawrence's hand first, then hers. She wasn't aware that she was crying until he touched her cheek with the backs of his fingers and said, "Stop that."

His voice was his own, and yet it was her mother's tone. All the things they hadn't been able to get right with the Kennedy deepfake, bloodlines seemed to handle just fine.

"Okay," she said.

"We'll be fine, kid. Like the doc's note says, we'll catch up in time.

Maybe we'll get another chance to talk and you can tell me how it felt, bailing out of a B-52."

Charlie slid out of the copilot's seat, and Marilyn Metzger slid into it.

"Do you mind if I stay up here?" she asked Hightower.

He shook his head. "It'll be nice to have some company this time."

"My sentiments, exactly."

Peaceful, she'd said of their endless experience in the cloud, and he had agreed.

Charlie hoped it would be again.

"Goodbye," Charlie told them.

She had just turned away when Marilyn Metzger spoke again. "Dear?"

"Yes?" Charlie looked back.

"Did you ever hear of Flight 19?"

Charlie shook her head, then regretted it, because Marilyn Metzger deflated.

"Sure," Lawrence piped up from behind Charlie. "They disappeared in the Bermuda Triangle. It was in that Spielberg movie. Happened in the fifties."

"It was 1945," Marilyn Metzger said gently. "And I don't know of Spielberg, but . . . it is good that you've heard about them."

"He likes the old shit," Charlie said.

Marilyn Metzger's smile was nearly as bright as her high-beam eyes.

"I'm glad someone does. Look into Flight 19 if you have a chance. And Martin Hazelton. Maybe you can refresh people."

"We'll try," Charlie promised.

When Lawrence offered his hand, she didn't hesitate to take it. She wanted to keep her balance as she stepped over the dead men.

The navigator's quarters, down the ladder and in the belly of the big plane, were strangely familiar, thanks to that replica in the lobby of BUFF Brewing. Even the ejection seat felt the same. Charlie didn't object when Lawrence insisted on buckling her into the harness.

She did okay with the process until he fastened the ankle restraints. Then she began to shake. Her hands went first, then her shoulders, her whole back trembling. She pressed her lips tight but even that didn't keep the tremble out of her jaw. The harness bit into her collarbone, pulling her hard against the seat, like being on a roller coaster. She wanted to throw up, but that would have required energy that her body no longer possessed. All she could do was sit there and shake.

Lawrence moved into his own seat and set about buckling himself in. Then they were locked in, side by side but in their own seats.

"They'll get us," Lawrence said. "There are so many people waiting down there."

His face was pale but his voice was calm. He'd zipped up the Crustacean Sensation letter jacket before harnessing in.

"What?" he said, frowning, and Charlie realized that she was smiling. It was a deranged smile, based on Lawrence's response, but that was okay.

"Nothing," she said. "I just . . . I like your jacket. I wanted to say that."

He looked bewildered, but he nodded.

"Once you pull that lever, it should all be automatic," he said.

The lever in question rested between Charlie's legs, just above her quaking knees. Her hands were free to move, but that was all. She was bound to the seat otherwise, and once the seat shot out of the plane, it was supposed to explode a second time, blowing her clear from it.

That was if everything worked *well*.

Sweat was pouring from her body now—too much of it, and it was too cold. Maybe she would just let Lawrence eject and she would stay in, with Hightower and Metzger. That wouldn't be so bad. Peaceful, they'd said. Yes, maybe she'd just stay on the plane and—

"Yank it up," Lawrence said, "and trust that it'll work."

"That's how Goose died," she said.

"Huh?"

"*Top Gun*." The words brought her back to the ground. To her world. The cloud might be peaceful, but she didn't belong on this plane. She hadn't volunteered.

"Fuck it," Charlie said, and wet her lips. "Let's go home."

"Okay." Lawrence wrapped his hands on the ejection handle, and she did the same. It took her three tries to get a firm grip. She simply could not stop shaking.

Lawrence said, "You want to go first, or want me to?"

"Together," she hissed through chattering teeth. "Let's go together."

"Okay. On three?"

She could no longer speak. It took everything she had in her to nod.

"All right," Lawrence said. "One . . . two . . . *three!*"

Charlie yanked up with all her might, and then the bomb went off.

Cold air and wicked wind snatched at her, grasping and greedy. She rose and spun, pummeled from all sides. Her mouth was open but she couldn't scream, because the force of the air hammering into her throat was too much, threatening to drown her with oxygen. When the ejection seat exploded and threw her clear, it felt like a loss, not a gain, her clutching fingers torn free from the armrests, her ankles wrenching, back snapping, head arcing before—

WHAM!

The parachute deployment hurt worse than anything else. She was sure she'd been ripped in half, saw a red mist that must be her own blood.

Then the mist cleared, and the sky was there, the sea below, and she was drifting.

Lawrence was below her—not far away, but too far to cry out for. His body was spinning, and it looked as if he was tangled in the lines from the chute, but she couldn't tell for sure because the wind was ripping at her eyes and the pain was a curtain between her and all understanding.

The only thing she knew for sure was where the sky ended and the sea began.

The cold came first, and then the blackness.

Later, she could recall nothing at all about being pulled from the water—not the sensation of the waves nor the sound of the boat engines, let alone the gloved hands of the Coast Guard swimmers who found her and cut her free from the parachute.

All she remembered was the sky, an expanse of blue broken by the black silhouettes of one plane and three helicopters. There were more planes up there, but she couldn't see them, only the big one, the B-52.

It circled once above Ash Point, flying low, as if the pilot wanted a visual confirmation of what was going on down below, and then it banked and flew northeast and began to climb.

Rising, rising, rising.

Charlie lost sight of it when a wave drove her under, and when she surfaced, the plane was gone.

The helicopters lost it soon after that, unable to match the big bomber's gathering speed. The F-16s had no such trouble. They tracked it over the cold, harsh waters known to fishermen as the Grand Banks, trying unsuccessfully to signal the aircraft, and although the pilot and the woman beside him would wave, they ignored all other hand signals. At orders from the Pentagon and the White House, no intercept maneuvers were conducted. Over the Grand Banks, arctic air pushed cold clouds into the severe clear day, and the

B-52 led the way into the storm. Just before it entered the cloud, one of the F-16 pilots reported that the plane appeared to be leaking fuel or oil, a black mist fanning out from the tail.

They lost sight of the plane shortly before sleet began to pelt the fishing boats below. Military installations in the United States, Canada, and Greenland reported the B-52 lost to radar at 17:02.

It did not return.

HOMEWARD
AUTUMN 2025

Charlie knew six days was too long to be hospitalized for a broken ankle and cracked ribs, but on Halloween she was still in the same room, and her father was at her side while they watched TV and waited on still more doctors to clear her for release.

Meteorologists dressed like vampires gave the trick-or-treating forecast before cutting back to the story of the two American teenagers who had stowed away on a historic B-52 after it was forced to ground at a decommissioned airfield during the unprecedented AI attack from unknown adversaries. The kids, who had survived an ejection from the plane, were unlikely to be charged, although surveys showed most of the American public wanted it to happen. Because they were minors, the government declined to release their names.

The plane's pilot, interviewed from the tarmac, offered a concise and compelling account of his horror at hearing the ejection alarm blaring, which led to his emergency landing in Halifax. He wasn't allowed to say much beyond "That's above my pay grade" and "They're lucky to be alive."

The story was getting less and less airtime. Even a great story got stale on a twenty-four-hour cycle. Besides, the unlikely stowaways were a footnote on a more troubling day. The focus remained on the real question: Who had instigated the high-tech attack on America's airline industry, and why?

There were still no answers. Passenger travel had resumed without incident. Congressional committees convened, intelligence agencies investigated, and pilot's unions petitioned for security reviews. It would all take time, everyone agreed on that.

Meanwhile, life went on.

Halloween night passed for Charlie like the five before it had. The doctors drew a lot of blood for a broken ankle and cracked ribs, and then the investigators arrived for another pass of questioning.

The interviews weren't so bad. She learned as much from them as she offered, and what she learned mattered a lot: Lawrence was alive, and so was Abe. She couldn't see them yet. She could when she answered all the questions and the doctors were satisfied with her condition. Rinse and repeat. One of their favorite new games was to tell her to embrace her delusions. She had been through a lot of trauma, they said, and that was nothing to be ashamed of.

"Go ahead and role-play," they told her. "Tell us what the pilot told you."

"We never talked to the pilot," Charlie said. "How could we have talked to him while we were stowed away in the bottom of the plane like delinquents?"

She was pretty sure they regretted having provided her with the TV at that point.

The blood draws and the interviews went on, but they became less frequent, and Charlie became more homesick. Ash Point was, strangely, what she thought of when she thought about home. Lawrence Zimmer was who she thought of. She missed the Crustacean

Sensation and his grandfather. She hoped they were really okay. It was one thing to hear it, but she wanted to see it.

Talking with her dad and the attorney he'd hired—a personal injury lawyer who had a billboard outside of Bangor, perhaps not the best equipped for dealing with DARPA—Charlie determined that, yes, it was a hell of a good deal to avoid federal charges in exchange for a simple nondisclosure agreement. She'd go home, go to therapy, heal her body, heal her mind. Stay silent.

Charlie attempted to negotiate the agreement. This caused the lawyer some heartburn, but he made a good-faith effort to extract information about Dr. Martin Hazelton and Marilyn Metzger and returned with photocopies of death certificates. Dr. Martin Hazelton had died at the Dennis Daniels Psychiatric Hospital in Sonoma, California, in July of 1959. Marilyn Metzger, staff assistant to Admiral Ralph H. Cutting, United States Navy, had been killed in a one-car accident on a rural road outside of Bloomington, Indiana, in September of 1962. Lost Man's Lane. Spooky name for a road, she thought, a little too on-the-nose, but it was the report they provided, and none of her questions generated anything else. Charlie gave up, gave in, and told them to draft the agreement.

It was time to go home.

Before they released her, she was notified of a final visitor: Dr. Layla Chen, chief archivist of DARPA.

They met on the second Monday of November, snow flurries in the air, meeting outside at Dr. Chen's request. The wind was rising and it was cold. Layla Chen was an energetic, slender woman with the keenest eyes Charlie had ever seen. They sat at a picnic table and Charlie asked the obvious question.

"Why did you ask to see me?"

Layla Chen could stare right into the wind without so much as wincing, her eyes so focused, it was as if she intended to bore through your soul.

"I've been authorized to let you know that some modifications will be made to your agreement," she said. "Some enhancements that I think will please you."

Charlie didn't say anything. Dr. Layla Chen removed a pack of cigarettes and shook one out, then offered it to Charlie.

"I'd have to be very dumb to smoke a cigarette given to me by DARPA," Charlie said.

Layla Chen smiled, slipped the pack back into her jacket pocket, and lit the cigarette. She smoked and blew it into the wind.

"You won't need to worry about college tuition. At any school of your choice. Your friend, Zimmer, is bound for Emerson, I understand."

"Emerson? He was supposed to go to the Maine Maritime Academy."

"His new financial situation appears to have redirected him. He tells us he would like to study poetry."

Lawrence Zimmer, a poet? And yet she could imagine it, a poet's heart hiding beneath the hard shell of the Crustacean Sensation. She would ask him to show her something he'd written, and she would not laugh. In fact, she had a strange feeling that she might cry.

"Good for him," she said.

"Indeed. You may also be interested to know that a private endowment will fund the construction of a museum at Ash Point. Groundbreaking will occur in the spring. It will be quite a structure: more than seven thousand square feet devoted to a single plane crash. Abe Zimmer has graciously agreed to serve as the director."

"You're covering all the bases, aren't you?" Charlie said. "Threatening us with federal charges on one hand, bribing us on the other. Wouldn't it have been easier just to kill us?"

Dr. Chen was no longer smiling.

"Why did you reference hearing your mother's voice?" she asked.

"Because I did hear it."

Layla Chen studied her, hunting for the lie. Well, good luck. There was no lie to be found.

"That's actually my one question too," Charlie said. "I understand the rest."

"Oh?" A glimmer of amusement returned to Layla Chen's eyes.

"Mostly. I mean, the phone calls weren't that difficult. Every expert on TV who was panicked when it happened now has a theory. You just prep an AI system with the videos that we all put there every day, all the American sheeple sharing their voices and faces without hesitation on an internet that you guys at DARPA created to begin with. Then you tell the system to call pilots. A few hundred calls, using voices that were easily culled from social media. Public data and artificial intelligence. Pilots and mothers and primal fears. Simple."

Layla Chen ashed her cigarette. "Artificial intelligence is a frightening new reality."

Charlie rolled her eyes. "Yeah, yeah. Now, I don't understand the Nightshade, of course, but you guys clearly don't, either, or it would be old news. We'd be using it to get from city to city and day to day. Apple would sell it in perfume bottles. Mist a little Nightshade, jump into next week in London, that kind of thing. The trouble is coming back, right? You need the watch for that?"

Layla Chen remained silent, her eyes revealing nothing.

"Okay, so you don't know how it worked," Charlie said, "but enough people were afraid that it *did* work to make them shut down American airspace and blame some faceless 'bad actor.' I might be missing the details, but the gist is clear."

"You have a remarkable imagination. That's both a gift and a curse."

Charlie ignored that, pressed on.

"But how did you get my mom's voice to come out of the plane wreck? And why?"

The winter wind blew hard in Dr. Layla Chen's face, but the woman never blinked.

"We didn't."

"Right, the investigation continues for the source of the attack, blah, blah, I know the drill," Charlie said. "I just want you to give me an idea. Imagine—hypothetically, of course—that you *wanted* to achieve this. I mean, you're at DARPA, where all the amazing shit that civilians can't even imagine is being tested. You're too smart to be completely stumped, right? You can at least make a guess. How did my mom's voice come out of that plane wreck? There's not even a radio in there. There's nothing but the rotting wires of an old microphone cord."

"Then there's not the necessary connectivity for the system you're describing," Chen said. Her voice was crisp, but she seemed troubled. She didn't enjoy scenarios that left questions. She did not like a mystery.

"My cell phone doesn't even get a signal at that wreck site," Charlie said. "But I *heard her voice.* And why would she have told me not to fly when I'm not a pilot?"

Layla Chen wanted the answer almost as badly as Charlie did. It was plain on her face.

"My best guess is that it never happened."

"Something funny? I was named after my great-grandfather. He's still in the air, as you know."

"He died tragically in 1962 is my understanding."

Charlie grinned and made a finger gun, giving her the point.

"Nice catch. I wouldn't have expected anything else from you. But while they've kept me locked up in the hospital, I—"

"You have not been in custody."

"Of course not. Painkillers must be sapping my brainpower. Sorry. While I have been reclining of my own free will in a hospital room where the only staff members have military clearance, I've been thinking about that voice and what it said: 'Charlie, you must not fly today.' I assumed Charlie was me. Could've been him, though. My great-grandfather."

Chen was trying not to look intrigued—and failing.

"It would be very interesting," Charlie said, "if DARPA's system for clearing the skies—"

"We have no such system."

"—if it used different methods at Ash Point, like the old loudspeakers, the Klaxon, whatever. You guys—sorry, sorry, the 'bad actors'— knew the plane originated from Ash Point. You told your AI enough information to understand the plane's origin story, and maybe it activated approaches that even *you* didn't anticipate." She looked out at the gray sea, followed the graceful descent of a gull, and then added, "Or maybe my mother's ghost gave me a warning."

Her voice roughened a little when she said that, but she didn't care.

Dr. Chen put out her cigarette, removed the pack, and withdrew another.

"Those things will kill you," Charlie said.

"I know it." Chen extended the pack to her again.

Charlie took the cigarette intending to throw it in the dirt or stomp it out, a gesture to prove she was no idiot, not dumb enough to smoke any cigarette, let alone one from DARPA. A voice in her head, though—one that sounded like her mother's—said that would be childish, a simple tantrum. She rolled the cigarette in her fingers, then shook her head when Layla Chen offered her a light.

"Your father says you want to go to film school," Chen said.

"That's right. Chapman, if I can get in."

"You'll get in." Chen blew smoke, watched it vanish. "It's a good fit for your skill set."

"My overactive imagination, you mean?"

"Yes. But there are other pairings. Some you may not have contemplated because they are not thought of as classical outlets for creativity."

"Like what?"

"You might consider DARPA, for instance."

Charlie laughed. "No fucking way."

"Who knows? Tomorrow you may feel differently. Tomorrow you may decide you want to light that cigarette after all."

"I won't." But still she did not throw the cigarette away. When Dr. Chen offered her a business card, Charlie accepted it, then put both the card and the unlit cigarette into her jacket pocket.

"Keep my card handy," Chen said. "Call if you wish. Anytime."

"Don't wait up for it. But thanks for the tuition. Free college never hurt anyone. I bet I'll have to take more than my fair share of blood tests at the student health center, though, won't I?"

"See, this is precisely why you should keep my card handy," Dr. Chen said with a smile. "You're a very perceptive girl."

Charlie froze.

"What?" Dr. Chen said, and for the first time there was genuine confusion in her eyes. That look, once more, of the thing she hated most: a mystery.

"Nothing," Charlie muttered. "Take care."

"You, too, *měinü.*"

Charlie tucked her crutches under her arms and pushed off the bench. The motion was still painful, but she was getting better every day. That was important. Christmas was coming, which meant she had a hill to walk up and a candle to light. The Ash Point vigil.

She walked away from Layla Chen, toward the hospital. Somewhere overhead, a plane hummed, but the gray sky hid it from her when she looked up.

We are off to meet the mystery, Marilyn Metzger had said.

Charlie limped ahead. She'd gone maybe twenty paces before Layla Chen spoke again.

"Miss Goodwin."

Charlie turned back. Layla Chen had her arms folded across her chest, and she was looking at the winter sky, not Charlie.

"You've pressed your powers of imagination to astonishing degrees tying an old plane crash during the Cuban missile crisis to the modern day and asking how DARPA"—she checked herself—"how *someone* might have cleared the skies. You are remarkably inventive. But you might wish to keep my business card handy while you allocate a little creative energy to the other question."

"What's that?" Charlie said.

Layla Chen's smile was cold and thin. "What if we hadn't?"

ACKNOWLEDGMENTS

As the old hype ads used to scream: *Only the most incredible parts of the story are true*! Writing this book, I often felt that way. The rabbit holes of research on this one were particularly rewarding, from the stories of Irving Langmuir, Vincent Schaefer, and Bernard Vonnegut, to the weather-altering efforts of Project Cirrus and Project Stormfury, to the grim stories of nuclear testing in Elugelab and Doom Town, and the terrifying days of October 1962, when the world narrowly averted nuclear holocaust with a bit more luck involved than was initially reported. And, oh yes, to our dubious, quite lucky history of losing nuclear weapons—and crashing those remarkable, still-in-use-today B-52 bombers.

The resources used in conjuring my fiction out of all this are too numerous to list here, but I'm particularly grateful for Ginger Strand's excellent book *The Brothers Vonnegut* and Annie Jacobsen's fantastic, frightening *Nuclear War: A Scenario*. Everyone should read that book. Vincent Schaefer's memoir, *Serendipity in Science: Twenty Years at Langmuir University*, gave me a marvelous window into a remarkable and romantic time in research science, and the beauty of a curious mind.

Anyone who ever flew—or still does fly—in an active-duty B-52 deserves our everlasting gratitude. The story of the heroic group at Elephant Mountain in Greenville, Maine, from January 24, 1963, deserves some special notice, as that's where this book has its roots. I encountered that wreck on a hiking trip with my wife, and the haunting story of their crash and the unlikely survival for two members in a blizzard lingered and refused to go away.

As for the Naval Surface Warfare Center, Crane Division—there's far less reality in that mix, but as I grew up nearby, urban legends of the place were always present, and I'd long wanted to add one to the mix. I hope the men and women who do real work out there understand!

I'd like to thank whoever sold a 1960s-era menu from the Dandale on eBay for providing an unusual spark of inspiration.

Then there are the saviors: Emily Bestler, editor and publisher and friend, whose patience and humor and enthusiasm make the work a joy, and Richard Pine, agent and friend, who gave me crucial pushes on this story.

Thanks to:

The wonderful team at Atria and Emily Bestler Books, especially Hydia Scott-Riley, Lara Jones, David Brown, Libby McGuire, Dana Trocker, Karlyn Hixson, Jimmy Iacobelli, Al Madocs, and David Chesanow.

Angela Cheng-Caplan and Allison Binder, the best film/TV reps anyone could hope for, and great people, as well.

Erin Mitchell, who takes care of so many things that I can't begin to enumerate them.

Early readers: Richard Chizmar, Eli Cranor, Brian Freeman, Gideon Pine, Bev Vincent, and Pete Yonkman.

ACKNOWLEDGMENTS

Always, always, Bob Hammel, friend and teacher.

My family—particularly my wife, Christine, who endured both the revisions and me during the process.

And, of course, there's *you*, dear reader, and whatever bookseller or librarian sent you this way. It's been fun. Let's do it again!